Game of Rogues

Also by Julie Anne Long

THE PALACE OF ROGUES SERIES
Lady Derring Takes a Lover
Angel in a Devil's Arms
I'm Only Wicked with You
After Dark with the Duke
You Were Made to Be Mine
How to Tame a Wild Rogue
My Season of Scandal
The Beast Takes a Bride

THE PENNYROYAL GREEN SERIES
The Perils of Pleasure
Like No Other Lover
Since the Surrender
I Kissed an Earl
What I Did for a Duke
How the Marquess Was Won
A Notorious Countess Confesses
It Happened One Midnight
Between the Devil and Ian Eversea
It Started with a Scandal
The Legend of Lyon Redmond

GAME OF ROGUES

 PALACE OF ROGUES 

JULIE ANNE LONG

AVON

An Imprint of HarperCollinsPublishers

FIRST EDITION

Interior text design by Diahann Sturge-Campbell

Library of Congress Cataloging-in-Publication Data

Names: Long, Julie Anne (romance author), author
Title: Game of rogues / Julie Anne Long.
Description: First edition. | New York, NY : Avon, 2026. | Series: The palace of rogues ; book 9
Identifiers: LCCN 2025038858 | ISBN 9780063464803 (trade paperback) | ISBN 9780063464797 (ebook)
Subjects: LCGFT: Fiction | Romance fiction | Erotic fiction | Novels
Classification: LCC PS3612.O49663 G36 2026
LC record available at https://lccn.loc.gov/2025038858

ISBN 978-0-06-346480-3

Printed in the United States of America

26 27 28 29 30 LBC 5 4 3 2 1

For Helen Kunic Davis—so grateful for your warmth, wit, and kindness, my lovely bookish friend. Thank you for everything.

GAME OF ROGUES

Chapter One

Lucifer's Fall might be a den of depravity, but it resembled a cathedral.

Honeyed light poured through a pair of tall, arched windows. Beneath them, exuberantly healthy ferns sprang from pots. Guinevere Woodville eyed this evidence of a well-trained and well-paid staff wistfully. When she'd departed their family home in Sussex for London two days ago, their housekeeper, Mrs. Haddock, had been moodily smoking a cheroot in the kitchen, one gouty leg hoisted on a chair. Mrs. Haddock had come to them with dubious references, a murky London past, and a large hairy mole on her left cheek. While she could not be relied upon to adequately nurture indoor plants, the suspicion that she might be a witch ensured the maids never balked at obeying her instructions. Mrs. Haddock did not steal the silver, and, most importantly, she was willing to work for the pittance the Woodvilles were able to pay. Somehow the ancient Woodville manor was maintained in a shambling semblance of gentility.

But during her interview for admission to the Grand Palace on the Thames yesterday, a darling little boardinghouse near the London docks, of all places, Ginny had watched as the maid called Dot slowly—torturously slowly, if Ginny was being honest—lowered the tea tray to the table, then leaped backward with a celebratory clap. The proprietresses, Mrs. Hardy and Mrs. Durand, had sighed happily. Imagine servants who took such joy in their work! Employers who took such joy in their servants! It was her dream.

But Ginny had learned to pick her battles, which was how she'd managed to raise herself and her three younger siblings into adulthood with their limbs, senses, and virtues intact. In so doing she'd fulfilled the first of the two promises she'd made to her mother before she died eight years ago. Which was two days after her father died, and three days after he'd driven the two of them in the Woodville high-flyer around a corner too fast one time too many.

Just a fortnight ago she'd been on the brink of fulfilling part of the second promise—ensuring the Woodville siblings made spectacular marriages—in the most triumphant imaginable way, thanks to a glorious bit of providence.

And then her brother had returned from London and thrown himself at her feet in sobbing hysterics, babbling about "Lucifer's Fall" and "the Reaper" and begging her forgiveness for what he'd just done.

The icy terror that washed through Ginny left in its wake the usual calm and preternatural clarity that overtook her when confronted with disasters.

It was only money (a lot of it); no one had died this time (yet). It conceivably *could* be remedied. And surely, no matter how scary, this "the Reaper" (how patently ridiculous was that name?) was just a man? They were not fundamentally mysterious creatures.

She had a fortnight to fix the unfixable. She would need to go to London.

But thanks to that frivolous concept men liked to call honor, her brother refused to divulge any more than a few bone-chilling details of his disgraceful evening. None were names, but one perhaps held a hint: *He had satyrs on his waistcoat buttons, and I swear they were jeering at me, Ginny! You would not have blamed me if you knew who it was.*

No amount of haranguing would budge him.

She was forced to turn to other sources for reconnaissance.

Mrs. Haddock also had a tendency to speak in cryptic aphorisms, which made her seem like a sage. Ginny had her doubts about this. But she *could* be a fount of surprisingly interesting information. When Ginny asked her, "Have you heard of a man in London called the Reaper who runs a gaming hell?" The housekeeper's head turned toward her slowly. Her eyes had gone so wide the whites showed.

And so apparently important was the message she was about to impart, Mrs. Haddock actually leaned forward and stabbed out her cheroot on the chipped saucer next to her elbow. "Now, you listen to me, Miss Woodville," she'd all but hissed. "Ye're a *good* girl, and you want naught to do wi' the Reaper. 'E be a *dangerous* man. One of the worst men in London. Beware the *strivers*. Them what come from nothin' and *strive* all the way to the top be right dangerous. And I don't care what women say about the size of 'is . . ."

She sat back abruptly and pressed her lips together, her expression cagey.

"Fortune?" Ginny guessed.

"I'll just go and see if the maids be done wi' the upstairs

dustin', shall I?" Mrs. Haddock pushed herself out of the chair and shuffled off.

Ginny had then hastily called upon her neighbor, the giddy young Lady Tomelty, who was in the country to rest between bouts of London socializing. She was married to a much older earl and could be counted on to say things she shouldn't, especially to an unmarried girl. Ginny asked her the same question.

"My goodness, where did you *hear* about Gabriel Marchand and his little sin palace, Lucifer's Fall? Not from your darling brother? Oh dear. The on-dit is that Marchand is *depraved*." Lady Tomelty gave a theatrical little shiver. "The men are desperate to be in his good graces and they all clamor to be members of his club and the ladies seem obsessed with him for—well, for reasons of *prowess*, I'm given to understand. I hear he does delicious things with ropes and whatnot."

She whispered all of this behind a gloved hand and then, maddeningly, pantomimed turning a key at her lips.

Ginny knew she could expect to blush every time she spoke with Lady Tomelty; she went in braced for it, because she felt it was worth the education. She had an inkling about what "prowess" meant. She wasn't entirely naive. But that didn't mean she wasn't also appalled.

On the whole, the Reaper sounded like a bad and terrifying man, and this suited Ginny. Without a villain to blame or defeat, the Woodvilles' latest predicament was merely ridiculous. Worse than that: pathetic.

No doubt many would consider her visit today to Lucifer's Fall a fool's errand. Viewing it that way was a luxury she could not afford. She had to start somewhere. Failure was unthinkable. She could see nothing beyond the horizon for the Woodvilles if she failed. The future might as well be an abyss.

Unlike Cerberus, the dog who guarded the gates of hell in mythology, the clerk who looked up from his desk when she approached possessed only one head. He wore spectacles and a crisply tailored blue coat. She could see the pale blur of her face in his gleaming brass buttons.

If he was shocked by the sudden appearance of a young unchaperoned woman, not a twitch betrayed it.

She handed her card to him. It was new, the lettering elegantly engraved rather than merely printed. For years she'd secretly yearned for such a fancy, expensive card; a few weeks ago, when the miracle that would have solved all of her family's problems forever occurred, she'd allowed herself this one frivolous indulgence. Now she felt mocked by her own optimism. She ought to have known that everything was bound to go to pieces again.

"The Honorable Miss Guinevere Woodville," the man read aloud. "Oh yes. We received your message yesterday." The light reflecting from his spectacles made it difficult to read his expression, but his pause was eloquent and his tone was desert dry. "How did you get in the building, if I may ask, Miss Woodville?"

"Your guard at the front entrance assumed I was someone named Martine who is apparently expected. I didn't disabuse him of the notion. He stepped aside and let me in."

She did feel a slight twinge of guilt about that. But surely it wasn't her fault they'd hired a gullible guard?

"Ah. I see." The man nodded gravely. "I'm Mr. Ogden, Mr. Marchand's secretary. Since you cared enough to lie, Miss

Woodville, I'll just see whether he has a moment to speak with you, if you would care to take a seat?"

Two tasteful brown leather chairs native to all places wealthy men congregate flanked his desk. She gingerly settled into one.

Well. This was almost too easy.

Mr. Ogden advanced about twenty paces to a room divided by a partial wall from the one in which she sat. More sunlight shone over the top of it, suggesting Mr. Marchand enjoyed another cathedral-like window in his office.

During their bass-voiced, murmured conversation, Ginny pulled in and released three long breaths. It did little to slow her galloping heart. Her palms were clammy inside her gloves; the cold tip of the knitting needle she'd tucked inside her sleeve pricked her skin. She would be prepared to defend herself if the need arose. She glanced down at her lap; the mirrorlike sea of marble made her dizzy. When she jerked her head up again she noticed the ormolu-trimmed sconces lining the wall and a sleek bronze statue of a woman in a toga, one bare breast exposed, tucked in an alcove. At the far end of the atrium, behind Mr. Ogden's desk, a door led into a hall.

Just in case, this morning she'd silently asked her mother to send her the usual sign that all would be well. She'd found it in the garden in front of the Grand Palace on the Thames: a tiny gray stone shaped like a heart. She'd collected twenty such stones over the years, and she kept them in a little wooden box on her writing desk. Whenever she felt sickeningly uncertain or achingly alone, Ginny sifted them through her fingers, remembered that she was still loved, and took courage.

For extra luck, she'd worn her copper-colored silk dress, because the Honorable Francis Balfort had once pronounced her "mesmerizing" in it. Her sisters, Felicity and Fiona, were a matched set of petite, blue-eyed, black-haired fairy princesses, like their mother. They almost instantly inspired daft, protective cooing in men. Ginny inspired what could best be described as appreciative wariness in them. She was long-legged and lush, with fierce, straight black brows over big, round whiskey-colored eyes. Her mouth was pink and full and her black hair billowed like bonfire smoke when released from its pins.

"You look wise and a little dangerous, as though you ought to be striding the moors, calling down the thunder," Francis, the third son of a duke, had once declared after he'd had three cups of ratafia at an assembly. After a long pause he'd added, "Apart from the freckles, that is."

She didn't bother anymore powdering the faint spray of golden-brown robin's-egg-like speckles on her cheeks. They were a deceptively whimsical feature on a girl who, by nature and by necessity, patently was not.

At last Mr. Ogden returned.

"Mr. Marchand is able to spare a few minutes for a chat, Miss Woodville. If you will come with me?"

Over the past eight years she'd learned the lengths she was willing to go to protect her family, and more than a little about shameless bargaining. She'd walked into the unknown nearly every day.

She stood, squared her shoulders, hiked her chin, and like a madwoman followed him into the Reaper's den.

Chapter Two

Ginny's father had once received a rifle from his friend and rival, the Earl of Sydenham. It had a lustrous walnut stock, a filigreed trigger guard, and a silver thumb plate engraved with her father's initials. It was a work of art that could blow a man's head off at two hundred paces.

Mr. Marchand was like meeting that rifle in the flesh.

He was standing in the sunbeam slanting down from the high arched window.

She'd needed to tilt her head what felt like an inordinate distance to discover his eyes were gray. The jolt she felt upon meeting them was, in fact, like touching the hot barrel of a gun.

Whereupon she was assailed by a host of inconvenient epiphanies.

The first was that this was not a man who could be mesmerized by a copper-colored dress. It afforded about as much strategic defense as an eggshell.

She didn't need to inspect him to be certain that his coat, trousers, and waistcoat were expensive, current, and exquisitely tailored, as tasteful as the surroundings, and also that all of this was sheep's clothing. No gentleman had need of shoulders that broad, for one thing. They were unseemly, nefarious shoulders, no doubt acquired by doing things like wrestling people to the ground. And no gentleman she'd ever met exuded the unsettlingly calm confidence of a predator in repose.

He was slapping her calling card lightly against his palm.

"Engraved," he mused. The rich timbre of his voice rustled across her nerve endings in a disturbingly pleasant way. "Impressive, Miss Woodville. I find I get so much more out of the experience if I can feel the words as well as read them."

Detecting a whiff of irony, she narrowed her eyes slightly. "My thoughts exactly."

He spoke with a gentleman's cadences. No doubt learned through parroting.

Maddeningly, she could read no conclusions about her in his eyes. They were remote and vigilant and cynical. It was easy to believe that the person looking out of them had seen things beyond the reach of her imagination. Despite her better judgment, she wanted to know what those things were, for the same reason she'd asked fellow boardinghouse guest Mr. Delacorte, a salesman of exotic remedies, if she could have a look in his medicine case last night, and why she had taken Mrs. Haddock up on her offer to teach all the Woodvilles how to roll cheroots. One never knew what kinds of knowledge would come in useful.

Finally, Mr. Marchand extended her card to her.

Too late she realized she ought to have magnanimously said "Keep it."

He arched a knowing brow when she took it from him.

She flushed. Clearly, he knew that engraving was expensive. This man knew the cost of everything, she would warrant.

A vast, glossy desk occupied the center of the room. On the wall flanking it was a painting of an elderly man, nude apart from an artfully draped scarlet robe, hunched over a writing table strewn with open books and decorated with a human skull. The man's bald head and the skull both glowed gold in the light of a candle.

"Oh, my goodness . . ." She was dumbfounded. "That's not . . . that can't . . . is that . . . is that a *Caravaggio?*"

Mr. Marchand turned his head. "So I'm told," he said shortly.

"It's . . . unmistakable. The chiaroscuro . . . that *red . . .*"

"Indeed. Caravaggio was by many accounts an ill-tempered, murderous thug who made extraordinary art, which I think says something amusing about the relationship between beauty and goodness. And there's a skull *right* there on his desk. All of that is reason enough to like it, don't you think, Miss Wood-ville?"

As an opening salvo this was brilliant. She hadn't the faintest idea how to respond.

"It was given to me to settle a debt," he added.

That "d" word seemed to pulse in the room.

She cleared her throat.

"Thank you for agreeing to speak with me, Mr. Marchand. I imagine you're a tremendously busy man."

"Oh? What do you imagine I do?"

She welcomed the bracing surge of irritation. *Fleecing aristocrats* was obviously the correct answer. *Whatever rogues get up to, possibly with ropes* was another. How very tempted she was. She was not incapable of coming out with that sort of thing.

Mr. Ogden's entrance saved her from sinking her cause within the first few moments. He slipped into the room and delivered a sheaf of papers and a little bundle wrapped in brown paper and string into Mr. Marchand's outstretched hand.

"If you'd like to sit down, Miss Woodville?"

Mr. Marchand drew out the chair opposite his desk. It was plump and upholstered in cognac-colored velvet, the first truly decadent thing she'd seen here. She settled in.

He took a seat at his desk.

There passed a moment of mutual assessment, during which she could all but feel his eyes rifling through her soul.

The merciless light of day revealed to her that Mr. Marchand was not young. Nor was he precisely old. His wavy dark hair gleamed mahogany where the sun touched it and picked out a few silver threads. His nose appeared to have been broken once, which somehow only added intrigue, and a thin white scar bisected one end of an eyebrow. It seemed improbable to her that anyone had been able to slice him; his face had clearly been chiseled out of granite, from the sharp edges of his jaw to the steep rise of his cheekbones. Except his mouth, which was rather beautiful. Supple and sultry. It looked as though he might actually use it to smile now and again.

She wasn't certain whether she thought he was attractive. It seemed the wrong word. One wouldn't say, "My, look at that attractive man-eating tiger," for instance.

Her breath had gone shallower. She'd tensed her stomach muscles. She didn't know if she didn't want to look away from him or didn't dare look away from him. They seemed one and the same.

He retrieved something from the little sheaf of papers Mr. Ogden had brought in.

"'Dear Mr. Marchand,'" he read. "'I would like to call

upon you at my earliest convenience to discuss an urgent matter. This is regarding an incident that took place in your establishment a week ago. I believe the members of your club unfairly took advantage of my brother's youth and naivete for personal gain, to devastating effect. I should like to meet with you to discuss ways to remedy the harm done. I am certain that together we may reach a mutually satisfying solution. Yours sincerely, the Honorable Guinevere Woodville.'"

It sounded rather brazen and incendiary when she heard it read aloud. She'd written it in the heat of urgency when she'd arrived at the Grand Palace on the Thames. If she had known ahead of time that Mr. Marchand possessed those shoulders, she might have reconsidered her approach. He did not look as though anything ever twinged him. Certainly not guilt or sympathy.

Mr. Marchand's expression still revealed nothing as he idly tapped his fingers on the desk. The sun picked glints from a gold ring on his finger. Instead of a signet, it featured an exquisitely wrought ivory skull. Of course.

"I confess I'm a bit puzzled by the assertion in your letter, Miss Woodville," he began politely. "I wonder if you would be so kind as to explain it to me?"

She cleared her throat. "I assume you are aware, Mr. Marchand, that my brother has inherited another title as a result of a distant relative's demise. As of a fortnight ago, he is styled both the Earl of Highgrove and the Viscount Woodville."

"I'm aware. He announced this at Lucifer's Fall a week ago when he climbed up on the billiard table and shouted"—he ruffled through the papers Mr. Ogden had brought in, which seemed to be notes—"'Huzzah! I'm an earl! I'm an earl!'"

This he read the way an actuary might recite a table of figures.

He looked up at Ginny expectantly.

Ginny was speechless.

"There must be some mistake, Mr. Marchand. Hogarth . . . doesn't typically climb up on things. He's . . . he's afraid of heights."

"Hogarth," he repeated carefully, after a long moment. As if he'd been given something unfamiliar to taste.

"We call him Garth at home," she expounded helpfully. "It's his second name. I know it's a bit unusual, but my parents were art afficionados like you." She tipped her head toward the Caravaggio. "Hence he was named for one of their favorite artists."

"I'm probably less of an art afficionado than an irony afficionado, Miss Woodville."

"Oh, I see. The way it's a bit ironic that your first name is Gabriel, the name of an angel usually referred to as heaven's messenger, while you run a gaming . . ."

Ye gods, his light eyes could, and did, get colder. They were downright arctic now.

"Hell?" he completed almost silkily.

Which is when she sensed it was wisest not to confirm or deny that that was what she had been about to say.

"Look around you, Miss Woodville." He swept out a hand. "Does this establishment resemble hell?"

"I cannot truthfully say, since I haven't personally visited the actual underworld. I've only ever read third-person accounts."

Something at last flickered in his unblinking regard. She could not be certain, however, whether it was amusement, or surprise, or incredulity. Or whether she ought to be worried.

"Your ferns are spectacular," she soothed.

"My—" He stopped and drew in what sounded like a patience-siphoning breath.

"Miss Woodville, since you were raised the daughter of a viscount, I suspect you've been sheltered from such distinctions, but Lucifer's Fall is a gentleman's gaming club. Like White's, only I daresay even more exclusive. Hence its popularity. It bears little resemblance to establishments often referred to as hells." Lest she feel comforted by this claim, he added, "I assure you, I would know."

This didn't surprise her in the least.

"I hope you'll forgive me if I inadvertently trod upon a sensitivity, Mr. Marchand."

"I have precisely zero sensitivities."

She would have loved to argue this point in other circumstances. "How singularly blessed you are in that regard."

Another of those minute little pauses ensued, during which she sensed she was being continually assessed, and it was impossible to know whether it was to her advantage.

"*To* the matter at hand . . . " he continued. He pushed the little paper-wrapped bundle over to her. "We finally managed to disentangle the Earl of Highgrove's cravat from the chandelier. He lost his grip while he was twirling it around his head whilst dancing on the billiards table. I'm afraid there's a slight singe mark where it struck a candle. Thankfully the cravat didn't become a wick and light the entire premises on fire. We were unable to repair the singe, but there's no charge for the laundering. Just one of the many benefits of membership at Lucifer's Fall."

This was a dizzying amount of new information to take in at once.

She gingerly dragged the bundled cravat toward her.

Despite everything, her heart squeezed at the idea of her shy, gangly brother dancing with happy abandon. Ever since their parents' accident, he'd been conservative in speech and motion, unfailingly punctual and scrupulously polite and thoughtful. As if in so doing he could forestall chaos and impose some sort of order on the shocking caprices of fate.

"Thank you." It was difficult to deny that laundry service was a clever benefit. "Obviously my brother got his money's worth from the evening." She said this a trifle bitterly.

Mr. Marchand merely nodded slightly.

"I don't think Hogarth has ever been drunk before. Not even at university."

"That much was clear to everyone witnessing the event."

Oddly, he didn't make it sound like a compliment.

"Hogarth is in fact quite shy, dutiful, and studious," she pressed on. "A very sweet young man. I'm fairly certain he's never gambled outside the pennies we use to play whist at home. He has always been cautious and responsible in all matters. He has never once put a foot wrong in his life . . . until he entered Lucifer's Fall."

Mr. Marchand was not taken in by her melodramatic pause. "It's difficult to predict what a gentleman might do whilst drunk. Overcome a phobia. Dance on tables. Gamble away his inheritance. That sort of thing."

And thusly he'd steered them to the crux of the meeting.

She gathered her nerve. "Given his obvious inexperience

and youth and naivete, I suppose I'm wondering why you allowed him to lose so much money."

She said this mildly. But her heart was jabbing away in her throat.

"Why I *let* him lose . . . " he repeated slowly, marveling. He studied her, idly tapping his fingers. "Miss Woodville, did you happen to read the sign at the front of this building?"

He said this mildly. She wasn't fooled. Nothing about him was mild.

"The one that says 'Lucifer's Fall'? It's a very fine sign. Discreet. Exquisite lettering."

"And are you familiar with the biblical story of Lucifer and his alleged plummet from grace?"

"Oh, that Lucifer? Yes, I've heard of him."

"Very good. Does the name Lucifer's Fall then strike you as the name of a nursery?"

"It wouldn't be my first choice for a nursery, granted. 'Kittens and Unicorns' might be more appropriate."

She didn't know how he'd gotten those faint lines around his eyes, but she was growing more certain it wasn't from laughing.

"Perhaps, then, Miss Woodville, you'll agree that the name of this establishment implies the nature of the risk inherent in entering it."

In other words, ruination and falling from grace were built *right* into the name.

"More of that irony you enjoy, I expect, Mr. Marchand."

"Indeed. I would have named it Kittens and Unicorns if I felt it captured the sort of experience my customers are seeking."

She considered pointing out Kittens and Unicorns would also be ironic, and thought better of it.

"But you *admit* there *is* a risk inherent in entering your premises."

"There is a risk in getting out of bed in the morning, Miss Woodville." He sounded indulgent and almost bored. This was her least favorite way for men to sound. "I was assured by the earl—Hogarth, if you will—when I interviewed him for membership that he has reached his majority. Is this not true?"

"He is twenty-one. I am older by three years." She was feeling older by the minute.

"In other words, yes, he has reached his majority. When he requested a tour of Lucifer's Fall, he professed flattering admiration for all we offer and told me he'd long yearned to be a member. He struck me as gracious, pleasant, and mature. He was also, he assured me, deep of pocket. Which is essential, as the gentlemen at Lucifer's Fall expect deep play from fellow members." Marchand returned to his sheaf of papers. "This"—he pushed a document over to her from his hatefully efficient little stack—"is the agreement your brother signed when he applied for membership at Lucifer's Fall, agreeing to the membership fees and to the rules regarding conduct, discretion, debts, and payments."

She glanced down at it. There was Hogarth's signature, tidy and even apart from big, silly loops on his "l"s.

It gutted her to think that her bashful brother had secretly yearned for something so louche. He'd never made friends easily. He snorted when he laughed, and he laughed when he was nervous. She could easily imagine Hogarth laughing and snorting during his tour of Lucifer's Fall, because he would have been desperate to impress Marchand, whose charisma was engulfing.

Ginny breathed carefully through a fresh surge of righteous anger.

Mr. Marchand thoughtfully drummed his fingers again. "Miss Woodville. You look as though you might have a brain in your head."

"Well. Faint praise is better than none, I suppose," she said brightly.

"So no doubt you understand that those not fortunate enough to be born into wealth and status must forge their own ways in life, using the skills and experience at their disposal. Would you agree that everyone is entitled to a chance to prosper?"

If he thought he could persuade her that running a gaming hell was a legitimate and perfectly reasonable vocation for any man, regardless of his social status, he was sorely misguided.

"Oh, I think I take your point," she said brightly. "And if you're referring to yourself, Mr. Marchand, I think it was very clever of you to discover a way to exploit wealthy men for profit."

He went rigid.

And then he leaned back so very slowly in his chair she was reminded of Dot lowering the tea tray. More accurately: of an arrow being primed for launching.

A scary glint in his eye suggested that he'd just been thrown his favorite red meat.

It was a moment before he spoke.

"Bored, wealthy men are indeed one of England's greatest

resources. But do we exploit chickens for their eggs? Do we exploit sheep for their wool?" He paused. "Do pretty, penniless women exploit wealthy men when they marry for money?" He'd lowered his voice confidingly, which started a traitorous, fuzzy heat at the back of her neck, as if he'd blown a breath there.

She cleared her throat again. She was parched from nerves; a gentleman would have offered her tea. She would not even have rejected a glass of something stronger. Marchand clearly intended to hasten her out of here.

"Quite apart from the fact that those are all debatable and perhaps even specious examples," she continued recklessly, and had the satisfaction of witnessing that scary glint flash again, "all the things you mentioned have in common some useful societal function."

"So your position is that any male recreation that serves no redeeming social purpose is contemptible." This he said neutrally, as though humoring a madwoman.

She was beginning to feel the impact of their exchange in her back teeth, as though they were instead swinging broadswords at each other. She resented Marchand's immovable calm in the face of her barely contained, sweaty desperation, his glossy confidence, the almost banal efficiency with which he conducted a business built on terrifying gains and losses and the destruction of lives, the fact that his waistcoat, striped in chestnut and pewter and done up with silver buttons, looked gorgeous with his coloring. Unusual yet tasteful, dashing without being gawdy. Perfection.

"There's always cricket, I suppose," she said. "It fosters sportsmanship, at least. And if a man takes a ball to the head and drops dead, it only destroys *his* life, not the entire team's."

"The risk is the *point*, Miss Woodville. The risk is the *fun* part," he said with sorrowful incredulity. As though he was disappointed in her powers of reasoning. "Man wasn't fundamentally intended to exist in ceaseless ease, like a pet. A little peril is the spice of life, particularly for a certain kind of comfortable gentleman. They find it stirring to feel a little frightened as long as they're certain they're safe. It's a game in every way to them—even 'the Reaper' nonsense." He gestured; his skull ring winked in the light. "If Lucifer's Fall were to vanish off the face of the Earth tomorrow, they would simply search out this type of experience in some other way, in some other place. I provide a valuable service by allowing them to forget their responsibilities for a time and indulge sometimes outrageous risks in a discreet, beautiful, safe environment."

This sounded like so much elegant hucksterism; she could imagine the gentlemen who applied for membership lapping it up. What stopped her from rolling her eyes was the unsettling grain of truth she sensed in it. *They were laughing right up until the high-flyer rounded the bend,* the neighbor who'd witnessed her parents' accident had told her. As though she would somehow find this comforting.

How could a man with a wife and four children be bored enough to be so reckless?

And even if he *had* been bored, how could he be so self-indulgent?

Had these qualities merely been lying dormant in Hogarth?

"But that's not the whole picture, is it, Mr. Marchand? A . . . business . . . such as yours depends upon the whims of fashion." She was proud of her strategically skeptical pause, and

Mr. Marchand actually nodded, as though he was amused. "It's about wanting to belong, to be accepted by your peers, to be a *part* of something. But if, for instance, the London Bridge suddenly acquired the sort of mystique that compelled men to flock to it, but they continually plummeted to their deaths from it, the public might eventually demand that the government block it off. Or even tear it down."

He tipped his head and gave her a "come now" look, as if to say they both knew that was a ridiculous example. "I *think* I understand what you're trying to say, Miss Woodville. But I can hardly help my mystique, can I?" He fanned his hands self-deprecatingly.

It occurred to her then that Mr. Marchand was toying with her.

Their contest of stares was interrupted by the slap of little running feet on marble floors.

To her amazement, a little boy burst into the room, waving what looked like half a sheet of foolscap.

"Help! What did I do wrong?" He shoved the paper in front Mr. Marchand.

"Fergus, you must ask politely to enter when I've a guest, and say 'please' when you request help." Mr. Marchand was stern but unruffled. He glanced at the paper, frowning slightly. "Look at this. Did you forget to do something?" He pointed.

The boy, towheaded and surprisingly clean for a boy of about seven years old, sucked his bottom lip in thought. Then his face cleared.

"*Carrying!*" the boy said and slapped his forehead. "Cor, I forgot about *carrying* the two. Sorry! Sorry, miss! Please! Thank you!"

Mr. Ogden all but slid into the office, panting as though he'd given chase. "My apologies, sir. I was just headed to the side entrance to take delivery of the Malbec order and he raced past me."

With one hand firmly on the boy's shoulder, he steered him out.

Ginny stared after them.

Then pivoted to look at Mr. Marchand.

A little silence ensued.

"That was a child, Miss Woodville." For the first time since she'd arrived, genuine amusement haunted his mouth.

"I recognized that, thank you."

"It's just that your eyes have gone the size of dinner plates in wonderment."

How Ginny loved a colorful turn of phrase. She wasn't about to let on.

"Is—" She stopped. It was impossible to imagine him in any sort of domesticity. And yet this impossibility only turned up the flame on her curiosity.

"He's an employee," he explained. "The road to iniquity is long. You have to start them out on it young or they'll never fully develop into rogues." He raised his voice a little. "He'll be taking over Mr. Ogden's job in a few weeks."

"Very amusing, sir." Mr. Ogden's voice echoed as he reentered the anteroom.

"Miss Woodville, where is your brother? Does he know you're here?"

The question made her wary.

"He's at home in Sussex. And no, he doesn't know I've come here, but I do not think he would be surprised. I've raised my siblings since we lost our parents eight years ago. And he knows I would do anything for them."

"I see. And what specifically was it you hoped to accomplish when you came here today, Miss Woodville?"

Her heart immediately leaped into a painful gallop. It was probably too late to attempt to ingratiate herself to him, but she suspected nothing she might have said or done would have made a bit of difference, anyway. Still, she needed to try.

She softened her gaze to something she hoped approximated limpid. "I understand this is an extraordinary request. But I would be so grateful if you would please speak to the person to whom Hogarth lost and ask him to tear up Hogarth's vowels. In light of my brother's youth and inexperience. In light of the grave and perhaps permanent damage done to his family."

She might have attempted a few tears, but she was certain they would have evaporated in the rays of scathing incredulity now pouring off Mr. Marchand.

"Miss Woodville. Regardless of your contempt for the nature of it, my business is successful because I never trouble a member to"—he paused, as if he could hardly believe he was about to issue the next words—"return money fairly won."

"I understand," she said humbly. "And I suppose it's only good practice to feed your members a new sacrificial lamb now and again. Someone from whom a large win is all but guaranteed."

She could not seem to help herself. If she could dent his armor even a little, she might leave here with her pride intact, if nothing else.

Mr. Marchand regarded her for a long moment of alarming stillness. His expression was thoughtful, his brow furrowed, his eyes hard and bright as dagger blades. She wondered if he was trying to decide which part of her to sink his teeth into first.

She took a breath. "I will be frank with you, Mr. Marchand."

"Will you? I wonder what you've been up until now," he said flatly.

"Discussions regarding the marriage settlements for my sisters, Felicity and Fiona, are scheduled for a fortnight hence. The success of these, *and* their marriages, and their futures, are predicated on the assumption of dowries that, as of a particular night Hogarth spent at Lucifer's Fall, no longer exist."

Marchand's head went back and came down in a nod of comprehension.

"I assume this applies to your dowry, too?"

She didn't reply. Yes, of course, her dowry, too. But this was quite beside the point, and she had no reason to believe she'd endeared herself to Marchand in any way. He would likely be pleased enough to tell her to go hang.

"No doubt you see the urgency, Mr. Marchand. I cannot bear to see my sisters' hopes crushed and their futures ruined, and I know Hogarth is devastated. If you would kindly share the name of the person to whom Hogarth lost, I promise I'll never trouble you again. I understand that *you* cannot speak to this person. But surely you cannot object if I had a word with him?" She beseeched him with her eyes.

This, in fact, was the information she'd been angling for all along. She knew the odds were very long of getting it from Marchand. But her chances of persuading a man of her own station—a man who might even have a daughter, who had a dowry—to take pity on her and her family were infinitely greater than budging the man in front of her.

Mr. Marchand was now studying her curiously.

And then he smiled faintly.

It wasn't a pleasant smile at all. He looked impressed and oddly . . . satisfied. No: vindicated. As if some unspoken suspicion had been confirmed for him.

"It seems you and I are not too different, after all, Miss Woodville," he said gently. The kind of "gently" that made the hair prickle on her neck in alarm.

He'd clearly chosen that sentence for maximum offense.

That's when she realized that not only did he recognize her tactics, but they were child's play to him. As simple as carrying the two.

"I expect you already know that if your brother were to violate any of his agreements regarding repayment of debt and confidentiality, it would mean the destruction of his reputation. I don't need to tell you that this, of course, would influence how his entire family is perceived. This"—he pushed another document over to her—"is his signed acknowledgment of his debts, which he also recorded in the book of wins and losses we keep. As a gentleman should."

Some tiny part of her was outraged that she was impressed with the thoroughness of the recordkeeping.

And then the plural of the word registered.

Or more like detonated.

"I was under the impression it was just the one debt."

"He owes fifteen thousand pounds to one member. And he owes the house four thousand pounds." He said this gruesome thing matter-of-factly.

Her stomach plummeted again and the room momentarily guttered like a candle flame in a breeze before her eyes.

"The house?" Her voice had gone hoarse.

"Me. I'm the house, Miss Woodville. Your brother is four thousand pounds in debt to me."

The blood migrated away from her skin as if fleeing far, far away from this fresh horror. She was all-over ice now.

"Once per year, members are allowed to borrow up to that amount against their accounts here at Lucifer's Fall. Which your brother did, against all advice, after he lost the initial amount. He then rapidly lost the four thousand pounds. The agreement he signed when he joined the club states explicitly that he has thirty days to repay it. I'm also given to understand that he won a few other wagers of a, and I quote, 'more whimsical nature.' My employee on the scene noted this." He gestured with his chin to his notes.

"Whimsi . . . I don't know what that means," she croaked.

"My records indicate only that your brother won an orange from Lord Grayford and a chamber pot painted with the king's face from Mr. Fenwick. Perhaps there were more so-called whimsical wins that went unrecorded."

Oh, for God's sake.

"Why didn't anyone *stop* him?" She was perilously close to shrill.

He was impatient now. "Miss Woodville, he's a grown man. He *chose* to do it. Surely no one knows better than a woman that it's men who invariably do the *choosing* in life. And while your brother's evening was eventful, it was not exceptional. Every evening at Lucifer's Fall is lively in an entirely different way. He was clearly having a wonderful time, until he wasn't."

It seemed inconceivable to her that he could discuss a life-shattering catastrophe so matter-of-factly.

"Perhaps the more important question, Miss Woodville, is why *you* let him do it. Since you raised him."

She stared at him. *Well played, Mr. Marchand,* she thought. It was so exquisitely timed and absolutely brutal that she sucked in a breath.

"My brother is his own man, Mr. Marchand, as you noted," she said coolly.

"I see," he replied dubiously.

Fear and loathing expanded in her chest. She had so far accomplished nothing unless it was gaining an enemy. She consoled herself with the conviction that not a tactic in the world would shift this man if he didn't want to be shifted.

He was studying her. *What do you see, Mr. Marchand?* She longed to know. His expression remained inscrutable. And yet she'd never felt so thoroughly *looked* at.

"Miss Woodville . . . How many women do you suppose have visited Lucifer's Fall for the purposes of haranguing me over the past five years?"

"Eleven," she hazarded.

"Close."

Distantly she heard men's voices and the clink of what sounded like bottles. And was that a woman's giggle? Perhaps Martine, whoever she was, had at last arrived.

Mr. Ogden breezed into the office and placed something in front of Mr. Marchand, who glanced at it, snatched up his quill, and dipped it.

"More than a few women, Miss Woodville. And while I do have some sympathy for their predicaments"—he scrawled his

name across the bottom of the paper and sprinkled sand—
"they, like you, inevitably come up against the uncomfortable
conclusion that, despite any initial impressions to the con-
trary, I'm actually a . . . Mr. Ogden, what was it Lord Gramercy
called me the other day?"

"A thoroughgoing bastard, sir."

"Thank you, Mr. Ogden."

Mr. Ogden left again, gingerly balancing the freshly signed
invoice, blowing sand from it.

Mr. Marchand regarded her evenly.

She was proud that she didn't even flinch, although that
"b" word entered her like a dart. She thought yearningly of
the Epithet Jar in the sitting room at the Grand Palace on the
Thames, presiding over civility.

"How efficient of you to delegate your epithets to Mr. Ogden."

"Are you complimenting my business acumen, Miss Woodville?" he said softly.

"I suppose I am," she said carefully. "Imagine what a triumph
you'd be if you'd decided to farm sheep instead. I suppose your
experience with hells necessarily consigned you to . . ."

She gestured broadly to the establishment at large and almost poked herself with her hidden knitting needle.

"Indeed," he said silkily. "We all play the hands we're dealt,
Miss Woodville. Just as women are so often consigned to using tears, swoons, or seduction to get what they want, because those are so often the only resources at their disposal.
Women have, in fact, done everything from threatening me
with bodily harm to offering the pleasure of their bodies to
me in exchange for forgiving a debt or for persuading their

husbands to stop gambling. No one, least of all me, faults any woman who attempts it."

Ginny had the strangest sensation that she was slowly being backed into a corner.

That he'd in fact been herding her neatly into a particular position during this entire conversation.

"I am generally disinclined to accept such proposals. However, given that your letter mentions your desire for the two of us to reach a mutually satisfactory solution to resolve your brother's debt, I have decided to offer that last option to you. Despite your contempt for the way I conduct my life."

Ginny's breath seized in her lungs. "I beg your pardon?"

"I'll call off your brother's debt to the house if you spend a night in my bed."

"In your . . ."

She stopped just in time. Because she had the horrible suspicion that if she asked what that would entail, he would tell her in no uncertain terms.

The silence was so total it was as though sound had never existed. The air seemed to cease circulating. Surprise obliterated her ability to form thoughts.

His polite expression was more surreal than any dream.

He simply waited.

Because he knew she was imagining it, and he wanted to witness her doing that.

And she *was* imagining it. How could she not?

It was her first realization that senses and sense were not always in accord. Because while her mind reeled in shock, her skin hummed and heated, as if coming alive in anticipation of being covered by him. A strange thrill mingled with queasy fear and unseemly yearning pooled low in her belly.

She could not look away from him.

And that bastard knew.

Just as she knew what she ought to say right now.

Perhaps driving her away had been the point of his proposition. But it was already several seconds past the time she ought to have shrieked in outrage and stormed out in a huff.

The longer she waited the more she incriminated herself.

But she would never again have a chance to ask the question that burned.

"Why me?" Her voice was hoarse.

"Because . . ." He leaned back in his chair and studied her again, as if he wanted to get his answer precisely right. "You have the look of a woman who has long yearned for someone to tell her what to do."

Her vision flickered in shock.

It was the worst thing anyone had ever said to her.

It was as if he'd casually rummaged through her soul and plucked out into the daylight her most painful, shameful fear: That for eight years, she'd been inadequate to the task of raising her siblings. To carrying out her mother's wishes. That she had been faking it all this time, and she had mostly failed. That their lives were merely shambolic, and if she'd been better at it, perhaps Hogarth wouldn't have gone crazy and gambled when the inheritance arrived. Perhaps he simply would have ordered his own engraved calling cards.

She had never hated someone more than in that moment.

"Well," she said brightly, at last. " 'Thoroughgoing' doesn't begin to describe it."

His smile was small, weary, and patient, as if, at long, long last, a slow pupil had grasped a concept.

"Shall I construe from your silence that you aren't amenable to that particular solution? Or were you simply taking a moment to imagine the evening we might share?" He said this appalling thing distractedly, whilst consulting his watch.

He was brilliant in a way foreign to her experience and terrifying in a way she could not have anticipated. None of her paltry weapons were equal to it.

"The former," she assured him coolly, struggling to match his hateful insouciance with as much aplomb. She was likely fooling no one, given every inch of her skin was on fire with outrage and her bright pink face was currently pointed right at him.

"Ah, well. We can't all have brilliant business acumen." He smiled sympathetically. "I'll just leave that offer on the table, shall I? Meanwhile, I'll await Hogarth's repayment. And, of course, his immense debt doesn't preclude your brother from enjoying his membership, should he choose to visit Lucifer's Fall again."

She wanted very much to tell him where he could leave this offer, which would require him to bend over and dexterously but roughly insert it into a narrow passage on his person.

She gave a start when he pushed back his chair abruptly and stood.

As if on cue, two liveried footmen bustled through the door. One settled a splendid many-caped greatcoat over his shoulders while the other thrust a gold-topped walking stick and hat into his hand. Marchand tucked the stick under his arm and began pulling on his gloves.

"Though it will no doubt astonish you to hear that other people seek my company, Miss Woodville, I've an engagement. Mr. Ogden, if you would kindly escort Miss Woodville off the premises and hail a hack for her. But as a token of our esteem, take her out through the special visitors' exit, not over the alligator moat."

The bastard winked at her.

"Oh, and Miss Woodville? You're not left-handed. The knitting needle should be tucked in your right sleeve if you want the slightest chance of actually skewering someone. Though of course you'd never have a chance of besting *me*."

He bowed, ironically. And in a flourish of coat and a glint of walking stick, he strode from the room and swiftly around the corner, flanked by the footmen, out of sight.

She stared after him.

She finally rose to stand on shaky legs, feeling as though she'd been swept up in a whirlwind then dumped ceremoniously on the ground.

She smoothed her hands over her skirts. They were clammy and damp inside her gloves. She had never changed temperature so often in so short a time in her entire life.

Mr. Ogden cleared his throat. "If you would be so kind as to accompany me, Miss Woodville," he said gently.

"Are there really alligators?"

"I'm afraid I'm not at liberty to say, miss."

Chapter Three

Mrs. Angelique Durand froze as she was lacing up her dress for dinner and stared, astounded, at her husband.

"Lucien, he's arriving *tonight?* And you're just remembering this now? You *told* him he could stay here?"

"Yes to all of those questions, and I'm sorry, to all of them, too." Lucien, Lord Bolt, was contrite. "I truly didn't mean to trample on our established order." The established order being that Angelique and Delilah Hardy, the owners and proprietresses of the improbably little jewel box of a building near the London docks known as the Grand Palace on the Thames, made all the decisions about guests. Their husbands, who were partners in an import and export endeavor called the Triton Group, were content to leave them to it. "Call it an impulse of bonhomie. Gabriel Marchand saved my life once in my wilder days. At the very least, he saved my skull. Someone was about to take a swing at it with a walking stick and he, ah, intervened in a timely and forceful way. I bumped into him near the warehouses this morning. We reminisced and traded war stories and he mentioned he was having a new roof put on his home, so he was looking for a place to stay for the duration. I told him about our little paradise here. I also suppose I was bragging a little, because I feel sorry for everyone who isn't able to live here."

Angelique knew his last sentence was both sincere and a tactic. It amused her, and it worked. She felt the same way. "How many times *has* your life required saving? No, don't tell me," she said hurriedly. "I still occasionally have nightmares about the one you told me about." In his infamously wild youth—well documented by the gossip sheets—Lucien, styled Viscount Bolt, bastard son of the odious Duke of Brexford and his late French mistress, had been kidnapped and hurled into the Thames in the dark of night. He'd been rescued from the murk by a Dutch ship about to leave port and had been presumed dead until his return, a decade later. "So what does Mr. Marchand do now?"

He hesitated. "By *do*, you mean . . ."

"Lucien."

"He is the proprietor of a gentleman's club."

She stared at him.

"Lucien Emil Jean-Luc Durand. I *know* you don't mean 'gaming hell.'"

"Every day I thank my creator for a wife who's smart as well as beautiful. For right you are. It's not quite a hell."

"Lucien."

"Let's just say gaming hells played a significant role in his past, just as they did in mine. And at these hells he learned how to become a successful business owner, just as these hells in my formative years are in part what gave your husband the air of danger you find so alluring. Speaking of which, have you seen my favorite stockings?" He was riffling through his clothes press.

Being married meant knowing that her husband, who had sailed the high seas and killed a pirate or two, had a favorite pair of stockings, which looked to her exactly like all of his other stockings. Why this pair of stockings was exceptional remained a mystery to her, but she always made sure it was handled with tender care when they sent out the laundry.

"Here." She scooped up a wrapped bundle on her dressing table. "The laundry was returned to us this afternoon so I haven't yet had a chance to put everything away."

"Ah! Thank you." He sat down on their bed to pull them on. "Marchand and I struck up a friendship of sorts at the Pit, which *was* an infamous hell, over a decade ago, because his job was to . . ." He trailed off again at Angelique's expression.

"His job was to stop thugs from bashing heads? In other words, his *job* was to actually bash heads? Lovely."

"Back *then*. And before you draw conclusions about him, one might say that this was Captain Hardy's job, too. The 'stopping thugs' part."

"I should *love* to see Captain Hardy's expression when you share this comparison with him."

Lucien laughed, because he would love to see it, too. Captain Hardy was the legendary blockade captain who had at last broken the back of the English smuggling trade. King George IV had even sent him a silver cup as a wedding present as a token of his gratitude and esteem. And while Hardy had become Lucien's good friend and confidant and partner in the Triton Group, they were different in as many ways as they were alike.

"Angelique, Marchand has done tremendously well for himself against formidable odds. He's an enterprising, hard-working, resourceful man of significant charm. I daresay he's wealthier than we are now. And who knows better than we do about creating something from nothing? Or about taking a gamble?"

Her wily husband was making good points. The Grand Palace on the Thames itself was a veritable monument to risk. When the former Countess of Derring, now Delilah Hardy, inherited the building from her late husband, the only occupants had been mice and spiders and possibly ghosts. Desperation, imagination, ingenuity, and hope had restored the building, and Helga's scones, Gordon the cat, the Epithet Jar, and their list of rules had turned it into the home of their dreams. Delilah and Angelique had taken the greatest risk of all by falling in love with and marrying Captain Tristan Hardy and Lucien Durand, respectively, when miracle of miracles, they appeared at the boardinghouse door and became guests.

From the very first they had vowed to never allow anyone they didn't like to live there for any duration. This lofty ideal didn't always stand up to the vicissitudes of commerce. Regardless, every guest was patiently cherished for the duration of their stay, whether they were someone the entire country revered (like a war-hero duke), or someone who needed to be dragged kicking and screaming out of the place by the British army (this had happened only once), or whether they were Mr. Delacorte, whom no one yet had been able to categorize, but no one ever forgot, and most people eventually loved. Though he was of a certainty an acquired taste.

"I can see, however, how both you and Delilah might want to exercise a bit of caution, considering the turmoil a certain recent guest has inspired."

Now Lucien was fighting a little dirty.

She hesitated. "*Turmoil* is a bit overstated, Lucien."

"If you say so," Lucien said dryly.

It was true that combining certain guests in the sitting room could be a little risky, such as mingling a duke with a scandalous opera diva, or mingling Mr. Delacorte with . . . well, anybody . . . but that was part of the thrill of the game. So confident had they become in their skill as social alchemists, Delilah and Angelique had invited Daniel Peck and his family to stay. They had never before had a guest quite like him.

They were beginning to think they never should again.

Mr. Delacorte was unexpectedly bearing the brunt of Daniel's stay. Which was a shame, because he'd also been attempting to teach Dot how to play chess, and this had qualified him for martyrhood even before Dot decided to give all of her chess pieces first names.

"But what of Mr. Marchand's character?" Angelique pressed.

Lucien regarded her evenly. "Do you trust my judgment?"

This was a mildly fraught question in any marital discussion.

"It is generally impeccable in most things," she admitted carefully. "From stockings to wives."

When he smiled, her heart performed lazy cartwheels. In her weaker moments she wondered why she would ever argue with him about anything. She felt absurdly lucky to sleep every night next to a man who had eyes the color of moss agates, the soul of a sardonic poet and made love with inventive fervor.

"I don't think you'll be able to fault his manners, Angelique. Which, as we both know, cannot be said about everyone who lives here."

Last night in the sitting room while Mrs. Pariseau was read-ing aloud from *The Arabian Nights Entertainments*, Mr. Delacorte had thumped his sternum lightly to release a little belch, to everyone's startled consternation. He'd been so caught up in the story he'd forgotten he wasn't alone. He was forgiven, as Mrs. Pariseau's captivating way of doing all the voices *could* sweep anyone away. Unlike cursing, belching in the sitting room was not subject to the one-penny fine imposed by the Epithet Jar, which Mr. Delacorte reliably kept jingling. It was how they paid for the daily newspapers. Mr. Delacorte firmly believed the Grand Palace on the Thames was smoothing away all of his rough corners.

"So what does Mr. Marchand look like?" Angelique won-dered.

"You'll be disappointed to hear that he's nowhere *near* as good looking as I am."

She laughed. "While that goes without saying . . ."

He grinned at her. "All jokes aside, allow me to put it like this: Mrs. Pariseau will love him."

Their longtime resident Mrs. Pariseau was a handsome woman in her middle years who was thoroughly enjoying her relatively monied widowhood. Adventurous of spirit and in-tellect, she never wanted to be married again, but there was nothing she loved more than a gorgeous man, unless it was arcane discussion.

And, every now and then, fanning the usual spirited sitting room discourse into something close to bedlam.

They adored her and they did like to keep her happy.

"It's for less than a fortnight, Angelique. What could happen? Mr. Marchand is nearly forty years old," he half jested. "One foot in the grave."

Lucien looped his arms around his wife and she settled into them with a sigh of resignation and contentment. He briefly rested his chin atop her golden-blond head.

They knew full well what kinds of mischief men that age could get up to without even trying. For instance, the Duke of Valkirk had acquired an unlikely scandalous opera singer wife at about that age as a result of living under their roof.

"But now I have to tell Delilah that you invited someone to stay without asking us first, and she won't love that, Lucien. She's kind and she'll allow it, of course. I'll do it, but I think you should apologize to her for forgetting. And we'll still want to have a little chat with him first, as we do with every guest."

"Fair enough," he said equably. He kissed her forehead, she fussed a bit with his cravat to straighten it, and they went down to join the guests for the cheerful chaos that was dinner at the Grand Palace on the Thames.

* * *

The little white boardinghouse was tucked in among the other buildings at the docks like a princess among cutthroats. It was closing in on eleven o'clock at night by the time Marchand found it, but the lamp was still out on its hook.

He paused before the door and tipped his head back to watch the half circle of the moon slip out from behind a cloud. Still seemed like a magician's trick to him, that, after all these years. He'd learned the difference between beauty and ugliness and between harmony and chaos thanks to the moon. It was the contrast between how he'd felt in his body when he looked up at it, and how he'd felt when looking at the squalor on the streets of St. Giles. Its soft, clean, remote glow had been the only lovely thing in his world for a long time.

Its light illuminated a rat fastidiously washing its little ears in the rivulets cascading from one of the modest gargoyles lining the roof edge. Nigh on twenty years ago, Marchand had gotten clean in much the same way, whenever he could. Small, hungry, dirty, frightened, perpetually, ferally vigilant and alone—he'd been a creature composed of instinct and nothing else, all his faculties forever pitched for threats. Certainly not superior to that resourceful rat.

How ironic that it had uniquely prepared him to be the ton's latest obsession.

A haze of glamour and enigma surrounded him now. When he appeared on Lucifer's Fall's betting floor, the members turned toward him like weathervanes, straightening their spines, smoothing their hair, unsettled and excited. He circulated among them, distributing charm, solace, encouragement, wit, diplomacy, mediation, and, if necessary, some light menace. He remembered the names of wives, children, favorite liquors, mistresses. They craved his attention.

They all felt cherished, and they were all a little afraid of him.

Marchand hoarded details like currency. A clenched jaw or slumped shoulders, a gleam in an eye, a spring in a step—he took note of such things the way one might study the elements to forecast the weather. He knew when Lord Galworthy was about to cast his accounts, when Mr. Dunhill was about to take a swing at Mr. Grissom, when Sir Randolph had a brilliant hand; he'd witnessed the furtive, tender looks and touches Lord Milton and Mr. Hanbury exchanged as they slowly fell in love. They were both married men, and they had children.

He judged no one.

This was less a magnanimity of character than a cynical—and almost heretical, given that he was English, and the English did love their classes—conviction that all men were the same under the skin. The only real difference between the ugliest of hells in which he had learned his trade and Lucifer's Fall was the smell. Instead of vomit and sour ale and gin and the funk of the unwashed, it was now rich man musk: bay rum, starch, expensive tobacco, polished leather, brandy, and whiskey. They loosened their cravats and sweated through their shirts over the kinds of wagers that elevated heartbeats to just shy of apoplexy. But the shiny faces and avid bloodshot eyes were the same in every hell, as were the motives. Some did it for the money, others did it for the reason a child loves being pushed on a swing, for the giddy highs between the lows. Others did it in order to feel anything at all.

He didn't care why they did it, as long as they did it in Lucifer's Fall.

His dinner companion tonight, Lord Charton, could trace his family lineage back to William the Conqueror. He would have been both outraged and wounded to know that Marchand thought all men were the same under the skin. He had chattered nervously, unwittingly desperate to impress an orphaned bastard from St. Giles.

And all through the dinner, the word "specious" in Miss Guinevere Woodville's voice had echoed in Marchand's head.

Marchand knew a lot of words now, but good dictionaries

remained outlandishly expensive and rare, so he didn't know that one.

He had a bit of a weakness for clever, spiky women, and that was the only reason he'd indulged that girl at all today. He knew she was frightened, but Miss Woodville also had a dangerous amount of nerve. And while God only knew he'd had cause over the years to be grateful to women who traded sex for money, he'd rightly suspected the very notion of that would horrify her. He'd made his offer strategically to get her out of his office, and he had no regrets.

He could also have told Miss Woodville that sanctimony was a luxury of the comfortable. So-called morality quickly went *right* out the window when one was desperate. If her family was indeed penniless now thanks to her brother's eventful night at Lucifer's Fall, she'd learn this soon enough.

She might even learn that she, too, had a price.

But he was confident he'd never see her again.

Hats off to the girl for getting under his skin, he supposed.

But his encounter with Miss Woodville wasn't the only reason his mood was edgy tonight. He always slept badly as a certain anniversary approached. It never failed to remind him that he'd gotten everything he needed and wanted a little too late for it to really matter, and that included Lucifer's Fall. In his weaker moments he could not shake the sense that this meant he'd failed, after all.

But nothing made him feel more alive than ambition. The Grand Palace on the Thames was *right* next to a livery stable. Never had a building location been better suited for a gaming hell.

Perhaps he'd call it Kittens and Unicorns when he owned it. Because he wanted it. And everyone had a price.

He raised the knocker on the red door and gave it a smart rap.

He waited. The rat, finished with its ablutions, scurried off.

After a few seconds he put his ear to the door. A muffled male voice muttered "Ow!" while a woman indignantly said what sounded like "The moon isn't even full!"

Marchand stepped swiftly backward when at last the peep hatch swung open.

A large pale eye appeared in the little window.

"Welcome to the Grand Palace on the Thames, the most exclusive boardinghouse in London!" The eye belonged to a cheerful young woman. This was all said in a breathless rush, as though she'd run a mile to get to the door.

"Is it? Well, then. Tonight must be my lucky night."

"I'm afraid that depends, sir. Curfew is in five minutes. And Mrs. Durand and Mrs. Hardy will want to speak with you first."

What on earth? Bolt hadn't mentioned a *curfew*. "As it so happens, miss, 'exclusive' is my very favorite word."

"Isn't it wonderful? I like it, too!" She seemed delighted with their accord.

"Forgive me. I ought to have told you, miss, that I'm Mr. Marchand, a friend of Lord Bolt's, and that I'm expected. I wonder if my valise and I might come in out of the drizzle."

Gabriel blinked when the peep hatch slammed shut.

Some sort of murmured conferral took place behind the door. And then he heard the slide of bolts and the clunk of latches.

The door swung open.

He stepped slowly, wonderingly inside.

A fine crystal chandelier sprinkled light over a black-and-white-checked marble foyer. He stared up at it, as momentarily arrested as if it were an earthbound constellation. Low fires burned in the rooms on either side of the foyer.

Before him stood a petite maid in a white cap and apron. The footman beside her was strapping enough to hurl thugs out of gaming hells. Marchand approved. It was the only sort of footman an establishment ought to have at the docks, a part of the city where one was slightly more likely to be stabbed than in, for instance, Grosvenor Square.

"How do you do? As I mentioned a few moments ago, I'm Mr. Gabriel Marchand."

The maid was staring at him much the way he'd stared at the chandelier.

She said nothing. Instead, a vivid shade of pink scrolled from her collarbone to her hairline.

As women often responded with abrupt silence and violent blushes when they first got a look at him, Marchand wryly accepted it for the tribute it more or less was.

"How do you do, Mr. Marchand? I'm Mr. Pike." The footman bowed, then added, dryly, "And this is Dot. If you'd like to have a seat in our reception room"—he gestured to the room to Marchand's right—"Dot will tell Mrs. Durand and Mrs. Hardy that you've arrived. May I take your hat and coat?"

The footman gave the gawking Dot a little nudge with his elbow.

Dot gave a start, dipped a curtsy, then whirled and bolted up the stairs.

Bemused, Marchand surrendered his coat and hat and walking stick to Mr. Pike, who ferried them away. He kept his valise with him.

In the reception room, firelight danced over a pair of softly worn pink settees. His feet sank into a thick, faded carpet patterned in similar shades. A cheery profusion of wildflowers were stuffed into a vase on the mantel; two silhouette portraits of women hung on either side of the fireplace. He wondered if they depicted the proprietresses.

Marchand had lived in crates in fetid alleys, in rooms crammed with a dozen other people, in tiny rented flats in crumbling buildings. When he'd finally bought his own London town house, he'd furnished it sparely but expensively. Some of his taste was innate; some of his taste was learned. He could now easily discern fine materials from not fine and genuine from fake.

As he took in this room, he found himself breathing shallowly through an odd, gathering tension in his chest.

Peculiarly, it felt almost like resentment.

But if he didn't know better, he might have called it yearning.

If he hadn't vanquished any inclination toward that most pointless of all emotions years ago.

He paced restlessly before the hearth.

Finally, he settled onto a settee, surrendering almost reluctantly to its comfort.

He idly contemplated how he might refurnish this room when he owned the building. These days, if he wanted something—anything—he generally got it. Resourceful ruthlessness was another of the gifts he'd taken from St. Giles.

He swiftly rose to his feet again at the sound of footsteps crossing the foyer. The two lovely women approaching—a brunette in maroon silk and a blonde in brown—were smiling at him as if he were the prodigal son returned at last. This mordantly amused him. People looked at him in a *lot* of different ways, but this was never one of them.

"Mr. Marchand, I'm Mrs. Hardy and this is Mrs. Durand." Mrs. Hardy was the brunette. "We were growing concerned! We're so delighted you've arrived safely."

He bowed. "It's a pleasure to meet you both. Lord Bolt made this place sound like a paradise when he told me about it, and I can see nothing to contradict his opinion of it. I apologize for arriving so late or for causing concern. My meeting with a potential new colleague went longer than I anticipated and hacks were surprisingly scarce this evening."

"Please do not worry about it, Mr. Marchand. I know Lucien wanted to be here to greet you, but you can blame me for his absence. I insisted he go on up to sleep, as he and Captain Hardy have an early start tomorrow morning. He is looking forward to your stay."

"I look forward to spending time with him again as well. I've never seen a man look so contented. I'm told the food here is remarkable. And I don't think I've ever seen a finer chandelier."

He was apparently saying all the right things, because the ladies' faces went brilliant with pleasure.

"We won't keep you, Mr. Marchand, as it sounds as though you've had a long day and no doubt you would like to get up to your room," Mrs. Hardy said. "We've got the fire burning hot and high in there for you. Perhaps you would like some drinking chocolate brought up, or some tea?"

The words "fire" and "chocolate" sounded absurdly seductive to Marchand.

"But first, why don't we have a seat here while you take a look at our rules to make certain you feel able to comply with them before you decide to stay." Mrs. Durand handed him a little printed card.

What the devil? Bolt hadn't mentioned any *conditions*, either.

The ladies and Marchand settled opposite each other on the pink settees.

He bent his head to read:

All guests will eat dinner together at least four times per week.

All guests must gather in the drawing room after dinner for at least an hour at least four times per week. We feel it fosters a sense of friendship and the warm, familial, congenial atmosphere we strive to create here at the Grand Palace on the Thames.

All guests should be quietly respectful and courteous of other guests at all times, though spirited discourse is welcome.

Guests may entertain other guests in the drawing room.

Curfew is at 11:00 p.m. The front door will be securely locked then. You will need to wait until morning to be admitted if you miss curfew.

If the proprietresses collectively decide that a transgression or series of transgressions warrants your eviction from the Grand Palace on the Thames, you will find your belongings neatly packed and placed near the front door.

You will not be refunded the balance of your rent.

Gentlemen may smoke in the Smoking Room only.

Most of those rules were sensible. But he wasn't at all certain how he felt about being required to dine and discourse spiritedly with a house full of strangers for the next few weeks. It had been *eons* since he'd been required to do something he didn't want to do. He was fairly certain he'd lost the knack.

Despite himself, he was pleased he'd squeaked in under the Grand Palace on the Thames's curfew tonight. Many would be surprised to learn that a man who oversaw veritable nightly orgies of spending and drinking was punctual to a fault.

"I'm curious as to what constitutes spirited discourse," he ventured politely.

"Oh, we have great fun in the sitting room," Mrs. Durand told him. "Our guest Mrs. Pariseau often reads stories aloud, and she does all the voices for the characters. Sometimes others take a turn. We like Greek myths, and horrid novels, and we've been reading *The Arabian Nights Entertainments* lately. And last night we all went around and said what tree we would be if we were trees, instead of people."

After a moment he repeated, politely, "Trees?" And by that he meant *you have got to be bloody joking.*

They nodded cheerfully in tandem.

He inspected them for signs of mischief, but both ladies were admirably inscrutable.

"Discussions can get a bit, well, *heated* at times, which is always exciting," Mrs. Hardy added.

"We've several avid chess players under our roof, too, if you play. But if you're feeling a bit shy about socializing, you can bring down a book or some correspondence and just quietly sit with us."

Shy? He narrowed his eyes. He had the sense that he was being lured into some sort of trap, the nature of which he could not quite identify. He tried to picture Bolt, who had once raced his high-flyer down Bond Street and often had to be extricated from fistfights, sitting about and comparing himself to a tree.

Though when he looked into Mrs. Durand's lovely hazel eyes it was a little easier to imagine how that had come to pass.

Domesticity was a religion to which Marchand did not subscribe. He did not aspire to a wife. And he was almost never at leisure. He worked; he went to operas and musicales and horse races and boxing matches; he took fencing lessons and fired guns at Manton's; he enjoyed short-lived but satisfying carnal liaisons that often ended tempestuously, because he was "not an easy man," or so he was frequently told, and which was certainly putting it lightly. He didn't suppose any of this would be changing anytime soon.

Though he'd gotten considerably more cautious about entanglements as he'd grown older. He'd learned the cost.

"Certainly I'm happy to comply with your rules for the

duration of my stay. I, in fact, also have a similar list of rules for conduct for my gentleman's club. Men in particular need to be told how to behave, don't you think?"

They all laughed together knowingly.

Lucifer's Fall's list of rules was shorter: Discretion, of course, as he'd told Miss Woodville, was one of them. Repeated violence—a man would be forgiven one or two thrown punches—would get a member suspended. Cheating was the cardinal sin. A man would be expelled from the club and the proverbial social earth salted of his name if he cheated. Marchand would personally see to it. He'd needed to do this only once before, to a nefarious viscount, and witnessing the results had apparently put the fear of God—or rather, Marchand—into the other members. The man had ultimately left the country.

"We've set aside a smoking room for men to temporarily escape the shackles of etiquette, should you find them too suffocating." Mrs. Hardy apparently sensed the run of his thoughts.

"Oh, thank God."

Thankfully they laughed at that, too.

"Have you ever evicted anyone?" He pointed to that particular rule on the card.

"Yes," Mrs. Hardy said simply.

His curiosity burned.

He thought better of asking them to expound. A warm room and drinking chocolate awaited him.

Surely he could follow a few rules in order to advance his agenda. Which was, of course, getting them to sell the building to him.

"Certainly I'm happy to comply with your rules." His staff was smart and well-trained. They could do without him for a few nights per week. "And drinking chocolate would be a very civilized way to end my day, thank you."

"We're *so* pleased you want to stay," Mrs. Hardy told him, sounding sincere. "Dot will bring up your chocolate." She produced a room key from a jingling set at her waist. "It's the third floor, last on the left. Mr. Pike will help you with your valise, if you like."

He thanked them, and politely declined Mr. Pike's assistance.

He wondered if they would have indeed thrown him out tonight if he didn't agree to the rules. He rather thought they would have, just as warmly as they'd welcomed him. Perversely, he approved. It hadn't before occurred to him that implacability could also be kind.

Chapter Four

Ginny's room at the Grand Palace on the Thames was soothing as a lullaby and snug as a burrow. But her view out the window was of an alley between buildings, and twice she'd seen the same two cats, one ginger (she'd named him Pumpkinhead), one black and white (she'd named him Inkblot), meeting apparently specifically to fight. They began by staring and yelling at each other, backs arched, ears flattened, before exploding into a brief, snarly cyclonic tangle, complete with great drifts of fur. Then they parted again.

It was like her own personal Punch and Judy show, and a perfect metaphorical representation of the inside of her head at the moment.

As the Grand Palace on the Thames rules allowed a few times per week, she'd decided to take her dinner in her room, and she'd sent her regrets regarding the sitting room gathering as well, though she genuinely rued not being present for the next chapter of *The Arabian Nights Entertainments*. She was simply not prepared to blithely socialize so shortly after she'd been emotionlessly sexually propositioned.

Every glancing thought of Gabriel Marchand sent heat

roaring over her skin as though she'd hurled another log on a fire.

Her emotions were ricocheting like a moth trapped in a jar between absolute fury at the cold *nerve* of the man, to a sick fear that she had failed to accomplish a single thing by her visit to him, to a dark fascination that regrettably refused to ebb.

It was as though Marchand had somehow infected her with a low fever. She had not ever considered herself an object purely of desire; more specifically, she had never considered herself an *object*.

To think that she might have peacefully lived out her life without knowing that something so primitive as *lust*—because she knew that's what all that heat and tingling was about—lived within her independent of sense and good breeding, like a dragon chained in a dungeon.

She closed her eyes and willed to mind the image of Francis's admiring gaze. His shyly ardent compliments would be balm right now. If she'd had anything like a dowry, he might have already proposed, and she never would have met Marchand. But Francis was the third son of a duke, and his wealthy parents were baldly practical about money and family connections.

She could hardly fault them. Her own family's budget had gripped her by the short hairs for the last eight years. It was often the first thing she thought of in the morning and the last thing at night. A family trust managed by her father's solicitor helped a little with the estate upkeep and funded Hogarth's education, and it would revert to her brother when he finally married. The rest of the money left by their parents—less than fifteen thousand pounds—had funded everything else over the last eight years, from household staff to food to clothing to animal feed to firewood.

And this was why the local butcher wandered freely through the Woodvilles' library on Friday afternoons and read what he found there to his heart's content, and why twice every month the best seamstress in the parish drove the Woodville curricle to visit her mother in a neighboring town, and why Hogarth's Latin tutor was the proud owner of a French horn she'd found in the attic (none of the Woodvilles played, but the tutor did). All because their limited family funds inspired Ginny to acrobatic heights of ingenuity when it came to negotiating discounts.

Necessity was the mother of confidence, and reticence was a luxury she could not afford. She'd been shy and overwhelmed by her new responsibilities at first, but she'd eventually learned to relish the challenge.

But for the past two years—and she'd never confided this to a soul—her breath would go nauseatingly short every time she opened the budget ledger. It was like watching the sands dwindling in a tipped hourglass. And while her darling sisters—level-headed, undemanding girls—seemed particularly easy to fall in love with and plenty of local boys did just that, the kind of grand matches her mother had begged Ginny to arrange for all of them required dowries that were at the very least not insulting.

She imagined how she would need to begin her sisters' marriage settlement negotiations now: "A funny thing about those dowries . . ."

What does your heart tell you, Ginny? That's what her mother used to say, whenever Ginny struggled with a dilemma or a decision.

She absently worried the little heart-shaped stone she'd found this morning between her thumb and forefinger, resentful that she was unable to dismiss the several brutally unsentimental points Mr. Marchand had made. Specifically, that men did the choosing. Her father had chosen to drive the high-flyer too fast, and her brother had chosen to gamble. It was mainly because of men that she was in this predicament.

Her mother had implored Ginny to *never* forget that she was a lady, with all that entailed regarding bearing and decorum, and to make sure her sisters never forgot it, either. The paradox was that the struggle to continue being a lady seemed to continually require Ginny to do things no lady would ever do, like visit gaming hells. She'd been able to travel to London in the company of a Sussex neighbor who was visiting relatives in Covent Garden. But apart from Mrs. Hardy and Mrs. Durand, she had no other chaperones in London and no plans to acquire any, and this was the sort of thing that would have given her mother vapors.

She buried her nose in the blossoms that were tucked into the little vase on her room's writing desk, and contemplated the two lists she'd spent the last hour scrawling on half of a sheet of foolscap included free of charge with her room. One column featured every member of the peerage with whom her family was acquainted in even a glancing way; it was long. The other was every London tailor or modiste she knew about. This included only Madame Marceau and Weston.

She had only two clues about the person to whom Hogarth had lost their inheritance. Hogarth's hysterical assertion about satyrs jeering from waistcoat buttons might not even be a clue. More likely he'd seen his own drunk little face reflected in their shiny surfaces, the way she'd seen her own in Mr. Ogden's buttons today, right before her encounter with the odious Mr. Marchand. But perhaps a tailor could tell her whether such a thing as satyr waistcoat buttons existed, and if they did, to whom they'd been sold.

Slightly more promising was the other clue: *If you'd known who it was you would have understood, Ginny.* This suggested to her that it was someone about whom she and Hogarth shared an opinion, and this unfortunately could be a number of people on her list. There was Lord Olyphant, for instance. A childhood friend of their mother's had married him. Hogarth occasionally imitated the man's excruciatingly slow, supercilious monotone to make Ginny laugh. Imagine *choosing* to marry Lord Olyphant, Ginny had once thought.

Imagine a time when she was so blithely ignorant of the caprices of fate that might lead a woman to do exactly that.

Do pretty, penniless women exploit wealthy men when they marry for money?

She shrugged her shoulders irritably, as if Marchand himself were standing behind her and whispering this in her ear.

Then there was the Earl of Sydenham, who had given her father that frighteningly beautiful rifle. Sydenham liked to claim that her father had stolen her mother from him, a joke that no one really seemed to enjoy but that everyone seemed to laugh at anyway.

If necessary, she would visit every member of the peerage one by one and ask them directly whether they were a member of Lucifer's Fall or whether they knew to whom Hogarth had lost all that money that fateful evening. *One* of them might crack when confronted with her copper dress and rank desperation.

But unless she got very lucky early in the process, tracking them down and visiting them one at a time meant lots of hack fares and solo journeys, not to mention withstanding the scalding embarrassment of those sorts of confrontations. She had only a fortnight in which to do it, too, and a little less than five pounds and a few shillings in her reticule.

And suddenly it felt as though a vise was tightening in her chest.

She closed her eyes and pictured Felicity's and Fiona's devasted little faces if she failed in her mission.

Felicity's fiancé was Lord Cambrough, an heir to a marquess. Fiona's was Charles Tarreyton, the second son of another earl. Both were attractive, good-natured, and not stupid. They were also sincerely devoted to her sisters. Both would rightfully feel betrayed and deceived, not to mention heartbroken, if they learned the dowries they'd anticipated had evaporated. The Woodville reputation would be destroyed, not to mention Ginny's own marriage opportunities. And poor Hogarth would never be able to forgive himself. He would be a shattered man.

Ginny knew she would suffer *anything*, do anything, to make this right for all of them.

I'll call off your brother's debt to the house if you spend a night in my bed.

She flinched away from Marchand's voice in her head again. *Almost* anything.

She glanced uneasily behind her at the soft bed, piled in blankets, draped in a pink knitted coverlet, and crowned with two cloudlike pillows, and pulled in a shivering breath, as if Marchand was waiting for her there.

Suddenly an absurd wave of homesickness for her siblings swept through her. She'd been away for only a few days but she craved the reassurance of people who loved her. A reminder of why she was doing all of this.

A cheerful word with Dot over tea might make her feel a little better. She'd last heard the downstairs clock chime half past ten, and the boardinghouse rules allowed guests to ask for a cup of tea as late as eleven.

She'd kicked off her slippers; they were lined up on the soft green and pink rag rug.

She stood up and stretched, then slid her feet into them and slipped out the door and dashed down the stairs.

She rounded the corner of the first-floor landing.

Then froze mid-step.

Her lungs seized.

If she'd been a forest creature, every hair on her head would have gone erect.

Mr. Marchand was coming up the stairs.

Mr. Marchand was coming up the stairs!

She prayed this was merely a hallucination, a fever dream born of the stress of the day, a trick of the light. Perhaps her vision would clear and it would prove to be Mr. Delacorte instead.

But the rank shock on Mr. Marchand's face dashed this hope.

Like the pair of cats in the alley outside, they remained tensely still, abject horror and antipathy ricocheting between their locked gazes.

Unfortunately he looked even more fascinating in the

shadowy light of the stairwell than he had in his office, if more sinister.

"Mr. Marchand, it is very bad of you to pursue me here," she finally whispered fiercely. "How *dare* you?"

"What on *earth* are you running on about, Miss Woodville? The notion that I would ever need to *pursue* any woman is comical." He said this with flat conviction.

The arrogance of him.

"I suppose it would be difficult for them to pursue you if they're tied up with *ropes*."

He blinked. "I beg your ever-loving pardon?"

They were conversing in hissing volumes.

She did not expound. She still had no idea what he did with ropes or why Lady Tomelty had bothered to mention it, but his confusion seemed genuine enough.

"A better question is what the devil are *you* doing here, Miss Woodville? I've already been generous to you with my time, despite the fact that you intruded upon my business through dishonest means without an appointment. If your intent is to continue bothering me about your brother's debts, I assure you it will not go well for you."

"Oh, my goodness, how very, very sinister, Mr. Marchand." She clapped a hand over her heart in feigned terror. "*I* came to London expressly to resolve my brother's predicament. Dear friends of mine told me to call here at the Grand Palace on the Thames for accommodation, as our very kind proprietresses were ladies to the core and would be glad to look after me. It's a very exclusive establishment, and Mrs. Hardy and Mrs. Durand thought I would fit right in. So I can't think why they would have allowed you to stay."

It was becoming clear that she simply could not sink any verbal barbs into him. His eyes lit up with relish at every challenge.

"My home is getting a new roof and repairs are being made to Lucifer's Fall, hence I needed other accommodations. *I* made arrangements to stay here several weeks ago. Lord Bolt is an old friend of mine."

She was taken aback. "But he seems so nice."

It was oddly liberating to say exactly what she wanted to say, unfiltered, even if this meant her worst, most sardonic self was unleashed. Because Mr. Marchand didn't even blink. His eyes merely widened with a dangerous sort of amusement. As if he dared her to keep talking.

"In light of our previous exchange, the *gentlemanly* thing for you to do—though I do understand that 'gentlemanly' might be a foreign concept to you, Mr. Marchand, based on your previous behavior—would be for you to leave and find other accommodations."

"Is that so? Tell me, Miss Woodville, how ladylike is it for a young, unmarried woman to show up unannounced at a gentleman's gaming establishment and lie in order to meet alone with the proprietor who is, according to your exacting standards, patently not a gentleman?"

This brought her up short. It was an excellent point.

She thought furiously.

She lowered her voice to a whisper. "What if I told Mrs. Hardy and Mrs. Durand that you propositioned me, Mr. Marchand?"

Her heart was racing by the time she'd finished her sentence. Because this might have been one risk too many.

Mr. Marchand narrowed his eyes. "What if I told them that *you*, to my great shock, sorrow, and dismay, propositioned *me*?"

"Wha—you—I did no such thing!" She nearly squeaked it.

"But no one would blame me for making that inference, given that you had come straight to see me after sending me a letter including suggestive language to that effect. It's the usual vague sort of thing ladies say when they're negotiating that type of arrangement. I could even produce your letter. It would be my word against yours."

That type of arrangement. As if it was a common occurrence.

Surely this wasn't true?

The things she didn't know, and didn't want to know but actually rather did want to know, a little bit, were legion. She flailed inwardly.

She decided he must be bluffing.

"How on earth would *I* know about suggestive language? Those can't have been ladies who wrote to you."

"So you admit you have no idea what *ladies* usually do," he drawled.

She sucked in a sharp breath and stared at him.

"You're an awful person." Her words emerged on a hush, oddly sounding more impressed than distressed. She supposed after a fashion she was. He was very good at whatever he was.

"*Yes*," he agreed almost exasperatedly. As if he'd been trying to convey this all along.

A silence during which they remained fused in a mutual glare lasted a few moments.

"Well. It seems we are both victims of the world's ghastliest coincidence, Mr. Marchand."

"Indeed."

"Surely, we can fix it so that we don't need to speak to each other, and we certainly never need to be alone together. The sitting room might be purgatory a few nights of the week, but I've endured worse," she told him loftily.

"As have I, Miss Woodville. Shall we shake on it?" The devil's eyes were glinting.

"Good try, but absolutely not." She swiftly clasped her hands behind her back.

"Very well, then. I look forward to ignoring you, Miss Woodville."

As he passed, she heard a soft rustling sound.

If she was not mistaken, he was chuckling.

Chapter Five

Mr. Marchand did not appear at breakfast or dinner the following day. But any hopes Ginny might have had about him suffering an attack of conscience and slinking away from the Grand Palace on the Thames in the dead of night were dashed when Mrs. Hardy and Mrs. Durand escorted him into the sitting room later that evening. He'd apparently merely been out all day advancing the cause of iniquity at Lucifer's Fall.

She watched Mr. Marchand take in the pianoforte, the little tables and chairs scattered about and the gently worn settees, the rugs and curtains, the pillows embroidered with things like "Bless our home" with bemused wariness. He looked big, glossily gorgeous and incongruous in this pleasant room where nothing precisely matched, including the guests, but everything somehow looked as though it belonged together, for that very reason.

He was clutching a book bound in red. It looked to her quite a bit like *The Ghost in the Attic,* from which Mrs. Pariseau had read aloud in the sitting room a few days ago. Perhaps he'd borrowed it. He didn't strike her as the sort of man who would take a fright about *anything*, let alone a ghost. Perhaps he hoped to acquire a few new ideas about unnerving people from it.

Ginny had settled in at a table behind Mr. Delacorte and the chessboard, and she'd been contemplating joining Mrs. Pariseau and Dot on the opposite side of the room. Captain Hardy and Lord Bolt were lounging at little tables, too.

Mrs. Durand clearly intended to take Mr. Marchand around the room to make introductions. She began with Mrs. Pariseau, a dashing widow whom Ginny liked very much.

Startlingly, Mrs. Pariseau launched right into flirting unabashedly. But then that was apparently the sort of thing widows were allowed to do with no compunctions.

"A *pleasure* to meet you, Mr. Marchand," Mrs. Pariseau told him. "You look like a man who has *quite* a vivid story."

Do I have a story about Marchand for you, Mrs. Pariseau, Ginny thought, bitterly.

"Indeed I do have a story. I heard *you* have an enchanting way with a story, too, Mrs. Pariseau." Marchand twinkled at her. "I'm looking forward to hearing you read aloud this evening."

Mrs. Pariseau delicately laid her heart with her hand and beamed at him. "We thought we'd read Greek myths tonight. Lots of mayhem and bad behavior mingling with moralizing. For adult ears only."

"Mayhem for adults is my favorite kind," Marchand confirmed.

He hadn't so much as glanced at Ginny yet, but she could not help but feel that remark was tailored just for her.

Marchand then shook hands with Captain Hardy and Lord Bolt, the handsome husbands of their proprietresses, who greeted him warmly, almost as if he wasn't dastardly. He was apparently already acquainted with both of them.

"I hear you're a tree now, Bolt," Marchand said, and Lord Bolt laughed.

Mr. Delacorte, whom she liked very much, was built a bit like an egg propped on legs, and he had thick, frisky eyebrows and rather lovely blue eyes. He sprang cheerfully to his feet. "Very good to meet you, Marchand. I'm in business with Hardy and Bolt in the Triton Group. And I also import remedies from the Orient and sell them to surgeons and apothecaries up and down the coast."

Marchand's eyebrows went up. He seemed intrigued. "Interesting line of work, Delacorte. Profitable?"

"Oh, I make a fair bit, a fair bit. If you ever need a little help with, you know, a certain struggle unique to gentlemen"—he extended his forefinger horizontally then let it slowly droop, by way of illustration—"it's one of my popular cures."

"Thank you." Marchand's composure stuttered for less than a second. "I'll keep that in mind should that tragic day ever arise."

At last Mr. Marchand was brought over to Ginny.

Heat rushed from Ginny's nape to her feet as she met his eyes again. For all the world as if he'd ignited some invisible fuse that traced the length of her spine. Her heart lurched then began beating at an absurdly swift clip.

"How do you do, Miss Woodville. A pleasure." He sounded grave and sincere, the charlatan. He bowed.

She dipped a swift curtsy. "How do you do, Mr. Marchand." She'd attempted to say it crisply, but she'd gone so breathless her words emerged sounding appallingly sultry.

His vanishingly swift, secretive little smile suggested he knew all about that invisible lit fuse and her shortened breath and her heart speed.

He at last settled in at a table across the room but directly in Ginny's line of vision, which was unforgivably provocative of him yet undeniably helpful, on the theory that it was a good strategy to keep an eye on ones' enemies.

She could not help but wonder what precisely he did during the day. Her own day had featured a fruitless journey to the establishment of Madame Marceau, the celebrated modiste, who had heard about etched silver buttons but was unfortunately unable to tell her where to find them, as none of her lady customers had yet requested them. Ginny would visit Weston tomorrow. She knew a visit to that exclusively male bastion would take most of her restores of nerve.

Ginny's head shot up when she sensed a fresh tension gripping the room.

This could only mean one thing: the arrival of Daniel Peck.

The primary trouble with Daniel Peck was that he was four years old. And while everyone who lived at the Grand Palace on the Thames had also once been four years old, none of them currently had children. They only vaguely remembered the age's bewildering, unfathomable customs, as if it was a distant land they'd once visited.

Five days ago, Daniel's mother, Mrs. Peck, had taken a suite for her two sons and their nursemaid at the Grand Palace on the Thames to await the return of her husband, who was traveling on a ship from Dover. Whereupon the family would return home to Northumberland.

Like a cherub in a Renaissance painting, Daniel was all dewy brown eyes, round red cheeks, black ringlets and shy smiles. Delilah and Angelique had been smitten during that first meeting. How refreshing it would be to have a child about the place! they'd thought, with wild optimism.

On the first night of their stay, Mrs. Peck brought Daniel (who nightly dined with his nurse in their suite) down to the sitting room after dinner while their nurse remained upstairs with the baby. The hush of happy anticipation fell. All the guests were prepared to be enchanted.

It began promisingly enough.

Daniel had bashfully fluttered his fluffy black lashes at Dot and Ginny and Mrs. Pariseau and smiled winsomely, captivating them.

But then things took an unexpected turn when Captain Hardy greeted him.

Daniel immediately burst into inexplicable, noisy sobs.

Lord Bolt fared little better: Daniel hid behind his mother and peered out at him, his little brow beetled in suspicion.

"Oh, he can be a little sensitive and fussy when he's tired," his mother explained with a little laugh. "It doesn't mean anything. Please don't let it hurt your feelings."

"It doesn't," Captain Hardy lied.

But then Daniel saw Mr. Delacorte.

He'd stared at him at length, with rapt, open-mouthed fascination, eyes alight with glee.

Such that Mr. Delacorte could not resist shooting a slightly smug look at the other men.

He'd bent to Daniel's height. "How do you do, young man?" he said cheerily. "I'm Mr. Delacorte!"

Daniel thrust out his belly, crossed his eyes, and bellowed, "'OW do you do! I'm Mr. Dewwacorte!"

Then he'd laughed uproariously.

Mr. Delacorte had staggered backward.

It was admittedly very funny the first four or five times Daniel did it, for Mr. Delacorte's expression alone.

"Isn't it fascinating?" Mrs. Pariseau said brightly, after Daniel had been taken off to bed that first night. "It's how children that age learn language, I suppose. Through repetition!"

But Daniel seemed to eke as much joy from it the forty-seventh time he said it as the first. It was apparently the very height of four-year-old comedy. Mr. Delacorte was obviously the funniest thing he'd ever seen in his life.

Everyone soon learned that this was not, alas, his only favorite thing to say.

Since that first night, all of his visits to the sitting room had been brief and harrowing as squalls.

Mrs. Peck released her son's hand and settled into a chair near Dot and Mrs. Pariseau.

Daniel immediately strutted across the room. "'ow do you do! I'm Mr. Dewwacorte!" He beat his puffed-out belly like a drum.

Mr. Delacorte regarded Daniel with a fixed, thoughtful expression that suggested he was imagining the child turning on a spit.

"Daniel, Mr. Delacorte doesn't like that," his mother said absently. She had settled in with an embroidery hoop.

The implication that Mr. Delacorte was the only one who didn't "like that" was almost funny.

"I want blancmange," Daniel replied to his mother in an exaggerated French accent: *Blahhhmajjjj.*

A slight rustling meant all the adults in the room were tensing for what they knew came next.

"The tart with dinner was nice, wasn't it, Daniel?" The Peck family had taken their meals in their suite this evening. "Helga is such a wonderful cook." Mrs. Peck said this warmly to Mrs. Durand and Mrs. Hardy, who offered her strained smiles.

"Blaaaaaahmaaaaaaaaaj," Daniel replied, his mouth open as wide as he could stretch it. "Blahmaa*aaaaaaa*j," he bleated like a sheep. "Blah ma ah *ah ah ah aj.*" He giggled.

He'd clearly heard the word somewhere and cherished it.

Daniel's "blancmange" record was thirteen times in one evening. Mrs. Pariseau had counted them to keep from going mad. A bit like a prisoner scratching the days off on a cell wall.

His mother seemed remarkably deaf to his foibles, in the way of all people accustomed to living with a ceaseless ambient sound, such as the distant gunfire of a constant battle.

Whispered conversations among Delilah and Angelique and their husbands had taken place about whether they ought to have a word about all of this with his mother. But he was a child; surely certain indulgences ought to be made? A new baby had disrupted Daniel's life. He was probably just bored. The discussions had been inconclusive, as of yet.

An anticipatory hush fell when Daniel meandered over to Mr. Marchand.

At whom he stared unabashedly.

Mr. Marchand finally put his book down and returned the child's unblinking regard.

Ginny held her breath. Surely Daniel would be devastated by Mr. Marchand's burning gaze. She braced herself for the child's roars of dismay.

"Daniel, pet, don't bother the gentleman while he's reading," his mother said vaguely.

"He's not a bother," Mr. Marchand replied.

Everyone forgave Mr. Marchand for this bald lie. It was his first evening in the sitting room. He would learn.

"Those are head bones." Daniel pointed at Marchand's skull ring.

"Indeed," Mr. Marchand agreed. "It's called a skull."

"A *skuuuullll*," Daniel crowed.

Lord Bolt surreptitiously dropped his head despairingly into his hands.

"I have bones in *my* head." Daniel knocked with a fist on his pate.

"Well, that's a very good thing," Mr. Marchand told him. "Otherwise your head might collapse like a blancmange. You need something in there to hold it up."

Someone in the room hissed in a revolted breath, but Daniel convulsed into giggles.

Ginny begrudgingly conceded the point to Marchand. Little boys loved disgusting things. Hogarth was all that was proper and polite now, but when he was seven years old, he had once skewered dog excrement with a stick and chased her with it.

"Can I hold it?" Daniel was emboldened to ask Mr. Marchand.

"My ring?"

Daniel bobbed his head.

"If your mother says it's all right."

Marchand glanced at Daniel's mother, who nodded her permission.

To Ginny's astonishment, he pulled that ring—probably worth a few hundred pounds—from his finger. "Be careful with it," he admonished.

Daniel accepted it with breathless care into his little hand, his mouth a perfect "O" of wonder.

He brought it up to his eye like a spyglass and squinted at it.

"It's made from the bones of pirates," Marchand told him.

"*Cor.*" Daniel was impressed.

From peering at it with his eyes, he moved it toward his nose and, for reasons known only to him, sniffed it. He paused speculatively, then darted a sneaky glance at Marchand.

"Do not put that in your mouth," Marchand said firmly.

"I wasn't going to," Daniel lied passionately, his eyes luminously aggrieved.

Marchand held out his hand, and Daniel obediently deposited the ring into his palm.

"Have you got any babies?" Daniel asked him, as Marchand pushed the ring back onto his finger.

Ginny was intrigued when Mr. Marchand didn't immediately reply.

"I do not have any babies," he said.

"*Lucky.* I've got a baby bruvver." This revelation positively thrummed with regret and disgust.

"I see. And how do you feel about that?" Mr. Marchand asked ironically, since how Daniel felt was clear.

"Babies are *dumb*. I hate him."

"Daniel!" But Mrs. Peck sounded weary, as though she'd heard this dozens of times.

"Babies *are* dumb," Marchand agreed.

At this, all the adults in the room went visibly rigid with shock.

Ooooh. Ginny was now on breathless tenterhooks. Perhaps Marchand would simply crack beneath the strain of maintaining gentlemanly behavior for whole minutes at a time, and they would be compelled to throw him bodily out of the place. She would *so* enjoy witnessing that.

"SO dumb!" Daniel repeated, hopping up and down, beside himself with glee at this show of solidarity. "Dumb! They don't know *anything.*"

"They *don't* know anything," Marchand agreed. Daniel giggled again. "But I will tell you something important, young Mr. Peck. Babies are small and dumb by design—on purpose, that is. And do you know why?"

Daniel shook his head like a wet dog.

The faint rustling Ginny detected was the sound of everyone tensing in case someone needed to leap up to clap a hand over Mr. Marchand's mouth. Captain Hardy was closest, and looked most capable.

"Babies are very, very small and fragile. Fragile means they can be easily hurt. Because he's fragile and doesn't yet know anything, he will count on you to help protect him and keep him safe and teach him how to do important things, like ride horses and swim and eat blancmange."

"Blaaahmaaajjjj," Daniel mouthed, still clearly fascinated by this speech.

"And this is how he will help *you* learn to be brave and

strong, all the things a good man needs to be. Being a big brother is one of the most important jobs in the world. As important as being a father or mother or an army captain." He lowered and softened his voice. "You want to grow up to be a good man, don't you, Daniel?"

Whether or not Daniel understood the entire substance of the message, he was clearly moved by the tone of it. His eyes had gone limpid with emotion.

The entire room was, in fact, captivated now. Even the fire seemed to stop crackling long enough to listen.

Ginny was unsettled and unwillingly enthralled. She recalled what Marchand had said about Caravaggio, the so-called murderous thug who created magnificent art. She supposed it was theoretically possible for a man to be an appalling rogue who was nevertheless good with children.

"So isn't it clever how that works, Daniel?" Marchand continued. "I think so. Your brother might be dumb now, but he'll grow up fast and get smart and you'll have lots of fun together. But right now he's only a little baby, and he will look up to you your whole life. I think you're *so* lucky to have each other."

Marchand said it very gently.

The tears of pathos welling in Daniel's eyes spilled onto his fluffy lashes and splashed onto his round cheeks. "Mama, I want to see my bruvver! I want to see him now!"

Mrs. Peck stared in drop-jawed astonishment at Marchand and Daniel.

At last she rose slowly, gingerly, from her chair. "Ah, of course, poppet. Let's go see your brother."

As she led a softly weeping Daniel out of the room by the hand, she cast an awestruck, grateful, and somewhat uneasy glance over her shoulder at Mr. Marchand, as if she suspected he might be a sorcerer.

The quiet rustling sound that followed was the room at large exhaling.

Perhaps Mr. Marchand simply had a talent for saying just the right thing to get someone out of a room fast, Ginny thought. He'd certainly demonstrated that yesterday afternoon when he'd propositioned her.

"Bravo, Mr. Marchand." Mrs. Pariseau mimed mopping her brow. "How did you know he was about to put that ring in his mouth?"

"Oh, what man can resist tasting pretty things?" he said easily.

Soft pink blushes winked on in all the women's cheeks around the room. Ginny felt her own face go warm.

"Don't you employ a few boys from Bethnal Green at your club?" Bolt asked.

Bethnal Green was a notorious workhouse known for exploiting orphans, who were often tricked into working for almost no wages under appalling conditions.

"I do. As often as I can, at least. I've hired a few from there who run errands for me and do some simple chores about the place. I can at least ensure they're safe and fed well and paid decent wages."

And maths, Ginny thought suddenly. *Someone is actually teaching those boys maths while they're at Lucifer's Fall.* Was Marchand actually paying a tutor for them as well? Perhaps he thought sprinkling in a few acts of charity with all the iniquity would increase his chances of getting into heaven.

"Lord Dominic Kirke came to stay with us not too long ago,

Marchand," Captain Hardy volunteered. Lord Kirke was a famously fiery Whig politician who fought for the rights of the vulnerable, including children.

Marchand looked surprised. "Is that so? I'm a Kirke admirer. I'd love to meet him."

"We can probably help arrange it," Bolt told him easily.

Ginny had been assured by Dot that the Grand Palace on the Thames was exclusive, and a visit from Lord Dominic Kirke seemed to confirm it, which was rather thrilling. Presence of a scoundrel notwithstanding.

"Should we resume reading the myths tonight, just for a change of pace from *The Arabian Nights Entertainments*?" Mrs. Pariseau held up the book of myths. "We last left off with the story of Daphne and Apollo."

Everyone concurred, as adult mayhem seemed like just the thing after a bit of child mayhem.

Mrs. Pariseau read all of the parts of the story with great feeling. The gist was that the sun god, Apollo, feeling very proud and full of himself for shooting and killing a powerful serpent with an arrow, had made fun of Eros, the god of love, for only being able to shoot *little* arrows. Whereupon Eros decided Apollo needed to be taught a lesson about pride. So he shot Apollo with an arrow that made him fall madly in love with a beautiful nymph called Daphne, whose father was the river god Peneus.

And then Eros shot Daphne with an arrow made of *lead*, which apparently made her find Apollo simply revolting.

A smitten, lust-addled Apollo chased Daphne thither and non to no avail, and poor beleaguered Daphne, seeing no escape from eventually being ravished by the sun god, frantically begged her river-god father to save her. So her father changed her into a laurel tree on the spot.

She was then forever out of reach of Apollo, who was doomed to suffer from lovesickness for eternity.

It was one of those stories that had everything: the perils of arrogance, desperate lusting, unrequited love, spiteful cherubs with arrows, transformation.

And everyone had a lot of opinions when Mrs. Pariseau finished reading it.

"Do you think what Eros did to Apollo was fair?" Mrs. Pariseau asked the room at large.

"I think Apollo asked for it. He insulted Eros's archery skills." Captain Hardy took marksmanship seriously.

All the men in the room nodded in solidarity.

"Then again . . . when you think about it . . . it wasn't Apollo's fault that Eros couldn't take a joke," Mr. Delacorte countered.

"But don't you think Apollo *needed* to be taught a lesson about arrogance?" Angelique chimed in.

"Maybe he could have bragged about his archery skills without actually making fun of Eros," Lucien conceded.

"What a pity they didn't have a cozy sitting room up on Olympus in which to debate their issues," Delilah reflected. "It's clearly mayhem up there."

"What I don't understand is why turning her into a tree was the only option. Why was that the first thing that sprang to Peneus's mind? *'I'll* show him—I'll make her a tree!'" Ginny asked.

"She was in a forest. Maybe he needed to make sure she matched the surroundings, if she was going to be there for an eternity," Dot shyly suggested.

"So by your way of thinking, Dot," Mr. Marchand said, "if Apollo was about to catch up to Daphne in the sitting room, Peneus would have been compelled to turn her into an Epithet Jar or a settee?"

Everyone chuckled except Ginny, who refused to be charmed.

Dot shot a nervous, speculative glance at the settee, as if it might have once been a nymph.

"Why not turn her into something like a dragon, so she could at least defend herself?" Ginny pressed, feeling oddly frantic for the poor fictional Daphne.

"Because even if she was a dragon, she would never have been able to kill Apollo. He's an immortal. His punishment is that *she's* not only forever out of reach, he will *suffer* over her forever," Bolt said.

"Isn't love sort of a punishment anyway, regardless?" Ginny said.

Good heavens, that remark caused a sharp silence she hadn't anticipated.

"Forgive me! I didn't mean it to sound so melodramatic. That is, the punishment is built into the reward. Because you don't get love without eventual grief. And you don't get grief without love."

That's when she noticed Marchand's cool social mask slip for a moment. He fleetingly looked stunned.

She saw it because she had, maddeningly, looked right at him.

She forcibly averted her gaze.

"Well now. Now that you mention it, Miss Woodville, it *is* diabolical to turn love into a punishment." Delacorte was a little indignant now. "I think I want to change my vote. If you think about it, that Eros *was* a right bas—"

All heads whipped toward Mr. Delacorte.

"—ket of trouble," he completed, darting a glance at the Epithet Jar.

"So many stories in myths are about nymphs being transformed into something else in order to escape a threat. As if there's no other option but to change yourself completely in order to avoid danger," Ginny said suddenly. How had she just realized this about a familiar myth?

Suddenly her chest felt tight from the injustice. If the Greeks were writing about it a thousand years ago, what hope did a modern girl have? Men always did the choosing; women always did the adapting. Just like Marchand had said.

"That's a very astute observation, Miss Woodville. Perhaps there isn't any other option but to change in those circumstances," Mrs. Pariseau suggested gently. "And perhaps that's the point the story is making. How else do we truly *transform*, if not through some sort of strife?"

Everyone contemplated this.

"But I feel as though I'm transforming every day I'm here at the Grand Palace on the Thames, and I don't feel a bit of strife," Mr. Delacorte declared.

"*No* strife? Be honest, Delacorte." Bolt tipped his head at the Epithet Jar, then at the chessboard, and added a surreptitious eyebrow hike in Dot's direction.

"And yesterday I found a piece of cheese that I accidentally dropped behind my bed a few weeks ago, and it had transformed quite a bit by just sitting there," Delacorte insisted. "Grew a fur coat."

"The maids ought to have found that, Mr. Delacorte." Angelique's tone suggested she was making a mental note to have a stern chat with Meggie and Rose.

"At least as a tree, Daphne is utterly off limits to Apollo. He can *never* have her. They are entirely different species," Ginny concluded.

She didn't look at Marchand, but out of the corner of her eye she thought she saw him smile almost enigmatically.

As if he somehow knew better.

* * *

Isn't love sort of a punishment anyway?

Miss Woodville's voice was once again echoing in Marchand's head as the smoke from four cheroots rose and mingled on the ceiling. The men had retreated to the smoking room after the myth reading, leaving the ladies to their embroidery and knitting and chatter. This room amused Marchand: Dense brown velvet curtains poured from the windows, squashy brown chairs surrounded an old battered table upon which a man could throw his booted feet, and a carpet in a scrolling pattern of browns and oxblood, the perfect stain-hiding shades, was spread across the floor. God bless and God help the women who understood men all too well.

Marchand was forced to concede that he hadn't hated the so-called spirited discourse. He'd never before heard the story of Apollo, Daphne, and Eros, but he found the notion of immortal gods behaving like conceited, petty asses entertaining. Eros had destroyed the life of that poor nymph just because his ego was wounded. It was in many ways a story about the perils of hubris, which ironically paralleled his own predicament. Because he'd been so bloody confident that he'd ruthlessly, cleverly dealt with the problem of Miss Guinevere Woodville, only to almost immediately find himself fixed in the accusing beam of her big brown eyes in a boardinghouse sitting room. Not only that, but according to the boardinghouse rules, he would need to endure her glare almost nightly. If this ghastly coincidence didn't have the ring of fate to it—or the knell of doom—he didn't know what did.

Granted, the view had its compensations. The lines of the girl—the way her long, slender throat glided into her collarbone and the way her hips flared from her waist, for instance—were more eloquent than any Caravaggio, as far as he was concerned. He was not one to disdain the opportunity to admire an elegant package.

Even if it contained a grenade.

Because he was quite certain that Miss Woodville was capable of being as unpredictable as a Greek god in a snit.

He'd contemplated leaving the boardinghouse for a hotel for perhaps half a second last night, and rejected it out of hand. Like Eros, he would be damned if anyone got the better of him, let alone a girl.

His own room on the third floor was insidiously cozy. There were bosomy-plush pillows on the bed and flowers stuffed into a little vase. Everything in it was soft. Lucifer's Fall's marble and gilt sheen was designed to bolster the egos of men of money and power; the whole of the Grand Palace on the Thames seemed designed to cushion spirits and falls. To . . . *envelop.*

While the men who gambled in Lucifer's Fall craved and curried his favor, few of them would ever invite him to their homes. (And *none* of them would ever introduce him to their daughters, but that went without saying). They all understood the social divide. It had never occurred to Marchand to mind as long as he made a profit and had a fine place to live.

But in the sitting room an epiphany had landed on him like a cinder thrown from a fire: The Grand Palace on the Thames was a *home*. Which made this his first stay in someone's actual home, the kind of home that had long been loved and lived in by people who belonged with and to each other. The realization had made him feel fleetingly furious and foolish and raw. As if he was the only one not in on a secret. As if he was pitiable for not recognizing how a real home ought to look and feel.

"What could have been" seemed everywhere he looked in this bloody place.

He was aware that everything tended to land on the raw at this time of year. The relentless coziness of the place, the surprise of Miss Woodville, the unexpected presence of a curly-haired little boy—taken separately, he could have managed well enough. Combined, however, they had nudged him off kilter. And normally it was as impossible to do that as it was to knock over that huge marble statue of the Duke of Valkirk in Hyde Park.

Isn't love sort of a punishment anyway? was a funny, jaded thing for a young woman like Miss Woodville to come out with. But she wasn't wrong.

"I'll give little Daniel the bit with the belly," Delacorte mused, breaking the silence. "That's not too far off the mark.

And the puffy cheeks. Was right funny the first four hundred and twenty-three times he did it. But why the crossed eyes? I don't look like that. Do I?" he demanded.

"Not at all," Captain Hardy assured him.

"I've been told I've nice eyes." Delacorte was indignant.

"They're lovely," Lucien agreed, and Captain Hardy laughed.

"Fine pair of eyes you have there in your head, Delacorte," Marchand contributed. "I bet they work really well, too."

"Like nobody's business!" Delacorte confirmed stoutly.

"I suppose pulling faces makes everything twice as funny when you're a child," Marchand told Delacorte. "It's like adding chocolate sauce on top of blancm—"

"Don't say it!" the other three men implored in unison.

Marchand grinned.

"At least I didn't make Daniel *cry* by just looking at him, like you did, Hardy," Delacorte said.

"It wasn't so much how I looked, as what I said," Hardy maintained. "Which was 'How do you do, Daniel.' And for some reason that shattered him."

"I'm very certain it was both how you looked and what you said," Lucien said remorselessly.

Delacorte nodded. "You have a look, Hardy."

"I have a *look*?"

"Do the look, Delacorte," Lucien urged. "Hardy's 'I'm going to have you flogged for insubordination' look."

"You *do* me?" Captain Hardy was stunned.

Mr. Delacorte planted his hands on his hips and glowered sternly, eyebrows drawn together.

Lucien and Delacorte laughed. Marchand thought it was wisest not to laugh, though all of this was impossible not to enjoy.

Captain Hardy was speechless.

His jaw dropped. "*When* have I ever planted my hands on my hips that way?"

"Well, that's just my interpretation of it. I was embellishing." Delacorte was unrepentant.

"So a bit the way Daniel embellished with his crossed eyes," Hardy retorted.

"If you like," Mr. Delacorte allowed pleasantly.

"It's probably not your fault, Hardy. That look. The army and all that. And I'm mostly immune to it now," Lucien told him. "It's useful in our business. Strikes fear into the heart of anyone who might dream of crossing you. Withers crops on the vine."

Captain Hardy half laughed, half sighed. "It's not too soon for Daniel to get used to it. Who knows? He might want to join the military."

"He's only four years old," Bolt reminded him.

"The military will straighten his eyes out for him," Delacorte said darkly.

"He stared at *you* as if you were a looby," Captain Hardy pointed out to Lucien. "Because you spoke to him as though he was applying for admission to White's. *Tally ho there old chum.*"

"*That* is a terrible imitation of Bolt," Mr. Delacorte told him. "But that is basically what you did, Bolt. I'd hide behind a woman if you used that voice on me, too."

"I wasn't *trying* to imitate Bolt," Captain Hardy said irritably.

Lucien's English was still subtly haunted by his mother's native French, and his cadences and word choices were, too.

"I'm inimitable," Lucien replied complacently.

"It's very disappointing when something so cherubic turns out to be so obnoxious," Delacorte said.

"Exactly what I said when I first met you, Delacorte," Captain Hardy said.

"Ha!" Mr. Delacorte was always a great appreciator of a well-landed joke. "Marchand . . . how did you come by your knack with the brats, er, bairns?"

Hell's teeth. Marchand's chest tightened. Though he was certain these men were well-meaning, a truthful answer would require saying a certain name aloud, and he just didn't want to do it in this smoky little room. He hadn't actually said it aloud to another human in years. The truth was, hardened bastard though he was, he wasn't certain he could trust his voice to remain steady if he did.

"Here's the trick," he told them. "Do you know when you go to a pub, and one of your friends gets too foxed? Sings sentimental songs one moment, picks fistfights the next, laughs hysterically for no reason you can comprehend the next, starts singing off-key nonsense songs, falls asleep in odd places, needs to be carried home?"

All the men nodded in recognition.

Delacorte had gone misty-eyed at this recitation. "Let's all go off to the pub after this! Say, how do you feel about donkey races, Marchand?" Donkey races were Delacorte's favorite pastime, a notch above singing bawdy songs in pubs.

"Very young children are a bit like that. You variously laugh at them and with them, humor them, scold them a little, sing along if you have to, and do your best to keep them safe. *Love* a good donkey race, by the way."

"Knew I liked you," Delacorte replied complacently.

"Children are like drunks. Huh." Hardy was bemused.

"No children among the three of you?" Marchand asked.

There ensued a little silence.

"We've both been married for about a year." Hardy gestured at Bolt.

"To our respective wives," he added after a moment.

"Thanks, Hardy, I think he grasped that," Bolt said.

Marchand knew very well that marriage was hardly a prerequisite for having children.

"How about you, Delacorte?" Marchand asked.

"None that I know of. One never knows, of course."

Everyone stared at him, a little nonplussed.

"I've traveled up and down the coast selling my wares to apothecaries and surgeons for years now, and I've enjoyed a few happy romps with a widow or two," Delacorte told him. Bolt and Hardy tensed. Mr. Delacorte had more than once shared a few too-detailed anecdotes about these romps. "I would be distressed to leave a woman alone with that responsibility, but none of us never know for sure, do we? Even if we're careful."

The other men in the room entertained the sobering and uncomfortable truth of this. Both by the possibility of inadvertent thoughtlessness (though none of them had ever really been rakes) and by the idea of possible little Delacortes running about.

"So what other wares do you sell, Delacorte?" Marchand asked, to change the subject.

"Oh, all sorts of remedies from the Orient, herbs and ground of bits and bobs of this and that, animal horns and testicles and what not. Some of them even work a treat—stop fevers, slow bleeding, heal wounds. Others don't do much at all, but people want 'em anyway."

"I'll be damned." Marchand was intrigued. "Which remedies are the most popular?"

"Oh, like I mentioned, the impotency cure is popular with apothecaries—they buy a lot of it. Especially the ones near St. James's Square, where all the gentleman's clubs—like yours, Marchand—are. Same with a certain headache powder. Works straightaway, but it can sometimes cause hallucinations. I've tried it. Had quite a few wild dreams. Though some people like that sort of thing. Bloke I know took it and when he looked in his own mirror he saw Queen Elizabeth scowling back at him. Gave him quite a fright."

"Was she sitting *next* to him when he saw her, or did the queen look back at him from the mirror? Was she *his reflection*?" Marchand asked.

"The latter," Delacorte said. "Kind of makes you wonder who *you* might see if you take it, doesn't it?"

"Bolt would no doubt see a tree," Marchand said slyly.

Lucien shot him a dry look.

They smoked contemplatively for a moment.

"If you had children, where do you suppose they'd sleep here at the Grand Palace on the Thames?" Marchand asked the room at large. "Have you enough rooms? Is there a nursery of some sort?"

"I just assumed we'd fill the annex ballroom with them," Hardy said.

Bolt gave a short, distracted laugh.

There was a pause. "I always thought it would be nice to

raise children in the country," Bolt confessed. "I've a house I inherited that I seldom visit. I was raised there."

Delacorte and Hardy looked at him, surprised.

One got the sense that Lucien had never before mentioned any longing to raise children in the country. And this Marchand recognized as a potential opening.

"You'd probably make a pretty sum if you sold this place today." He gestured, indicating the Grand Palace on the Thames. "Might never have to work at anything ever again." Marchand casually blew a stream of smoke ceiling-ward. "I recall when your annex wing was for sale, I was disappointed I'd missed the opportunity."

"Both buildings actually belong jointly to our wives," Bolt told him. "I bought the annex building and gave it to Angelique in the hopes she would marry me. Ironically, before that, I was eyeing it for a gaming hell, too."

At Marchand's expression, Bolt gave a short laugh. "Yes, it was mad to give her a building. I was in love. What can I say? I would have given her the moon. I've never regretted it. She promptly gave half ownership to Hardy's wife, because Hardy's wife gave Angelique half of the Grand Palace on the Thames when they became partners."

Despite himself, Marchand found himself admiring the efficiency and pure trust implied in this partnership. And therein lay its strength, he was sure.

And therein also lay the reason that persuading them to sell might be trickier than Marchand had anticipated.

"If they ever want to sell . . ."

He had the sense he'd just uttered a sacrilege, judging by

the quality of the silence and the closed, cautious expressions that greeted those words.

But all it really took was a seed planted, he knew.

It would grow, or it wouldn't. He would certainly look for opportunities to nurture it.

Nobody took up the question.

"I have a hunch that all of you would be wonderful fathers, in different ways," Marchand reflected, into the silence. "It might require combining forces, however. Hardy for the discipline, Bolt for, oh, let's say grace, Delacorte for the comedy. Like that."

He'd made all of them smile, and damned if that wasn't a good feeling.

"You never know. If you stay here too long, *you* might even accidentally leave here with a wife, Marchand. Lots of people seem to do that," Delacorte said wistfully.

Marchand snorted. "She'd need to rope and tie me first."

Chapter Six

Dinner at the Grand Palace on the Thames was a merry, chaotic sport in which everyone won, most particularly Mr. Delacorte. Tureens sloshing and brimming with hearty things were swiftly passed in every direction, and Ginny learned quickly that one needed to be nimble and alert to avoid mid-air collisions. Tonight she'd nearly taken a butter dish to the temple because her eyes were on her plate. She'd been applying herself diligently to the fish stew and herbed potatoes in an attempt to avoid looking directly at Mr. Marchand, who had somehow contrived to sit almost directly across from her.

Today she'd endured a stingingly awkward visit to Weston's on Old Bond Street to inquire about satyr buttons. All the gentlemen behind the counter had eyed her reprovingly, clearly keenly disturbed by the invasion of a young, well-bred, unchaperoned woman into their masculine sanctum.

"Good heavens, miss. No. That travesty of a button sounds like something George Stultz would do to waistcoats," the gentleman at the counter sniffed, when she'd inquired about the satyr buttons. "You might try at *his* shop."

She'd departed with a scorching blush and returned at

once to the Grand Palace on the Thames, her quotient of bravado spent for the day, though she was painfully aware that shame was pure indulgence given the urgency of her mission. She did not look forward to her visit to George Stultz's shop tomorrow.

Ironically she had Mr. Marchand to thank for the miracle that happened next.

Because her traitorous head inevitably lifted and turned as if of its own accord, and her gaze collided with Mr. Marchand's.

Whereupon she swiveled it sharply away again, toward Lord Bolt.

Who had just rotated his torso to pass the bread to his wife.

When he did, candlelight glanced off the silver buttons on his waistcoat.

Ginny saw that they were etched with little galleons.

She went so abruptly still she was nearly bashed in the head by a tureen of peas Mrs. Pariseau was trying to hand off to her.

"If you'll excuse me, Lord Bolt . . . " she ventured. She took the peas and passed them on.

He looked over at her and smiled.

"My brother mentioned admiring buttons similar to the ones on your waistcoat. He said they were etched with satyrs or some such. He's a lover of mythology, like Mrs. Pariseau. I thought they would make a charming gift for his birthday, but I don't have the first notion of where to find them."

All of these things were fundamentally true.

Something glinted in her peripheral vision. She instinctively knew it was Mr. Marchand's gunmetal gaze. He'd gone still.

"Ah! It sounds as though your brother may have seen the Earl of Sydenham's buttons," Lord Bolt told her. "He was wearing a waistcoat of that description a few weeks ago in White's. My tailor knows someone who knows someone who does the silver etching on buttons. I'd be happy to find his name for you, Miss Woodville."

Hope went to Ginny's head so violently she nearly swayed from it.

If you knew who it was, you'd understand, Hogarth had told her.

Her father's friend and rival. The one who claimed her father had stolen her mother from him, and who had gifted that handsome rifle to him.

Of course. The Earl of Sydenham.

"Thank you, Lord Bolt. I would be much obliged."

* * *

"Miss Guinevere Woodville. It *is* you. My God. I thought my ears had deceived me when Farnham told me you were waiting in the foyer."

Ginny had in fact been cooling her heels in the Earl of Sydenham's foyer for nearly ten minutes. She'd slipped out of the Grand Palace on the Thames after dinner in the wake of Mrs. Pariseau, who was off to meet friends at the theater, because widows were allowed to gallivant without men. She'd shared a hack with her as far as Covent Garden.

In parting, Ginny had assured the slightly skeptical Mrs. Pariseau that the friends she was visiting would see her safely home. Then she'd taken the hack the rest of the way to St. James's Square.

Perhaps the earl *would* see her safely home, for old time's sake. One never knew. Just in case, she'd tucked a knitting needle in her sleeve again for protection, in anticipation of needing to hunt alone for a hack later.

Sydenham was the same floridly handsome fellow she remembered from the last time he'd visited her parents more than a decade ago, though he'd gone significantly grayer and ever-so-slightly balder. She knew a fleeting surge of desperate resentment that her father was not alive to go grayer, too. She liked to think her father would have kept all of his hair, just to spite Sydenham.

"I am so very abashed to intrude upon your evening, Lord Sydenham, and in such an unusual manner, but—"

"Who is there, dear?" A woman called from the top of the stairs. "I thought I heard a young lady's voice."

The Countess of Sydenham swanned into view. A plume swayed languidly from her purple turban with every step of her graceful descent, and light bounced from the toes of her satin slippers.

"It's . . . ah, Miss Guinevere Woodville, dear." The Earl of Sydenham still sounded a bit dazed. "She seems to have come for an . . . after-dinner visit."

He said this last a bit ironically. There really was no such thing as an after-dinner visit among the types of social calls Londoners paid one another. Which was one of the many reasons Farnham the footman had been reluctant to admit Ginny to the town house at all.

The other reasons were the fact that she was a young woman and alone, of course, because heaven forfend.

Ginny didn't blame him, because she'd had about plenty

of time to entertain second thoughts about being there while he'd gone to fetch the earl. She'd ultimately decided she was glad she hadn't waited until morning. If fortune favored her, she might even be able to return home as soon as tomorrow with good news for Hogarth.

"Guinevere Woodville? As in *Viscount* Woodville?" The countess was amazed, too.

". . . and now the Earl of Highgrove," Ginny prompted. "Perhaps you already know this, but my brother, Hogarth, inherited the title."

"Yes, I believe we did hear! Oh, Miss *Woodville*." The countess was in the foyer now. She took Ginny's hands in hers and studied her fondly. Her wide blue eyes reminded Ginny a bit of Dot's. "Look at you, a woman grown now! And so very pretty! I remember you so well as a little girl. The freckles were so charming! Not that they still aren't, of course, but there's always powder, isn't there? Your parents were such good fun. So *madcap*. We do miss them very much. You have your father's eyes."

"Ah—thank you, you're very kind. And we miss them, too. Very much."

The Earl and Countess of Sydenham had not once visited the Woodville children after their parents' deaths.

There ensued a lull.

"Are you in some kind of trouble, dear?" the countess prompted.

Which was a polite way of asking her what the devil she was doing in their foyer.

Ginny pulled in a long, courage-bolstering breath. "I have urgent need of counsel on a particular matter. I could not think of another friend in London to whom I could turn. Otherwise I would *never* intrude upon you without sending a letter first. Nor would I ever come alone. I feel rather at odds right now."

She wanted them to know that she at least knew *how* to behave like a lady, even if she wasn't doing it now. She owed that much to her parents, particularly her mother.

The earl and countess exchanged a glance.

"Well, do come through into the drawing room, my dear." The countess at least sounded kind. "We'll have a chat."

In the drawing room a few steps away, a leaping fire picked out the glints of gold leaf and ormolu. Velvet was everywhere.

Ginny settled onto a crimson settee opposite the Sydenhams.

She considered where to begin. She decided it was best to get straight to the point. "I wondered if you had seen my brother lately, Lord Sydenham."

"Why, is he missing?" the earl smoothly replied, just as his wife exclaimed, "You just saw him at Lucifer's Fall, didn't you, dear?"

The earl pressed his lips tightly together.

Against a curse word, if Ginny had to guess. She knew the look.

The countess placed a gloved hand delicately over her lips at her faux pas.

A tense silence followed.

Apparently, the earl didn't believe Lucifer's Fall's little rule about protecting the privacy of members extended to wives.

"I believe Hogarth lost a very good deal of money to you at Lucifer's Fall, Lord Sydenham," Ginny pressed on.

The earl sighed. "Well, he did, indeed," the earl decided to confirm with matter-of-fact cheer, since they all knew about it. "It was a *very* lucky night for me."

Ginny's heart was pounding sickeningly now. She prayed to every god she could think of for the strength to say what she needed to say next.

"In honor of your friendship with my parents, I wondered if you would consider tearing up his vowels and canceling his debt."

She was both horrified and thrilled to have gotten the words out. It felt utterly brazen.

They echoed in her ears like a gong clash.

The silence that followed was surely the longest and most awkward in English history so far.

A bead of sweat slid from her neck into her cleavage as the earl and countess regarded her in wary amazement.

"You'd . . . like me to just . . . forget . . . the debt?" The earl issued all of these words gingerly. As if giving Ginny an opportunity to apologize or explain away this latest hideous social transgression.

She was nauseous with shame and nerves. "Yes."

His eyebrows dove into a frown for a full five seconds. Suddenly, all at once, his expression cleared. "But that's not how it works, my dear." His relieved tone suggested he'd thought about it and concluded she was just misguided or naive, not soft in the head. "Winning *money* is the *point* of five-card loo. It's why it's worth playing at all. It's what we pay the exorbitant membership fees at Lucifer's Fall in order to do. I spent a good deal of money playing in order to make a good deal of money. Your brother seemed to really be enjoying himself, and I could not deny him the chance to play against me for old time's sake."

I'll just bet you couldn't, Ginny thought.

"But you see, Hogarth did not mean to get so carried away." She tried to keep her tone bright, even though there was a peculiar ringing in her ears.

"Oh, certainly, certainly. I understand. But that's the thrill of it, ain't it? Letting it sweep you up." The earl made an expansive sweeping gesture. "He was entering into the spirit of the thing, as it was his first night there. It was stirring to see him in action."

She wondered if the earl was one of those who saw Hogarth dancing on a billiard table.

"I know it's a bit alarming to lose the first time you do it, Miss Woodville, but your brother, now that he's an earl, can always win more!" the countess soothed. "You can buy so much on credit and no one ever asks you to pay for it, when you're an earl. And one can't *always* lose, just like you don't always win, isn't that right, dear?" she said to her husband.

Ginny understood two things simultaneously: These people were *daft*. Mad. As. Hatters.

But then, so was she.

Because here she was, trying to talk them into giving back fifteen thousand pounds.

They were also, she suspected, considerably craftier than she was.

"It's just that the particular sum you won was very much spoken for." Her lips fought her mightily when she tried to turn them up into a smile. It was an attempt to make her words sound something other than desperate.

The countess laughed merrily. "Oh, *all* money is always spoken for, my dear. We've been thinking about ordering a new barouche with the winnings. We've only got the one, and it's nigh on two years old now. We'll name one of the horses on the team after your brother."

The earl and countess laughed at this together.

Ginny heard noises resembling a laugh emerging from her own stiff lips. *Imagine* having more than one barouche.

She took a breath. "It's just that both of my sisters are engaged to be married, you see. We're due to enter negotiations for the marriage settlements within a fortnight. And surely you understand about dowries . . ."

"Oh, how lovely! Our congratulations to little Francesca, wasn't it? And . . ."

"It's Fiona and Felicity."

"We'll send over a little gift. Perhaps a silver creamer?"

I have a suggestion for a gift, Ginny was awfully tempted to say.

"They looked so much like your mother," the earl suddenly recalled. "The twins." His tone was wistful.

"They do." Her heart began pounding. "They've grown up to look *just* like her."

Perhaps this was it. Perhaps sentiment would be the thing that brought him around.

She prayed again to the same legion of gods. She reminded herself that she'd found a stone heart, and surely it must mean something.

"Miss Woodville, did your brother *tell* you that he lost to me?" the earl asked suddenly.

Bloody hell.

Her gut immediately turned to ice.

She thought she'd gotten lucky, but the earl was unfortunately finally realizing a few things.

Another torturous little silence sifted down.

"No, sir. He refused to tell me. Hogarth has a *very* strong sense of honor. He said he would rather *die* than tell me." There was no harm in exaggerating just a little. And in truth, Ginny did want to kill Hogarth, a little bit.

She didn't expound, because she needed to buy a few more moments to think.

Something she ought to have done more of before she arrived.

The earl's brow creased. "Then how—"

Suddenly Farnham the footman appeared again in the doorway. "Forgive my intrusion, Lord Sydenham, but you've another caller." He delivered this news on a peculiarly nervous hush as he proffered a silver tray, upon which rested a single card.

The earl frowned. "Who could it be at this—" He snatched the card up and read it.

He shot to his feet.

Then he sat down hard again.

Then he stood up again and sat down again, and smoothed his hair.

The countess leaned toward him. "Dear, why the agitation?"

He showed the card to his wife.

"Oh!" She excitedly patted her own hair. "Good heavens. How unusual. But should we? With Miss Woodville here? I don't know, dear. It's not quite proper, is it? It's not the done thing. He's—but—"

Ginny found herself smoothing her own hair, reflexively. Who on earth could cause such a stir? The *king*?

The earl hesitated.

"Bring him in, if you would, Farnham."

The footman disappeared.

And returned with Mr. Marchand.

Mr. Marchand brought the woodsmoke scent of the night in with him on his coat, as though he'd materialized out of fire and brimstone. His cheeks were ruddy from the chill. He'd pushed back his hair. He looked excruciatingly dashing.

He was a fresh shock every time she saw him, Ginny realized then. Every time she needed to reacclimate to the fact of his shoulders and cheekbones and the whole fact of him.

His eyes found her the way an arrow finds a bull's-eye, and they flared in triumph—clearly, he'd somehow known she'd be here, and felt vindicated—and burned with a distinct warning.

She glared back at him.

For a mad moment she considered bellowing the epithet that immediately sprang to mind. How liberating it would be to incinerate what was left of her reputation. To burn it all down completely in front of an audience who would probably waste no time making sure all of the ton knew. It was so exhausting clutching at the shreds of her dignity.

The earl and countess didn't notice, as they were busy gazing admiringly at Mr. Marchand.

"To what do we owe this rare honor, Mr. Marchand?" said Lord Sydenham.

"I was in the neighborhood and I thought I'd bring the Malbec you enjoyed the other evening. It's a marvelous vintage. I got some in especially for you."

"And how thoughtful of you to remember how much I

enjoyed it, Marchand. I know Malbec is not all the rage at the moment."

"It is among those of us with excellent taste," Marchand assured him. "My apologies, Lord Sydenham. If I'd known you were already entertaining a charming guest, I would never have dreamed of intruding."

Liar, she silently mouthed to Mr. Marchand.

"You're not intruding at all." The earl sounded aghast at the very notion. "It seems to be our night for unusual but charming callers. May I present Miss Guinevere Woodville."

She sullenly rose to her feet. "How do you do, Mr. Marchand?"

"How do you do, Miss Woodville?" He bowed like a courtier, the fraud.

"This is the Mr. Marchand who owns the gentleman's club we were discussing, Miss Woodville. Isn't that a coincidence?" The countess was thrilled. "It's as though we conjured him with a magic spell!"

Ginny yearned to point out that anything that conjured Marchand was really more of a curse than a spell.

She dipped a perfunctory curtsy and sat down again.

"Stay and have a bit of that Malbec with us, Mr. Marchand," the countess coaxed. "Give Farnham your coat and the bottle. He'll open it for us."

"That's a very kind offer, but I wouldn't want to interrupt your visit with Miss Woodville."

Dashing her hopes, he was handing off his coat and the bottle of wine to Farnham before he even finished his sentence. He clearly intended to stay.

"Miss Woodville won't mind, would you, Miss Woodville?" the earl insisted.

Marchand arched a brow at her. The glint in his eyes told her he was savoring the internal battle he knew she was waging between what she wanted to say and what she ought to say.

"Why should I mind?" she said pleasantly enough, through a clenched jaw. Everybody sat again.

Marchand took a chair across from her, because heaven forfend she should ever be spared a view of him.

"We were, in fact, just discussing a visit her brother, the Earl of Highgrove, recently paid to Lucifer's Fall," Sydenham said.

"Were you now," Marchand said flatly.

"Miss Woodville is the daughter of an old friend of mine, rest his soul, the Viscount Woodville. Her brother is now the Earl of Highgrove. And Miss Woodville just popped in a few minutes ago, out of the blue."

"How unorthodox of her," Marchand said lightly.

Ginny scowled in her heart, because she didn't dare scowl with her face.

"Her family was always a bit free-spirited," the earl told Marchand, sotto voce.

This sounded as though he was actually apologizing for her family to *Marchand*, of all people, which made Ginny grind her teeth.

Marchand nodded sagely. "I understand. I've known a few libertines in my day, too."

Now he was deliberately goading her.

"Oh, I'm certain you have," the countess enthused, almost on a purr.

Ginny felt compelled to protect her family's honor. "Oh, it's not quite as exciting as all that, Mr. Marchand. My father liked fast horses," Ginny said. "Other than that, we're a bit dull and respectable."

Mr. Marchand tipped his head skeptically.

"In fact, my brother never seemed interested in gambling until he heard of Lucifer's Fall. I don't mean to be unkind, Mr. Marchand, but I'm rather regretting that he did. Ha." She tried to say it lightly for the benefit of the earl and countess. It emerged more tautly than she preferred.

"My dear, if Lucifer's Fall didn't exist, all the men would just go someplace else to gamble," the countess said earnestly.

"We'd go someplace else to gamble," Lord Sydenham affirmed, as if nothing had ever been more self-evident.

"They'd all go someplace else to gamble," Marchand echoed grimly, to Ginny.

The Earl of Sydenham accepted a glass of Malbec from Farnham, who had returned with glasses on a tray. "I was explaining to Miss Woodville, who has quite charmingly and naturally been sheltered from gentlemen's customs surrounding wagers, that gentlemen don't typically, on a whim, tear up another man's vowels if they've won fifteen thousand pounds at the gaming table."

Every single time she heard that figure Ginny's head went tight with disbelief. One of these times she would keel over into a swoon. Perhaps expire. Perhaps that would be all for the best.

"Ah. Is that what Miss Woodville asked you to do?" Marchand managed to sound only mildly curious.

The earl nodded sorrowfully and indulgently.

"Why, I'm afraid asking someone to return money they

rightfully won would be considered outrageous, Miss Woodville," Marchand said gently.

The expression in his eyes was not gentle.

"Outrageous!" the earl repeated, as if relieved to hear just the word he'd been looking for all night. As if he'd been given permission to use it. "But forgivable, in light of the circumstances of her naivete."

He smiled fondly at Ginny.

Her lips spasmed into a grimace.

"One thing still puzzles me, however, Miss Woodville," the earl said. "How *did* you know that your brother lost to me, in particular, if he didn't *tell* you that he did?"

An alarming stillness came over Marchand. He fixed his eyes on her with an intensity she realized was a warning.

And that's when she realized she had him by the proverbial short hairs.

Because if she wished, she could merrily lie: *Oh, Mr. Marchand and I had a long, cozy chat aaaalll about you, Lord Sydenham, all about your habits and foibles and your mistress, make that mistresses, he told me everything, and he told me to go ahead and ask you to give the money back, as you'd be happy to do it.*

The power to foment chaos briefly inebriated her.

She and Mr. Marchand held a few seconds' worth of eloquent conversation using their eyes only. His were surely scarier than hers.

She could feel impulse and reason warring within her.

Reason was winning. Simply because she couldn't predict what would happen if she did say all of that, or anything approximating it. It would be satisfying to watch Marchand scramble to undo the damage, but her own reputation and her family's would be dented in the scuffle, too.

Then there was the little matter of the fact that they currently lived under the same roof at a boardinghouse by the docks, and Mr. Marchand would doubtless volunteer the information to Sydenham. Perhaps he'd invent a few choice things about her of his own. She had no doubt that he would fight like a trapped wild animal.

"I pressed and pressed Hogarth for the answer," she faltered. "Which was difficult for him. Because of, ah, honor. All he finally told me was that he lost to someone he *greatly* esteemed. And that the chance to play with this person was the reason he wagered at all. Since he is not gregarious by nature, and I knew Lucifer's Fall's members are generally members of the peerage, I thought of you at once, Lord Sydenham. I fondly remembered your kindness to our family and your warm relationship with my father. And I know how much my parents admired you. Hogarth does, too. It was a lucky guess, I suppose."

A silence terrifying in its length greeted this masterpiece of invention.

"That was very clever of you, dear," the countess assured her, finally.

The corners of Marchand's mouth betrayed that he was suppressing a smile. He shook his head slightly.

But the earl's expression had gone softer. She exulted, but she could not yet exhale. She did not yet know how to convert the softened expression into the return of fifteen thousand pounds.

"Do you know, I had a thought, Miss Woodville." The earl's

voice was drifty and musing, as if he'd spent that silence poring over memories. "I know how we can make your brother's little wager more fun."

"Debts are so much better when they're fun," Ginny replied weakly.

"The late Earl of Highgrove—the one whose title Hogarth inherited—once bought out from under me at auction a Chinese vase from the Ming dynasty. An *exquisite* thing. Unassuming on first glance. Deceptively simple but beautifully wrought. Like my wife."

"Oh!" his wife said, sounding confused.

"It's worth several hundred pounds. Its small, flawlessly round shape spoke deeply to me for reasons I cannot fully explain." The earl cupped his hand and made a hefting motion. "It's white, with a pattern of blue lovebirds frolicking among entwined lotuses. I was distraught when I learned the antiquities dealer who had acquired it specifically *for* me had sold it out from under me. I was willing to pay a hundred pounds more than it was worth. I can only assume the earl, your cousin, offered him a considerably better deal. Unscrupulous, if you ask me. Your family does like to steal things from me. Ha! I jest. I jest, of course. I have never been able to forget that vase."

Just like he'd never been able to forget her mother.

"The vase sounds lovely." He was only making her uneasy in a new way. Chinoiserie was very popular; much, much cheaper stoneware imitations of Ming vases abounded. Only the wealthiest of people could afford an *actual* Ming vase. They were exceedingly rare and obviously coveted. She'd never even seen one up close.

"Find that vase and bring it to me within a fortnight, Miss Woodville, and I'll tear up your brother's vowels."

She stopped breathing.

The air shimmered oddly, as if she were dreaming, or about to ascend to heaven. She was experiencing a violently sudden change of internal atmosphere.

Marchand was frowning slightly.

Her breath came shallowly and goose bumps rose on her arms as she was once again flooded with that prodigal feeling known as hope.

She hadn't the faintest bloody idea where that vase was. The late earl might have sold it yet again; he might have been buried with it, for all she knew. A housekeeper might have accidentally turned it into smithereens while dusting. Perhaps the solicitor knew.

"Done," she told him.

"Shall we shake on it?" The earl extended his hand, and she took it, unable to resist flicking a glance at Marchand, whom she had refused to touch only yesterday.

"So witnessed," Mr. Marchand said shortly. The deal was official.

But for some reason Marchand looked faintly troubled.

Deal thusly sealed, Ginny didn't want to be in that room with *any* of these people for one moment longer.

"Thank you, Lord Sydenham, Lady Sydenham. Your offer is gracious beyond words. I'm certain you'll want to spend some time chatting with Mr. Marchand, so I'll bid you good night. It was so very lovely to see you. And it was a *pleasure* to meet you, Mr. Marchand. No, don't stand, please! I can see myself out. I remember the way. Thank you so much for your kindness and hospitality. And I'll see you again when I bring your vase to you in a fortnight!"

She leaped to her feet, bobbed the world's swiftest curtsy, trailed a gaily waving hand, and bolted.

She was already in the hall before anyone could reply.

She could hear her own shoes echoing absurdly on the marble, as though she were being chased. *Click click click click.*

She might even have fluttered Farnham's coattails with the breeze she created as she passed him when she dashed out the door.

Chapter Seven

Outside, she was shocked to discover that the day was still suspended between sunset and nightfall. Less than an hour had elapsed while she was inside, even though it had felt like an eternity. The sky was striped in beige and indigo and the shadows were long and rapidly getting longer. Lamplighters had already begun their work. Her path was somewhat illuminated as she jogged along. *Please let there be a hack, please let there be a hack.*

Unfortunately it was a peculiar hour for anyone to be coming and going, and hack drivers knew it. None came along.

And then—predictably—she heard boot heels on the pavement some distance behind her. She nearly growled in frustration.

She knew exactly who was bearing down on her before she even turned.

She accelerated to a ridiculous trot.

She glanced over her shoulder. The unmistakable silhouette of Mr. Marchand was looming.

He merely needed to lengthen his stride to be upon her in seconds.

And then she passed what looked like—and surely it was kismet, because how else would she have been able to see it in this light?—a bright stone right there on the pavement. Was it shaped like a . . .

It was!

It was speckled white and gray and shaped like a heart! *Exactly* when she needed it. She whirled and lunged for it.

Just as Marchand's foot was about to come down on it.

His reflexes were extraordinary.

He performed a high kick to avoid crushing her hand, hopped backward on his other leg, flailed his arms like windmill blades, and spent a second or two teetering north and south in a valiant effort not to topple.

He managed to right himself, but not before he lost his hat.

It was now tumbling down the pavement.

When he turned to give chase to it, she snatched up the little stone.

It would be ridiculous if she continued running. So she waited.

Mr. Marchand returned to her, hat in hand. His hair had flopped over his brow. His furiously affronted expression reminded her of the Woodvilles' pet goat, William, who was outraged whenever they dragged him away from eating everything in his favorite flower bed.

A nervous laugh escaped her.

Laughing was a mistake, judging from Mr. Marchand's expression.

"Help me understand, Miss Woodville. Do you find it funny to lunge at my ankles like a rabid spaniel?"

She was tempted to fan the air, such were the waves of irritation radiating from him.

"No, I swear to you. I'm very sorry. That is, I *wasn't* lunging at your feet. I didn't mean to laugh. It's . . . it's just you reminded me of William."

"Who in God's name is William?"

He was so exasperated that it was nearly impossible not to laugh nervously again.

She decided it was wisest to say "No one you know."

"Then why did you lunge at my feet?" he persisted.

She was certain the truth would madden him, which she would also enjoy. So she told him.

"I saw a rock that I needed. You were about to step on it."

"A rock you *needed*."

She nodded.

"Was it a diamond?" Dripping with sarcasm, that.

"Oh, God. If only."

"You do understand that rocks aren't currency?"

She did not dignify that with an answer.

There was a little pause.

"Why did you need a rock?" He asked it as if he was curious despite himself. As if he *resented* that she'd made him so curious despite himself.

She contemplated whether she ought to lie or tell him the truth.

"It was a sign from my mother."

She said this specifically in order to see yet another new expression on his face.

And it was everything she'd hoped for.

"A sign from your mother," he repeated, in that neutral humor-the-madwoman voice she had come to loathe.

"Yes. A sign that I'm on the right path when I need advice. I ask her. And heart-shaped stones always appear when I need them."

The quality of the silence, and his mood, palpably changed then.

She retrieved the stone from her reticule and displayed it to him on her palm. He peered down at it without comment.

Then he impatiently pushed his hair off his forehead and fussed a bit with the cant of his hat on his head.

"So by your way of thinking, the right path was under my foot?"

"No, no. Of course not. That's not how it works. And the very notion of you would, in fact, send her to her grave all over again. No offense meant."

Every offense meant, in other words.

Surprisingly, he said nothing more.

The sky was flooding with deepening indigo now. The lamplighters had nearly finished with this particular part of the street.

She asked the question that tantalized her.

"How did you know I'd gone to the Earl of Sydenham's residence, Mr. Marchand?"

"Your eyes lit up with the zeal of an owl spotting a juicy rat when Bolt mentioned Sydenham's waistcoat buttons at the dinner table."

"The waistcoat buttons are the only thing Hogarth would tell me about that night. And that's the second time you've mentioned my eyes, Mr. Marchand. Careful, or you'll be writing love poetry about them next."

This caused a beat of silence.

"It's the funniest thing," he mused. "I started writing a poem about them just this morning, but I encountered a hurdle when I couldn't find a rhyme for 'pain in my arse.'"

She honored this with the impressed wordless moment it deserved.

"Farce," she suggested quietly. "Parse."

His expression was a picture then. Complicated. Perhaps amused. But the predominant emotion seemed to be amazement.

"In truth, it is difficult to *miss* your eyes, Miss Woodville, because you never take them off me." His voice had gone dangerously low again.

If she blushed in the near-dark, hopefully he wouldn't notice. It was true that if a room contained him, there seemed no compelling reason for anyone to look elsewhere, because for God's sake.

"Well, that's only good sense," she admitted frankly. "You've demonstrated an inclination to do the unexpected, Mr. Marchand. I feel I should at all times be braced."

He took this in with equanimity. "You should never play five-card loo, Miss Woodville. You'd give yourself away every time. You'd lose a fortune over and over again."

"What a *terrible* pity to hear it. I guess that means I won't be able to ever again set foot inside your pretty, pretty gaming hell." She sounded like a child, and she didn't care.

"It's not a hell. It's a bloody paradise—or it was, until you walked into it."

"Mr. Marchand. 'Hell' is a relative word. Lucifer's Fall was the location of the third worst thing to happen to my family. And if you're about to say 'your birth was clearly the first worst,' ha, now you can't, I said it first."

"Miss Woodville, anything can happen to anyone anywhere. One street over, one can buy a lovely ice or be run over by a carriage. Though I'm flattered you think I'm capable of such a scathing rejoinder. I wish I'd thought of it," he added.

"'Rejoinder' is quite a fancy word for a rogue."

"After you make your first fifty thousand pounds, they let you use any words you wish."

That figure dropped on her like an anvil.

He remained quiet and let her marinate in the realization that he was very wealthy. Mr. Marchand was not a gloater, but he was a dirty, dirty fighter and he knew that had shut her up.

"Do you have any idea what your little visit to the earl could do to my business?"

"I imagine I can't stop you from enlightening me."

"Are you familiar with what the black plague did to Europe?"

"Oh, *honestly.*"

"When word that an earl's sister has gone rogue, tracked down a member of Lucifer's Fall at his *home,* and actually had the temerity to ask him to *give back* the money he fairly won, news of your little visit will spread from earl to duke to MP to every single member of Lucifer's Fall. They will rightly assume the confidentiality that is the cornerstone of their membership at Lucifer's Fall, which they *absolutely count upon,* has been breached. And just like that, I will have lost their trust, and then their business, and then I will be ruined. And regardless of your contempt for my livelihood, Lucifer's Fall is the second best thing to ever happen to me. Correction: It did not *happen* to me. I built it. From nothing."

Damn him, now she was wondering what the first best thing to happen to him was.

"From nothing? Not from the bones of your enemies?"

"Essentially the same thing." Then with a mildness that made the hair on the back of her neck prickle, he added, "Do you doubt me?"

Beware the strivers, Mrs. Haddock had said. Perhaps she *was* a sage.

She shook her head slowly.

"I'm afraid I won't allow you to ruin me, Miss Woodville."

He said this evenly, but it was no less unnerving for all of that.

She'd never had a more civil yet terrifying conversation. She was far, far out of her depth. She had swum out into the middle of the ocean and unsurprisingly, there were sharks.

She did, she realized, she *did* want someone to tell her what to do. In the absence of that, *she* would have to figure it out herself.

She cleared her throat. "Mr. Marchand . . . please understand that I'm going to get my family's inheritance money back no matter what it takes, because I have no other option. That is a bald fact. Ruining you is not my intent, but if it somehow seems necessary in order to achieve my goal . . . that will be unfortunate, but it will not stop me." Her voice shook. "If all I'm left with is revenge, if all I'm able to do is go from house to house asking every member of Lucifer's Fall to give all their money back, then maybe that's what I'll do."

He took this in.

And then, the corner of his mouth actually lifted almost ruefully. "Fair enough. On the whole, I approve of ruthlessness."

Was that what she'd become? She liked the power of the word even as it made her feel bleak. It was simply love that made you ruthless. She had promised her mother, and that was love. She took care of her siblings, and that was love.

He'd probably never loved anyone or anything but the reflection in his mirror and his gaming hell.

"Though I should warn you, no one has ever gotten the better of me, Miss Woodville."

"Likewise, Mr. Marchand." She had no idea if this was true, but she liked the way it sounded.

He paused, seeming to consider what he was about to say. "Did you actually think it would work? Confronting the earl about the debt? Asking for the money back?"

"God, no. Not for one minute. I felt like an idiot. And I felt like an idiot at Lucifer's Fall, too. What do you take me for?"

He stared at her. "I honestly have no idea." He sounded grimly bemused. And as if he were talking to himself.

"If a tiger chased you up to the edge of a gorge that was about, oh, fifteen feet wide, wider than you've ever jumped before, Mr. Marchand, and your choices were either giving up and being eaten by a tiger or attempting to leap to the other side, what would you do?"

"I would seize his whiskers and give them a tug. I hear they don't like that."

She fixed him with a quelling glare.

"Leap," he admitted tersely. "Always leap."

"Exactly."

Thusly two leapers frowned at each other, wary of, and not precisely pleased by, this tenuous evidence of some sort of accord.

"So . . . more desperate than mad, but a little of both," he said half to himself, as if he'd finally decided upon the answer to her "what do you take me for" question. "Miss Woodville, whether you know it or not, you're as much of a gambler as any man who walks into Lucifer's Fall."

She went warily still, as though he'd winkled out yet another one of her secrets. She hadn't quite thought of herself that way before. Perhaps taking risks ran in the family?

"I recognize a negotiation technique when I see one, by the way," he added somewhat grimly. "I know you asked for the impossible first when you came to my office."

"Guilty as charged, I suppose," she said. "But! Look where it got me." She couldn't suppress a note of marvel in her voice. "All I need to do is get the vase for him."

"Do you actually know where this vase is?"

"Haven't a clue. See, you couldn't tell I was lying, could you?"

At this news, his hands went up to grip his head as though he were afraid it was going to launch from his neck.

He lowered them with some apparent effort.

She gave a start when he put two fingers against his lips and whistled sharply.

She hadn't even noticed the hack approaching. At last.

The carriage pulled to a halt. The horses snorted softly, and shook their heads, sending their tack jingling.

When Marchand reached across her to pull open its door, she took a few steps backward, into the street.

Suddenly he lunged toward her and seized her by the waist.

She shrieked. "What the devil are you—So help me *God*, if you don't unhand me, I'll—"

He lifted and deposited her neatly, and more or less gently, on the carriage seat.

"You'll do what? Dispatch me with that knitting needle you have tucked in your sleeve?"

She froze and stared at him.

"Ah, sir, er, madam. Is everything . . ." The driver nervously called down.

"We're fine," they replied in irritated unison.

"Look down, Miss Woodville."

Rattled, she peered where Marchand pointed.

And beheld a little tower of horse manure, surrounded by a moat of urine. A common feature of London streets.

She would have stepped right in it if he hadn't scooped her up with the ease of flicking lint from his shoulder. She was not petite.

"I realize you're more or less knee-deep in shite at the moment, so to speak, but I assumed you would prefer not to *actually* be knee-deep in shite. I'm afraid there wasn't time to debate it. I leaped, if you will." After rather too long a pause he added, almost reluctantly, "I apologize for startling you."

She could think of a million cleverly scathing little things to say, most involving the word "shite," but as much as she'd like to, she couldn't fault his reasoning, or his gallantry, even if it was more reflex than gallantry.

"Thank you, Mr. Marchand," she said, resignedly. Subdued.

"You're welcome, Miss Woodville." He sounded faintly sardonic.

To her utter chagrin, her throat suddenly was tight.

And then—oh, God, no! Now her eyes were burning.

Why was she about to *cry*? Why *now*?

It was just because for those brief seconds she'd been airborne in a rogue's arms she'd felt weightless for the first time in nearly a decade. No one had lifted a burden from her for at least that long. The contrast between that moment and everything that came before was stark.

Now she knew what awaited her if she ever, ever let down her guard: Of a certainty she would fall apart, and that terrified her.

He peered at her.

"Oh—you're not—are you *crying*?" He sounded bewildered and aghast.

Which was almost funny.

"No." She sniffled.

He made a scoffing sound.

"All right. But not because I'm upset."

"Of course not," he said soothingly. "What do you have to be upset about?"

He had the blackest sense of humor she'd ever experienced. She resented it because she actually quite liked it. Probably for the reason a razor likes a strop.

"I'm just . . ." She did not feel safe completing that sentence in front of him. *Embarrassed. And frightened. And exhausted. I can't shoot darts at you from my eyes, so tears will have to do.*

She swiped the back of her hand at her eye.

He sighed heavily. "Here." His voice was quietly gruff. She glanced up to find him holding a handkerchief. "No need to weep on your fingers like a . . . like a peasant."

This surprised a laugh out of her but she bit it back. Because she could just imagine how unbearable he would be if he thought he could charm her.

She took his handkerchief.

The driver politely cleared his throat. "Sir?"

Marchand's arm shot straight up. "One moment, if you would, my friend."

The driver leaned over and plucked what appeared to be a shilling from Marchand's fingers.

A very faint scent, perhaps bergamot, clung to Marchand's handkerchief, which was brightly clean and very soft. For some reason this small, elegant comfort made her eyes well again. She kept her head down, sniffed, and gamely undertook her usual methods for gathering her wits: squaring her shoulders, taking deep breaths.

Marchand remained quiet. He was probably watching her the way he would watch a gambler sitting across from him: for tells, for sudden moves, for information he could use as ammunition.

She realized she was dragging her fingertip over the initials embroidered on the edge of his handkerchief. She tried and failed to ascertain what the letter in the middle might be.

"Embroidered. Interesting. I find it's much more rewarding when you can feel the letters as well as see them," she quoted, ironically.

He huffed a soft sound that might have been a laugh. "It's a funny thing. I told myself that when I made my first one hundred pounds, I'd buy only the finest handkerchiefs I could find, with my initials stitched into them. And I swore I'd never be without a clean handkerchief again. That was a decade ago."

She slowly lifted her head. She studied him in wary surprise.

The new-fallen night was interrupted only by the lamps on the hack, but his eyes still seemed almost beacon bright in this light. She didn't know why she found this reassuring instead of unsettling. He would be easy to find in the dark.

"I suppose that sounds a bit stupid," he added.

She studied him.

"Very," she agreed, gravely.

His smile began slowly, but it soon took over his whole face. His entire overwhelming self—the innocent boy he must have once been, the intimidating man he was now—seemed distilled in the wry tilt at the corner of his fine mouth. His eyes had nearly vanished in amusement. He was all unguarded warmth.

It knocked the breath from her and wrung her heart like a rag.

Holy mother of God. No man had ever possessed a weapon as dangerous as that smile.

But then she realized she was smiling, too, which made her wonder whether she might have been the one to do it first.

She wiped the smile off her face and thrust the handkerchief back at him.

He took it.

"Thank you," she said again.

He nodded and tucked it away.

"By the way, a small folding knife tucked in your bodice or garter would be more practical than a knitting needle," he said pragmatically. "But you shouldn't carry a weapon unless you're fully prepared to use it. Because you're right-handed, you really ought to keep the needle in your other sleeve, so you can slide it down into your dominant hand and really get a bloke in the gullet." He pantomimed a thrust upward and she winced. "Or just shriek like a bird of prey if someone seizes you the way I did a moment ago. That ought to terrify them into dropping you."

No man had ever said "bodice" or "garter" to her in conversation before, let alone "gullet," and she wasn't certain she wanted to get used to it. A dose of Francis Balfort's cautious, genteel admiration would be soothing right about now.

"I didn't shriek like a bird of prey." She said this as a matter of rote, because she probably had. She actually found this vivid assessment funny. "And I don't think I've ever used the word 'gullet' in a conversation before."

For some reason, he smiled slightly again. He shook his head, as if in response to some conversation with himself.

"You are going back to the Grand Palace on the Thames, Miss Woodville. I will not be traveling with you in that hack, for reasons I hope are obvious to you, given that you were raised the daughter of a viscount. You're going to need your reputation, since you clearly have nothing else, and even if we're enemies, I want the playing field to be fair. And I don't want to be evicted from the boardinghouse, because the scones are worth committing crimes for and that bed is sinfully comfortable. Henceforth, you will not be wandering about the city unchaperoned. You're a danger to yourself and others when you do that."

"While it's hilarious that you think you can tell me what to do, I do not *wander*. I'm not a toddler, Marchand. I always have a plan."

"That's what I'm afraid of."

The hack driver cleared his throat. "Sir, beggin' yer pardon, sir, but will you and yer wife ah, yer doxy . . . ah . . ."

"She's not my anything, good sir, unless it's my pain in the arse."

But Marchand sounded less rancorous and more grimly resigned, which she supposed was something of an improvement.

"Just lovely, Mr. Marchand. You've *such* a moving way with words."

He deftly came out with what looked like another shilling, a princely sum for a hack driver, and handed it to the driver. "For your time and patience, with our apologies."

The driver whistled. "For that much I can drive the two of you around while you tup back there if that's what this is all—"

Marchand and Ginny made nearly identical aghast noises.

"Number eleven Lovell Street will do just fine, thank you," Marchand told him. "Please take her there."

He shut the door on Ginny, probably with some relief.

The hack rolled away, and she peered out the window at Marchand's figure receding into the dark, where *he* no doubt felt safe.

Chapter Eight

Spirits fueled by coffee richly enhanced by cream, a scone baked in heaven's ovens, not one but two serendipitously found heart-shaped stones, and one sparkly grain of hope, Ginny embarked on her search for the vase the following morning.

Her plan, and she thought it was a good one, was to seek out the late earl's solicitor to request another look at his will, in case any special bequests had been made. The Woodvilles had been provided with a copy of it, but she didn't recall a mention of a Ming dynasty vase. Perhaps he would know where such a valuable piece had gotten to.

His offices were in Bond Street, and Dot had informed her that hack drivers knew they could frequently find passengers at the Grand Palace on the Thames.

So she went out into the little park in front of the Grand Palace on the Thames to wait for one to pass.

She lifted the little latch on the wrought iron gate, and froze.

The park already had an occupant.

"Oh, it's you," she said.

"Why, good morning to you, too, Miss Woodville." Mr. Marchand was sitting on a bench.

His dark brown wool coat fitted to distracting perfection the wedge formed by the taper of his shoulders to his waist. His buckskins hugged the contours of the kind of thighs that could crack a walnut, should a person risk getting close enough to tuck one between them. The shining toes of his boots reflected a plump white cloud overhead. He was, as usual, almost too much to absorb.

"I've been wondering about something for a few days, Miss Woodville. As a young, unmarried woman of aristocratic lineage, shouldn't you be trailed everywhere you go by some sort of glowering dowager who would rap me with a fan for even attempting to speak to you?"

She sighed. "Yes," she admitted glumly. Because that was indeed usually how it was done.

Amusement glimmered in his eyes. "A lady's maid not in the family budget?"

She stared at him in icy silence. He was too clever, and he also sounded faintly sympathetic, which stood all the bristles of her pride on end. There was no reason he ought to know any more of her business than he already did. But this was, in fact, exactly the reason she didn't travel with a companion everywhere. And though she perpetually felt a little underdressed without a chaperone, she was also getting a little too used to it, and beginning to appreciate its benefits.

"What do you think I did with the rest of yesterday evening?" he asked.

"Debauchery," she said firmly.

"I was in by curfew," he replied piously. "Debauchery requires a considerably greater investment of time."

"I imagine you would know," she said politely.

But he didn't look at all debauched. He looked bursting with vigor, and his face even gleamed from a fresh shave. He'd either done that himself or taken himself off to the barber at an ungodly early hour. She'd seen her own bleary-eyed father at the breakfast table the morning after a particularly exciting party, his hand trembling as he attempted to spoon sugar into his coffee. She knew exactly what excess looked like.

Those faint shadows remained under Mr. Marchand's eyes, however. She hoped his conscience kept him awake and prodded him with pitchforks.

He cast his gaze upward. "Looks like a pleasant day for vase hunting. You said last night that you always have a plan. So what is your plan?"

She could think of no reason not to tell him. "I thought I would call upon the earl's solicitor to ask if he knew of any bequests of a vase from the Ming dynasty. I don't recall seeing any in the copy of the will with which we were provided, but I didn't memorize it."

"Mmm. The solicitor. Clever way to start."

She didn't know why she felt a surge of satisfaction at his approval.

And then he ruined it. "I know a cleverer way."

"You'll save both of us time if you're not coy about it, Mr. Marchand."

"*Coy?*" He was amused. "I know exactly where the vase was last seen."

She stared at him. "How . . ."

"A vase fitting that precise description has apparently been seen at the home of a longtime lady friend with whom the late Earl of Highgrove, ah, enjoyed close relations. Her name is Mrs. Henrietta Parker. She, in fact, has many friends in London, all of whom speak highly of her and visit her often, and several recall seeing such a vase there."

She suspected "longtime lady friend" with whom the late Earl of Highgrove "enjoyed close relations" was a long way of saying "his mistress," and she could feel a blush coming on. The euphemism was almost worse because all those words gave her more time to picture everything they entailed.

"Shall I assume you spoke with one of her visitors?" she said stiffly.

"Several of her visitors," he said cheerfully. "Over port last night.

"I know everybody," he explained almost pityingly, to her stunned silence. "And I was discreet in my inquiries. So no one knows a wayward sister of an earl is on the loose and looking for a vase."

"Were *you* one of her visitors?" She told herself she asked only because she was curious.

"I haven't had the pleasure of her acquaintance. She is about seventy years old, about the same age as the late earl when he expired. Lest you begin to feel too optimistic, I'm told she embarked on a trip to Italy some time ago, but was expected to return this month."

"*When* this month?"

"I don't know, Miss Woodville. I made inquiries. I'm not a mage. But we're now three weeks into the month."

Then she realized something. "If the late earl gave the vase to her, and she's sentimental about it, and it is indeed worth hundreds of pounds, I likely don't have a prayer of getting it from her." Panic began to creep like toxic smoke under the door of her optimism.

"Come now. Surely, you're a better negotiator than that. You find out what somebody needs or fears, and you go from there. I thought you were ruthless. Desperate times call for whatever measures will work."

He issued this startlingly cold-blooded point of view matter-of-factly. As though "need" and "fear" were the sole motivating factors in anyone's life.

Upon swift reflection, she supposed that wasn't far from wrong. Hadn't he identified what she'd needed and feared and used it to try to negotiate her into his bed for one night? Likely, he'd viewed it as giving her something that *she* wanted. Quid pro quo.

Nice men did not do that sort of thing.

Safe men did not do that sort of thing.

And yet. She was beginning to get an inkling of how someone might become the kind of person who *did* do that sort of thing.

"If you choose to pursue this avenue, I will accompany you to Mrs. Parker's home," he said. "As it's not St. James's Square, the possibility of being stabbed or abducted is marginally higher." He said this dryly. But one never knew.

She noticed he was not asking her whether she would *like* to be accompanied.

Still, she saw the wisdom.

And who else could she possibly ask?

Last night he'd saved her from manure and put her into a hack by herself, and she supposed in his world that counted as chivalry.

"If all of this is just a ploy to lure me into the dark, confined quarters of a hack with you, Mr. Marchand . . ."

"*Once* again," he said patiently, "I have never needed to lure any woman anywhere in order to do anything with them, nor have I needed to stalk them. I assure you, eager volunteers abound. I expect it's only a matter of time before you throw yourself at *me*, Miss Woodville."

She huffed out a disgusted breath.

In truth, she was very disappointed to realize that she found his frank way of saying shocking things—as if they were ordinary, everyday, inalienable truths—a little erotic. Every moment spent anywhere near him was a revelation. For instance, now she knew she could dislike someone profoundly even as the things they said started up an indecorous tingle in her nether regions.

"Secondly, why would I subject myself to the mortal peril of being proximate to your knitting needle? Heaven forfend."

He'd elevated "sardonic" to an art.

They both turned at the sound of hooves and wheels on cobblestones. It sounded like a hack.

"I have business elsewhere in town this morning, Miss Woodville. If you still feel you need to visit the solicitor, might I suggest at least taking along Dot, if she's available? Because men can be awful, as you know. I will meet you in front of Mrs. Parker's residence at two o'clock this afternoon. Here's the direction." He held out to her a folded scrap of foolscap.

He'd been prepared with it.

He was very efficient, for a devil.

Marchand whistled sharply when the hack pulled into view. It stopped.

She gestured to him that he should go ahead and take it.

"What, I ask, do you have to lose, Miss Woodville?" He tipped his hat to her, pulled open the door of the hack, and rolled away.

* * *

When a hackney cab delivered Ginny to the house on Finster Street at two o'clock, Mr. Marchand was already waiting at the blue wrought iron front gate. He looked tall and forbidding, the heart-stopping angles of his face distinct even from a distance.

A breeze pushed gossamer shreds of clouds across a pale blue sky. Though it was a rare sunny day, the shades were drawn on every window of the town house, except for those upstairs, which were bare of coverings. Their blank darkness seemed oddly sinister. The walk hadn't been swept in some time; sun-crisped leaves skittered across it and others had banked in front of the door.

By contrast, curtains fluttered in the open windows of several nearby houses, and their walks were tidy, too.

"I've never been in this part of London before," she mused. It was charming. She could imagine herself living here.

"It's where all the mistresses live," Marchand told her, spoiling her fantasy and reminding her too vividly of his recent indecent offer.

"Is that so?"

"Yes, and all the rogues live on another street, and all the merchants on another, and all the aristocrats on another. It's a very efficient system."

She sighed.

He was frowning up at the house. "I would have thought Mrs. Parker's staff would keep the house looking spruce in her absence, so as not to attract burglars."

So he thought something was amiss, too.

He touched the gate.

They exchanged a glance when it swung open.

It shouldn't have been unlocked.

He turned to scale the steps up to the door, and she followed him.

"Ought we to knock?" she asked.

He seized the knocker and rapped.

They waited.

He put his ear to the door. "Nothing is stirring in there."

He rapped again, with the same results.

He tried the doorknob.

The door was locked.

He pressed his lips together in thought.

"Perhaps one of the neighbors will know whether Mrs. Parker has returned?" she suggested.

Marchand scanned the street, then returned to staring at the door.

"Give me one of the five hundred and eighty-two pins you use to hold your hair in place, Miss Woodville. But be careful, because one wrong choice and the whole structure will come down."

"Nonsense." He was more or less correct, of course.

"The hairs that have already escaped their confines prove my point. The rest seem just as anxious to do that."

She gave a short self-conscious laugh. The curls at her temples were purposeful, but she was not going to stand here and explain hairstyles to a rogue on a dead earl's former mistress's front stoop.

He watched her pull a pin with fixed avidity, as if he was picturing with relish all of it coming down.

Which made her feel not unpleasantly warm. Her hand was a little clumsy as she handed it over, and she was ostentatiously careful not to brush his fingers. "What are you going to do with it?"

"Use it to protect myself from your advances, of course." He dropped to his knees and guided the pin into the lock.

"You're going to break into the *house*?"

He jiggled and maneuvered it for a few moments with seeming deliberation. This obviously wasn't the first time he'd done such a thing. "Yes."

"But . . . what if the neighbors notice?"

He paused and looked at her. "What if they do?" He sounded amused.

Oh, God. As she'd said to him the night before, he'd proved he was all too capable of the unexpected.

What did she know about this man?

"What if there's a bolt on the inside?"

"Then I'll go in through the servant's entrance, or a window," he said distractedly.

"And are we going to *steal* the vase?"

He stopped to fix her with a reproving stare. "For heaven's

sake, Miss Woodville. No, we're not going to steal it. What kind of monster do you think I am?" His affront was wholly feigned. "We'll ascertain whether it's even in the house, and then . . . decide how to proceed from there. But I definitely think something is a bit off, and I want to know what it is. I'm worried she might have been robbed, or otherwise harmed. Call it an instinct."

He returned to jiggling.

And then something gave with a click.

She caught her breath.

Marchand tried the doorknob.

When it turned, she caught herself just as she was about to clap her hands in delight. What kind of lady felt triumphant instead of chagrined that they were breaking into a house?

"Stay behind me," he whispered. "I'm not leaving you out here alone."

Which is when she noticed he had a gun in his hand.

He had a gun in his hand!

"Why the *gun?*" she whispered indignantly. "Where did that *come* from?"

"You should always have a gun in your hand when you break into a house. Close the door. Quietly."

Dense, cold, musty air engulfed them. She saw at once that the candles in the sconces wore a fine coat of dust, as if they hadn't been lit or replaced in some time.

He put a finger to his lips and an arm out to stop her. They listened.

She heard it then, too: Low, desperate voices, in the cadences of a furious argument.

"Give it to me. Give it to me now."

"Do you want it like this?"

"Yes, damn you! I want it!"

Her heart was now pounding so hard her chest felt bruised.

"Are they arguing about the vase?" she whispered to Marchand.

He was frowning and looking perplexed.

Which was none too comforting.

"Stay behind me," he whispered again, unnecessarily, because she hardly inclined to dart ahead of him. "And walk quietly."

Why on earth she obeyed him instead of hiking her skirts in her hands and running out the door was beyond her. It was too late; curiosity was her besetting curse.

They moved through the foyer, toward what she suspected was a drawing room, the usual architectural configuration in a town house like this one. The door of it was ajar about a foot.

As they drew closer, other sounds, confusing ones, gradually became audible: a rhythmic smacking of some kind, as though someone was striking a smooth object. A peculiar dry scrabbling, like mice living in upholstery. A kind of creaking noise, the sort a rocking chair in motion might make. Muffled oaths. All in all, it sounded like some kind of scuffle.

She threw a sharp, frightened look up at Marchand.

Oddly, his expression had subtly transformed to one of pure bemusement.

Gently, very, very slowly, he pushed the parlor door wider.

She peered past him into the dim room.

Her eyes were immediately drawn to something pale near the back wall.

She froze, transfixed in disbelief as her vision adjusted.

It appeared to be a vast pair of white buttocks.

The buttocks were bobbing up and down on the settee, which was swaying and squeaking violently on spindly legs. Two feet, clad in women's sensible walking shoes, were perched on either side of the buttocks. What looked like serviceable wool stockings were bunched around their ankles.

The owner of the feet gave the buttocks a loud smack. "Give it to me faster!"

The buttocks complied with speed.

"Argh! Oh no! *WHY*?" Ginny shouted before she could stop herself, and slapped her palms over her eyes as if someone had cast acid into them.

Marchand leaped between her and her view of the heaving bodies and fanned out his arms.

He could do nothing to drown out the shrieks, grunts, oaths, squeaks, and rustles as the lovers scrambled apart and attempted to reassemble themselves.

There fell a silence.

"Miss Woodville, why don't you wait in another room while I have a conversation with . . ."

He swung the gun in the direction of the settee.

"Mr. Benson and Mrs. Cartwright," the man breathlessly volunteered. "Is you robbers? Please don't shoot us. We ain't robbers, neither."

She noticed that none of the names were Henrietta Parker.

". . . while Mr. Benson and Mrs. Cartwright get sorted out."

He did not have to make that suggestion twice.

Chapter Nine

G inny found another smaller drawing room on the same floor, which was also dusty, musty, cold, and empty apart from a single settee. The floors were bare.

She hoisted the blinds and parted the curtains to allow in some light, then sat down and waited, numbly contemplating her choices and listening to the unintelligible murmurs of conversation coming from the next room.

Once again, she was both mortified and fascinated.

Presently, Mr. Marchand found her.

He studied her from the doorway for a moment before approaching.

"It seems Mrs. Parker unfortunately passed away in Italy a few weeks ago. Mrs. Cartwright was her housekeeper and Mr. Benson was her butler, and they received word of it only a week ago via letter."

"I see. How sad." It *was* sad.

"Mrs. Cartwright was upset, and needed comforting, so, ah, Mr. Benson was cuddling her."

Ginny stared at him balefully. Judging from the heat, her

face was a uniform shade of crimson. "Oh, for heaven's sake, Mr. Marchand."

The corners of his mouth twitched upward. "Do you need smelling salts?"

"Why, have you got any?" she said somewhat bitterly.

"No. I was just curious."

This made her bark a short laugh. But it tapered into a sigh.

He cleared his throat.

"I imagine it can be a little distressing to witness that sort of, ah, intimacy, when you didn't expect to. It's natural to feel . . ."

She was amused at his caution and almost touched by his attempts at sympathy.

"Disturbed? Inconvenienced? Embarrassed? Deeply regretful?"

"If those are the things you feel, then those are the things you feel." He looked amused. And not at all uncomfortable.

Imagine being the sort of person who wasn't even a little nonplussed by happening upon unexpected fornication, complete with buttock smacks.

"Doubtless it's more picturesque when *you* do it."

He went dead silent and abruptly still.

She knew a surge of deep satisfaction at robbing him of words. He wasn't the only one who could be unexpected.

"Probably not," he finally said smoothly. "I'm sure it depends on the angle at which it is all viewed. Or the perceived attractiveness of the participants."

She closed her eyes. "Oof," she muttered, miserably.

She opened them in time to find a fleeting grin vanishing from his face.

"I would have thought your legendary prowess would make a difference to how things looked, regardless of the angle," she countered.

"My *what?*"

Ginny was delighted at his astonishment. "Prow. Ess," she repeated, relentlessly emphasizing each syllable.

Which made him frown darkly.

"Who on earth have you been talking to?" He didn't add "young lady" at the end of that sentence but his tone implied it and somehow that was even funnier.

"Lady Tomelty. Your prowess was the on-dit, she claimed. I did a little research on you before I came to London."

He scowled, which was a fearsome thing to witness.

Then he tipped his head back. "Giddier than a champagne bubble?" he guessed. "Blond? Pretty as a trinket? About thirty years old?"

"That sounds like her."

He remained quiet. His scowl hadn't entirely disappeared. She was reminded of the gargoyles on the roof edge of the Grand Palace on the Thames.

"She shouldn't have spoken to you that way. At all. Even I know that," he said almost reflectively. As if he was realizing a few things about Ginny's shambolic upbringing and recent history.

Which was quite ironic, given that he had recently made her an offer that no man should ever make a gently born unmarried lady.

That no *gentleman* should make, anyway.

The word that adequately captured whatever Marchand was hadn't yet been invented.

"No, she shouldn't have said it. But how else would I learn anything about anything?" she said matter-of-factly.

"I've met Lady Tomelty exactly once, at a sort of salon. Her husband is a member of Lucifer's Fall. She has no firsthand knowledge of that or anything else about me, and that includes prowess. This I swear on my life. So I'm not certain what precisely you've learned."

"That such a thing as prowess exists and that some people consider it a good thing."

He smiled faintly. "Touché. It's not *un*important information."

"Rather disappointing to hear that the prowess bit about you is not true and you're another grunty scrabbler like our friends in the other room, however," she said sadly.

He went rigid again. Clearly thunderstruck.

Ginny was enjoying herself now.

And then amazement, hilarity, and a fairly serious warning not to trifle with his dignity mingled in his expression. One got the sense that Mr. Marchand was seldom truly taken aback, let alone crossed.

She knew the most ridiculously delicious triumph. Startling him might really be her only line of defense against his intimidating aplomb, even if it was probably unwise to test her luck and his patience.

Though in every way, in every respect, her every action was already well past unwise.

"Prowess usually takes two," he replied evenly enough. "It's not a skill you possess that fits every instance. It's not like shoeing a horse."

She was starting to regret the track she'd set them both upon, because she immediately felt warm again.

"Well, that's a relief. I'm so glad to hear it's not like 'shoeing a horse,'" she said with the irony it richly deserved.

"It's more like a dance. If one partner is graceful, but the other routinely treads on or trips over feet or prefers reels to waltzes or doesn't move at *all* . . ."

She'd never met anyone so unafraid of not blinking. She considered it a personal challenge to hold his gaze, but it was like being handed two shillings plucked out of a fire.

A night in my bed.

He was willing to forgo the *four thousand pounds* he was owed for that privilege.

And it was probably less to do with her charms than the fact that he had so much money he could do frivolous things with it.

Perhaps.

Or perhaps he knew things about her that *she* had yet to discover.

His words were smoldering inside her like little coals now, someplace where rational thought could not reach to quench them.

If Mr. Marchand decided to suddenly lunge and ravish her, replicating the scene in the drawing room, there probably wasn't much she could do about it. The house would become an orgy house.

Although she was somewhat comforted by the notion that she'd probably already proved that she was more trouble than she was worth.

"Probably you shouldn't be saying those sorts of things to me, either," she said primly. Also wickedly.

He sighed heavily, as if she was exhausting.

"I haven't yet asked them about the vase. I thought we'd go in and have a chat with them together so we could both hear what they have to say. They seem like pleasant enough people. Unless you would find it too awkward."

"All right." She might as well have yet another mildly excruciating conversation, the only kind she seemed to have lately.

* * *

Mr. Marchand brought in chairs from the dining room so they could sit across from Mr. Benson and Mrs. Cartwright. He'd opened up the blinds, too.

Chatting with a man whose buttocks she'd seen before she'd seen his face was unprecedented for Ginny. His face was broad and mild and friendly. His hairline began at about the middle of the top of his head; he sported jowls. He wore a neat butler's uniform.

She could not help but steal a glance toward Mrs. Cartwright's shoes. She seemed to have managed to pull up her stockings snugly. She wore a cap and apron, both white and tidy, and a blandly deferential expression.

Both of their faces were red, and she suspected her own was, too.

Marchand's wasn't.

She had never once imagined the Woodville servants making love, and now she wondered why. She would never have figured either of the two people sitting across from her for passionate spankers, and she was doomed to wonder that about everyone she met from now on.

"I hope you'll forgive our intrusion. It's just that we were concerned about Mrs. Parker," Marchand said. "And given the outward condition of the house, when no one answered the door, it struck me as ominous."

Ginny had explained that she was a relation of the late earl's.

"Your cousin, the earl, was a nice man, Miss Woodville. We saw him often. It's very sad for us to lose both of them. Perhaps they wanted to be together." Mrs. Cartwright said this.

"I'm sorry for your loss, too," Ginny told them.

Mr. Benson reached out and squeezed Mrs. Cartwright's hand. Perhaps they *had* been comforting each other, along with the spanking.

"Mrs. Parker passed away whilst she was in Italy," Mrs. Cartwright told them. "We had the letter a week ago, and we at first didn't know what to do or where to go. We've been living here, but we haven't been paid for the past month's work as usual."

Judging from the condition of the house, she'd ceased cleaning right about then, too. Perhaps they'd been lovemaking with abandon all over the furniture instead in the interim.

"Then the landlord learned she'd cocked up her toes and he told us he would pay us to pack up her house and clear out her belongings as best we could as soon as we could. Mrs. Parker was mad about her knickknacks, wasn't she, Benson?" The butler nodded. "They was *everywhere*. Little porcelain dogs and shepherdesses and vases and dishes. Had to dust each and every one of them every day for fifteen years, all them nooks and crannies, never broke a one of them. Got to know them like they was me own children. And still she didn't think to leave a *will*," Mrs. Cartwright said bitterly. "And me out of a job. She had no children. We took the lot of the knick-knacks to Fleegle's Emporium of Wonders on Farwell Street. Got three whole shillings. Sold off her furniture, too."

Ginny recognized the name of the shop. It was where her sister Felicity's fiancé, Lord Cambrough, had whimsically purchased a little china pig for her. Felicity collected them.

"Do you recall in particular a little blue-and-white porcelain vase with flowers and birds on it?" Ginny asked. Her heart was thundering.

"Oh, she had a good dozen blue-and-white vases! She did so like her chinoiserie." Mrs. Cartwright pronounced this "chinwossy." "She didn't love one more than another, because she loved everything the earl gave her. But I do remember the one with the birds. Had funny dark lines on the bottom, like a child had scribbled on it? The earl gave it to her, so she was right fond of it anyway."

"It had sentimental value to the earl as well, which is why we are inquiring," Mr. Marchand said smoothly. "Miss Woodville's family would like to keep it in his honor. When did you take them to Fleegle's, if I may ask?"

Ginny almost wished she could reach out and grasp Marchand's hand as she awaited the next words.

"Two days ago."

"Thank you for your time," he said briskly. "I wonder if you would mind if we had a look about the house?"

"You're the one with the gun, Mr. Marchand," Mr. Benson said. "Would it make a difference if we minded?"

"None whatsoever," Mr. Marchand confirmed.

* * *

Ginny and Marchand performed the quickest imaginable search, side by side, wordlessly. He wouldn't let her wander about alone, on the off chance anyone else was lurking in the closets or bedrooms.

But the upstairs rooms were all but stripped of furnishings, fixtures, and carpets. A scrap of ribbon remained on one floor. She picked it up and held it briefly. She knew a swift stab of sadness for the woman whose house this had been. Her throat went tight again. Nearly every trace of Henrietta Parker had been erased. No dishes, cutlery, or pots and pans remained in the kitchen.

She looked up to find Marchand watching her.

Finally, he touched Ginny's elbow as a signal. They bustled out of the house, leaving Mr. Benson and Mrs. Cartwright sitting somewhat forlornly side by side on the settee. Still holding hands.

She wondered if they'd resume what she and Marchand had interrupted when they departed.

"Do you think they're in love?" she asked Marchand. "Mr. Benson and Mrs. Cartwright?"

She asked it mainly to see how his expression would change.

"Well, they must be, Miss Woodville." He said it indulgently, on a slow drawl. "Whatever else could it be?"

The driest irony she'd ever heard.

The man clearly possessed not a shred of romance.

"But they're not married."

"Matrimony is hardly a prerequisite for what they were

doing." He was very amused. "Neither is love. Nothing but appetite is required for that, Miss Woodville."

She felt a bit foolish. But when she pictured Mr. Benson's and Mrs. Cartwright's linked hands, she was tempted to argue the point.

Suddenly she noticed there were two hacks waiting outside the house.

She turned toward Marchand wonderingly.

"They've been waiting there for some time. I arranged for them before I arrived," he told her. "Nearly anyone will do anything for the right price."

They regarded each other for a beat of silence.

"Nearly," she reminded him.

The lowering light was behind him. In it his face was pale gold and his eyes were silver and his edges were gilded. He looked exactly like a person who could persuade anyone to do anything.

"You will take one hack back to the Grand Palace on the Thames, Miss Woodville, because Fleegle's Emporium of Wonders, whatever the devil that is, won't be open after dusk. And I will take the other back to Lucifer's Fall to address a little business before I return to the boardinghouse. I'm prepared to escort you to Fleegle's tomorrow afternoon about two o'clock."

His presumptuous ordering her about still abraded her nerves, but less than it had even hours ago. His sheer competence, and the money he threw about like he was Midas himself, made her nervous. She was afraid to get accustomed to it, but it wasn't easy to resist. It was as though a too-tight belt she'd worn around her rib cage for years had finally been loosened a few notches. She wondered if it was a strategy, on his part. If she didn't put up a bit of a fight, sooner or later he'd order her to lie back and hoist her skirts and she would obey out of sheer habit.

She could see no reason to argue with him about her own personal hack, however.

Instead of lifting her this time, he offered his hand to help her up, and she took it.

She was shocked when her cheeks went warm as he closed his fingers around hers.

She ducked her head briefly and released him swiftly.

When she looked up again, she caught an expression she could not quite interpret fleeing from his face. She might have called it rapt if he'd been any other man.

As far as she was concerned, he'd been instrumental in her family's catastrophe, but he also could have easily let her twist in the wind. She was still a lady.

She remembered her manners, because he deserved that much.

"Thank you for your help today," she said almost shyly.

He touched his hat. "Anything to keep you from ruining me, Miss Woodville."

Chapter Ten

"This is Mrs. Cartwright's worst nightmare. The dusting!"

Ginny was agog at the sight of row upon row upon row of little vases, dishes, bowls, match keepers, salt cellars, and more stretched on into infinity in Fleegle's Emporium, which was milling with people picking things up and putting them down again.

"It's a lot of people's worst nightmares," Marchand said grimly. "Imagine the crashing sound after one mighty sneeze."

"Or if you swung a cricket bat in here," Ginny said.

Marchand had in fact presented a cricket bat to her a half hour go when he'd returned to the Grand Palace on the Thames. He'd been at Lucifer's Fall all morning interviewing new guards to replace the one he'd fired for letting her in, or so he told her. He'd been out at Lucifer's Fall last evening, too, as the boardinghouse rules allowed. While she'd played a rousing game of whist with the ladies, Ginny worked up a little resentment by imagining him strolling through a thicket of drunk heirs happily engaged in losing their fortunes. It was an attempt to offset something that felt disconcertingly like disappointment. The room felt diminished by Marchand's absence.

"Apparently, this is one of the 'whimsical' things your brother won," he said when he handed the cricket bat over to her. "It was sent to him care of Lucifer's Fall. And look, it's even signed by Silver Billy Beldham." Silver Billy was a famous batman. Her brother worshipped him. "It might actually be worth something." Marchand had paused. "Not anywhere near as much as Hogarth wagered for it, of course."

Ginny had sighed heavily and brought it up to her boarding-house room, muttering beneath her breath about her brother.

"Let's speak to Fleegle's proprietor," Marchand said now.

They waited in line as several people ahead of them made purchases.

Mr. Fleegle turned out to be a bald gentleman with a long, regal nose and bushy white eyebrows. He flicked his eyes over the two of them and adjusted his posture to ever-so-slightly straighter. Likely he smelled money.

"Good afternoon, sir. Would you be Mr. Fleegle?" Marchand asked.

"Yes, sir. And you would be?"

"A potential customer. Mr. Fleegle, would something you purchased from a customer three days ago already be out on your shelves?"

"Anything pretty we received three days ago would have already been sorted and recorded by our staff and put out on the shelves. Anything ugly we use for target practice for the fun of it or sell for skeet."

"How do you determine ugly from pretty?" Ginny wondered. Only slightly ironically.

"Taste, my dear." Mr. Fleegle tapped his temple. "You have to be born with it."

"How interesting! One learns something new every day, don't they, ah, dear?" She turned to Marchand.

He fixed her with a quelling look.

"A vase to which we are sentimentally attached was inadvertently added to a box of knickknacks and brought here by a woman named Mrs. Cartwright," Mr. Marchand informed him. "You purchased it from her for three shillings. Do you recall this, Mr. Fleegle?"

"Quite a lot of gewgaws, dogs, and things? Shepherdesses? Several vases? Little bowls?"

"That sounds like it," Marchand confirmed.

Ginny crossed her fingers in her skirts.

"We put some of it out on the shelf, if I recall. I sold some of the shepherdesses to a bloke who wanted to line them up on a fence and shoot them for target practice."

"Oh no!" Ginny's hand flew to her heart, as if he was talking about murdering real shepherdesses. *Men.* For heaven's sake. "Do you have any shepherdesses left?" she asked.

"I think I see one on that top shelf over there, where the staff usually puts out knickknacks that look like people." He squinted, and pointed.

She pivoted to stare sorrowfully at the homely little shepherdess that Harriet Parker had allegedly cherished.

"Do you keep an inventory list or record of purchases?" Marchand asked.

"What kind of establishment do ye think we are, fine sir, that we wouldn't keep a list?" Mr. Fleegle said this with cheerful indignation. "We get so many similar things in that we number the items, then cross them off our list when they're sold. V125 for a vase, and so forth."

"No description of the item, such as color and shape?" Ginny pressed.

"Not really necessary, is it, if it's numbered? And we really haven't the time for that. Much more efficient this way."

"It's a clever system," Ginny confirmed disconsolately.

"How many vases did you sell over the last few days?" Marchand produced a handful of coins and was hefting them in his gloved hand, and Mr. Fleegle thumped what looked like a ledger up onto his counter and opened it to a marked page.

"Five," he told him. He took the coins.

"Do you recall anything distinctive about the vases sold, or the people to whom you sold them?" Marchand asked.

"If I'd known you'd be in with a handful of coins asking for such things, young sir, I might have made more of an effort to pay attention. We don't sell things on account here. The transactions are all in coin. We mark sales out of the book as they're made. We don't sell antiquities, as you can see. No one even needs to sign a receipt."

"Efficient," Marchand finally allowed, after a moment. Somehow tersely.

"Thank you, sir, for your time," Ginny said, feeling thwarted.

"You're both welcome to have a look at what we have. If it's blue-and-white vases you love, we've *lots* of chinoiserie. We keep them along the back wall." Mr. Fleegle gestured to a cluster of blue-and-white odds and ends on a series of shelves about twenty feet long. "And people often come in to buy odds and ends and then go on to sell them again at market stalls about the city. If you don't find that vase in the shop today, you may yet find it somewhere else."

"Thank you, sir." Ginny turned to Marchand. "I'll take the far end of that section while you take the part nearest the door."

She smiled when his eyes widened somewhat warningly at her audacity. She doubted anyone ever ordered him about.

But somehow she wasn't surprised when he obeyed.

* * *

Marchand idly plucked up a small white vase patterned in a tracery of vines and flowers, glanced at the bottom, and put it back down again. His search was perfunctory. He had the peculiar sensation that he was floating over himself, watching *Gabriel Marchand,* of all people, pick up and put down knick-knacks.

He in truth had learned nearly a decade ago how to spot Ming from not-Ming fairly quickly—he didn't own any, but in the first flush of his wealth, he'd contemplated buying a piece as an investment, and had ultimately decided it was too dear for him. There was something softly, subtly otherworldly about the glaze on Ming porcelain, something uniquely grace-ful about the forms it took—and he would wager his eyeteeth that not one scrap of Ming was currently in this shop.

So why was he doing this?

He felt sympathy for but no real guilt about Miss Woodville's plight. And while vase hunting distracted him from dwelling upon the beautiful yet excruciating anniversary he would be marking a day from now, that wasn't the entire reason, either. Though it seemed related in some way he was unable to quite put his finger on.

It was more as though he'd stepped into some sort of undertow against which he had no defenses. St. Giles had prepared him for a *lot* of things. But not this.

A case could be made that it had begun when Miss Woodville first appeared in his office. And he supposed he could assign that cozy bloody boardinghouse some blame.

But if he was forced to trace the origins to a single moment, it would be when he'd swept the soft, scented weight of Miss Woodville up in his arms and deposited her into the hack outside of the Earl of Sydenham's town house. During those few seconds, something within him had unexpectedly righted when she was in his arms, as if she was ballast and he'd long been a listing ship.

He was certain Miss Woodville somehow sensed it.

She'd begun to test her power over him.

She could never win a contest of wills against him, of course. He couldn't help this. Winning was what he did; it was how he was made. And he knew that girl was all untapped sensuality—pupil flares and flushed cheeks did not lie. He did not for an instant believe she would take him up on his original offer, but he was confident that in a matter of days, if he really wanted to, he could be admiring the firelight-burnished curve of her round white arse as he took her from behind in front of his hearth. And she might wonder how on earth she had come to be on her hands and knees in front of a bastard from St. Giles, but he would know. Because he would have subtly, gradually steered the both of them right up to that moment.

He was smarter than that.

Few women were more dangerous for a man like him than a virgin aristocrat with a messy life.

As he idly picked up another vase he surreptitiously admired the sway of her walk as she moved down the aisle. The bands of muscle across his stomach went taut in a reflex as old as time. As if his body was preparing to pounce.

Darkly amused, he drew in a steadying breath, put the vase down, and picked up another one.

"Pardon me, madam, but I couldn't help but overhear your conversation with Mr. Fleegle a few minutes ago. Are you looking for a white vase with blue flowers and a pair of lovebirds on it?"

Marchand's head shot up alertly. A strange man was addressing Miss Woodville.

"Yes!" Miss Woodville confirmed eagerly. "I *am* looking for a vase with birds on it!"

Marchand narrowed his eyes. The man was dressed a bit like Mr. Ogden, though everything about him was considerably less crisp and shiny. His boots were scuffed, his coat was rumpled, his hair was a bit greasy. Something about the glittery intensity of the bloke's gaze plucked a warning note from Marchand's intuition. Every decent man knew better than to directly approach a young woman to whom he'd never been formally introduced, unless she was on fire and needed to be extinguished.

Marchand began casually inching toward them.

"Me name's Cook, madam. I was in yesterday with a friend who buys up everything he can find what's got birds on it. Right popular, those. He sells them again in the southeast of St. James's Park, by the fountain, near all the other vendors. I'm certain he bought a vase what sounds just like that one. We'll be there between three o'clock and five o'clock today, if you want to"—the man froze when he noticed Marchand's eyes boring into him—"have a look. I hope ye find your vase, miss."

He shrunk away. Then he speedily looped around the shelves in the middle of the shop and exited, the bell jingling on the door behind him.

Marchand handed off the last chinoiserie fake—just flowers, no birds, no marks on the bottom—to an elegantly dressed matron standing near him, who had been reaching for it. She smiled meltingly at him and murmured her thanks. He nodded politely.

"Ginny? Miss Woodville? I thought I heard your voice!"

Marchand swiveled again. *Ginny,* was it? Who on earth were all these men appearing out of nowhere? Was Fleegle's known for assignations? It was remarkable he hadn't heard about it, if so.

This new male voice sounded refined. Also, absolutely delighted to see her.

But Marchand stiffened when an utterly stricken expression flashed across Miss Woodville's face.

"Oh, my goodness. Lord Cambrough. What a wonderful coincidence!" Miss Woodville—Ginny—darted a nervous look in Marchand's direction before she curtsied.

He understood at once: It would be *dire* for her if anyone she knew saw her with the Reaper, of all people.

He turned his face away and feigned rapt fascination for the bowl he hefted in his palm. But he kept his body angled slightly toward her so he could surreptitiously monitor the proceedings.

"You forgot to call me Henry, *Ginny.*" Lord Cambrough, a

lanky, good-looking young fellow, swept off his hat to reveal wavy blond hair. "After all, we'll be family soon."

He sounded playful, but Miss Woodville now looked positively queasy. "Ha! Of course, *Henry*. I do look forward to that happy day, and I know Felicity certainly does, too. I'm certain the two of you will have a long, happy life together. What brings you to London?"

Ah. So Lord Cambrough was her sister Felicity's fiancé.

Marchand put the bowl down and reached for a vase.

He knew it was probably only a matter of seconds before Lord Cambrough asked a question that Miss Woodville couldn't possibly answer without lying.

Unless she wanted to lay waste to her reputation.

No wonder she was terrified.

Marchand's mind whirred. He would need to solve this problem quickly.

"I'm in London for my uncle's birthday celebration," Lord Cambrough told her, "and then it's back to Sussex after tomorrow. I'm looking forward to our meeting about the marriage settlements. You'll be there, of course."

"Oh, of course I'll be there, Henry. I have everything well in hand. I'm looking forward to it, too." The pitch of Miss Woodville's voice had gained a strained half octave. "And I'm looking forward to your wedding, too."

"I was nearby and thought I'd pop in to see if I could find another silly little china pig for Felicity's collection. You know how much she loved the last one I gave her."

Cambrough sounded charmingly besotted with Miss Woodville's sister.

"What a sweet idea. I do hope you find one. She will adore it." Ginny sounded rushed and rote.

There fell what could only be described as an awkward pause.

"What brings *you* to London, Ginny?" Cambrough asked Ginny brightly.

"I'm lodging at an exclusive little boardinghouse called the Grand Palace on the Thames. I'm here to attend to a bit of official family business. I'll be back in Sussex soon."

"Ah. Well, that sounds grand. I thought you might like to know that Balfort is in London for a few days, too. I just serendipitously encountered him at White's. I know he would want me to extend his warmest felicitations. He spoke very fondly of you."

Who the devil was Balfort, and why was he warmly thinking of Miss Woodville? Marchand immediately wanted to know.

But Ginny blanched. "Well. I should like to see Francis soon, too." She said this almost weakly.

Francis, was it?

The elegant matron was next to him again. She was inspecting a bowl.

Marchand leaned toward her and whispered something to her. He surreptitiously produced a one-pound note.

She nodded just once, very subtly, and took the note.

Just as Lord Cambrough asked the fatal question.

"So who are you out with today, Ginny?"

Miss Woodville merely beamed at Henry as if she hadn't heard him.

Whereupon Lord Cambrough swiveled his head this way and that about the shop, struggling to connect someone in it to Ginny.

His questing gaze collided with Marchand's.

The boy blinked, frowned darkly, and returned his attention to Ginny, his brow furrowed with almost comical alarm.

"You're not . . . surely you're not . . . are you here *alone*?" He delivered the last word on a hush, as though it were an epithet. He followed it with a nervous little laugh, in case she found the very notion insulting.

"Oh no." Ginny laughed merrily. "No, no, no, no, no. Certainly not. Can you *imagine*?"

Cambrough's eyebrows were decidedly worried now. "I find that I cannot."

Ginny cleared her throat. "Well, as it so happens, I'm wiiiith . . ."

She made the word last so long Henry was compelled to lean forward in suspense.

"Mrs. Tuffet," the matron interjected as she strode over to them, Marchand's pound note payment tucked out of sight into the wrist of her glove. "I'm Miss Woodville's neighbor, Lord Cambrough, and she was kind enough to accompany me to London, as we both had business here. Isn't that thoughtful of her! It's madness for young women to travel alone, don't you think? And I'm terribly sorry to rudely interrupt, but we *really* must be going at once, Miss Woodville, or we'll be late to our soiree. It's a pleasure to meet you, albeit so briefly, Lord Cambrough."

"Oh! A pleasure to meet you, too, Mrs. Tuffet, was it?" Henry was confused yet visibly relieved.

Marchand watched as Miss Woodville strode out of the shop arm in arm with a woman she'd seen for the first time twenty seconds ago.

* * *

"Thank you, once again, for the rescue, Mr. Marchand. You're a very resourceful man."

Ginny said this a trifle acerbically. Because while she was indeed grateful, she was also very embarrassed. Mr. Marchand had not only quickly recognized her grave social peril, he'd had the presence of mind to solve her problem with a deft bribe to a stranger.

When she relived the moment she'd said "wiiiith . . ." to Lord Cambrough with desperate, feigned cheer, she nearly shriveled with mortification.

She'd actually marched a good thirty yards down the street arm in arm with the woman Mr. Marchand had paid to lie. She was a widow, Mrs. Tuffet explained during their walk.

Mr. Marchand eventually caught up to them, collected Ginny, and bustled her around the corner after they waved good-bye to the helpful stranger.

Ginny had watched the woman go somewhat wistfully. What an injustice it seemed that a husband usually had to die before a woman could run about town freely.

She was now sitting across from Mr. Marchand in a grubby little pub. It seemed unlikely that anyone with whom she was acquainted would wander in. Although it was becoming clearer and clearer to her that anything could happen at any time, so there seemed no point in relaxing her guard, ever.

Her heartbeat, in truth, had not yet recovered from the abject terror of watching Lord Cambrough's expression subtly change when he suspected she might be wandering around by herself in Fleegle's Emporium of Wonders. Gently bred young women simply didn't *do* that, *particularly* in a not-quite-savory neighborhood. Unless, of course, they were helplessly eccentric, in the process of going mad, or up to something truly, unforgivably, disastrously disreputable.

Like gallivanting around with one of the princes of London's demimonde.

If Henry had entered the shop a few moments earlier and seen her with Marchand, speaking with Mr. Fleegle . . .

. . . if he'd then told Francis what he'd seen . . .

The cascade of potential ramifications chilled her blood.

Most young men possessed of titles and pedigrees stretching back to William I—like Lord Cambrough—wouldn't enthusiastically marry into a family of eccentrics. While there was a slim chance Felicity's engagement would survive the disappearing dowry, a disreputable sister on top of that would likely be the final nail in its coffin.

She would rather die than destroy her sister's happiness.

Lord Cambrough's family would *never* mix socially with a man like Marchand. Her reputation would be tainted forever if her association with Marchand was known.

But it seemed to her that her two overlapping worlds, the secret one in which she was suddenly living, and the one she'd lived in every day for the last twenty-four years, were blurring at the edges, bleeding into each other. Because it struck her as irrational that the man sitting across from her, the one who had just rescued her from certain social devastation, could be the agent of her social destruction simply by virtue of being who he was—an impresario of a gentleman's gaming club. She might as well be sitting across from a lit grenade, for how dangerous this association was.

Yet she'd never felt safer.

Mr. Marchand seemed pensive, and she was drained by the scrabbling farce her life had become.

But surprisingly she rather liked sitting in the grubby pub. It was novel. It was dimly lit. The table wobbled, and it had been carved with Epithet Jar words and various initials. She traced one with her gloved forefinger.

Marchand was enjoying an ale.

They didn't serve tea or coffee here. He'd poured a little bit of the ale into a glass for her and she was staring at it. She'd never tasted ale. It was admittedly pretty, deep gold under a creamy crown of foam.

"'Ginny'?" Marchand finally quoted. Amused.

"None of my siblings could pronounce Guinevere, let alone spell it, when we were little, so it stuck."

"I see. Miss Woodville . . . how long have you lived alone with your siblings?" He seemed to have been doing some wondering about things during the silence.

"Since I was almost sixteen years old. Eight years."

"And you raised them with no other adults around?"

"Well, not precisely. The neighbors regularly looked in on us and have been very good to us. So did various relatives, when they could. But they knew we didn't want to be separated. And everyone knew I'd be equal to the job of running the house. It was my mother's wish, after all." She said this both proudly and defiantly. "I suppose we were lucky, after a fashion. We never felt abandoned."

"Your mother specifically requested that *you* look after your siblings?"

She was feeling interrogated now, and a trifle defensive. He was clearly trying to understand how her life had come to such a pathetic pass.

"Yes. Well, I'm the oldest. My sisters are twins—four years younger than I am. They're very precious and sweet girls, quite innocent but level-headed. And Hogarth is clever but a bit timid in many ways. He's also very sensitive. But *I* am the capable one. I always have been. And *I'm* not timid. My mother knew I would be able to manage it."

He nodded thoughtfully. "Did your parents *tell* you that you were these things or did you decide that you were these things?"

The question surprised her. "Well, yes, they told me this. But my sisters *are* precious, Mr. Marchand. Hogarth is shy. I *am* capable."

"I believe you." But he said it only after a hesitation.

She bristled at the note of skepticism. It always seemed only a matter of time before Marchand made her bristle.

"And there's no other money attached to Hogarth's new title? No property that can be sold, no other income?"

These were admittedly probing and personal questions, but she supposed the two of them were past being precious about that sort of thing. "There's one other property entailed. We may eventually be able to earn rent from it, but it could be some months before we find a tenant, provided we ever do. The land surrounding it would be decent for raising sheep.

That is, if we were able to actually buy some sheep. We *do* have all sorts of animals at home, but no sheep. And we also have a big house and very little money left."

He took this in. "I overheard your conversation with Lord Cambrough, of course. And I'm struggling to understand why you're the one negotiating the wedding settlements for your sisters, and not your brother or your solicitor."

"I'll be better at it," she said shortly.

"But your brother is a grown man. He's an earl. He's the one who ought to be managing the estate. And he's the one who ought to be negotiating the settlements. As the head of the Woodvilles, he ought to be looking after his family, and that includes you. If he can arrange for membership in Lucifer's Fall, he can certainly handle that responsibility. Is he impaired in some way I missed when I met him?"

She thoroughly resented this question and punished him with a moment of sullen silence.

Mainly because, in her heart of hearts, she knew he was right.

She had completely forgotten what it was like for a man to *want* to take charge of something.

"But I promised I would look after him, Mr. Marchand. Remember, he was just a young boy when my parents died. And . . ." She took a breath. "He's been afraid of heights since my parents' high-flyer accident."

Marchand's head went back then came down in a nod of comprehension. "I see."

"He's not impaired. But surely you understand why I'm protective of him."

Marchand poured a little more ale into her glass, his brow still furrowed.

She sipped it and wrinkled her nose. Which made him smile slightly.

She drank a little more to please him. She would not ever crave ale, she decided, but it wasn't horrible.

"I want you to know," he said quietly, finally, "that I think the Earl of Sydenham is a bastard."

She went still. Stunned.

"Treating someone else's grave financial predicament as a game is despicable. He ought to have either forgiven the debt, rejected your request outright, negotiated the amount down, or offered a fair exchange on the spot. Not send you on an absurd hunt."

She recalled how uncomfortable Marchand had looked when the earl had introduced his little plan about the vase. Viewed one way, she supposed Marchand's blunt offer to exchange money for sex *was* more honorable, even if it was still on the face of it odious. He seemed to understand that her body was the one commodity with which she could freely barter.

How absolutely surreal it felt to entertain these sorts of thoughts.

But with his words, some of the tightness in her chest eased. It was a relief to hear that someone else recognized the gross indignity of her circumstances. Even if that indignity more or less had its origins at Lucifer's Fall.

"I never liked him," she admitted. "The Earl of Sydenham always maintained my father stole my mother away from him."

Marchand snorted softly. "Can anyone truly be stolen from anyone else?"

"My thoughts exactly! I once overheard him say to my father, 'I'm an earl, and you're only a viscount. She'd have to be a looby to choose you over me, ha ha, I suppose I dodged a bullet.' Even when I was very small their banter made me uncomfortable. It didn't seem funny at all. My mother loved my father, clearly. She *chose* him."

"Men and their honor, Ginny," Marchand said simply. Dryly.

She fell quiet.

"Mr. Marchand, I would like to go to the park to see if that man named Cook and his friend have the vase."

"Absolutely not. Those men want to rob you."

She was *never* going to love the way he issued orders. "But what if they *do* have the vase?"

"Even so, I am very certain they want to rob you," he repeated dryly. "And they don't have the vase. I can say that with about one hundred percent certainty."

"But if they *do* have the vase, I can have it as soon as today," she insisted, a little desperately.

"They're going to try to *rob* you, Miss Woodville." He was exasperated now. "I know that corner of the park. It's near all the gentleman's clubs. It's an excellent place to do some robbing, if you're of a mind. I'll hand that to them. And if there's anything I've learned definitively from my storied career, it's when a man is up to no good. If we both go, they'll rob both of us, or kidnap you. Maybe a little of both. Or worse. You will not be going. And I will not take you there."

How had her life come to this? Was she really a hairbreadth away from a possible kidnapping because of a *vase*?

"Do you genuinely think there's a possibility of all of that robbing and kidnapping?"

"I wouldn't say it if I didn't. You might be sheltered, Miss Woodville, but surely even you know there's a higher chance of being robbed than finding a Ming vase in a park. I need you to believe me." The last words were terse and adamant. She could tell he was very nearly offended that she was arguing the point.

"But there's a *chance* of finding it." She could hear the anguish in her voice.

Whereupon he fell abruptly, grimly silent.

They sat that way for a time. Staring down each other yet again.

"Honestly, Mr. Marchand, who would look at you and think, 'I can successfully rob that man'?"

This made him give a short, humorless laugh. "You'd be surprised at how many bloody stupid people live in London."

But fear had her in a vise again. She simply could not relinquish what seemed like her only chance to repair this Hogarth-wrought disaster. She could all but feel again the wind of the abyss whistling beneath her feet.

"Mr. Marchand . . . I . . . I don't know what else to *do*." Her voice broke.

He did not reply. The grim line of his mouth tightened.

His expression remained implacable.

She drew in a long breath, and exhaled at length. "Very well. If you won't go with me, Mr. Marchand. I'll go on my own."

She said it softly and evenly.

It was a test, and they both knew it.

He didn't like it one bit. Surprised anger flashed in his eyes.

His expression now was thoroughly forbidding.

The little hairs at the back of her neck buzzed as if in anticipation of a lightning storm.

'E be a dangerous man. One of the worst men in London, Mrs. Had-

dock had called him. He probably was, for many reasons. Not the least of which was that he was the reason that she, Guinevere Woodville, was discovering she had a taste for danger.

He'd been right when he'd accused her of being a gambler. Because she'd essentially just made a reckless wager. And as she waited for his reply, she teetered on the dizzy verge of an exultation she was afraid to examine too closely.

It had little to do with the vase, and everything to do with the man.

Because she knew what his answer would be.

And she thought she knew why.

He drained his ale. He referred to the time on his pocket watch.

"I'll go with you," he said quietly.

* * *

"There *are* vendors here. Look, Mr. Marchand!"

In St. James's Park they passed tables ladened with meat pies, fresh flowers, fruit, baskets and pottery, various tonics in dark bottles, and bundles of dried herbs. The latter made her think of Mr. Delacorte. All of these wares were presided over by cheerful, beckoning merchants. Potential customers clustered about. It looked quite benign, even festive.

Ginny's mood was improving by the second, which it probably had no right doing, given her circumstances. But she was outside on a fine enough day, in an interesting park she'd never before visited, accompanied by a huge, glowering man. Hope, while gasping for breath, had not yet been entirely extinguished.

Then Marchand flicked cold water on her mood.

"Miss Woodville, if someone sees you with me, they will make the kind of assumptions about you that I am certain you will not appreciate. I am neither unknown nor inconspicuous in these parts. You might want to keep your head down if you don't want to become gossip sheet fodder."

She kept her head down.

Mr. Marchand's tense alertness and surly mood discouraged any impulse she might have to chat.

He remained unhappy with her. In the hack on the way to the park he'd tried to convince her to go back to the Grand Palace on the Thames while he went to investigate the alleged vase merchant instead. She'd refused. It wasn't that she didn't trust him to do it. It was that she *needed* to see that vase with her own eyes. If it was there, she wanted to bear witness to the miracle that would make all of her problems disappear.

She also suspected he was unhappy with himself.

Because he'd agreed to do it because he simply couldn't help himself.

A disorienting realization was taking shape as they strode along in silence. Here she was, willingly following deep into a park a man she'd known for mere days. A man who not only *wasn't* a gentleman, but who had frankly propositioned her. Logic insisted there was a greater than zero possibility that he would drag her into a bush and ravish her, despite his pattern of nearly chivalrous behavior.

And yet here she was with him, anyway. Not one particle of her thought she should run away.

So far, all Marchand had done was look after her in a way that no one else had done for almost a decade.

She wondered if it was pathetic that this was all it took to make her follow a strange man into the woods.

After all, people look after sheep for a time before they enjoy a mutton feast.

"I would be delighted to be wrong about Mr. Cook's intentions," he finally said. It sounded reluctantly conciliatory, but he gave the man's name an ironic frisson. As if he was certain it was an alias.

Presently she heard the gurgle and splash of a fountain. She risked a look up then.

They had entered a somewhat unkempt little grotto—the grass and flowers overgrown, grass raggedy at the edges of the walkway—surrounded on three sides by tall shrubberies and hedges.

And in the middle of it a little wizened man stood behind a table scattered with knickknacks. He wore a brown cap.

His eyes were small, bright, and twinkly, like a bird's.

She gasped, thrilled. "Are you the man with the bird vases?"

He bowed. "Why, I am indeed, miss! I'm 'appy to know my reputation precedes me. Come 'ave a look! Mayhap yer 'andsome fella will buy a few trinkets for you."

Ginny turned triumphantly shining eyes on Marchand.

She recoiled when she saw how cold and remote his were.

He all but glued himself to her side as they approached the table. Her heart kicked painfully in anticipation as she sought out flashes of blue and white among the bowls and vases and little birds. She hoped the two pounds in her reticule would be enough to make the vase hers when she found it.

But it became apparent in seconds that the vase wasn't there.

Her eyes passed again and again over the array of wares, her breath going ragged, her entire being desperately resisting the moment when the truth must inevitably sink in and obliterate hope.

She dreaded turning to Marchand and seeing confirmation of her folly reflected in his face.

Her head shot up when the shrubbery behind the table began to rustle violently.

And out popped the man she'd seen in Fleegle's.

In his hand was a pistol, and he'd aimed it right in the dead center of her chest.

Black spots of terror scudded before her eyes.

She staggered backward, encountering the hard wall of Marchand's chest, as the two men swiftly rounded the table.

The pistol was still trained on her.

"I'll just 'ave yer wee bag, miss," said the man with the gun. "And you there, big guv, 'and over yer walking stick if ye dinna want a hole in yer 'ead and turn out yer pockets. I can tell by jus' *lookin'* at ye that ye've got a beauty of a watch, so don't even think of 'iding it from us."

Later, Ginny would remember what happened next mainly as a series of distinct sounds, and not even loud ones, which somehow made it all the more terrifying. *Crunch thud grunt crash thud thud.*

It was over in seconds.

Marchand had rammed an elbow into one man's throat while chopping his walking stick up beneath the forearm of the man pointing the pistol and kneeing him in the groin. The pistol went flying and the thugs buckled.

The final *thuds* were the sound of two grown men hitting the dirt from a standing position.

That sound reverberated through her as she stared down. A scream congealed in her throat.

Her knees turned to water.

Marchand seized her elbow before she collapsed. He bent to sweep up the thug's gun. He tucked his walking stick beneath his arm and managed to lock the gun with one hand. Then he swept his arm around her, holding her close to his body, and steered her wordlessly, swiftly back up the path. Leaving the two would-be thieves moaning in a litter of broken crockery.

Chapter Eleven

Marchand furiously shoved his newly acquired pistol into his inside coat pocket. He might as well hurl it into the shrubbery. It was an old and cheap stick and odds were good that bastard wouldn't have even gotten off a shot if he'd managed to pull the trigger.

His skin was still all over ice.

That bastard had aimed it at Guinevere's heart.

Those thugs were very, very lucky Marchand hadn't done murder.

He realized he was rushing Ginny when she stumbled; he curled his arm around her more tightly to steady her and slowed his pace. She was trembling. It sent a fresh wave of fury through him and a nearly painful surge of protectiveness.

He reserved most of the fury for himself.

What bloody good were any of his instincts if they dissolved in the face of a girl's doe-eyed entreaty? *He'd known better.*

What was happening to him?

She'd *known* he could not say no to her.

He didn't like that at all.

And he didn't like *one* bit being played. For she had indeed played him.

And now here they were.

Just below his feet something small and bright nestled in the grass nearest the stone path snagged his eye. He swiftly bent to pluck it up and tucked it into his pocket as they passed. Miss Woodville didn't seem to notice.

When at last they came upon a bench close enough to the main street to hear carriage wheels clattering over cobblestones, he stopped. "Sit," he suggested quietly.

She collapsed onto the bench.

He removed the pistol from his coat pocket, snapped it open, dumped out the powder and shot, and dropped it in the shrubbery.

Then he shrugged out of his coat and settled it over her shoulders. It all but engulfed her.

She immediately burrowed in and gripped it closed in her fist.

He sank down next to her and finally allowed himself to exhale. He hadn't needed to fight quite like that in many a year. It amazed him that his body had still known exactly what to do. He supposed it was the way a musician's hands always remember a song.

Merry, teasing voices—a woman's, a man's, mingled with children's laughter—floated on the breeze to them from the nearby path. It was both jarring and soothing.

"Are you angry with me?" she ventured finally. Her voice was a little frayed.

He decided to tell her the truth. "Yes. A little. I'm much angrier at myself, however."

She accepted his verdict somberly. "I'm sorry." She sounded subdued.

He shook his head. "I understand why you needed to do it, Miss Woodville."

Neither spoke for a time. Merely breathed, and listened to the rush of wind and the voices.

"You might have mentioned you thought we would be robbed," she said finally.

Damn the girl. He laughed.

She pulled his coat more snugly about her. "How did you know how to . . . how to do what you did back there? All the . . ." She gave the air a chop with one hand.

"Experience."

"At hells?" He had to admire her commitment to being sardonic even in times of danger. "Did you fight a good deal at hells?"

"It was less about fighting and more about defending. My first job at a hell was at a place called the Pit, and I was the person who, shall we say, helped keep order. You get a feel for when trouble is about to ignite by just watching and listening. Someone might clench their jaw, or utter the wrong word a little too loudly. Someone might look *too* nonchalant. Pickpockets often do. More than once I had to wade into a brawl well underway. You tailor your approach to the circumstances and the men involved—height, weight, presumed strength, presumed weapons. Like that."

She gaped at him, then closed her mouth again. "That is *fascinating*," she said, sounding a little too sincere.

Which amused him. She really ought to have been appalled.

"You notice everything," she quoted. She was recalling what he'd said about the buttons.

"I notice everything," he confirmed quietly. Her knotted hands, the lush rose curve of her lips, the golden speckles on her cheeks. Everything.

"Do you think there are any more thieves where they came from?"

"I'm here," he said calmly.

She studied his face. He knew a wayward impulse to remove his glove and slide his thumb across the curve of her cheek just to see if it was as soft as it looked. Finer than Ming, surely, that curve.

When she exhaled slowly, relaxing into, trusting, his protection, he felt gratified all out of proportion.

"Do you sing?" she asked.

He gave a short, startled laugh. "Do I *sing*? Not well."

"I thought it might be soothing to hear a little song after our fright." Her eyes glinted with mischief.

He sighed and shook his head slightly. For days now her audacity had been perforating his armor like kitten claws. He decided he would tolerate it as long as it diverted him, and not a moment longer.

"The only songs I know are unfit for your ears. There's one about a bloke named Colin Eversea that goes on for days. He gets up to despicable things. Man after my own heart."

"Sing it like a lullaby, under your breath. Maybe I won't even notice the lyrics."

"No, Miss Woodville," he said sternly, "and here's the reason. When you nurse an injured wild animal back to health— let's say it's a fox—you have to be careful not to allow them to get too accustomed to their cozy indoor accommodations, or they won't be fit to live in the wild again. Too much exposure to bawdy songs and cutthroats and the like and various other discomforts and you might get used to them, which will make you unfit to marry an aristocrat. And that's how you're going to survive. A big country house, or a London town house on Grosvenor Square? *Those* are your natural habitats."

Her lips curved slightly. "Oh, very well."

"Surely you've some hopeful suitor hovering in the wings," he added idly. "Your sisters can't be the only Woodvilles in demand."

He felt peculiarly tense in the silence that followed.

"Francis," she replied almost abstractedly.

"Francis?" He knew the oddest combination of relief and antipathy toward Francis, whoever he was.

Then he recalled that her sister's fiancé had mentioned Francis in Fleegle's Emporium of Wonders.

"He's the third son of a duke," she said offhandedly. "Francis Balfort."

"Of course he is. My point exactly," he said shortly.

Francis was not yet a member of Lucifer's Fall. Perversely, Marchand considered this a mark in Francis's favor. Possibly he had a few mild outdoor hobbies. Francis might hold on to his fortune and was in all likelihood not disaster-prone.

"My mother's last wish was in fact that we all make the kind of marriages befitting the Woodville title. Grand and appropriate and titled. I vowed to her that I would make certain of it."

"Ah."

He didn't know why this information should settle heavily

on his chest. Because he admired the way Miss Woodville hewed to her responsibilities as though they were commandments handed down on stone tablets.

And he also understood that her promises were, after a fashion, monuments erected to the memories of those she'd lost. A little like those heart-shaped rocks.

He understood this because he'd long held on to his own pain and loss as if it were the island he'd washed up on after a shipwreck. It anchored him even as it had stranded him.

"So what is Francis like?" he asked.

"He's nice," she told him.

"Sounds perfect for you," he said dryly.

She smiled. She cleared her throat. "I've never heard that Francis has done anything with . . . ropes . . . for instance."

She delivered the word "ropes" on a hush, as if she were a smuggler and it was the password.

He sighed. "I'm going to need you to translate whatever it is you keep trying to say about ropes, Miss Woodville."

A slightly worrisome silence ensued. He suspected it was the sound of Miss Woodville gathering her nerve.

She was studiedly looking away from him now, straight ahead. "Lady Tomelty said you did, ah, things with ropes. In the same conversation where she mentioned your prowess."

"What the *devil?*"

Her eyes were lit up with wicked amusement when she pivoted toward him again. She was absolutely thrilled to have thrown him.

"I didn't know what she meant," she confessed. "She implied that it was depraved. And yet she made it sound like a good thing. It's all very puzzling."

"I couldn't tell you what it meant if I wanted to, either." This wasn't true. He could definitely hazard a guess.

He cast about in his mind for memories of assignations that had gotten a bit adventurous. Some most assuredly had, but ropes had not factored in any of them, and none of the details were anyone's business, least of all Miss Woodville's. He told no one *anything* about that side of his life, he was discreet, and he was not precisely promiscuous. Especially as he grew older and understood thoroughly the risks versus the satisfaction of such liaisons.

It was both disconcerting and amusing to know he'd infiltrated the London gossip stream so thoroughly. And, at least from the sound of things, flatteringly.

Perhaps because if he had any credo at all, it was that leaving a naked woman unsatisfied constituted failure.

"She said it as if it was something everyone knew," Ginny pressed on.

"She must have me confused with someone else, as impossible as that seems."

"*So* odd that people persist in just making things up about you." She did not sound convinced.

"Can you blame them for being fascinated?" He leaned back and indolently stretched out his legs.

She snorted.

In the silence that followed, he could all but feel her next question forming. He was pretty certain he knew what it would be.

"*Do* people do things with ropes?"

"For God's sake, Miss Woodville," he said, pained. "You have really got to stop talking to Lady Tomelty."

"Then why would she say it?"

He sighed and gave this some thought. "Do you like blanc-mange?"

"Yes. Is blancmange somehow involved, too?"

It certainly could be, if you want it to be, he could have said. A vision of the no doubt creamy contours of Miss Woodville's thighs flared into his mind's eye, and honestly, who could blame him? Men were capable of such dualities: hovering protectively near a female who was quaking in his coat while reflecting on the velvety insides of her thighs. He was fully in control of his impulses, if not necessarily the way his groin tightened.

"Blancmange is delicious on its own, right? Rich and satisfying and decadent. You don't necessarily need to add chocolate sauce to enjoy it. Or clutter it up with fruit. Would you agree?"

"Blancmange *is* nice, yes, Mr. Marchand." She humored him.

"But if you had blancmange every single night, and it was the only dessert you were allowed to have, you might want to try variations."

She took this in.

She cleared her throat. "Ropes are a variation on . . ."

"Yes."

When she fell quiet, he would have given nearly anything to hear the contents of her thoughts, while at the same time realizing he was better off not knowing.

"Spanking, too?" she asked after a moment.

"Yes."

"I see," she said politely.

He stretched his arms out across the back of the bench. "But no such frills are needed when two people simply want each other very, very badly."

He said this idly, almost drowsily, as if it were a comment on the weather.

After a long moment, her shoulders rose and fell as she pulled in a long, long shuddery breath.

If she asked him what he meant by that, he decided he would tell her.

Explicitly.

She was testing her power over him by again and again inching over the usual boundaries of propriety that constrained a girl like her.

He found her bold innocence erotic. And she knew it.

If he was a better man, he wouldn't encourage it.

If he was a stronger man, he would not take the bait.

Or up the ante.

As it was, he felt as though he was leaving a sensual little breadcrumb trail leading right to his bed and this seemed both inadvisable and impossible to stop.

"Thank you very much for the loan of your coat," she finally said politely. "It's helped with the shakes."

"You're welcome, Miss Woodville."

"I'm embarrassed to be such a ninny."

"Why? If you weren't afraid of cutthroats, I'd be even more concerned about your sanity than I already am."

"But I want to be afraid of nothing."

"Good luck with that," he said dryly.

"How did *you* get that way, Mr. Marchand?"

"What way?"

"Afraid of nothing. How did you manage it?" Her voice had gone small and urgent.

He knew a fresh surge of irrational fury that she'd been

compelled to withstand so much fear that she wanted to be strong enough to never again feel it. It struck him as both valiant and wrong. If *she*, a gently raised aristocrat, felt that way, more than one man had failed to protect her. And it ought to have been easy for all those spoiled men with whom she'd been raised not to fail her. What was the point of them, otherwise? What was the point of men?

Clouds had parted over them and sunshine was slanting warmly down across his thighs. Apart from an ongoing slight ringing in his biceps from the blows he'd just struck two men, sitting on a bench with her was strangely as pleasant a moment as he'd had in a long time. Though of course these days every lovely moment brushed up against the edges of a sorrow, a regret about what might have been.

He hated to interrupt this miniature idyll with the truth.

But he did anyway.

"Have you ever eaten a rat?"

She turned her head slowly and studied him at length. "But we just had breakfast."

He laughed.

But he could read in her expression that she inferred a very good deal from his question. Her eyes were troubled, soft, and wary.

Which meant she'd probably landed on the truth.

He didn't think he'd ever outright told his story to anyone, not as a narrative: *Once upon a time a boy was orphaned on the streets*, that rot. As jaded as he was, within him lingered a superstition that if he gazed backward upon his past too long, greasy black tendrils of it would reach out to snatch him back.

"I'm not fearless, Miss Woodville. I just grew up in the St. Giles rookery. I was orphaned at the age of six. I never knew my father. And I think the shortest answer is that when fear— and it comes in a wide variety of forms, like fear of hunger, fear of death—is all you know from the beginning, you don't call it fear, you just call it life. And you learn how to live within it the same way a fish born in the ocean learns to swim. On some days, it even feels as though you've mastered it. Invariably something happens to humble the devil out of you and prove you wrong. And from that you learn a new set of lessons. It's a series of adaptations, day after day after day. That, and being willing to do almost anything to survive."

He imagined telling her the rest. The things he'd never told anyone. He could turn it into a verbal house of cards, layering grimy detail upon brutal anecdote, watching her lovely clear eyes go more and more pained and unnerved and repulsed until he finally said the thing that permanently appalled her.

On the other hand, Miss Woodville was a chance-taker by nature. She would consider it a personal challenge to not even blink as he told her worse and worse things. But he knew she would feel it, that she would picture it, and he knew darkness left a stain if you let it settle into your imagination. He found he could not abide the thought of ever doing that to her.

"You would do anything to survive? Lie? Cheat? Steal?" She paused. "Sing?"

"Mmm . . . never, ever cheat. That's a good way to get killed in the rookeries. My philosophy is to keep things as simple as possible, and lying only complicates everything. I'd lie when absolutely necessary. But never when doing business. Likewise, stealing. I mainly stole only to eat or stay clothed, not for profit. Notice, I said mainly. Probably because I was able to get odd jobs from about the time I was five years old. These days, I do none of those things. But probably only because I no longer have to."

She seemed subdued. But she was regarding him thoughtfully, and, surprisingly, without a shred of judgment. Rather, with something like awe.

He could not deny it was pleasant to be looked at that way. Or that he felt a slight sense of relief.

As if a belt long buckled too tightly had been released a notch.

The breeze lifted one of the spirals of black hair at her temples. He felt as though he could watch that lift and flutter for a very long time and never be bored.

"That's why you're so elegant and clean," she said finally, almost to herself. As if she'd been drawing a series of conclusions in her mind.

He stared at her and felt a wayward flash of anger and a peculiar little flicker of fear, as though she'd just picked his pocket. She had leaped to that correct assumption with an almost surgical precision. He was not at all accustomed to being readable.

Now she looked uncertain. "I'm sorry. I just . . ."

"You're right," he admitted. "It's remarkable how many of the things we take for granted are, in fact, luxuries. Food. Shelter. Cleanliness," he said shortly.

"And it's why you hire boys from Bethnal Green. Because you grew up in the rookeries, and you want them to have better lives." She didn't phrase it as a question.

"I hire them because they're cheap and quick and grateful." He was feeling a little self-conscious now.

"Oh, certainly. And the tutors you hire to teach them maths probably work for nothing. I happen to know that tutors do not like to work for nothing."

He hesitated. "I don't hire tutors."

Her jaw dropped. "*You* teach them maths!" Again, it was not a question. It was an amazed realization.

He did, in fact, teach them maths. As best he could.

Any moment now her questions would get a little too close to the bone and he needed to put a stop to that.

"So did you ask anyone else about me before you disrupted my life, Miss Woodville?"

"Yes. One more person."

Her honesty amused him. "And?"

"She said you were dangerous. One of the worst men in London."

He gave a short, stunned laugh. "You didn't want to take a moment to soften that news?"

"I always feel as though you would take it as a personal affront if I attempt to soften anything."

He smiled. For one moment, all he could do was sit there and *like* Miss Woodville.

"Well considered, Miss Woodville. And for all I know, your friend may be correct, though there hasn't been a vote lately. I might have been usurped from the top spot. Who said this to you?"

"Mrs. Haddock."

"Oh, *her.*" He had no idea who Mrs. Haddock might be.

She laughed. Albeit somewhat cautiously.

"I suppose it's all a matter of perspective, like anything else," he allowed finally.

He was surprisingly not wholly displeased to hear himself described that way. He'd spent so many years being afraid that there remained considerable satisfaction in being thought of as formidable.

He realized then that he could live with anything anyone chose to call him. He knew who he was. That was the only thing that mattered.

He wondered if the thieves had dragged their carcasses off into the shrubberies by now.

"Isn't it funny how we're sometimes comforted by weight?" Miss Woodville touched the sleeve of the big coat draped over her. "And sometimes oppressed by it. We describe responsibilities as a weight. And they do sometimes feel like an actual weight."

She was thinking again about her duty to her family. He supposed it was never far from her thoughts.

She slid out from beneath his coat very carefully, smoothed it gently, and handed it back to him with a tender care that moved him.

"That's what life is, I suppose," he said abstractedly, because his coat now smelled very, very faintly of lavender after being close to her body. He surreptitiously brought it close to his face. "Nothing but paradoxes."

As he pushed his arms into the coat sleeves again, he accidentally-on-purpose dropped the flint and steel he carried in his pocket. It was a tactic. When he bent to retrieve it, he surreptitiously tucked the little object he'd found on the pavement next to Miss Woodville's walking shoe.

He sat up again.

"Do you think we saw all of the vases in the shop?" she asked.

"It certainly felt that way."

"Mr. Marchand . . . what if I don't find the vase? Doesn't it feel as though we've reached a dead end?"

He was mordantly amused that they were a "we" now.

"Well, I don't lie, cheat, or steal, Miss Woodville, but that doesn't mean any of those options are off-limits to *you*. I suppose the question is, what are you willing to do to get what you want? I think a person only truly knows themselves when they know the answer to that question."

If he knew Miss Woodville, she was thinking about the offer he'd made in his office. One night, four thousand pounds, at least some of her problems solved.

But that offer was beginning to feel like a sword dangling from a single thread over his head.

Some part of him was sorry now he'd made it, for reasons he preferred not to examine too closely.

"But I think there's still a chance you'll find the vase," he concluded quietly, into the long silence. He didn't think there was a chance in hell, truthfully. He just wanted to soften some of the tension in her expression. He had come to realize that her eyes were especially beautiful when lit with hope.

"What makes you think that?"

"Anything is possible and things can always get better before they get worse again. Life is a tide that rolls in and out." He stood. "Are you ready to go? Make sure you watch where you step this time."

She glanced down at her feet.

And gasped.

"Mr. Marchand!" she said triumphantly. She snatched up the little stone he'd placed there—because that's exactly what he'd found—and held it aloft. "My third one in London! And I do think this is my best one ever. *Look* at the red stripe. Do you believe me now? It can only be a sign, don't you think?"

She displayed it on her palm and he dutifully looked at it. "That's a rock, all right," he confirmed.

"Probably the closest I'll ever come to holding your stony heart in my hand," she said with mournful mischievousness.

"No doubt." He stepped forward to scan the street for a hack. Serendipitously, one was approaching. He raised his hand to hail it.

When he reflexively dropped his eyes to the ground, he realized he'd been looking for heart-shaped stones for days now.

Chapter Twelve

Delilah hummed contentedly as she installed Tristan's just-mended shirts into their clothes press, then she turned to trip lightly back down the stairs.

The boardinghouse seemed unusually quiet today. She knew its ambient sounds so well—the murmurs of people coming and going, the precise pitches at which certain stairs creaked beneath the weight of guests, the distant clank and clunk of Helga and her staff doing magical things with pots and pans and rolling pins in the kitchen. And then there was the occasional crash of a tea tray, because Dot's inner thoughts and outer actions did not align as frequently as Delilah and Angelique would prefer. It was, in fact, becoming increasingly clear that the inside of Dot's head was a bit like an itinerant carnival, brimming with distracting wonders and perils that led to dropping tea trays.

But Dot hadn't dropped a tea tray in weeks. Just as Mr. Delacorte hadn't uttered an epithet in the sitting room in weeks.

Both milestones made Delilah feel proud and wistful. Perhaps the Grand Palace on the Thames *was* refining both of them, as Mr. Delacorte continually maintained. Perhaps her own gentle and genteel influence had made some little bit of difference. She'd once been a countess, after all.

Though she *wished* Dot would remember to change the flowers in the reception room. They were now quite, quite dead.

On the third floor, she stopped abruptly. The candle in the third sconce had mysteriously winked out *again*.

It was *always* that candle. Yet they'd never been able to detect a draft near it.

Perhaps Dot's fervent belief in ghosts had finally attracted one.

When Delilah was alone it was easy to imagine they might have a ghost or two. After all, centuries worth of drama, skullduggery, hardship, and no doubt romance had played out between the walls of this building long before she'd inherited from her perfidious late husband. Its past lived on in the form of the word "rogue" still faintly visible on the sign hanging outside. She had come to love this building so much she could easily imagine wanting to spend eternity here.

Suddenly she noticed the wallpaper curling a bit away from the baseboard near the sconce. Perhaps errant moisture was dousing the candle flame? Perhaps there was indeed a rogue draft not even the clever Mr. Pike had been able to vanquish?

She bent over to inspect the wallpaper.

Which is when two fingers clamped onto the flesh of her bottom and squeezed.

"*SHITE!*" she shrieked and whirled about.

To find Daniel Peck staring up at her.

His eyes were twice their usual saucer size in absolute astonishment.

His little hands were clamped over his mouth.

Her heart was thundering. She covered it with her hand and pulled in a breath.

Delilah was stunned. She had never so much as muttered that word aloud in her life—not as a verb, noun, or adjective. Ever. She'd been a *countess*, for heaven's sake, and before that the daughter of a baron, scrupulously raised to be as perfect as possible. It simply did not ever spring to her lips.

"All right. I ought not have said that word, Daniel," she said carefully. "But you pinched my bottom. You startled me. That wasn't nice at *all*. You mustn't ever do that to people."

"*It's a bad word?*" His face was brilliant with thrilled realization. "You said a bad word!"

Oh, dear God. She could foresee where this was going, and she knew there was nothing she could do to stop it.

"Daniel, sweetheart. Where is your mother? Your nurse?" Delilah craned her head desperately down the stairs.

He turned around.

"Shite!" he incanted merrily under his breath, as he hopped down the stairs. "Shite shite shite shite shite."

One "shite" per stair.

* * *

That evening, someone else at the Grand Palace on the Thames uttered an astonishing word.

"Check," Dot said quietly.

All the guests were in for the night, and every single head swiveled toward Dot and Mr. Delacorte in surprise.

If Dot had indeed checked Mr. Delacorte's king, it would be quite a milestone.

More specifically: It would be a miracle.

"Check, I *think*," she amended. "Am I right, Mr. Delacorte? Is it a check?"

Mr. Delacorte peered at the chessboard.

"I'll be da—" He darted a look at the Epithet Jar.

Dot's bishop had been lurking behind the knight she'd just moved. Voila! It was now checking the king.

Delacorte was cautiously pleased with his pupil.

He gently moved his knight to block her check. "Well done, Dot."

"All the credit goes to Sir Percy," Dot said humbly. "He did it on behalf of the queen. He is in love with her."

"Who is Sir . . ." Mr. Delacorte stopped. He did not want to encourage this.

Dot pointed to the knight she'd just moved.

Behind Dot and Mr. Delacorte, Ginny had been dealt into a game of whist with Mrs. Durand and Mrs. Hardy. Given that the trail for the vase seemed to have gone cold, she felt a little guilty about thoroughly enjoying the evening's dinner—a stew with lots of things in it, all of them delicious—then going on to recreate with a game of cards. Though she supposed even people on the way to the gallows enjoyed a last meal.

A pistol had been aimed at her today, besides. She needed to replenish the strength that a few moments of potent terror had leached away. She could not sustain hope if she was starving. And rules were rules.

And whenever she was alone in her room, fear began to crowd her once again.

Her other option for financial salvation (albeit by way of a salacious offer) had taken a little table along the wall. He was once again in her line of vision.

He'd brought a few half sheets of foolscap and a pot of ink and a quill into the room with him.

She noted with undue fascination how he gripped his quill tightly and wrote at a deliberate, careful pace, his brow furrowed in concentration.

Have you ever eaten a rat? When she imagined the frightened, starving boy he'd once been, her breath went short. How and when had he learned to read and write? How had he acquired an entire *building*? Not to mention employees and a fortune?

His very survival struck her as a miracle worthy of a myth. He might as well be a demigod.

He looked up abruptly, intercepting her gaze just as she was thinking this.

You never take them off me, he'd said about her eyes after they'd both departed the Earl of Sydenham's house.

He'd known she'd be looking.

But then, he'd grown up needing to notice everything.

She flushed and dropped her eyes to her hand of cards.

He'd made it very clear how much he noticed about her.

The ways in which he made it plain that he desired her were somehow both elegantly subtle and wholly shocking. It was in the amused smolder in his eyes when he fixed her in his gaze. In the way his eyes lingered on her mouth. It was in the contrast between his polite restraint and solicitousness and the way he toyed with the elasticity of propriety. He was frank, rather than insinuating. All of it was hopelessly compelling.

None of it bore any resemblance to Francis's shy, glowing, respectful admiration.

After their misadventure in the park this afternoon, Marchand had sent her back in a hack by herself to the Grand Palace on the Thames.

"I'm off to Lucifer's Fall, because I have a meeting with Mr. Ogden to negotiate the price for new linens for the tables on the gaming floor," he'd told her, as he helped her board the hack. When he'd offered his hand to help her up into the carriage, she'd taken it without thinking. "No rest for the wicked."

He'd smiled at her expression.

"It's the mundane things that keep the industry of debauchery profitable, Miss Woodville," he told her, ironically.

It was only when he'd stopped speaking that she noticed she was still gripping his hand as if he were the very thing tethering her to earth.

And he was allowing her to do it.

Little by little, in increments, she'd begun to feel safer with him than without him. That realization had made her tug her hand away as if she'd been burnt.

Expressionlessly, he'd nodded, touched his hat, then closed the hack door.

She flexed her hand absently now, reliving the way it had felt to touch him. Then she flattened it deliberately on the table, as if to punish herself for thinking about him.

Suddenly a familiar tension rippled about the room. Daniel Peck's arrival was nigh. This time he'd brought an entourage.

Mrs. Peck was leading Daniel by the hand. And trailing them was his nurse, who was carrying something.

Or, rather, a little someone.

The baby!

"Mr. Marchand?" Mrs. Peck said almost shyly.

Mr. Marchand glanced up, surprised. "Good evening, Mrs. Peck."

"Daniel wanted to show his baby brother to you."

To Ginny's shock, Mr. Marchand suddenly looked as hunted as a boy cornered in an alley.

He visibly pulled in a long breath, then rose to his feet almost gingerly.

The nurse carefully settled the bundled-up baby in his outstretched arms.

Everyone else had also stood up when Mrs. Peck entered. And now they craned their heads to peer at the baby, who had a shock of black hair and merry brown eyes.

The baby gazed at Marchand as if he was a marvel, which was the way most people seemed to gaze at Marchand. Ginny found it interesting to witness that it apparently began at birth.

"How do you do, new little sir," Marchand said gravely to the baby.

The baby enthusiastically waved his fists and made muffled little duckling sounds.

Ginny's throat knotted. How safe that baby must feel right now. Her skin hummed, remembering how Marchand's arm felt curved protectively, possessively, around her, as he led her away from the carnage of crockery and cutthroats.

Who had held Mr. Marchand when he was a baby, or a child?

How could a man be both safety and danger?

Mr. Marchand was communing silently with the baby, to whom he'd offered his finger to grip.

"I see you've held babies before, Mr. Marchand," Mrs. Peck said.

His head shot up as if she'd accused him of a crime. "I beg your pardon?" he said sharply.

"Most men go at it as if they've been handed a sack of potatoes," Mrs. Peck explained, sending warning glances at the other fellows in the room, who apparently were going to be given a chance to hold the baby, too.

"I find the 'try not to drop them' approach works best." Marchand's voice had gone abstracted again. "It only makes sense to support the wobbliest parts of them."

"His name is Roger," Mrs. Peck told him.

Roger the baby made more adorable snuffling sounds.

Ginny's heart suddenly felt too big for her chest.

Marchand finally gently handed the baby back to the nurse.

"Thank you for sharing him with me, Daniel," he said politely.

Daniel toed the carpet shyly by way of reply.

Roger was then passed about the room by all the adults as if he were a sort of benediction. He didn't cry or fuss at all. It was as though he understood his job was to transform all the adults in the room into mush.

And then the tiny human was placed into Ginny's arms. He flapped his little starfish hands as she gazed at him, transfixed.

She was suddenly certain she would kill for Roger, if necessary. A shocking gust of emotion nearly swayed her: a fierce yearning bound up in painful hope and an amorphous but exhilarating fear. As if she stood on a high peak and could see in every direction. She wanted her future to feature lots of Rogers.

She pulled in a steadying breath.

Her heart skipped when she glanced up to find Marchand's eyes fixed on her.

But she was stunned to see he'd gone pale.

He looked away from her with some effort and aimed his eyes unseeingly at the far wall.

His stillness alarmed her.

She gave Roger back to his nurse, who passed him to Delilah, who cuddled him a bit before she passed him to Captain Hardy.

And as Delilah admired and was amused by the way her darling husband held the baby—as carefully as he would hold a loaded musket—she noticed an ever-so-slightly mutinous look move across Daniel Peck's face like incoming inclement weather.

Because it was one thing to proudly show off a newly beloved baby brother. It was quite another to feel *invisible* when your newly beloved baby brother was in the room. Daniel clearly had not anticipated this.

Delilah hadn't yet told a soul about the afternoon's pinching and swearing interlude. Not even her husband. She hadn't had a chance.

Foreboding encroached. Because she had a sense of Daniel now, and she knew he was mulling the *perfect* way to direct everyone's attention back to him. She knew what conclusion he was bound to draw.

As if he could read her mind, Daniel glanced at Delilah and smiled impishly.

"Quickly. Say 'blancmange,'" Delilah murmured to her husband. "Do it. Hurry. Loudly. It's urgent."

Captain Hardy stared at her in amazement. He'd just handed the baby to Mrs. Pariseau. "What on . . . why on earth would I . . ."

But he was helpless against her pleading expression.

"Blancmange," Captain Hardy dutifully said. His voice raised.

Lucien shot him an astounded, wounded look.

Captain Hardy shrugged.

"*Blahhhmajjjj,*" Daniel crowed, and laughed merrily. Everyone winced. "*Blahhhmajjjj!*"

Then he slapped his stomach and puffed up his cheeks. "I'm Mr. Dewwacorte!" He strutted over to where Mr. Delacorte and Dot sat at the chessboard.

Mr. Delacorte dropped his head into his hands.

"I'll tell you why later," Delilah promised Tristan on a whisper.

Everyone gave a start at an abrupt rustling sound.

Mr. Marchand was swiftly, clumsily, gathering his papers and inkwell.

Then he stood.

"I'll just bid everyone good evening, shall I?" he said.

To Ginny's astonishment, he bowed to the company at large and strode out of the room he'd been in for all of fifteen minutes.

He didn't look back at her.

* * *

One of Dot's secrets—and she had many little ones—was that every sunny, clear day, she made a point of crossing the foyer for the pleasure of being sprinkled with the little rainbows thrown down by the crystals of their beloved chandelier. This usually happened in the morning, after breakfast, and that time was nigh.

She clutched in her fist a bundle of violets. Yesterday, she'd forgotten to replace the fading flowers on the mantel in the reception room, which she was supposed to do the day before, because she had forgotten to do it the day before that. Now they were drooping over the lip of the vase like swooning maidens.

This morning, Delilah had asked her to do it again, somewhat reproachfully. Dot's cheeks had gone hot with remorse.

Unlike Mr. Pike, who had been hired after a long, largely fruitless, often undignified search for a footman who could write and spell, thump an intruder on the jaw if necessary, lift heavy things, and more, all while working for a modest salary at a boardinghouse near the unglamorous docks, and was therefore rightfully prized, she had merely come along with Mrs. Hardy, the former Lady Derring, like baggage. She understood she was prized, too, but mainly because Mrs. Hardy and Mrs. Durand were kind and very patient.

So lately she had taken to answering the door—her very favorite thing to do, because it was like opening a gift every time—with "Welcome to the Grand Palace on the Thames, the most exclusive boardinghouse in London!" in an effort to be admired for her bold initiative. The bit about it being exclusive was the new part. But no one had yet remarked upon it.

Would Mr. Pike ever have thought to add the bit about "the most exclusive boardinghouse"? Of course not! He had no imagination.

But Mr. Pike remained her competition. Because he had gotten a delicious taste of answering the door, decided he liked it, and he wanted to keep doing it.

Dot had at last agreed to allow him to answer it only on Wednesdays that fell on a full moon. He maddeningly persisted in behaving as though she hadn't been very, very serious about this.

It was grossly unfair that her nemesis should possess shoulders that went on for ells, and make her heart stutter when he looked directly into her eyes. He was also stubbornly kind.

A few weeks ago, when they had all gone to a donkey race, Mr. Delacorte had intimated that Mr. Pike had a sweetheart. This news had unexpectedly landed like an anvil on Dot's heart.

It had been quite a revelation for her, in more ways than one.

She had not quite regained her footing around Mr. Pike in the aftermath. She felt, oddly, as though he had gotten the better of her. She had not expected to feel like poor Apollo, heartsore over Daphne, a tree.

Violets firmly clutched, she took a long gliding step in the little shower of rainbows, closed her eyes, and rotated, imagining she was Daphne. "Now I'm a tree," she whispered.

She opened her eyes to discover Mr. Pike frozen on the stairs, wearing an expression of utter bemusement.

Her face was instantly scorching.

They stared at each other.

"Good morning, Mr. Pike."

"Good morning, Dot. What are you doing?"

The trouble with Mr. Pike was that he was not shy about asking awkward questions. Such as when he'd discovered her rubbing lamps in the sitting room, and she'd been forced to tell him it was because she wanted to ascertain whether they might be harboring any genies. One never knew, after all.

"I was just about to replace the flowers in the vase in the reception room," she said with dignity. She gestured with the violets.v

"I see. Does this require turning about three times with your eyes closed?"

She paused. "Sometimes," she decided to say, cagily.

He bit back a smile. "I thought I heard you say something about a 'tree,'" he persisted.

Finally she sighed. "In the sitting room at night we've been reading Greek myths. Peneus turns Daphne into a tree to save her from Apollo's, ah, attentions." Her blush renewed itself. She said all these things as if Peneus and Daphne and Apollo were people with whom Pike might be acquainted.

He took this in.

"Shame on that Apollo," Mr. Pike finally said. "He sounds like a brute."

"He was heartsore," Dot explained.

"Oh." Pike was confused. "I was just on my way down from having a look for drafts on the third floor," he volunteered.

One candle in a specific sconce on the third floor persisted in mysteriously snuffing out, and it was particularly maddening to Mrs. Hardy. Dot could have told them the search for the cause was futile; obviously it was ghosts.

"Mr. Pike . . . do you think you'll always be a footman?" she asked suddenly. "Or will you ever transform into something else?"

He blinked. "That eager to be rid of me, are you?" he said dryly. He hesitated. "Mr. Hawkes did mention to me once that he thought I would do well working for the Alien Office." He'd lowered his voice. "In intelligence."

Dot was surprised. Mr. Christian Hawkes—now styled Viscount Redvers—was a former renowned spymaster who had come to stay at the Grand Palace on the Thames. Pike had once worked for a very wicked earl, and Hawkes was able to send the earl to prison for a terrible crime in part because of Pike's help.

Suddenly she was sorry she'd asked. The possibility of Mr. Pike leaving to become something else seemed as awful as the possibility of him having a sweetheart. Inconveniently, she did not want to imagine either thing. But imagining was what she did best. She couldn't seem to help it.

"I think that would be a very fine thing," she said bravely. Because it was the kind thing to say, and she thought it would be true. No one had better shoulders for a career involving catching enemy spies.

She was glad she'd said it, because he looked very flattered.

"What about you, Dot? Do you think you'll always be a . . ." He trailed off, as if he could not quite find the right word for whatever Dot was.

She hesitated.

"I might want to be a story writer." She almost whispered it.

This little inspiration had been germinating for some time. She'd never told this to another soul. She'd never even dared say it aloud to herself.

Pike merely nodded. "I can't think of anyone more suited for that job."

She smiled at him radiantly.

Whereupon he looked almost stricken, as if he'd taken a blast of sunlight in the face.

She yelped exultantly when someone knocked on the door.

Then spun and tore across the foyer toward it.

"*Damn.*" Pike leaped the last two stairs and gained on her.

She got there first and opened the peep hatch.

"Good morning!" she said to a pair of brown eyes and woolly eyebrows that appeared to belong to a man. "Welcome to the Grand Palace on the Thames, the most exclusive boardinghouse in London!"

"Well, good morning, miss!" The man on the other side of the peep hatch sounded relieved to hear her cheery tone. "I have a delivery for the Earl of Highgrove. It's a prize he's won."

She glanced at Pike, standing over her shoulder now. He shrugged.

To Dot, it sounded a bit like a prank.

"I'm afraid we haven't an Earl of Highgrove currently in residence, sir."

"I went first to Lucifer's Fall, where I was told that Mr. Marchand would be willing to accept the prize on behalf of the earl. But Mr. Marchand was not in. I don't know *where* to find the earl, but I was told Mr. Marchand was currently staying at this boardinghouse. And so that's where we came." The man sounded a bit desperate.

Mr. Marchand was a name she at least recognized.

"I'm sincerely hoping you'll take her off my hands," the man added. "We're both getting a bit tired, and she's a bit cranky."

Dot was very taken aback. She was very certain a "she" should not ever be delivered as a prize.

She exchanged a concerned look with Mr. Pike.

"One moment, sir," she said a little too brightly to the man, and hastily closed the hatch.

"Hold on—isn't the Earl of Highgrove Miss Woodville's brother?" Pike whispered.

As if summoned, Miss Woodville crossed the foyer then. She was wearing a marigold-colored pelisse. To Dot, she looked like sunshine on two legs.

"Miss Woodville," Dot said quietly. "I have some unusual news. A man standing outside the door has brought a delivery for the Earl of Highgrove, care of Mr. Marchand." She paused. "He says the delivery is a 'she.'"

Miss Woodville froze.

"Oh, God," she croaked.

Dot and Mr. Pike gazed at her in silent commiseration.

"What would you like us to do?" Mr. Pike asked quietly.

"What's the trouble?" Mr. Marchand entered the foyer, looking as though not a thing had ever troubled him in his life, clean shaven and dashing in a dark gray coat and dark trousers. "Because your expressions and the presence of Miss Woodville suggest there is one."

Miss Woodville shot him a dark look.

"Someone has brought you a 'she,' Mr. Marchand," Miss Woodville said tautly. "Or, rather, someone has brought my brother a 'she.' Apparently, *she* is one of the things he won at Lucifer's Fall."

Miss Woodville and Mr. Marchand locked eyes in an exchange more complicated than any conversation Dot had ever heard.

"Is something the matter?" Delilah called from the first-floor landing, where she stood with Angelique and Mrs. Pariseau, who was on her way to the museum.

Dot put a finger to her lips and beckoned them with swoops of her hand. They scrambled down the stairs, each of them wearing identically worried expressions, although Mrs. Pariseau's was also just a little thrilled. It wouldn't be the first time a drama had unfolded in the foyer.

"The Earl of Highgrove, Miss Woodville's brother, won a prize. A man has brought this prize to the door." Dot was thoroughly enjoying the opportunity to pause dramatically, which she did until everyone leaned closer. "He says the prize is a 'she.'"

Delilah, Angelique, and Mrs. Pariseau reared back, and they all hissed in breaths between their teeth.

"*And* he says that she's tired and cranky," Dot added, with relish.

Mr. Delacorte, happily full of breakfast, ambled through the foyer then, blinking in the sunlight. He was whistling softly and carrying his case of unusual medicines, on his way to visit a few apothecaries.

He halted when he saw the crowd. "Well! What's the occasion?"

Dot took a breath in preparation for launching into her story again.

Miss Woodville was still staring accusingly at Mr. Marchand.

"Miss?" the man called plaintively from the other side of the door.

"I'll take care of it," Mr. Marchand said grimly.

He opened the door a few inches, slipped out, and closed it behind him.

Dot put an ear to the door and a finger to her lips while everyone crowded around her.

They staggered backward when the door swung open again seconds later.

Mr. Marchand reappeared in the doorway. His expression implied he was very carefully suppressing some unidentifiable emotion.

"Why don't you all come out and meet her?" he suggested neutrally.

Quizzical glances darted between all those gathered.

Mr. Marchand stepped aside, flung open the door, and beckoned with a flourish.

Everyone nearly tripped over one another to get out into the courtyard.

Whereupon Mr. Delacorte stopped abruptly and clapped a hand to his chest.

A beatific smile spread slowly across his lips. A near-celestial radiance suffused him. His expression suggested that, like Job, he'd at last been rewarded for all the trials and noble sacrifices he'd lately endured. The torment of chess with Dot. The slings and arrows of Daniel's crossed eyes and belly thumping.

"It seems your brother won a donkey, Miss Woodville." Mr. Marchand gestured.

A little brown-and-white donkey, saddled and haltered, switched her tail and flicked her long ears. She sported long, long eyelashes and limpid, sweet brown eyes, much like Daniel Peck's.

"*Eeee AWWW!*" she announced.

Mr. Delacorte beamed toward the sky, as if God himself had dropped it at their door.

"We can't keep a donkey," Miss Woodville said despairingly. "We don't *need* a donkey. Why did Hogarth wager for a *donkey?* We already have William, who eats enough for a whole herd of goats."

"Hold on—William is a *goat?*" Mr. Marchand was indignant.

Ginny was impressed that he'd remembered what she'd said about William.

The donkey stretched out her neck, bared her teeth, and chomped the blooms off the violets Dot was holding.

Chapter Thirteen

After much fussing over and patting of the donkey, who quickly ate the rest of Dot's flowers and seemed inclined to eat the little garden in front of the Grand Palace on the Thames as well, arrangements were made to board her for a few weeks in the adjacent livery stables by virtue of an intricate bargain with the stable owners involving a dozen of Helga's scones, a week's stay free of charge at the Grand Palace on the Thames, tickets to a program at a bawdy theater (which Mr. Delacorte had in his coat pocket), the current contents of the Epithet Jar, plus two pounds and two shillings and four pence, donated from the pockets of Mr. Marchand and Mr. Delacorte and the reticule of Miss Woodville.

If the donkey had a name, the man who delivered her was unaware of it. Hogarth had won her from the Earl of Kildere's third son.

Mrs. Pariseau went off to her planned visit to a museum; Delilah, Angelique, Dot, and Mr. Pike returned to their chores; and Mr. Delacorte went off to get the donkey settled at the livery stables.

That left Mr. Marchand and Ginny in the courtyard.

Ginny suddenly felt a little shy.

In the bright daylight, he looked tired. Her heart twinged. She recalled how pale he'd gone before he'd abruptly departed the sitting room the previous evening. She studied him for other signs of languishing, but apart from faint shadows beneath his eyes, he was his usual intimidatingly splendid self.

"You might as well add one pound and a shilling to my brother's debt total," she finally said.

He smiled. "Already done."

She gave a short, pained laugh. "I wonder if this is the last of the so-called whimsical gifts Hogarth won."

He cleared his throat. "About that . . . Miss Woodville, I have something important I feel I should share with you. You may want to sit down for it."

Alarm surged through Ginny. Perhaps he *was* desperately ill.

He gestured to the bench in the little garden, and she stumbled over to it and sat down warily.

He sat across from her on the other bench, at a chaste but still pleasantly disturbing distance. She was aware of but perilously unconcerned about the fact that they were both growing comfortable with this sort of proximity to each other. Her mother would have keeled in a swoon.

She breathed in, and the scent of the nearby blossoms plus eau de Marchand—bay rum and soap, a dash of tobacco—made her head briefly light.

"Miss Woodville . . ." He leaned toward her like a doctor about to deliver difficult news. Her heart slammed. "I'm wondering if it's time to consider the possibility that your brother might just be a little, well . . ." He paused suspensefully. ". . . stupid."

She froze.

His eyes were glinting. The devil.

"Oh, my *God*," she breathed in mock wonderment. "You've hit upon it! That's precisely it! He's *stupid*."

He nodded slowly.

She laughed, but her laugh evolved into a despairing groan. "What I can't be certain of is whether it's a permanent, fatal sort of stupid, or just a young man sort of stupid, because aren't all boys a little stupid until a certain age?" She turned to him beseechingly.

"The aristocratic ones are, of a certainty," he agreed equably.

"You weren't, naturally."

"Oh, I was stupid. But there's a sort of grandeur to the way Hogarth is going about being stupid. A purity. An innocence. A divinity."

"Have a care, Marchand."

"Sorry," he replied insincerely, stretching out his legs.

"How on earth will he survive, let alone raise a family? How can I stop him from doing stupid things now that he's started? What if he does it again, even if I actually ever find the vase, which doesn't seem at all likely anymore?"

"Here's the paradox: You stop him from doing stupid things by not stopping him from doing stupid things."

"I assure you, that's not an option."

"Miss Woodville, you—emphasis on *you*—cannot keep the young earl in cotton batting the whole of his life. And that is part of the problem, I'm afraid. He seems to have saved up all the stupid things he's never done before and done them in one night."

She bristled. "But I *promised* I'd look after him. And besides, I *want* to look after him. I'm good at it. It's what I'm best at, in fact." Was this true, or was she just reflexively arguing a point?

"But I suspect Hogarth has probably been very, very careful not to put a foot wrong in order not to let you down in any way for all these years, too, and this, believe it or not, could be in part the result."

That brought her up short.

Damn Marchand and his bluntness and pointing out things she didn't want to face. It was a relief as much as it was a trial.

She pondered this assertion.

"I should tell you, Mr. Marchand, that Hogarth did not precisely shame himself at university. He's not *that* kind of stupid. In fact, he greatly impressed all of his tutors."

"What were his best subjects?"

"Fencing. Mathematics."

"You're having me on."

"I'm quite serious. Even the fancy kind of mathematics. Formulas like hieroglyphics." She waggled her fingers in the air, pantomiming the scrawling of equations. "That sort. The reason he went mad at the betting table had nothing to do with his ability to *calculate* things."

"Hmm." Marchand was pensive.

"Do you know, Mr. Marchand, my brother would tell me only two things about that whole night at Lucifer's Fall. He said that I would have understood *why* he did it if I'd known with whom he was wagering. And I think I do understand, now that I know it was Sydenham. And—this is the odd one—he told me that Sydenham's satyr waistcoat buttons were jeering at him."

"Jeering?" Mr. Marchand said it so sharply she gave a start.

"It might have been 'leering.' I expect it was just because Hogarth was drunk."

"Well, he *was* that," Mr. Marchand mused.

He fell silent for a time.

"Marchand . . . what is the point of me if I can't keep him from being stupid for the rest of his life?"

"Guinevere."

Her head swiveled toward him abruptly, her eyes wide at the sound of her first name. The word was gentle, but etched in amazed exasperation.

"What is the point of this shrubbery?" He reached up and drew a leaf between his fingers.

"It's decorative? It . . . looks fetching against this bench?"

"And?"

"It's . . . a home for birds and insects and little rodents. A prop for lectures from supercilious men of dubious character."

His eyebrows flicked. "So birds and insects no doubt think of it as one thing, and you think of it as another, and what do you suppose the shrubbery believes its purpose is?"

"But *do* shrubberies think, Marchand?" She tipped her head and wrinkled her nose.

"The shrubbery just *is*. It basks in the sun and soaks up rain and puts out flowers in the spring."

"But I'm not a shrubbery?" she reminded him.

He sighed. "It's a matter of perspective, isn't it? What the *point* of anything is? You are a grown woman. You don't need a point. But should you be so inclined, *you* can decide the point of you."

He was again making the kind of philosophical sense that unnerved her because it called into question the way she'd lived her life to date.

"You don't understand. I'm *good* at it," she said stubbornly. "I *like* looking after him."

Did she? Or was it all she knew?

Was it all she knew because her promise kept her connected to people who were forever gone?

She didn't like the way these thoughts felt, because they threatened to reorder an existence that was already in a state of upheaval.

Her head suddenly ached.

He read something in her expression.

"Close your eyes," he ordered. But gently. "And turn your hand palm up."

"Speaking of ordering people about," she muttered. But she obeyed.

Her breath hitched when his fingertip touched her palm.

He delicately, slowly, traced a simple shape across her palm with his fingertip.

Her breathing went shallow.

Ohhhh, this devastating bastard. It was so subtle, so clever. So *revelatory*.

Shivery tributaries of sensation fanned out from where he touched her; in their path, cells stirred awake to participate in this little pleasure. The hairs on the back of her neck lifted. The ones on her arms prickled to attention. Her nipples were practically stinging. *Here, here, and here,* her body seemed to say. *This is where you want to be touched by him, in case you didn't yet know.*

And just as all rivers reach the sea, apparently this sensation, which was in truth hardly a touch at all, was destined to convene right between her legs in a hot, heavy pulse of longing.

He'd touched her for all of five seconds.

And in those five seconds, like those seconds during which she'd been airborne when he'd lifted her into the carriage, she'd felt an extraordinary, elemental freedom from . . . herself. Or rather, she'd felt more purely herself than she had in years.

Imagine what he could do with his fingers over the span of a night, a wicked little voice that sounded remarkably like Marchand's whispered inside her head.

One night of pleasure, and at least a few of your problems would be solved.

Finally, reluctantly, she opened her eyes.

"I didn't feel a thing." Her voice was a traitor: It creaked.

He smiled at her, thoroughly, almost sympathetically, amused.

"You know, I honestly expected seduction to be a little fancier. Perhaps with . . . nets?" she hazarded.

"Nets?"

"I'm only guessing. I didn't mean to shock you, Marchand. My goodness, look at you, clutching your pearls in alarm."

"If I *wanted* to actually seduce you, I wouldn't have to *try*. You'd just fall into my hand like a ripe plum before you even knew what's happening to you." He sounded bored. He cupped his hand, illustrating, presumably, the plum.

She made a soft little scoffing noise. "I'm certain you kiss the way a little boy kisses his grandmother."

A speculative, knowing, almost pitying little smile curved his lips. As if he knew a thousand things about her that she had yet to discover.

She felt that smile in her nether regions as surely as if he'd traced a shape there, too.

"Are you off to negotiate prices for wax candles at Lucifer's Fall or some such today?"

She looked up at him, surprised, when he didn't reply.

Finally he said, "I usually visit my son on his birthday. And his birthday is today."

He'd looked away from her. His voice had gone gruff.

Her mind blanked in shock.

"Your son," she repeated carefully.

Her capacity for absorbing surprises was nearing its limit.

A half-dozen distinct emotions collided in her chest like billiard balls, all painful and unsubtle. From sort of a surprising and nearly unbearable, melting tenderness to curiosity to stunned amazement.

But the worst, the most distinct, the most shocking *and* unworthy . . . was jealousy.

It, in fact, pressed the breath from her.

Who had borne him a son?

When?

Where was she now?

Suddenly *so* many things she'd noticed about Marchand made more sense. His kindness to the boys from Bethnal Green, his deftness with Daniel Peck. The baby. Missing pieces of the picture of him were flowing into place.

"My son," he confirmed, again.

He did not expound, and the way he'd said it called to mind a door being firmly shut.

"I . . . I . . . didn't realize you'd been married."

He turned toward her and tipped his head with a wry "come now" expression, as if she ought to have known better. Then shook it slowly.

One day she would not blush when he matter-of-factly revealed such details of his extraordinary life, and that was the day her mother would roll over in her grave.

Today was not that day.

"Silly me. Wedlock. Such a quaint notion."

"It's not a quaint notion," he said shortly. "But he *was* born out of wedlock. As was I. As I'm certain you're aware, it's not generally a cause for rejoicing. But these things happen commonly enough."

Not in her world, they didn't. Her parents would have been horrified to know with whom she was casually conversing. These things were disastrous and scandalous in her world, though even she had heard the cautionary tales of girls who had been seduced and abandoned. It was why girls—the aristocratic ones, anyhow—were so scrupulously guarded.

The girls born and raised in St. Giles must be so terribly vulnerable.

She wanted to know all about it, and yet she wasn't certain she could bear hearing it for a dozen complicated reasons, all of which were less of a revelation to her than they ought to be.

Despite everything, she appreciated how Marchand never made excuses and never apologized for himself.

"Your son . . . so he's not the boy I saw in your office?"

He shook his head.

A new thought rattled her. "Mr. Marchand . . . are you married to anyone now?"

She didn't know why she'd so blithely assumed that he wasn't. Suddenly there seemed no reason he couldn't be, for when had Marchand behaved in an expected way? What did she really know about the rules of the demimonde?

But the sickening plummeting sensation in her stomach was well-nigh unendurable.

She waited what felt like a gruesome eternity for his answer.

"No, Ginny," he said almost gently. "I'm not married. If I was, I wouldn't be gallivanting around with the likes of you." He paused. "Probably."

She transferred her gaze to her thighs, confused and unnerved by the relief that gusted through her. She felt unworldly and young and off-balance.

He noticed. He was quiet.

"So," she finally said. "Your son. I take it you'll be making a quick visit to Newgate Prison to visit him?"

That was a risky joke even for her.

He turned to study her.

"I'll be going to visit him where he's been since he was five years old. Under a stone at Broadview Cemetery."

Holy. Mother. Of God.

She squeezed her eyes and fists closed against the brutal jolt of shame. It was like being dropped from the top of a building.

She sincerely wished *she* were under a stone in Broadview Cemetery. Anything, *anything* to avoid experiencing the excruciating aftermath of her hideous glibness.

Her entire torso was on fire from mortification.

There was literally nowhere to hide from her own awfulness.

"Mr. M-Marchand . . . my God . . . I'm . . ."

She cracked her eyes open. His eyes were brilliant with wry hilarity and crinkled at the corners. He shook his head to and fro. To and fro. The bloody man was mercilessly, thoroughly enjoying her discomfiture.

"I would never want you to be anything other than who you are, Ginny."

"A perfect arse?"

"That, too."

She exhaled a gusty breath and squeezed her eyes closed. "I really am terribly sorry. About what I said *and* about—"

"Oh, for heaven's sake. I know you are," he said affably enough. "Thank you."

But he wasn't all right.

He'd been handed a baby last night and what she'd witnessed was a man struggling not to come apart in front of other people. He'd bolted from that room because he'd needed to be alone with the enormity of his memories. He was suffering stoically, but greatly, such that his usual aplomb was no match for it. It showed. Only a little, but it was revealed in the tension in his face and the shadows beneath his eyes.

She was suddenly frantic to do anything she could to help ease it.

"Well, let's go and visit him," she ventured softly. "Unless you'd rather go by yourself . . . because you think I'm too much of an ass."

He quirked the corner of his mouth. "Don't you have a busy schedule of annoying people today?"

"Do you really want to risk letting me wander about the ton on my own?"

A smile briefly haunted his lips. He didn't move, and he didn't reply.

She was stunned to realize that he was, in fact, steeling himself for the journey ahead of him.

And it slashed her heart.

She rested her hand softly on his arm. "Gabriel," she said gently.

He glanced down at her hand, then slowly up at her. His expression suggested wonderment. His breath was held.

"I'm coming with you," she said.

Chapter Fourteen

MICHAEL GABRIEL MARCHAND
1810–1815
BELOVED

The blossoms Marchand brought with him from the park in front of the Grand Palace on the Thames fluttered in the breeze in front of the stone.

"I didn't want him."

They were the first words he'd said since they'd boarded the hack at the Grand Palace on the Thames. They were barely audible, and they punched Ginny airless.

She stared at him, stunned.

But this was Marchand, after all. So she waited.

"Whining, frightened, brainless creature. Me, that is. I was." He flashed a ghost of his usual smile. "But the baby was helpless, too."

He took a long breath.

"His mother was an opera dancer. She was charming and clever and pretty. I met her at a gaming hell I worked for called the Pit. Our liaison suited and amused us for almost a

year, until it didn't, and just as things were about to end between us, she learned she was enceinte. Neither of us wanted a
child. She disappeared when he was only a few weeks old, and
I haven't seen her since."

The notion of a mother abandoning Marchand's baby
panicked Ginny as if it had been her own child.

She knew full well how devastated and terrified that girl
must have been, especially if she hadn't any family to support her.

Ginny thought of how it had felt to hold baby Roger and
she knew she didn't have it in her to bolt. No matter the con-
sequences.

"So just like that, she was gone, and it was me and him
alone," Marchand continued, "and he was only a few weeks
old. I held him, the day I realized she'd gone for good. And I
looked into his face . . . and I could see that he *knew* what he
had in me. He knew I was an unprepossessing, shiftless, callow
fool who thought he was so clever, so fearless, so tough, even
though I know now I was anything but, and he'd concluded
his situation was not promising. I swear his expression was . . .
wry and resigned and *merry*. As though he was thinking, 'Very
well, if it has to be you, let's get on with it.' There was already
an entire person in this . . . in this wee thing."

His voice trailed.

"I set out to prove him wrong. I was going to be worthy.
I did all the things you were supposed to do. I found a wet
nurse, but paying her meant I couldn't afford rooms of our
own. I pestered every parent I knew about how to raise a boy.
I was going to win at being a father the way I eventually won
at everything else. He was mine and I was his. He was the first

person who ever truly belonged to me. He was my family, and I was never going to let him go."

His face was taut and pale. In the stark light of the day, he looked weary and older than his years.

A tiny part of Ginny howled in silent protest at this unbearable proof that he was only human. The selfish, frightened child in her had come to rely on a vision of him as invincible. He was the first true source of strength she'd known in over a decade.

She understood now how he'd come by his strength and calm self-possession.

It had its origins in both the loving and the loss.

Her stomach turned in on itself. She was suddenly frantic to go back in time so she could save him and Michael from any hurt at all. Why would fate visit so many tests upon one person?

She thrust her hand into her reticule and fished about. She came out with one of the cheroots she'd absently tucked in there for God only knew what reason after Mrs. Haddock taught her to roll them.

She stepped forward to hand it to him.

His eyes flared in surprise, then he shot her a look of wry humor and abject gratitude and took it wordlessly.

He strode a few feet away from her to light it with the flint and steel in his pocket, and sucked it into life. He politely aimed the smoke away from her, but the wind was anarchic and it blew it all about. Smoke wreathed him as though he'd materialized there, fresh from the underworld. The breeze ruffled his hair and flipped the ends of his coat. A little of his tension visibly eased.

"He was one of the smartest and funniest people I've ever met, Ginny. I swear this to you. Had a way with a pun. Liked to make up his own jokes. They always started with 'Papa, guess what?' I would say 'What?' And he'd say 'The sky is green!' And that was absolutely *hilarious* to him because I guess the notion to him of a green sky was outrageous." He paused to smile faintly. "He would stop to pick a flower and carry it about in his pocket all day without crushing it, then give it to me before I put him to bed at night. Then hurl apples for the pleasure of watching them explode."

Her chest ached. "Little boys do like to watch things explode."

"It's one of the greatest pleasures in life," he agreed somberly.

With excruciating, exquisite clarity she could picture a tiny boy with Marchand's tumultuous hair and bright eyes and dimples. She would never be able to meet him, to hear his laugh, and she suddenly couldn't breathe for grief.

"I saved my money from all my shite jobs, so that one day we could get a proper room for just the two of us to live in. A real home. We lived with a slew of others. Sometimes I took him to work with me. I eventually learned how to invest money. I learned about maths and accounting. I talked a bloke into teaching me to read. I decided I was going to have my own gaming establishment, and that I was going to send him to Cambridge or Oxford one day. I was on my way."

He paused at length.

"Not quite six years," he finally said. His voice was hoarse. "That's all we got. A fever swept London, we both caught it. And he—"

He stopped abruptly.

She could hear him breathing.

"I'm so, so terribly sorry." Her voice was shredded. "I wish I could have met him."

He looked across at her and watched her for some time. He smiled sadly, faintly, ruefully, as if he was picturing just that. Her heart twisted.

"This might sound ridiculous, Ginny . . . but I had never felt like such a failure when I realized I couldn't afford to have a fancy verse carved into his headstone. Because you see, this was well before I founded Lucifer's Fall. I'm a rich man now, but I was too bloody poor to honor this spectacular person, because back then I was hardly better than a thug with few prospects." His voice frayed. "It infuriated me. It infuriated me that I didn't even *know* any fancy verses because let's just say that I wasn't any squarer with our alleged maker or the book about him then I am now. And so I didn't know what his stone should say."

Ginny understood what he meant. "On my mother's stone it could have said, 'Loved peaches.' And decades from now people might come across her stone and think, 'Ha, isn't that quaint' or 'How disrespectful! That's all her family could think to say?' And maybe they would laugh at it. But peaches were her favorite fruit, and 'peach' was my father's nickname for her, and fanning out from that word are a thousand memories, and when anyone says 'peaches' it conjures her for me as clear as day."

He listened to this with a smile. "Michael's could have read, 'Laughed hysterically at every fart. God took one look at his sleeping face and created the angels in his image.'"

She made a sound, almost but not quite a laugh, as her heart cracked in two.

She laughed. "I'll probably catch a pox of some sort, and mine will read, 'Died as she lived. Covered in spots.'" She absently gestured to her freckles.

She had come to love the way he looked at her when she said things like that. With a sort of awe, mingled with a hilarity that transcended laughter. And something more somber and intent she could not quite interpret.

Finally he gave a slow, very slight shake of his head. As if he could not quite reconcile the wonder of her.

More than anyone she'd ever known in her life, he made her feel singular. He seemed to relish aspects of her character she'd never considered of any worth. He took her for what she was, probably because she'd revealed more of her true colors to him than to any other human being. She'd even discovered a few *new* colors because of him. How odd that nothing in her life had ever felt quite so luxurious as being known.

"Anyhow, Ginny, according to the stonecutter, I could afford only a few little words or one big word. The decision tormented me. I couldn't sleep. I dreamed about Michael. This was the last thing I would be able to do for him and I wanted to get it right. So 'beloved' is the word I chose. I thought it was a good word. Because it's the only thing that matters about any of us in the end, isn't it?"

He said this quietly. Almost defiantly.

As if, for the whole of the time since Michael died, he'd been in search of absolution, some acknowledgment that he'd done the right thing.

She was impotently furious she couldn't go back in time so she could tell him then that the word was perfect. Devastatingly correct and to the point. Just like Marchand.

"You found the best word," she told him with absolute conviction. "There's no better word."

He looked at her sharply in that way he had, as if he were sifting through her mind for lies and truths. Then gave a shallow nod.

When he exhaled and tension in his shoulders at last eased, she felt as though she'd achieved something of worth.

He stubbed out his cheroot on his flint and steel box then tucked it inside. He strode over to stand before his son's headstone and matter-of-factly handed his handkerchief to her.

She hadn't realized tears were coursing down her face.

He didn't fuss. He didn't say a word. They were just two people, feeling what they felt. In his presence now, sadness felt as safe and natural as an exhale or a heartbeat.

"Do you want to be alone for a moment to have a chat with him?" she asked. "I'll wander off."

He shook his head. "I talk to him all the time," he said simply.

She hesitated. "I talk to my parents, too." Her voice was hoarse.

He just nodded, as if to say, of course.

He was studying her thoughtfully now, as if he was considering what to say next.

"Ginny . . ." He paused. "You may hate me for saying this . . ."

Oh, God. She looked up at him warily.

". . . but it was always too much for you."

"I beg your pardon?"

"Raising your siblings, managing the house, all on your own. What happened to you, what your mother asked of you. It was too much for you. It could have flattened anyone. But you . . ." He trailed off.

The way he'd said "you" was so richly complicated, so savored, it sent a rush of delicious sensation down her arms.

He gave a soft laugh. "Here *you* are. Still standing."

She took this in, and waited for defensiveness to rear, for temper to flame. But it was gone. All of it. She recognized truth when she heard it. It was a relief to accept it. It had been too much for her.

"It's too much for any of us, really," he added. "Life is. Including me. Somehow, we get on with things."

The wind sighed through the long grass at the edges of the cemetery.

"I don't hate you."

She nearly whispered it.

And a thousand unspoken things thrummed in those four words.

"I know," he finally said very gently. Like a wizard apologizing for the spell he'd cast upon her.

She reached into her reticule and retrieved the little red-and-white-striped heart-shaped stone she'd found by the bench in the park and held it up. "Do you mind if I leave this for Michael?"

He glanced at it, then back at her.

"But that's your best one." He said this with only a little irony.

She knelt and propped the heart-shaped stone snug against the headstone, right beneath the "B" in "beloved."

They both stood back and gazed down at it.

"I suppose the best thing about stony hearts is that they're indestructible," she said. "They never stop loving."

He turned his head swiftly toward her.

She'd at last become strong enough to hold his gaze.

She thought, in fact, she'd be willing to hold it for eternity, as long as he looked at her the way he was looking at her now, and the moment was long but not long enough, somehow.

"The night sky without stars," he said finally. As though he'd long been working out a conundrum in his head, and this was his best theory.

"I beg your pardon?"

"Your face without freckles," he explained.

Her breath snagged.

His expression was intent and somber. The rhythm of the wind through the trees sounded like breathing to her.

A fear that was very like elation, or an elation that was very like fear, filled her chest with an odd radiance and stole her breath.

Finally, he tipped his head in a "let's go" gesture.

He strode past her, trailing his fingertips in a caress across Michael's stone as he went.

Marchand's stride was a little too long and swift as they followed the path that meandered through the cemetery back to the street. Almost punishingly so. She struggled to keep up.

One would have thought he was trying to flee her.

Or flee *something*.

She trailed him, deeply regretful that she hadn't buttoned up her pelisse. A gust of wind yanked at her hem and flipped it out behind her like the tail on a kite. If she wasn't careful, she'd be airborne in a moment.

She gasped when she almost collided with him.

He'd stopped abruptly and turned.

In a single smooth, decisive motion, he looped an arm around her waist, pulled her up against his body, and cradled her head with his other hand.

His mouth came down on hers.

A small, wild sound hummed in her throat.

He kissed her like a lover, not like a virgin who had never been kissed. It was tender yet ruthlessly carnal and almost frighteningly hungry. Her entire being at once surged to meet him, greedily. She opened to him and the taste of him at once went to her head like a drug. Molten need poured through her. She reveled in his textures, the velvet heat of his tongue, the scrape of his chin against her cheek, the drum of his heart against her hands. He held her against his body as though he'd recaptured something once stolen from him. And she could feel vibrating in him everything he kept leashed.

He fanned his hand at her back and slid it down, down to the base of her spine, along the curve of her arse, dragging one finger right along the seam of it, and it was so lasciviously, devastatingly erotic her knees nearly buckled. He pressed her up against the hard jut of his cock, and pleasure bolted through her body.

When the tenor of the kiss gradually became deeper, became slower, became an expression of things they didn't dare admit to themselves let alone to each other, she could feel herself unraveling. Her eyes began to burn with tears.

She was suddenly scared to death.

He sensed it.

He lifted his mouth from hers.

His heart drummed beneath her hands. She savored it wonderingly.

Around her, the world spun.

"Just as I suspected." Her voice was shockingly kiss-scorched. She whispered just an inch or two away from his lips, "You kiss like a granny."

His eyes were starry, kiss-hazed, and amused.

He traced the arc of her bottom lip with his fingertip. Magical, that. That caress set tiny bonfires everywhere in her body.

"That's *very* funny, Ginny," he murmured. "Given that it's you who needs a stick to walk now."

He lowered his arms from her and stepped back just a few inches.

She nearly buckled.

She attempted to take a step.

She wobbled drunkenly.

He had kissed the bones right out of her legs. She was fairly certain he had ruined her equilibrium forever.

She righted herself. For a moment they stared across at each other.

His expression evolved from raw wonder to closed and guarded as she watched him.

She wondered if it merely reflected hers.

Suddenly she wanted to run. From him or from herself, she wasn't certain. For some reason it felt all of a piece.

She tried another step. She was still unsteady, but she managed to stride ahead of him.

"Do you want to borrow my walking stick, Guinevere?" he called solicitously.

She didn't turn around.

Little by little, she found her footing again, as she walked ahead of him, and she buttoned up her pelisse. As if in so doing she could seal off forever every inconvenient, dangerous thing she felt.

* * *

But when they at last passed through the gates of the cemetery and reached the main road, he drew abreast of her. As luck would have it, a hack was rolling by. Marchand didn't even need to raise a hand. The driver, catching a glimpse of a gold-topped walking stick and those shiny boots, pulled his horses to a halt at once.

Marchand reached for her waist and swung her up into the hack as though she weighed nothing. As if they did this all the time. As though he'd claimed her.

Her heart knocked against her chest like a fist.

They gazed at each other, silently. He appeared to be deciding what to say.

"I've some business to see to that will take me out of London for a day or two. So I won't be returning with you now to the Grand Palace on the Thames."

She was stunned.

Her heart plummeted in dread.

He correctly read her expression.

"I'll return," he promised. Gently. A little ironically. As if it was ludicrous to think he could stay away from her.

Her heart revived with such a sharp jolt it robbed her breath.

Infinitely reassuring, infinitely maddening as usual, he closed the hack door and vanished from view.

Chapter Fifteen

Marchand paused at the foot of the long drive to take in the rambling, centuries-old house. He dismounted from his hired horse, a patient bay gelding, and loosely tethered him to a shrub. He knew his visit would be brief.

As difficult as it was to intimidate him at the advanced age of thirty-six, the weight of the realization—less a realization than a confirmation—that he and Guinevere Woodville had been raised in different galaxies required a bit of an internal adjustment. It was helpful to be reminded that it was only through some perversion of fate that he'd come to be kissing her nearly senseless in a cemetery.

Every glancing thought of that moment sent twin spikes of lust and fear through him. Hope had no business anywhere near how he felt. But there it was, glimmering like daybreak on the perimeters of his life now, shortening his breath. He couldn't seem to stop it any more than he could stop the sun from rising. But what would he hope for, anyway? *Papa, the sky is green.* That was how outlandish it was to imagine a life with her. There was a better than excellent chance that her family and friends would bloody well disown her if they saw her consorting with him, or anywhere near him. And nothing meant more to her than her family and friends. He understood that painfully clearly.

That she rightfully belonged to him and with him felt like an inalienable truth. How could he know that after just a few days? As surely as he'd known he would die for Michael from the moment he'd held him. Truth was truth.

The way she held him felt to him like truth.

The way she looked at him felt like truth.

The way she kissed him felt like truth.

And the way she'd held that baby last night felt like his destiny.

He did not know how to reconcile the ferocity of his possessiveness with the seeming futility of their circumstances.

But what did he really know for certain? He knew he'd only truly loved and been loved by one other person in his entire life, and that was Michael.

The dangers upon which he'd been trained in his youth had mostly been immediate in nature—thieves, violence, hunger. He'd seldom had the benefit of recognizing a danger so far in advance. And yet he'd still been almost helpless to avoid this one. Because just like hope, devastation hovered on the periphery of his awareness, too.

Imagining making love to her sent need coursing through him so violently his limbs all but trembled.

But if he made love to her, it might destroy both of them.

He suspected she would never fully know peace until and unless she finally fulfilled her mother's final wish. And that meant she would live out her life ensconced in a house like the one he was staring at now, the word "Lady" instead of

"Honorable" engraved on her calling cards. She would prob-ably sit across from a man named Francis at the breakfast table.

Then again, he may have already robbed her of a chance at peace, merely by virtue of existing.

And that gutted him.

Would he have forgone the experience of knowing her? Of holding her in his arms?

He was not that selfless of a man.

He had no map for any of this. He was fumbling in the dark, with only instinct to guide him.

But the enforced domesticity of the Grand Palace on the Thames had cornered him into an uncomfortable realization: He'd been wrong about what he really wanted and who he re-ally was. It had nothing to do with turning the Grand Palace on the Thames into a gaming hell.

No matter how uncomfortable that realization, he was not one to take for granted the gift of that epiphany.

Discreetly but determinedly, nervously but with a sense of irrevocability, he'd already gotten a change of course un-derway.

That change of course was part of the reason he was here today.

He'd made his decision about this trip to Ginny's family home sometime during the visit to Michael. He'd known he'd needed to leave straightaway if he wanted a seat on the royal mail coach that afternoon, so he collected a few things in a valise from his residence, had a look to see how the repairs of his roof were going (slowly), then asked Mr. Ogden to send a message to the Grand Palace on the Thames to let Mrs. Hardy and Mrs. Durand know he would be away.

He'd found a room in an inn in Sussex before the end of the day. That was where he realized he'd become a bit of a snob about inns. There were no comfortable rugs on the floor, no little flower in a vase. He'd miss Helga's magnificent morning scones.

But he did like how warmly the faces of the innkeepers lit up when he inquired how to find the Woodvilles' residence. They clearly thought highly of the family.

He walked up the drive.

A luxuriously woolly goat was nibbling the bright flowers growing with unchecked abandon around the perimeter of a fountain in the center of it.

"You must be William," he said to it. "Something tells me you're not supposed to be out here eating those."

William lifted his head and eyed him benignly with his wise, oblong amber eyes.

Marchand gently looped his hand under the rope collar around William's neck and led him up to the door. The goat clopped behind him complacently, right up the steps, as if he'd done it a dozen times before.

He'd needed to knock twice, much more emphatically the second time, before the door opened a crack.

A woman with chaotic eyebrows peered out and flicked her gaze over him.

"We already have a goat. We don't need another one," she said, and began to close the door.

He thrust his booted foot into the crack.

"Are you Mrs. Haddock?"

"Who wants to know?"

"I'm Gabriel Marchand. I hear you've been spreading rumors about me, and I've come for a reckoning."

It was a wicked impulse, but he'd been unable to resist it.

She gasped so mightily she nearly sucked his cravat through the door crack.

"Forgive my little jest, Mrs. Haddock. My name is, however, Mr. Gabriel Marchand. I've come to call upon the master of the house. The Earl of Highgrove. Is he in?"

"What do ye want wi' that boy, Mr. Marchand? If you 'arm a hair on his head, I'll put a curse on you that withers yer nether regions."

He rather approved of the unorthodox gate-keeping.

"As intimidating as that sounds, why on earth would I harm him when he owes me money, Mrs. Haddock?" he said matter-of-factly. "How would I collect? I come in peace."

They stared at each other.

"That makes sense," Mrs. Haddock allowed, reluctantly.

"I think he'll speak to me. Can you have someone take this goat back to his usual quarters? He was eating the flowers. I'll go have a word with his lordship."

She opened the door with great reluctance, and Marchand stepped inside.

Mrs. Haddock led him up the stairs, and though he was very curious to see where Ginny usually slept, even he knew it would have been extraordinarily untoward to ask. He saw no signs of her sisters. Perhaps they were out doing what fiancées of aristocrats did, tra-la-la-ing through the vast green grounds, making daisy crowns. He didn't know. He already suspected that he would do anything at all for them, if needed. If Ginny asked.

Hogarth was in shirtsleeves and stockings and leaning precariously back in his chair in the way young men often do, reading a book.

"Mr. Marchand here to see you," said Mrs. Haddock.

"Oh dear God!" Hogarth shot to his feet and the chair crashed to the floor. "That is, good afternoon, Mr. Marchand. What a pleasant surprise."

"Good afternoon, Lord Highgrove." He bowed. "I hope you'll forgive my intrusion. I don't want to give the impression that I'm collaring you in your den, as it were."

"Not at all," Hogarth said politely, though everything about his posture and expression suggested he was screaming inwardly. Sometimes aristocratic manners amused Marchand.

Marchand turned and stared at Mrs. Haddock until she melted away. Then he closed the door.

"I won't take up too much of your valuable time." He said this only a little ironically. "I'm given to understand that you excelled in mathematics and fencing whilst you were at university."

Hogarth blinked, and hesitated. "Well, I don't like to boast . . ."

"Yes or no?"

"Yes."

"Do you think you could impart this information to another human who is just learning mathematics and fencing?"

Hogarth looked puzzled. "To . . . you?"

Marchand sighed. For God's sake. "To a room full of young boys and perhaps girls. Around the ages of nine and ten or so. Some older."

"Certainly I could. I often tutored other students. I know how to, ah, impart information so that they actually permanently learn it."

"That's everything we want out of learning. All right. Perfect. I would like to offer you a job doing that."

"Er . . ." Hogarth looked awkward, sympathetic, and regretful, as if he didn't want to embarrass Marchand by informing him that earls simply didn't take "jobs."

"The pupils will be boys and perhaps some girls who are residents of the workhouse at Bethnal Green. And if you perform your duties reliably and consistently for three days per week, for a period of three years, I will forgive your debt to Lucifer's Fall entirely."

Hogarth's breath rushed from him in a shocked gust.

"But, if at any point you shirk your duties, or miss them for any reason other than catastrophic illness, loss of limb, or family death, your debt will be restored in its entirety, and I will *not* fail to collect it."

"But . . . that's extraordinarily generous of you, Marchand. How did you . . . why are you . . ." Comprehension flared in his face. "Oh. I think I know."

Gabriel could read very clearly the conclusions Hogarth was drawing about why he was visiting today.

None of the Woodvilles had any business gambling.

He admitted to what Hogarth probably already knew. "Perhaps this will come as no surprise to you, but your sister appeared at Lucifer's Fall and we had a conversation."

A parade of expressions chased one another across Hogarth's face. Amusement was definitely one of them. He clearly had a sense for how that conversation had gone with Ginny.

"Here are my stipulations, Lord Highgrove. You are going to tell your sister that this was your idea. Not mine. You will write a letter addressed to me at Lucifer's Fall, describing everything I've just told to you as though it were your very own idea, which occurred to you because you were aware I employ children from Bethnal Green. I will then inform your sister that I think it's a noble and excellent solution to your debt to the house. Do you think you can handle this assignment and its parameters better than you handle your liquor?"

"Of course." Hogarth shrugged with one shoulder.

"All right. Now point to the body part you like best."

"I—er—I suppose—" Hogarth pointed to his groin. Blushing scarlet.

"Good man. As it should be. That's the part I'll remove with a sword if you fail at this."

"Ha ha!" Hogarth's face creased in merriment.

"Hogarth. I wasn't joking."

"Honestly, Marchand. You can't persuade me that you're a thug. Despite all the . . ." He gestured eloquently with both hands at Gabriel's general person and demeanor.

"'Thug' was once an actual position I held at a place of employment. It was on my calling card.

"Written in blood," he added, when Hogarth's eyebrows slanted skeptically.

This was maddening in a new way. Perhaps *all* the Woodvilles were uniquely maddening.

"You don't have to threaten me," Hogarth said, almost gently. As if he were soothing a wild beast.

"Yes. Based on your previous performance, I am entirely convinced that threatening you is just the thing."

Hogarth paused.

"Why is this so important to you?" he asked suddenly.

"Because if you do fail at this, you will break her heart."

He realized at once that he had revealed entirely too much of his hand. It was stunningly unlike him, and a measure of how enmeshed he now was.

Too late he pressed his lips closed tightly.

"Why the devil are you worried about my sister's heart?"

Hogarth said this sharply. He suddenly sounded very much like a brother who would happily call Marchand out and skewer him.

Which Marchand appreciated.

And he hesitated scarcely more than a second.

But it was long enough to incriminate him.

"Marchand . . . are you sweet on my sister? On *Ginny*?" Hogarth was stunned.

"Sweet? *Sweet?*" Gabriel made a series of disgusted little noises, as if he'd just accidentally ingested a flying insect.

"It seems like—"

"I'm not sweet."

"All right."

"*Nothing* about me is sweet."

"I believe you," Hogarth said, soothingly. But he looked troubled, indeed, as well he might. Given the immense gulfs in their respective life stations.

They stared at each other in wary silence.

"Your sister is . . . in many ways one of the most difficult humans I've ever met. And I'm sure you can imagine the kinds of people I've met. But what she has is . . . valor."

Hogarth's eyes might be like Ginny's, but such a different spirit shone out of them. Less fierce, but still soulful. More innocent and mild and somehow infinitely, objectionably . . . kind. Marchand understood fully why Ginny wanted to protect him, because now he found himself wanting to protect him, too.

But he also knew that protecting Hogarth meant making sure Hogarth could protect himself.

"True valor is a rare quality in this world, Lord Highgrove. And because she cares about you, you might just crush what remains of it if you disappoint her again. But if you make her proud, it will be one of the finest moments of her life, and she deserves fine moments. I daresay it might even be one of the finest moments of *your* life. And you deserve those, too. Do you comprehend me? I don't know how to teach you to care if you don't. Because you bloody well ought to care."

Hogarth was still frowning at him thoughtfully.

Finally he said, hesitantly, "I *do* care, Marchand. My family is the *only* thing I care about. I made a mistake. A terrible mistake. Perhaps the first in my entire life." His voice cracked. "I have scarcely been able to bear it."

Marchand quietly took this in.

"Then why did you do it?" But he asked it more gently than accusingly. He genuinely wanted to know.

Hogarth didn't speak for a time. Then he drew in and exhaled a long breath. "There is something you don't understand about Sydenham."

The back of Marchand's neck tingled with portent. Because this was the other thing he'd come to speak with Hogarth about today. Something Ginny had said in the garden at the Grand Palace on the Thames had sparked in him a suspicion that had at first seemed almost absurd.

But the more he entertained it, the less outlandish it seemed.

He needed to be careful. The web of connections between the aristocrats and wealthy men who sustained his business all but guaranteed that anything Marchand said would be repeated.

"Did the earl do something you consider untoward on that notable evening?" he asked evenly.

"He insulted my father." Hogarth said this somewhat thickly.

"And so you retaliated by giving him all your money?"

He said this deliberately to make Hogarth bristle, because he knew too well that being challenged was really the best way to find one's spine. Provided he truly possessed one.

"They were friends and 'cheerful rivals.'" Hogarth gave these words an ironic, somewhat bitter lilt. "Sydenham and my father. At least that's how my father put it. But there was always an edge to their exchanges and it made me uncomfortable when I was a boy. Mainly because I heard Sydenham claim more than once that my father stole my mother from him. I heard him say it quite a few times. They both played it off as a joke. How can a person be *stolen*? It seems to me my mother made her choice when she married my father, even though he was a viscount and Sydenham was an earl and considerably wealthier. And at Lucifer's Fall that night, Sydenham said to me . . ." Hogarth paused. And dragged in a steadying breath. "'Such a pity your father killed your mother. She'd be alive today if she'd married me.'" Hogarth's voice had gone thick. "And *again*, he played it off as a *joke*. I think he might have been drunk. I simply could not let it stand."

Marchand was not easily horrified. But that was an egregious thing to say to another man, drunk or not.

"Unforgivable," he told Hogarth quietly.

"It just struck me as *unconscionable* to assert that to my face," Hogarth continued, "whether or not there is some truth in it. And I'm not naive, Marchand. I know there's some painful truth to it. My father *could* be reckless. But I wanted to win. I wanted to humble Sydenham thoroughly and wipe that smug expression from his face. Just *once*. I wanted to do it for my father and for my mother." His voice thickened. "And I *was* winning . . . well, and also losing, quite a bit"—his eyebrows dove in confusion—"and then suddenly I lost and lost and lost some more. And I couldn't seem to even see clearly or concentrate at all. I'd never been drunk before that night. I swear to you I didn't know being drunk was *like* that. I was, in fact, so drunk that I could have sworn the satyrs on his waistcoat buttons were jeering and winking at me." He flushed red.

That was exactly what Ginny had told him.

The suspicion that had been coalescing on the periphery of his awareness for days finally settled into a cold spot in Marchand's gut. He could trace its origins back to a certain conversation in the smoking room of the Grand Palace on the Thames.

"Lord Highgrove . . . do you remember if Sydenham gave you anything to drink? That is, did you accept a drink specifically from him, rather than from one of the waiters on staff?"

"He was the only one who did bring drinks to me. I thought it would be rude to decline his offer."

"*He* brought them to you? Not the waiter?"

Hogarth nodded. "Brandy. He wanted to toast to my father's memory."

Damn.

Inwardly Marchand cursed quite a bit more colorfully.

He knew what he needed to learn next.

But deciding what he would do if his suspicions were confirmed would be sticky indeed.

"I don't know if your debt to Sydenham can or will be resolved," Marchand told him, carefully. "I believe your sister is doing her best. But in truth, it ought to be you, Hogarth, who is attempting to resolve it."

Hogarth swallowed. "I know. It's just that she's . . . she's always taken charge. I'm so used to her taking things on . . . and it's hard to say no to Ginny."

Truer words were never spoken, Marchand silently conceded.

"The donkey you won was delivered, by the way, and is resting comfortably in a livery stable."

Hogarth brightened. "I won a donkey?"

Marchand sighed.

"All right," he said briskly. "Please write that letter today and send it to me care of Lucifer's Fall in London. Within a fortnight, I will write to you with information on when and where your instruction will begin. I will have my solicitor draw up a contract for you to sign, which you will do, in London, in my presence. As of now, if we shake on it, I will consider your debt settled unless or until you otherwise violate the terms of the contract. And you can tell your sister when she returns to Sussex. I need to leave now in order to get the coach back to London."

Hogarth exhaled windily. "I cannot thank you enough, Marchand."

He extended his hand and Marchand shook it. Then he turned to leave.

Then he paused, and turned back.

"Lord Highgrove . . ." He hesitated. Then decided he could not forgo this opportunity, because he might not ever have it again. And he wanted to do it both for this young man and for Ginny. "Most men of any worth make mistakes of magnitude at least once in their lives. But when you care about others in your life more than you care about yourself—and that means more than you care about your pride, or your honor—you don't make *those* sorts of mistakes. The kind that cause utter destruction. Perhaps this is something that can only be learned the hard way. I don't know. It's just something I've learned, and if it has any value at all I just felt I should tell you. Do you understand me?"

Just the faintest hint of sullen rebellion flickered over Hogarth's face. No man likes to be lectured by another man. Particularly not by a man who is far from his social equal.

But the expression was fleeting. Hogarth nodded somberly. "I understand. Truly. Thank you."

"*Sweet*," Marchand muttered as he jammed on his hat and headed for the door.

Chapter Sixteen

The word "shite" hovered over Delilah like a guillotine with a fraying rope.

She sat now at her dressing table, plaiting her hair, relieved to have gotten through another evening without hearing it echoing throughout the sitting room in Daniel's voice. She knew it was only a matter of time, however. Her pride balked at telling his mother about their little encounter on the stairs. So far, she'd told only her husband, very briefly, shortly after she'd forced him to say "blancmange" aloud. Even making *that* confession had felt torturous. She didn't know why. Tristan had been a *sailor*, after all.

Still, she had inwardly writhed in embarrassment when his eyes had widened in amazement.

She whirled when she sensed said beloved husband standing in the open doorway of their room. Staring at her.

He entered, and quietly closed the door.

"Tristan . . . why are you looking at me like you've never seen me before in your life?"

"Because I don't know who you are anymore," he said gravely.

Alarm surged through her. "W-what do you mean?"

"I thought I'd married a refined lady. Somehow well above my station. Instead, tonight I find myself going to bed with a salty-mouthed sailor. I don't know, Delilah. I might need a little time to adjust."

She snatched a glove off her dressing table and threw it at her laughing husband, who caught it adroitly.

Truthfully, she loved it when he teased her. It was a side of him that he shared almost exclusively with her.

"I'm glad *you* find it funny, Tristan."

"And I'm sorry to tease you if you're embarrassed about it." He deposited a kiss on top of her head as he deposited her glove back on her dressing table. Military habits died hard. He never flung his clothes about, even if he was able to get out of them with breathtaking speed.

He did that now and got into his nightshirt and she tried not to stare, but that nightly revelation of her husband's magnificent body was like getting a birthday present every evening, and it remained one of the best things about being married to him.

He slid into bed and sighed happily.

"No, I don't mind. It *is* funny, I suppose." She climbed into bed next to him, pulling their blankets and quilts up over both of them. "It's just—Tristan, *have* I changed since you've known me? Because I think that's exactly what's bothering me. It never would have *occurred* to me to shout that word in any context before. Not even accidentally. I was raised to be a lady, with all that implies. I'm *horrified* that it just came out of me like that. Mr. Delacorte thinks we're influencing him, but what if it's the other way around? What if I'm transforming like the cheese Delacorte found under his bed?"

She burrowed into his arms and they both sighed contentedly.

"Sweetheart, why, exactly, are you horrified? I'm a little aroused."

She laughed, then stopped. "Wait—are you?"

"Well, I generally am a little when I hold you like this . . ." He pulled her gently closer. "But no, just hearing you bellow 'shite' doesn't instantly inspire an erection. But I'll tell you why it makes me happy. Do you think it's possible you've never before felt safe enough to shout that word?"

"Safe? I'm not sure I know what you mean."

"You've told me before how you were raised to please, and how you've always been aware of the need to be proper, to conform to everyone else's needs and expectations. But here? You're safe here to be wholly yourself. And nothing is more beautiful to me than that, because all I want from life is for you to feel safe to be exactly who you are. So in light of all that, your 'shite' is music to my ears. It makes me feel like I've done my job in making you feel secure."

"Oh, Tristan." She was moved; she shifted to kiss his shoulder. "Do you know, I think you might be right."

"Delilah, I know you hold yourself to an exacting standard, but I promise you do not have to be flawless. *I* do, but you don't."

She snorted softly and gave his ankle a little nudge with her toes. "Silly. You *are* perfect, however."

It was his turn to snort. "I would love you even if you were Delacortian in nearly every way."

The "nearly" amused her. "You're legally required to. For better or for worse are right there in the vows."

He laughed shortly. "If Daniel had pinched *me*, I'm afraid I might have punted him over the banister out of pure reflex. You were well within your rights to add to his vocabulary in such a colorful way. And while I can't call out a four-year-old for pinching my wife's arse, he needs to know in no uncertain terms that such behavior is neither appropriate nor allowed. He needs to understand that it's disrespectful."

"What if his father does it, and that's where he learned it?" she whispered. "Pinches women. Or at least pinches his mother."

Tristan went still a moment. He sighed heavily and laid an arm across his forehead. "Regardless, we have to say it to him and hope the lesson sticks before his father gets here. I think we have a responsibility to the world at large to curtail a bottom pincher if we can."

They silently reflected on this.

"I could do it. I could tell him," Tristan said. "I want to. But do you know, briefly, I almost wanted to die, when he burst into tears when I spoke to him that first time. The *mortification*, Delilah. And trust me, more than once I've made a grown man cry as blockade captain. That was part of my job. It's child's play for me. I'm hard as bloody nails. Or I can be. So . . . why did it destroy me?"

"My poor dear." Her husband was *not* hard as nails, not all the time, but that was their secret and she cherished it.

"He looks like a damned puppy. Christ, his eyes filling with tears. The lower lip quivering. The horror."

Delilah was trying not to laugh. "I'm so sorry."

"Delacorte and Bolt say I have a *look*."

"The stern one?"

"You know it, too?"

She merely squeezed his hand.

"I was raised by the military, as you know. Giving and taking orders was about the extent of the affection exchanged."

"If we are so blessed, you will treat any child of ours the way you treat anything else you love. Like me. You don't order me about, do you?"

"That's because I want to live to see another day. Also, I want to die when you cry, too."

She laughed softly. "You're going to have to be stern now and again, and that's how he or she will feel safe and know how much you care. And I will be so grateful, because you know I struggle with being stern." It was true; Angelique, a former governess, was considerably better at it, in an amusing way, and all of their servants knew it. "Any child we might have will have the perfect balance of parents."

"Marchand says that between me, Bolt, and Delacorte a child raised here would get everything he needs from a father."

She laughed. "Mr. Marchand seems unusually wise with regard to children. I wonder what his story is?"

"It's actually a little like mine. St. Giles included, according to Bolt. And I expect a man like him won't ever feel safe sharing all of his secrets until the right woman comes along."

She knew this was true of her beloved husband.

"Why do I have the feeling that being a father will be a thousand times harder than being a blockade captain?" he murmured.

"One is about war, the other is about love?" she guessed.

"And as Eros demonstrated when he shot Apollo, love is even more challenging."

"It almost seems greedy to want more out of life than we already have. I feel lucky every single day," he told her. "And yet . . . a little Delilah . . . a little Tristan . . ."

Her heart felt swollen as she imagined a little boy that looked just like him. "We'll make it work the way we've made everything work so far. And if for some reason it doesn't happen for us . . ." Her voice had gone a little thick. "We'll make that work, too."

They fell quiet.

"By the way, Tristan?"

"Yes, love?"

"My favorite look of yours is the one that comes over your face . . . when we've just, ah, joined . . . and I'm under you . . . and I've just wrapped my legs around your back . . ."

"Oh, I think I can oblige you with *that* look, milady," he murmured.

* * *

It had felt almost sacrilegious to do something so mundane as play spillikins with Mrs. Pariseau in the sitting room a mere few hours after she'd been kissed into weak-kneed oblivion. It was Ginny's valiant attempt to prove to herself that nothing had really changed. But she'd played badly. Her blood had been heated to lava temperatures a few hours earlier and had only just now ebbed to a distracting, low simmer. She blamed that for her unsteady hands.

Well, that, and a lingering, wild, piercing exultation that made every breath feel like the first she'd ever taken.

This exultation would not and could not and should not last.

But she decided she wanted to be alone with it as long as it did, to savor the feeling.

So finally she excused herself so she could pace in her own little room.

She walked from door to window over and over. Giddy. Enervated and frightened.

She'd been raised within the confines of a set of beliefs about class and aristocracy. She was a lady and proud of it. She'd grown up thinking she knew precisely how gentlemen and ladies should behave, what kinds of friends she ought to cultivate, what constituted goodness and morality. There was a right kind of man and a wrong kind and a right kind of woman and a wrong kind. At no point had she thought to question any of the things her parents had taught her. Why would she? Everyone she knew felt the same way.

But now it was as though the kaleidoscope of her life had been given a twist. All the pieces were the same, but everything looked different.

She understood now that Lucifer's Fall, that alleged palace of sin, was after a fashion Marchand's monument to love and his fortress against loss. He had been born into chaos and survived the unthinkable and had still managed to embrace life with grace, humor, courage, panache, and a healthy helping of insufferable arrogance. She could only begin to imagine all of the things he'd been compelled to do to become the person he was today, so very many of them unsavory.

All of those experiences were the scaffolding upon which his extraordinary character had been built.

The daughter of a viscount could hardly veer farther away from her upbringing than passionately kissing a rogue in a graveyard. And not just any rogue. An orphan bastard who had once eaten a rat, rammed a cutthroat in the larynx with his elbow, was apparently wealthier by far than the Woodvilles, and had been instrumental in divesting the Woodville heir of his fortune, but who had essentially looked after their daughter as though she was infinitely more valuable than the Ming vase they were seeking.

One might even say—though this felt like the height of heresy—better than the father who could not have been bothered to drive his high-flyer carefully.

She could too vividly imagine how stricken her parents would be if they'd known about him, however. How betrayed they would feel.

But, oh, God . . . when she was in Marchand's arms, she could feel how badly he'd needed to be held.

Almost as desperately as she'd wanted to hold him.

Her heart twisted.

She could not bear to be the reason he suffered another single moment of pain or loss.

And yet it seemed inevitable.

You can decide the point of you, he'd said.

"Mama. *Help. Me.*" She whispered it fiercely, pressing her fists to her forehead.

Was she merely bewitched by him, or had she changed? If she had, when had this metamorphosis taken place? Wasn't it possible that when Peneus turned Daphne into a laurel tree to save her from Apollo, Daphne had thought, "Huh! I suppose I'm a tree now! Why does it feel like I was *always* meant to be a tree?"

Then again, Daphne probably still missed her nymph family. She wouldn't even be able to talk to them if she was a tree.

Loneliness and fear whistled like an icy wind through Ginny's soul at the thought of being so thoroughly cut off from the people she loved.

She at last carefully sat down at the writing desk and drew a half sheet of foolscap toward her, then dipped her quill.

She loathed conceding defeat. As she'd told Marchand once before (though with considerable bravado), no one got the better of her anymore. She was so accustomed to finding a solution that she could not quite accept she had exhausted every avenue. The back of her neck went damp from nerves as she wrote:

Dear Lord Sydenham,

I hope this message finds you and the countess well. I fear I write with disappointing news. After a concerted search and a number of inquiries, I regret that I am unable to locate the Ming vase that once belonged to the late Earl of Highgrove. Its fate remains unknown. I wondered if I may call upon you tomorrow at two o'clock to discuss different terms for the repayment of the debt. If you would kindly send word to me care of the Grand Palace on the Thames at 11 Lovell Street, I should be most grateful.

Yours sincerely,
The Honorable Guinevere Woodville

She would ask Mr. Pike, the footman, to take it to the earl first thing tomorrow morning.

She did not feel optimistic about her chances. But the earl had extended hope to her once before. Perhaps he'd do it again.

She wrote a list of her remaining options as cold-bloodedly as she was able.

When she was done, it looked like this:

Spend a night in Marchand's bed.

Her palms grew damp as she stared at the words. She sat and experienced the slow, heavy thud of her heart, the flush of heat through her body, the sharp pulse of longing between her legs, as for the first time she felt herself seriously contemplate it. Not out of outrage. But as a rational form of salvation. As a choice she would make for herself.

This frightened her so much she threw the foolscap on the fire, as if it were cursed, and went to bed.

* * *

Over the past few mornings Ginny had begun to find the rhythmic sound of Mr. Delacorte crunching on fried bread at breakfast almost soothing. She'd already eaten the scone brought into her room by the maids earlier, because only a fool would pass up that opportunity. But she did like eggs and kippers, too.

They were the only two people left at the breakfast table.

Ginny examined the reflection in the side of the coffee

urn. Purple shadows curved beneath her eyes. She'd tossed and turned fitfully the night before. Her bed was no longer a sanctuary. The very word "bed" conjured Mr. Marchand.

Last night, in her imagination, he'd touched her everywhere, in every conceivable way. Her skin had come alive with such yearning awareness that even the soft slide of her night rail over it was as sensual as hands.

She longed for him to return and equally dreaded it.

Suddenly Mr. Pike appeared in the doorway.

She'd asked him to take her message to the Earl of Sydenham this morning, and she'd seen him leave with it.

As if in a dream, she watched him move over to her, carrying a little silver tray.

On it was a message.

She peered down at it.

It was sealed with an "S" pressed into red wax.

Her heart gave a single, hard jolt.

She gingerly accepted it. "Thank you, Mr. Pike."

He bowed and backed away.

She held it for a long moment, simply breathing, looking down at it, heart pounding sickeningly.

While it remained unopened, hope remained.

It rattled in her hands as she broke the seal.

Dear Miss Woodville,

The news about the vase is indeed disappointing, but I don't think another discussion is worth my time or yours. I look forward to the fifteen-thousand-pound payment at the end of the month.

The countess and I send our best to you and your family.

> *Yours,*
> *Lord Sydenham*

She stared at it until the letters swam beneath her vision. Her head rang as if it were made of metal and had been whacked with a spoon.

It seemed she wasn't constitutionally capable of accommodating the total eradication of hope.

"Miss Woodville," Mr. Delacorte said gently. He sounded concerned.

Her expression must have told him something was amiss.

Possibly he'd said her name more than once and she was only now hearing him.

She looked up at him blankly.

"Would you like to come with me to visit your donkey?"

She blinked. Of all the things anyone might have said to her then, somehow it was the only right one. It was kind, it was ridiculous, it interrupted her despair, and she liked donkeys.

"Yes, please," she said meekly.

Off they went.

* * *

The donkey seemed content in the livery stable surrounded by horse friends. Patting her and feeding her carrots restored Ginny's spirits somewhat. Mr. Delacorte went off with his medicine case to visit apothecaries, and she returned to the Grand Palace on the Thames.

"Miss Woodville, you've a guest!" Dot greeted her at the door, her eyes dancing. She lowered her voice to a conspiratorial hush.

Ginny's heart lurched again. What if it was Sydenham, having a change of heart?

And a guest *would* arrive when she smelled a bit like a donkey.

"Did he happen to volunteer his name?"

"Mr. Balfort."

She sucked in a sharp breath.

Francis! But how?

Then she recalled that Cambrough had said that Francis was in London, too. How odd that she hadn't bothered to retain that information.

Her head swiveled to look where Dot gestured.

There Francis stood in the pink reception room, smiling at her.

"I'll sit with you, if you like," Dot whispered.

Ginny thought hurriedly.

"That would be best, thank you, Dot."

* * *

"I felt rather daring calling upon you at a *boardinghouse,*" Francis confided, his eyes sparkling. Dot had brought in tea; Ginny poured it and now Francis held a cup. She knew how he took it: one little spoon of sugar. "I hope you don't mind. It's not the most genteel of neighborhoods, is it, but it's rather nice inside. If a trifle worn. And I've brought a new book of poetry. I think you'll like it, Ginny. I ought to have said . . . you're looking . . . so lovely."

He was babbling, a little.

She felt slightly removed from her body, like a spectator watching a play. It had been only a few weeks since she'd seen him, but Francis suddenly seemed like a character in a book she'd read, not someone she'd known fondly for a good portion of her life, someone she'd expected to marry. She oddly felt epochs older than him, and he was older than her by a year.

"I do like it here," she told him. "Everyone is very kind and the accommodations are so comfortable." Out of the corner of her eye, she noticed Dot beaming at the praise.

"I've never been to Fleegle's," he confided. "I've heard of it." He lowered his voice. "Cambrough said he thought he saw that chap called the Reaper there. That's a little unnerving, don't you think? Cambrough has seen him only once before, in the Galleria. He has his own *gaming hell*. Quite a dangerous fellow. I'm glad you were spared the sight of him. Of course, he's not welcome in White's, so I would never meet him. Gaming is not how I prefer to spend my time." He sniffed.

It's not a gaming hell, a voice in Ginny's head said. It sounded like Marchand's.

"How thrilling and unusual to have seen him," Ginny replied, chilled to the bone.

"London can be such a colorful place," Francis said. "It's not always safe."

You don't say, Francis.

"Indeed. But I feel very safe here. It's quite good to see you, Francis."

And she wasn't lying. He was a kind, merry person as well as undeniably handsome—and he knew it but was still not too arrogant about it. He was clever but not dazzlingly so; he didn't yammer on and on about himself like so many men liked to do. She'd always liked the way he seemed just a little in awe of her and just a little shy.

She could not remember why she'd liked this now. Perhaps it was because she'd had no basis for comparison.

Then she realized: She'd felt steadily admired, which was quite a fine feeling.

But she had not felt *seen*. And now she knew the difference.

The difference between him and Marchand was the difference between a scribble and a Caravaggio.

This epiphany introduced a new flavor of despair into the exciting blend of emotions already churning within her.

"When Henry told me you were in London, I simply could not resist the temptation to come and see you," he said.

This sounded very nearly ardent, and Ginny went sharply silent, awash with trepidation.

"He mentioned you were in town on family business," he added, into her sudden silence. "I imagine it's something to do with preparation for the marriage settlement meetings for Felicity and Fiona?" This he said almost bashfully.

"Yes." It wasn't completely a lie.

She was overcome with a sudden vertiginous dread.

It occurred to her that Francis might be here to *propose*.

It would be a dream come true and her worst nightmare.

It was not something she ever imagined occurring while she

smelled faintly of donkey and sported purple circles under her eyes and had spent the entire previous night imagining the hands of another man roaming her body.

But she wasn't mad. If he proposed, she knew there could be only one answer.

* * *

Like a green lad's, Marchand's heartbeat sped ever-faster the closer his hired hack drew to the Grand Palace on the Thames.

And once he'd disembarked, he paused again outside of it to admire the little gargoyles on the roof edge. And to heighten anticipation.

Because Guinevere Woodville was inside.

When he opened the door, the cheerful warmth of the place seemed to rush forward to greet him.

He drew in a long breath to settle the absurd, utterly uncharacteristic twang of nerves.

He took a few steps into the foyer.

Then froze beneath the chandelier.

Ginny was sitting in the reception room on the pink settee.

Across from her sat a very handsome young man.

In other words, a man her *own* age.

The man was long limbed and lean, and at a glance Marchand could see he was wealthy. It was something about the posture, the shine on the boots, the Byronic cut of his curly hair. He looked like the young men who clamored to become members of Lucifer's Fall. But Marchand didn't recognize him.

Ginny was smiling at him fondly.

Marchand's breathing went shallow.

A pot of tea and cups occupied the table in the middle. Which suggested this was a formal social call of some duration.

Dot occupied a chair in the corner, an embroidery hoop in her lap. He supposed she'd been recruited for the occasion. Because, of course, young, unmarried aristocratic ladies could not visit with aristocratic men without witnesses.

God only knew what they could get up to.

His absolute rigidity must have drawn their attention.

Although his glowering could have done it, too.

Ginny shot to her feet at once. The brilliant delight that flared unguarded in her face evolved into alarm, then caution.

Then guilt.

When her eyes went pleading, his gut pulled itself into a knot.

Of course, she had no reason to feel guilty at all.

He had no claim on her.

Just as there was no real reason for jealousy to be pouring through him in black, toxic torrents.

He, in fact, couldn't breathe for it. It was a sensation utterly unprecedented in his life. He had no defense against it. He simply stood there, amazed, and boiled in it.

"Miss Woodville," he replied politely, when he was finally able to speak. "Good afternoon."

He looked pointedly at the young man sitting across from her, then back at Ginny, then back at the man, who had the refined features one might find on someone whose ancestors had mated with only attractive people over the centuries. He'd risen to his feet, too. He was regarding Marchand with the pleasant, open expression of someone who easily trusted because he'd never doubted for a moment that the world was arranged in his favor.

"May I introduce my friend Francis Balfort? His father is the Duke of Balfort. He's visiting London and learned from our mutual friend Lord Cambrough that I was in London as well. I happened to accidentally meet Lord Cambrough in a shop the other day."

Ah, yes. Fleegle's Emporium of Wonders, specifically.

"How do you do, Mr. Balfort. I'm . . ."

He halted abruptly. Ginny's eyes had suddenly gone terrified and beseeching.

And then he understood: She was afraid he was going to say his own name.

That realization drove right through him like a sword.

Two things shocked him: how savagely that hurt.

And how wholly unprepared he was for how savagely that hurt.

His mind momentarily blanked.

"I'm Mr. Gabriel," he completed quietly.

Two bright pink spots of shame flared high on Ginny's cheeks.

She turned away toward the window.

The two men bowed to each other.

Francis obviously didn't recognize Marchand by sight. But given the young man's age and social rank, it was all but impossible that he wouldn't know Marchand's name. Many of his friends and their fathers were likely members of Lucifer's Fall.

And Francis's expression would change pretty rapidly if he knew the Reaper not only stood right in front of him, but was personally acquainted with Miss Guinevere Woodville.

Ginny's reputation and future prospects would be in ashes in seconds.

For an instant, a primitive, unworthy instant, Marchand imagined the aftermath of that. Would she then be forced to turn to him, if she had no other prospects?

He was a man who would do nearly anything to get something he wanted. But when he realized he would rather die than do that to her or to himself, he grimly realized just how far gone he was.

Dot was studying him curiously.

He prayed she wouldn't interject.

"How long will you be staying, Mr. Balfort?" Marchand asked. "Have you taken a room at the Grand Palace on the Thames?"

Too late he realized he ought to have replied "A pleasure to meet you" first, but he was not in the mood to lie. And besides, life was short, and Marchand would have decisions to make right away if Balfort was staying. Such as whether poisoning him or throwing him off the roof would be the better option.

"I'm returning home to Sussex in an hour or so. I just thought it was a lovely coincidence that Ginny was in London, too. Like kismet. I've been traveling a bit and it's been too long since I've seen her." He cast a blushingly wistful look at her that made Marchand feel dirty, jaded, and a thousand years old.

"Three weeks," Ginny said.

"Nearly four," Francis retorted merrily.

Ginny was so pale her freckles stood out in stark relief. She had definitely sensed the tenor of Marchand's mood. She kept her eyes fixed on him, as if she didn't trust him not to do something—how had she put it?—unexpected. "I suppose it is."

"What's that in your hand, Mr. Balfort?" Marchand asked.

The boy was holding a little book.

"I was just reading a favorite poem to Ginny," he said.

"Do you write poetry?" he asked the boy.

He looked at Ginny, and he could see in her eyes—eyes that, as far as he was concerned, were the only poem the world had ever needed—that she remembered their conversation outside the Earl of Sydenham's house.

"I've given it a try," Balfort admitted. "Do you, Mr. Gabriel?"

"Oh, yes. Lately I've been struggling with one particular rhyme."

A tentative smile appeared on Ginny's lips.

An awkward silence ensued.

"Remind me, when did you intend to return to Sussex, Miss Woodville?" Marchand finally said to her.

"In about a week." Her voice was frayed. "I've a commitment to attend a meeting on behalf of both of my sisters in Sussex. I'm very much looking forward to seeing my family and friends."

"And I am very much looking forward to your return," Balfort admitted fervently.

Oh, to be so innocently, transparently, faultlessly honest, Marchand thought. To feel so *entitled* to hope.

"I'll leave you to your visit," Marchand said and made for the stairs.

* * *

Francis departed an hour later.

Haunted both by the last thing Francis had said to her before he'd bid her farewell and by the gutted expression on Marchand's face when he'd lied about his name, Ginny wearily climbed the stairs.

She paused at the window on the second floor. She'd caught a glimpse of her cat friends. They were crouched outside, staring at each other, ears flattened.

They were squaring up for another fight.

"Who are you rooting for?" Gabriel's tone was casual.

She gave a start.

She hadn't even heard his approach.

She didn't turn around.

She could already feel the heat radiating from his body. It took every ounce of her will not to lean back into him.

"Pumpkinhead—I call him that because of his big round ginger head—likes to do a lot of staring first, while Inkblot—I call him Inkblot because of the black blot on his white face—likes to get right into it first. I've never noticed an actual winner. The fur really does fly, however. In big tufts. And then it's over."

"These are friends of yours?" He sounded amused.

"They're the nightly show from the window in my room."

"I'm envious. My room is at the end of a corridor opposite a candle that snuffs out mysteriously. But I've an excellent view of the tops of ships."

"Seems an exhausting way to go about a life. One fight per day, every day," she mused.

"When you understand that they're probably fighting over the rights to a female, it makes sense."

She fell silent.

Suddenly *she* was seething.

Not necessarily *at* him, but because of him.

And because of herself.

Because of her life.

Because the notion of him fighting Francis over her was ridiculous.

Francis would be dead in three seconds.

"How was your journey?" she asked politely, hoping to steer the conversation elsewhere.

"It was fine. Did Francis leave?"

"Yes," she said shortly.

"Did you enjoy your little visit?"

Anger surged at this characterization of it. "It was nice to see him."

"Nice," he repeated, after a moment. As if that word were a profanity.

There was a pause.

"Did he propose?"

"Good God, Marchand." Her temper flared. "Mince a word now and again."

"Did he?" He was relentless. He never, ever was intimidated by passion or fervor, and God how she loved it.

She felt a flush of shame. "No," she said softly.

"Why not?"

She didn't answer that.

"Dowry problems?"

She felt like kicking him.

She didn't want to tell him the truth, because she knew it would hurt him, because it hurt her, and it was all of a piece now for the two of them.

And yet there was no avoiding the truth of what Francis had said before he departed.

Ginny swallowed. "He said that he'd heard the Woodvilles' circumstances have changed for the better, and he hoped to have an important conversation with me when I returned to Sussex for the marriage settlement discussions in a few days. He did not use the word 'marriage' or 'married' and he doesn't know anything about . . . what happened with Hogarth at Lucifer's Fall. All the losses."

The horrific eradication of her dowry, in other words.

Did Marchand truly understand the humiliation she would feel if Francis had asked her to marry him, and she'd accepted—only for him to learn later that she had no dowry, after all?

Did he understand how humiliated she would feel if she had to tell Francis outright that despite their recent inheritance, she currently had no dowry? That it had all disappeared, because her brother had gambled it all away at a gaming hell? And was then compelled to watch Francis's sweet face fall, to see betrayal and hurt in it?

The notion of any of these scenarios curdled her blood.

How was it that Marchand, who had known so much fear in his life, did not seem to recognize how terribly *afraid* she was? About her future. About her feelings about him. She wasn't worldly. He was too much for her, yet exactly enough, and she feared nothing else would ever be enough again.

She was miserable, and she was aroused, and neither condition seemed likely to be eased soon.

He was quiet for some time.

"Ginny . . ." When Marchand turned her name into a sigh in her ear, spangles immediately stood all the little hairs on her nape erect, and a pulse of what she knew to be pure lust throbbed between her legs. "Here is the thing . . ." This, too, was more breath than words, uttered drowsily. He leisurely feathered his lips down her throat, and she sighed and arched into him, in thrall to these new, glorious sensations. She couldn't help it. She would take them while she could. "I might be little better than a street rat dressed up in a rich man's clothes . . ." When he touched his tongue to her ear, a soft moan spiraled from her; she was half angry, half astounded. "But I don't understand what kind of man can't make his own money for a woman he wants." His lips, his tongue, his breath were on the bare place below her hair, at her nape; she could feel his erection hard against her bottom and the heat pooling at the crux of her legs, as if ready *now* to receive him, and she sighed helplessly, softly. "A man who wouldn't go to the ends of the earth for a woman he wants strikes me as no kind of man at all." The words were incendiary, infuriating, but he delivered them like a mesmerist, and she found herself turning as unresistingly as a flower in the breeze to abet his wandering lips as pleasure sparked to life everywhere across her body. "A man who wouldn't buy her everything she needs, keep her safe forever, give her children, never let her know a moment's worry or want again. Would pay *any* price for the privilege of being with her. But then, as we both know"—his tongue, and then his teeth, delicately toyed with the whorls of her ear, as her breath came in staccato tatters now—"I'm not a gentleman."

Anger and despair and lust and wonder warred within her like those cats outside. His jealousy was darkly satisfying, even erotic. But she knew at the root of it was deep pain, and that scared her. She desperately hated being the cause of his suffering. She hated being the cause of her *own* suffering.

Everything he said was everything she had ever wanted to hear from a man, and she had never realized it until now.

But were these really things *he* wanted, were these really things he was offering her, was this really proof that he could indeed read her very soul?

Or was it possible that he was just playing dirty because he was jealous, and wanted to win?

"Funny. I don't feel a thing." She didn't recognize the slow, pleasure-drugged sound of her voice as he drew his tongue along the cords of her throat.

"No?" She heard the dark laughter in the word. His fingers lightly skimmed the length of her arms, then his hands covered her hands, which were clasped in front of her.

Then he lifted them and she let him, because God help her, she thought she would let him do whatever he wanted to do to her now.

He brought them up to her breasts.

And then he guided her hands in a rough caress over her bead-hard nipples.

Her head fell back hard as shocking pleasure cleaved her; she bit her lip to muffle her cry.

Her breath came in speeding, ragged gusts.

"Everything you felt just *now*, Guinevere?" he whispered. "That's what *I* do to you."

He gently took his hands from hers.

She didn't turn as she heard his footsteps on the stairs, leaving her.

* * *

In his cozy room, which was softer than a goddamn hug, Marchand brooded.

The brooding embarrassed him.

He was altogether appalled with himself, in general. It was sobering.

He had no experience of this kind of jealousy—the possessive, mindless, reactive kind. He'd behaved little better than the feral boy he'd once been. As if he'd been cornered by thieves in an alley, about to be robbed of a crust of bread he'd stolen. He'd fought like a demon back then for something he'd felt was rightfully his. He yearned for the right to do that now.

But he'd just been an *ass* to her, and now he had a rampaging erection.

He took care of that, adroitly and swiftly, while picturing his hands covering her breasts. He saw stars when he came.

The relief was temporary. The jealousy flowed right back into his veins, cutting off his air.

He needed to learn it like an enemy, so he could discover which weapons he could use to disarm it. He was a grown man, jaded and seasoned and intelligent enough. He could surely rationalize it away.

But that was the trouble: What he felt for her had begun somewhere within him that cynicism hadn't killed. Some unprotected place where he was still a boy innocently in thrall to the moon. It had sneaked up on him; it now bound him like vines.

The problem with being accustomed to assessing threats was that it was a matter of moments before he realized his jealousy was mainly fear. Fear of both the known and the unknown. Because it was one thing to *hear* about Balfort anecdotally.

It was another being compelled to stand in the same room with a man who would more than likely share Ginny's bed for the rest of her life.

And to understand that sweet, calf-eyed boy was, all things considered, probably a better choice for her.

His entire being rebelled against the notion so powerfully that it felt as though his rib cage were being ripped apart by two mighty hands. He struggled to breathe through that suffering.

Jealousy was also pain.

He was ashamed of that, too. He ought to have been past that by now.

Because he knew too bloody well what it felt like to have his heart gouged out and his world turned to ashes. He recalled too well the slow, painful, halting climb up out of the depths of loss while presenting himself to the world as shrewd, dangerous, and invincible in order to survive. He knew what it had been like to learn himself all over again in the absence of a person he loved.

It ought to have made him even harder and even braver. He wanted to be harder and braver.

It had instead made him humbler. And more patient.

And very wary of pain.

He knew too well the savage price exacted by love. Grief was built right into it, as Ginny had mentioned in the sitting room. That poor bastard Apollo, yearning eternally.

He allowed himself one weak moment to rail at the superfluous cruelty of fate.

Anyone who knew him superficially—which was nearly everyone, except Ginny—would have been surprised to learn his greatest gift wasn't knowing precisely how to punch a man in the kidneys. It was that he knew how to care. He knew now definitively that it was what made him feel whole. It was what he'd been missing. Whether it was wading into a fight in a gaming hell or tucking a little boy into bed, or looking after spoiled aristocrats at Lucifer's Fall, or escorting the beautiful, maddening daughter of a viscount on a chase around London. He took care of people.

Mainly, he wanted to take care of her.

He had a look at his pocket watch.

There was time to get a hack to St. James's Square.

There he would pay a visit to an apothecary and ask the questions that had been forming since his chat with Mr. Delacorte in the smoking room.

If he was right about the suspicion he was pursuing, there was a possibility he could keep Ginny safe for the rest of her life. If that was all he would ever be able to offer her, then by God, he was going to bloody well try.

Chapter Seventeen

Ginny took advantage of the four-nights-a-week-in-the-sitting-room rule to hide in her room that night, right after dinner. She wished Marchand were more subtle about staring at her during dinner, but then, she wouldn't know he was looking at her if she hadn't been looking at him. She'd, in fact, been dangerously unaware of anyone noticing their mutual fascination.

Dot had loaned her *The Ghost in the Attic.*

She didn't read it.

The turmoil taking place inside her was sufficient drama.

She crawled into bed instead and listened to the wind rattling the window.

There were the things she wanted, and the things she needed. She might have made a list and put them into columns, as she'd done with the clues about Hogarth's gambling debt, except they swirled like leaves kicked up in a storm. She could not discern one from another.

What she wanted was to know every single thing Marchand could teach her about sex.

But her body begged to differ. Her body insisted this was

not a want but a need, as surely as hunger was a need. *It's an appetite,* he'd once said to her, with something like condescension, outside of Henrietta Parker's house. He had shown her that desire could bank and bank as though it was leading somewhere very important, somewhere extraordinary. He had shown her it had gradations. This afternoon, he had lit her body on fire and left it smoldering, and obviously he was the only one who could quench it.

What she wanted was not to want him.

But that would mean she never would have met him.

What she wanted was to never have met him.

Because now her life was distinctly before him and after him, no matter what happened.

Her throat was thick.

She rested her forehead on her hands.

What she both wanted and needed was to return to Sussex able to tell Hogarth his debt to the house had been paid, and that they would have at least *something* with which to negotiate marriage settlements for Felicity and Fiona.

What she wanted was to stop being afraid. She wanted one *damned* moment when she was not afraid. Because fear was sawing away at her being and she had begun to feel as though it was only a matter of time before it snapped completely. She wasn't certain Marchand truly comprehended this.

And then she told herself that there was a certain symmetry to it. Her family's recent misfortunate had originated with Gabriel.

Why *shouldn't* he also be the path to salvation?

With the four-thousand-pound debt forgiven, she could perhaps negotiate a marriage settlement of two thousand pounds each for Felicity and Fiona, plus a percentage of the anticipated rent of the entailed estate they had inherited, once they found a tenant. It was still paltry. But it wasn't *nothing*. It wasn't insulting. It might be enough to save her sisters' futures.

But she would still need to explain why the dowry amounts were so low, when the understanding had been so different when their fiancés proposed.

It left nothing for *her* dowry, of course. That hardly seemed to matter when she didn't even have a marriage proposal yet. She would survive, somehow.

This was the dangerous run of her thoughts when lust and desperation colluded.

One night out of her entire life.

One night in Gabriel's bed, and she could get both what she wanted and what she needed.

And surely no one else would be the wiser?

She closed her eyes and pictured herself moving up the stairs, down the hall toward his room. Knocking on the door.

His eyes would go hot when he saw her. She felt the jolt of his gaze now, as if she stood before him.

With that thought *want* pierced right through her, as if her body was telling her, adamantly, that she was on the right track.

She could quench a curiosity. Solve a mystery.

She could look up into his fierce eyes as he covered and claimed her.

The rush of blood to her head at that thought nearly made her sway.

She could eradicate at least one fear. The bliss of that. The *bliss* of that.

She would walk away with a memory.

But what kind of memory? Would she cherish it? Would she bury it, because it would bring crippling shame every time her thoughts touched on it?

Or would she be just another desperate woman in the annals of time who had done exactly what she needed to do when offered an option?

Could she be just that pragmatic?

To get what she wanted, she decided she could.

And as her resolve began to solidify, her heart began to thud, thud, thud as if it were falling down one stair at a time.

She sat up on the edge of her bed. *My room is at the end of a corridor opposite a candle that snuffs out mysteriously.* It seemed kismet now that she knew this. And perhaps he'd deliberately told her for this very reason.

Was he lying awake thinking about her, even now?

The clock downstairs struck eleven o'clock.

Slowly, as if in a dream, she reached for her pelisse and slid her arms into it. She took up her lit candle.

And set out to take another mad leap into the unknown.

* * *

Nerves somehow compressed time. She hardly recalled her journey up the stairs to his room.

Finally, she tapped at his door with two knuckles, on the theory that a decisive knock would echo like a gunshot at this time of night.

The courage that had propelled her up the stairs was

dwindling as the cold bit through her night rail and even through her pelisse.

She decided she would not knock a second time. She would count to five, and then flee down the stairs if he didn't answer.

On four she heard the scrape of the bolt sliding.

The door opened.

"Guinevere." He looked stunned.

He wore only a shirt and trousers. His sleeves were rolled up. His feet and throat and forearms were bare. Aggressively masculine-looking curly hair sprang from the V at his throat and the hair on his head was tumbled every which way. She sensed he had rolled out of bed and hastily dressed.

All this ungarnished gorgeous manliness went to her head like a punch.

"Good evening." Her voice had gone thready.

And that's when her nerve sputtered out.

She could say nothing more and merely stared. There was no light at all in which he did not look fascinating, and that included flickering candlelight.

She tried not to glance at his trouser fall, behind which was his penis. If all went according to plan, she would become better acquainted with it.

"Is that what you came to say?" he whispered. Still tense, but a little amused now.

She still couldn't find her voice. "I." It emerged more as a croak than a word.

"Is anything wrong?" he asked urgently.

Her heart swelled. God help her. It sounded as though he was ready to do murder for her, if necessary.

She swallowed. "I'm . . . I thought . . ."

He wasn't helping her at all. Likely because he'd just fully realized she was wearing only a pelisse over a night rail. His eyes traveled the length of her and returned to her face, and now his eyes were dark and fixed.

Queasy with fear and shame, and despite all that, despite the madness of what she was doing, there was a nearly unbearable, pulling yearning between her legs.

Why hadn't she rehearsed this?

"I'm . . . I'm here about your offer." Her pounding heart made her voice tremble.

It sounded as though she were applying for a job.

"My offer." He repeated it carefully. Whispering.

He was going to make her say it out loud?

She swallowed. "I've decided to . . . when first we met, you said you would . . . if I . . . one night . . ."

He pulled in a long, long breath. "Oh. I see."

The following silence was deafening.

A draft tugged at the candle flame.

"I'm afraid that's no longer possible," he said.

Oddly, the fact that he'd said it so kindly made the words ring as stunningly hateful, because she was at once excruciatingly embarrassed.

Even though there was nothing of condescension in them.

She felt like a child who had just done something ridiculous.

"Go back to bed, Guinevere." He said this slowly, firmly yet so tenderly.

Why was his voice shaking?

She remained frozen.

"*Go*," he repeated, urgently. Hoarsely.

What would he do if she reached out and touched him now? What if she traced that open V at his throat, as she longed to do?

She knew the two of them were fuse and flame.

He would combust. He would seize her like he had the day in the cemetery.

He closed the door.

And threw the bolt.

She stared at it, stunned.

She enjoyed one merciful instant of numbness before humiliation poured through her body in acidic torrents.

Like a ghost, she returned to her room, on legs she couldn't feel. Later she couldn't remember getting there at all.

* * *

Gabriel slid to the floor and pressed his back against the door.

"Holy Mother of GOD . . . " he breathed.

What the bloody hell had just happened?

How had he not anticipated this?

He stared, stunned, into the shadowy depths of his room. Reeling as if he'd taken a fist to the jaw.

You mad bastard, his body howled. *You mad, idiot bastard.* She'd been right *there*, within reach. He'd seen the curve of her breast beneath her night rail outlined in candlelight and shadow, and he could, right now, have been peeling that night rail over her head and touching his tongue to her nipple. Sliding his hands over her satiny skin. *Why are you surprised? Wasn't this always the game plan? Why are you not exulting?*

He'd barked "GO" at her instead.

It had been pure instinct, a reflex, originating someplace more primal than desire. A survival instinct.

Who, exactly, was he protecting?

And if it was her . . . why was he shaking?

***

At first, Ginny wished she could wad herself up into the smallest imaginable ball like a handkerchief, tuck herself into some dark, hidden corner, and quietly finish expiring from shame.

It was almost gruesomely funny that this was not an option, as the rules of the Grand Palace on the Thames required her to join the other guests at dinner and in the sitting room. She might have offered herself up to be ravished in exchange for money and been rejected, but she still played spillikins. She had even offered a suggestion for the name of one of Dot's knights.

"You can call him Judas," she said. "Because he betrayed the queen. And now she wants to destroy his entire army."

"Ooooh!" Dot approved, while Mr. Delacorte made an incoherent sound of near frustration.

Her passage home was booked a few days hence on the mail coach.

Maybe she could saddle up Hogarth's donkey and leave for Sussex now, and contemplate her utter failure to resolve anything at all during the entire, slow journey home.

The worst part was the sense of betrayal she felt.

What if everything she thought she knew about Marchand,

what if every memory she'd collected precisely the way she collected stone hearts—every look and word exchanged, the expression on his face in the churchyard as he gazed across at her, the way he held her, the way he kissed her—had been a lie? A strategy?

Had this been his objective, after all?

Because she *had* fallen into his hand like a ripe plum.

Perhaps he thought he'd *won*, and he had nothing left to prove now.

And perhaps that was the reason he felt he didn't need to expend any effort making love to her. She scarcely knew a thing about all of that, after all. Ropes and spanking notwithstanding.

She refused to meet his eyes in the sitting room or at the breakfast or dinner table, but he scarcely took them off her. She knew because she could *feel* his gaze, for the same reason she knew she would be able to feel him present anywhere, in a crowd or if she was blindfolded in a dark room. If he'd addressed her directly, she would have taken great pleasure in aggressively shunning him and letting everyone in the room wonder why.

She could barely eat. She put a few things in her mouth at each meal and didn't taste them. Misery blunted every one of her senses, as if her whole being had donned mourning.

* * *

Marchand told himself: *It's better if she hates me now. It will ultimately be so much easier for both of us.*

But every time he saw her at the dinner table or in the sitting room, he felt freshly destroyed. Unlike him, she had not developed a useful, hard shield between herself and the world. Her suffering was palpable. He could hardly breathe for witnessing it. She was *furious*, that much was clear. No doubt she felt humiliated. She probably felt betrayed. She was entitled to feel all of it.

Perhaps she was gravely disappointed he had not taken her to bed.

If that was the gratifying case, well, two of them suffered torments over that.

On the whole, he suffered because she suffered.

But he suffered for his own reasons, too.

For the first time in his life, he'd dishonorably reneged on a deal, when he'd vowed to himself that he would never be that kind of man.

He told himself that his reasons had been noble. He was saving the viscount's daughter from something she'd regret, no matter how desperate her straits seemed now.

But he suspected in this instance that "cowardice" was masquerading as "noble."

And lurking beneath the cowardice were reasons he simply did not want to face.

And he suffered because he'd asked Hogarth to send the letter describing "his" plan to repay his debt to Lucifer's Fall. The royal mail between London and Sussex was usually swift, but it hadn't yet arrived. He ought to have stood over the boy and demanded he write it in his presence, so he could take the letter back to London with him.

He'd just been so eager to return to the Grand Palace on the Thames. To be wherever Ginny was.

He'd imagined presenting Hogarth's letter to her and watching her face go soft with joy and pride, savoring the miracle of it.

He'd wanted to be her bloody hero.

But Marchand was accustomed to getting on with things. He knew from experience that despite outer circumstances, if he didn't keep kicking to stay afloat, the waves would eventually suck him under. And he'd always valued his own worthless life, although God only knew why. Perhaps he'd somehow known he would wind up someday kissing a beautiful girl in a churchyard, which would make everything he'd done to survive up until that moment worth it.

He found he could hardly countenance the notion of burdening her with the truth about his feelings. He wouldn't know *how* to tell her, anyway. He'd never done such a thing in his life.

Because he could not know for certain how she felt.

Even the possibility of witnessing pity in her soft eyes if he told her the truth made him want to shrivel. It would haunt him bitterly for whatever remained of his days. How could she possibly understand that making love to her would destroy him if he had to let her go?

He'd asked Mr. Ogden to make a certain appointment for him two days hence. On his calendar for that day Marchand wrote the word "retribution."

He took ice-cold satisfaction in the anticipation of meting out punishment and settling a grave wrong.

Before she returned to Sussex, if all went according to plan, he would be able to give Ginny's life back to her and to the people she loved.

So it seemed to him that he had arrived at the solution for what he could do for her. Perhaps it was the only point of him.

And for that, he thought he could endure anything. Even her hate.

* * *

The need for solace finally drove Ginny outside to the little park in front of the Grand Palace on the Thames after lurking in her room for the better part of two days. It seemed as good a place as any to look for a stone heart, even though she'd already found one there. Lightning could very well strike twice.

No stones immediately leaped into her line of vision, as they had that magical day in the park next to Marchand. Gordon did, however. The plump striped cat who roamed the halls of the Grand Palace on the Thames was sleeping beneath a shrub, and he hopped up next to her on the bench. She scratched him under the chin. The purring was admittedly consoling.

"I hope you don't have any fights with Pumpkinhead and Inkblot," she told him sincerely.

"*Prrrp*," he trilled, noncommittally. Promising nothing.

Her head shot up when she heard the squeak of the gate.

She went so rigid so abruptly that Gordon shot straight up and then vanished in a tabby blur.

Marchand froze before her.

She was literally caged in by a wrought iron fence.

His expression suggested that of a man silently shouting "Bloody hell!"

It was the first time she'd looked at him for two long days, and it might as well have been the first time she'd ever seen him. The impact on her was entirely the same. In the bright daylight, he looked magnificent, intimidating, and exhausted. Exactly like a man who hadn't slept at all since she'd interrupted his sleep two nights before.

Her heart, that traitorous organ, yearned to go to him to offer comfort.

She fixed things. She couldn't seem to stop wanting to do that. Even for people who destroyed her.

"I didn't know you were here," he said stiffly. "My apologies for the intrusion, Miss Woodville. I'll leave."

But when he turned away, every cell of her body howled in protest.

He froze as if he'd heard her soul crying out to him. He hesitated.

Then she watched his shoulders move in a sort of resigned breath.

He pivoted to face her.

"You're upset," he said quietly.

That was a significant understatement.

"Nonsense," she said firmly. She refused to give him the satisfaction of knowing how thoroughly emotionally ravaged she was. But her voice shook.

He steeply arched a skeptical brow.

"It wasn't my intent to embarrass you," he said evenly. "And I'm very sorry if I did."

Ugh. That careful, formal tone.

"I wasn't embarrassed."

That won her an almost impatient look. As if lying bored him.

"And there's nothing shameful about the choice you made," he continued.

She merely stared at him.

She saw him tense to leave.

"I know," she said swiftly. "But the fact that *you* lost your nerve doesn't surprise me a bit, Mr. Marchand."

At once, that familiar, challenging light flared in his eyes.

"I suppose I ought to have known that you wouldn't keep your word," she pressed on recklessly. "For all your big talk about never lying, cheating, or stealing. Once a rogue and all that. The joke is on me."

He pressed his lips together. His eyes were both flinty and wounded. She'd hit her mark.

"You're hurt," he claimed correctly.

"Wrong again, Marchand."

He didn't honor this lie with a response.

Tension tugged at his eyes, about his mouth. He was suffering.

"Was it because of Francis?" she blurted. "Are you . . . are you . . . punishing me because of . . ." Her voice broke.

He looked tormented now. "No. Absolutely not."

"Then why—"

"Because. I. *Can't*, Ginny," he said slowly and evenly, laying all of those words down like bricks. This time there was a warning in his voice.

But did she also hear a hint of a plea?

She nodded sardonically. "Ah, I *think* I understand now," she said on a faux hush. "And I'm so *very* sorry to hear about your impediment. I guess Lady Tomelty had it wrong, after all. Perhaps Mr. Delacorte has something in his case to remedy it."

Marchand spun on his heel and stormed out the garden gate.

She jerked when he all but slammed it behind him.

She closed her eyes and dropped her face into her hands. She drew in ragged breaths through a nearly unbearable pressure in her chest. She wanted to scream. She wanted to sob.

She thought her entire being might fly apart.

She'd dragged in three ragged breaths when she heard the latch on the gate lift again.

She froze.

She heard the muffled crunch of his slow footsteps toward her.

Slowly, cautiously, she lifted her head.

Her heart turned over hard at Marchand's expression.

It was tormented. Furious. Hunted.

Yearning.

He was breathing audibly.

"I look for heart-shaped rocks on the ground everywhere now," he said. "Every. Bloody. Where."

She froze.

"I beg your—"

"My eyes can't be on the ground, Ginny. I need to be on the lookout for perils."

She was stunned.

"All right," she said carefully.

"And I don't think you're pretty at all."

The bastard let her sit with that for a torturous few seconds.

"No. You're *alarmingly* beautiful, in an entirely unique way that somehow seems different every time I look at you. And I . . ."

Goose bumps raced over her skin. What was happening here?

". . . and that makes it difficult to concentrate, let alone breathe. I need to think, Ginny. I need to breathe."

Her own breath left. She couldn't say a word. She was riveted.

"I've never—never—brought anyone to see Michael before. You're the first. *The Ghost in the Attic* has nothing on the inside of my heart, Ginny, I can't go *showing* the inside of my heart to people."

"Gabriel . . ." she said softly.

He raised his voice. "And dear God, Guinevere, you are"—he paused to huff out a breath—"*stubborn* beyond belief. And clever in ways that require me to constantly pay attention. And gentle in a way that makes me . . ." His voice frayed. "That I . . ."

His fury sputtered out.

He was subdued now. Drained, but clearly implacable. "As I once said," he said slowly, "I simply will not allow you to ruin me."

There was no sound but the rush of the breeze through the shrubberies around them. She could all but feel his beautiful, savage, battered heart lighting on her palm. Crushable as a butterfly.

"Making love to you would ruin me, Ginny. And that's why I can't."

The ferocity of his yearning poured from him in rays. But his will was as palpable as a wall. It was as though he were fighting for his very life, which of course was all he'd known how to do since he was a boy.

"I see," she finally said.

She wasn't certain she did, entirely.

What if she never saw him again?

She looked at him as if it might be the last time, hoarding every second he remained in her vision. She was afraid, too. Because she didn't know how to comfort him. She couldn't, when clearly she was the source of his torment.

"Gabriel . . . ?" Her voice was threadbare.

"Yes, Ginny."

"Do you know . . . do you understand . . . how frightened I am about money?"

Pain fleetingly tensed his features. "I know," he said quietly.

Where did that leave her?

Something remained unsaid. Something she desperately needed to understand.

I look for heart-shaped rocks on the ground everywhere now.

And then she remembered the one that had magically materialized near her foot.

And then she thought she understood, and once again her breath was robbed. *Oh, Gabriel.*

He was terribly afraid of being hurt. And ashamed of being afraid.

But how could she know for sure?

What if she nudged him again? Not by goading him. But by

testing, one last time, the strength of his resistance, to see if it would give way. To see if the ultimate truth would emerge if she gave him one final push.

The rogue in her made her do it.

She leaned forward and said softly, "One night. One night in your bed. I'll do anything you want me to do. And after that, my brother's debt to you will be paid."

He closed his eyes, taking those words like a blow.

Her heart was pounding so hard the blood sang in her ears.

When he opened his eyes again, his expression was once again as unreadable as any expert gambler's.

"I'll give you my answer this evening."

He turned on his heel and closed the gate behind him as he left.

Chapter Eighteen

When Marchand returned to his room, he discovered the flowers in his vase had been replaced before they could finish dying. Just one of the little ways the Grand Palace on the Thames tenderly cared for their guests. *Protecting them from the illusion that all things must die*, he thought mordantly.

He'd learned early in life that sex was an appetite, a commodity, an escape. He'd never truly been innocent. In St. Giles, everyone did indeed do what they needed to do in order to survive another day. He'd fended off the advances of both men and women when he was younger. Later, he'd found surcease from loneliness and the endless struggle of survival courtesy of women who took his money. Together, they'd helped each other get through another day.

He was grateful to the women who took pains to show him what it meant to be a lover and not just a fucker. But the beauty and mystery of women's bodies taught him that, too, because they begged for exploration. He savored the power to make a woman lose her mind with pleasure. He believed it ought to be an equal exchange.

He'd never considered that his own battered, orphaned,

bastard hide might possess any specific intrinsic value to anyone because it contained *him*. He knew he was good looking, and he understood that came with advantages. But when he thought about it at all, he'd assumed his worth was measured in how much money he had, or in what he could do for someone else. It hadn't bothered him. He'd never known any different.

He hadn't considered that his touch—*his* touch—could be a soul-baring gesture of radical trust. That the way he touched could be a confession. A gift freely given. He'd never before thought: *I want to kiss* her *there in the hollow of her throat, so I can feel* her *pulse against my lips, feel the hum of* her *moan of pleasure, so I can savor the stunning miracle that this particular maddening, beautiful woman exists in the world at the same time that I do.*

He'd never before thought: *I want to watch her eyes go hazy when I trail my fingers over her skin. I want to watch the play of emotion and pleasure on her face as we make love.*

In the cozy, loving confines of this room, he was forced to think about all of that now.

When he touched her that way, there was no way Ginny wouldn't know that he loved her.

And God help him, he understood now what a gift that trust was.

He wanted her trust, freely given.

But he also wanted her to be able to choose to whom she gave it.

He wanted to be chosen.

He had never once been chosen in quite that way. Not in his entire life.

He wanted to be naked with her in every sense of the

word. Equal. Not as part of a financial transaction involving a giver and a taker. He wanted to *share* with her something entirely new.

In so doing, for the first time, he would be in some ways as innocent as she was.

His heart ached for the girls in St. Giles who had never had that choice.

He also understood devastation lay on the other side of it. Because after he made love to her, he would need to let her go. And she would take a piece of him with her.

He hadn't lied. She would indeed ruin him. For any other woman.

He'd considered as he stood there in the garden just telling her that he'd go ahead and strike the four-thousand-pound debt from his books. But what if she thought he was willing to pay any price *not* to have sex with her? Very darkly amusing.

And then . . . and then she'd tested him yet again.

Now he was curious about her motives.

He thought he understood why she'd taken that one last risk.

He loved that about her as much as he rued it. She was never boring, that girl.

And if he was right about her reasons, it meant for him a glimmer of hope that he hardly dared nurture.

Ah, Guinevere, sweetheart, he thought. *Just as I told you before that I wouldn't let you ruin me, I also told you that no one ever gets the better of me.*

And so, though he was as afraid now as he'd ever been in his life, he harbored one spark of hope.

He knew there really was no other way to know the truth for sure.

He was going to need to call her bluff.

* * *

Little battles of both the overt and covert varieties raged all over the sitting room that night.

While Dot indecisively twiddled a pawn between her fingers and hummed tunelessly, Mr. Delacorte waged a heroic inner battle against the urge to bellow "Just *move* the bloody thing!" But if she *did* move the bloody thing, he would win a rook. Which on the one hand would be satisfying—who didn't like winning a rook? But on the other hand would be maddening, because he'd explained several times that she *shouldn't* leave her rook exposed like that. And Dot would then be crushed. And he would feel as though he'd failed as a teacher. What would they call him when he became a martyr? St. Stanton, his first name? Or St. Delacorte? He imagined himself depicted on tapestries in churches, riding a donkey.

At the opposite end of the room, Mrs. Pariseau, Delilah, and Angelique were earnestly debating what book they ought to read aloud tonight, while Delilah's conscience continued wrestling with the fact that she hadn't yet told Mrs. Peck that she'd shouted "Shite!" in front of her son. Like a draft or a leak, she sensed the longer it remained unattended, the worse it would get.

Mrs. Peck had not yet brought Daniel down for a nightly visit.

Ginny occupied her own little table. She had only herself to blame for the agony of anticipation that made her incapable of doing anything but staring at the page of the book she'd brought down to the sitting room with her. The words had gone blurry.

She inwardly waged a battle over what she would do if he summoned her.

But she thought she already knew. There was only one thing she wanted. And only one way to get it.

Unbeknownst to Ginny, inside Gabriel Marchand, who as usual wasn't shy about staring at her, a battle over a decision had already been concluded. He had brought correspondence into the room and was apparently writing a letter at a little table.

Just as Mrs. Peck entered the sitting room holding Daniel by the hand, Dot at last, at long, long last, moved that pawn.

Mr. Delacorte sighed heavily. He made a *tsking* sound as his black queen sailed confidently across the diagonal to take Dot's rook. "Dot, do you remember what I told you about that particular pawn? You left your rook exposed, and my queen was waiting *right* there to take it. A better move might have been—"

But Dot was already clopping her knight over to the F3 square. She sat back and gave a gleeful clap. "Ha! Now your queen is in jail!"

Delacorte froze.

He stared at the board.

On the back rank, courtesy of the positions of two knights, a few pawns, and a bishop, his queen was well and truly trapped.

Lord Bolt, sitting at a table with Captain Hardy, leaned over and gave a low whistle. "Well. Look at that. She got you. You aren't getting out of that one. Not with your queen, anyway."

This was one of the most dire things that could happen in a chess game, everyone knew.

Delacorte reeled. "Dot . . . did you . . . did you *plan* that? Have you been planning that? Did you do that on purpose?"

His voice had gone a little croaky. Surely Dot hadn't been silently planning a *tactic*?

"Well, it all began when Adolfo decided to make the ultimate sacrifice," Dot explained.

"Who the *bloo*—" Mr. Delacorte darted a glance at the Epithet Jar. "Who is Adolfo?"

"The rook! He decided to sacrifice himself! That way, Sir Horatio, her true love, could be the one who heroically trapped your queen. She can't get out now. She's in jail!"

"Yes, we all see that," Delacorte said tensely. "Horatio is . . ."

"This knight." She pointed to the knight that had sealed off his queen's escape from the back rank. "He yearns for her, but she's married to Theodore the Second."

"Is Theodore the king?" Despite herself, Ginny was invested in this story.

"Yes!" Dot was thrilled with Ginny's insight. "You see it, too?" She looked triumphantly at Mr. Delacorte, feeling vindicated. "And little Peter helped." She pointed at the pawn.

"And her bishop is clearly there to administer last rites to your queen, Delacorte," Captain Hardy contributed.

Mr. Delacorte shot him a filthy look, and Captain Hardy grinned.

"Perhaps you should name your pieces, too, Mr. Delacorte,"

Dot said kindly. "That way you might be more careful with them."

He opened his mouth.

Then closed it again.

"How badly do you want to curse right now?" Lucien asked him.

"SHITE!" Daniel Peck bellowed.

Delacorte and Dot jumped so violently that the chess pieces keeled over and rolled, as if in agony. They hadn't noticed Daniel creeping up to the table.

Everyone in the room gave a start.

Mrs. Peck, who had just sat down, shot to her feet.

"Daniel Edward Peck!" She was blazing with embarrassed fury. "Where did you learn that word? From Mr. Delacorte? It was Mr. Delacorte, wasn't it, Daniel?"

Everyone stared at Mr. Delacorte.

Whose mouth dropped open.

Eventually nothing but an arid squeak of outraged injustice emerged from it.

Delilah couldn't bear it. She rose at once. "It was me."

A shocked gasp went up.

"Oh, *honestly*," Captain Hardy said irritably. "It's just a word."

Another gasp went up at that.

"Was it your first time?" Mr. Delacorte asked Delilah sympathetically.

Mrs. Peck was staring at her, aghast. "Mrs. *Hardy*! I was assured this was a genteel, exclusive boardinghouse. Why on earth . . . please help me to understand!"

Delilah was scarlet. "Mrs. Peck, Daniel was wandering alone on the third floor. I was bent over to look at a bit of peeling wallpaper. He pinched me and . . . that was the word that burst forth. He startled me badly."

"He pinched you? Where did he pinch you?" Mrs. Peck's tone was now indignant.

"On the third floor," Delilah repeated hopefully.

"But *where*?"

"Oh, it hardly matters, does it?" Delilah said desperately. Although she knew it rather did.

"On the bottom!" Delacorte cheerfully guessed. As though there would be a prize for the first correct answer.

"Thank you, Mr. Delacorte," Delilah said grimly. She was scarlet now.

Mrs. Peck's hands went up to cover her mouth. She was now clearly distressed. "Oh my good heavens. I'm so, so sorry, Mrs. Hardy. I'll have a word with our nurse! Four-year-olds can be so slippery. Daniel, why on earth did you *do* that?"

Daniel stared mutely at his mother with his big calf eyes. Clearly, he hadn't the faintest idea why he'd done that. He was four years old. Reason and impulse had not yet begun to work as a team.

"Round," he finally said.

"Round?" His mother was confused.

"And squishy."

Delilah closed her eyes.

"All right, that's enough." Captain Hardy stood. "Your son pinched my wife, Mrs. Peck. He frightened her. She shouted. She has already apologized to him, and now I think Daniel should apologize to her."

Daniel's face began to crumple.

"Daniel, do not cry," Captain Hardy requested reasonably.

So surprised by the conversational tone was he that Daniel, perhaps accidentally, obeyed.

"It hurts to be pinched, and it's an unkind thing to do," Captain Hardy continued gently and matter-of-factly, trying his best not to sound like a blockade captain. "You scared Mrs. Hardy. And while she is an adult, adults have feelings, just like you. You wouldn't like it if she pinched *you*, would you?"

He was careful not to sound accusing. He was presenting Daniel with a simple yes or no question.

Daniel shook his head.

"Daniel, tell Mrs. Hardy that you're sorry for pinching her." Mrs. Peck nudged her son.

"I'm sowwy for pinching you," he whispered.

"I accept your apology, Daniel," Delilah said with dignity. "And I'm sorry again for shouting a naughty word."

"Now, Mr. Peck, we would like you to put a pence in the jar," Captain Hardy told him. "Those sorts of words are not allowed in this room, so there is a small penalty."

As it turned out, Mr. Delacorte had an available penny. He passed it to Mrs. Peck, who gave it to Daniel, who bravely strode over to the jar and dropped in the penny.

Everyone began to cheer, then stopped abruptly when it occurred to them that it might just encourage Daniel to shout "SHITE" with abandon.

"Now, Daniel, sweetie," Delilah said, "do you want to come with me to see if Helga has any apple tarts left in the kitchen?"

"TAAAARRTS!" Daniel roared, and gave a gleeful hop.

Delilah led him off by the hand. He hopped the entire way down the stairs to the kitchen.

When Mr. Marchand abruptly stood, it was as if someone had swung a hammer at Ginny's heart like a gong.

It leaped into her throat.

"Well, on that note, I'll bid everyone good night," he said. "It's far too salty in here for my delicate constitution."

To good-natured laughter, everyone bid good night to him.

He didn't so much as glance at Ginny as he passed her table on the way out of the room.

In fact, so subtle had he been that she didn't notice the small, ragged scrap of paper on the table in front of her until he was gone.

She stared at it.

She turned it over with shaking hands and read:

Come to my room at eleven.

Chapter Nineteen

At about two minutes after eleven o'clock, Marchand greeted Ginny at the door of his room in the same attire that had made her lightheaded a few days previously. In other words: He was already half undressed.

She'd decided to wear her copper-colored silk for the occasion, instead of her night rail.

"You're a little late. I was beginning to worry that your courage had failed you," he said.

"When has my courage ever failed me?"

"Exactly how I reassured myself during those long moments of anticipation," he replied, somewhat silkily.

He stepped aside so she could enter the room.

The click of the door closing behind her seemed deafening.

She would be shocked if he couldn't hear the pounding of her heart, which sent the blood ringing in her ears.

The room was shadowy in the corners. But the fire was leaping so healthily high that Lucifer himself would have been right at home. It smelled headily like Marchand in here. Notes of bergamot and leather and bay rum, a little sweat.

The covers of his bed were turned down neatly.

At the sight of this her head went so light with fear and nerves, she nearly swooned on the spot. It seemed the scene was set for their transaction as surely as one would lay the table for a banquet.

He was quietly watching her take in the room.

"Would you like some brandy? It might help with the nerves."

She opened her eyes. "Yes. Certainly. Please. If you're having some."

"And then we'll get right to it."

"Oh. Ah. All right."

It's not like shoeing a horse, he'd once told her.

She barely heard the glug of the brandy over the pounding of her heart. Her breath sounded inordinately loud and ragged in her ears.

He handed the glass to her.

His eyes widened when she tossed all of it back, then coughed and spluttered.

She handed him the glass, and he laid it gently aside on the table near the settee.

"Now, I'd like to remind you that our agreement was that you'd let me do anything I wanted to do. Anything. *Anything at all.*" His voice was all silk, sin, and promise. "Is that correct, Guinevere?"

Oh, Christ. She *had* said that. What had possessed her to say that?

"Yes." She whispered it.

"I'd like you to stand in the middle of the room and take off your dress."

A long silence ensued as she took in this request. "W-what will you be doing?"

"I'll be sitting over there, watching you take off your dress." He pointed to the settee.

"Oh."

There was another little silence.

"You can begin now," he said politely.

He settled back on the settee with a brandy snifter cupped in his hand.

Her hands were shaking so violently that it was long seconds before she was able to seize hold of her laces. For a moment, she seemed in danger of knotting them rather than tugging them lose.

He never took his eyes from her, and he didn't move a hair.

She fumbled some more, clawing to loosen the laces further.

He'd been so still that she gave a start when he suddenly raised his eyebrows.

Finally she was able to spread the laces wider apart.

The sleeves of her dress sagged to her shoulders. The whisper-slide of the silk over her skin was like gentle hands.

She pushed one sleeve lower. Then lower still.

Marchand remained still, quietly observing this extraordinarily awkward show.

But his gathering tension was palpable.

Was he really going to allow her to do it?

All she had to do now was shimmy out of the whole dress and let it pool to the ground at her ankles.

She stopped.

The tension, and the silence, stretched like a drawn-back bowstring.

Of course she couldn't do it.

But he'd already known that.

He'd done a magnificent job, however, of making his point about the folly of testing him.

All she wanted now was to make sure this extraordinary man felt safe to tell her the truth.

His eyes widened as she slowly moved over to the settee.

His breathing seemed suspended as she gingerly lowered herself to sit next to him.

The silence stretched.

She could hear the in-out rush of his breath.

"Gabriel . . . ?" she whispered.

"Yes, Guinevere?"

She was very nervous. "You win."

"I beg your pardon?" But he didn't sound surprised. His voice was so gentle.

"I'm afraid I can't . . . I can't do this." She swallowed. "Not like this. And I understand now. Why you can't. And . . . why . . . we shouldn't."

"Oh?" The word was so tender. He was hoarse. "Tell me why, Ginny."

He was going to make her do it.

Oh, she was scared to death.

But what choice did a leaper have but to leap?

And so, joyously, recklessly, she did just that.

"Because I love you, too."

He stopped breathing.

She witnessed her words utterly transform him. Soften him. Illuminate him. Until it seemed to her that he glowed in the firelight like a painting of a medieval saint.

He drew in a long, shuddering breath, as if he'd at last been released from a locked box.

"Yes." His voice was graveled. "I love you, Ginny."

For a moment they merely sat in the presence of this glorious, hopeless thing they had inadvertently created. Ginny had never realized that love was an atmosphere. It felt like infinite peace bound with wild joy.

She watched the play of light and shadow over his face, committing the way he looked in this moment to memory.

She could feel the cool air of the room against her back, which was still exposed by her loosened laces.

"Well. I suppose I should be going," she said thickly.

For the space of several breaths, he didn't reply.

"That's probably best." His voice was hoarse with sorrow.

She willed her body to rise.

It simply wouldn't respond. It was as if she'd commanded it to do something that was fundamentally unnatural to it, like flying.

Here is where I belong was its silent protest. *Wherever he is.*

But her body would need to learn to do without him.

Her heart would need to learn to do without him.

Sitting with him now, it suddenly seemed dizzyingly inconceivable to ever be without him. The future yawned like a chasm.

It's all too much for any of us, he'd said. *Life is.*

He blurred as her eyes filled with tears.

She was scarcely aware that she had dropped her face into her hands until she felt the tears slipping through her fingers.

"Guinevere." It was an aching whisper. "Oh, sweetheart. Ginny, don't cry."

He leaned forward. She felt his hands gently cradle her face.

She lifted her head. His eyes had gone glittery with tears, too. She saw herself reflected in his pupils.

He collected her tears with feather-light strokes of his thumbs.

He leaned forward and pressed whisper-soft kisses on her damp eyelids. One at a time.

He laid his lips lingeringly on her forehead.

And when she tipped her face up, their lips brushed.

She could feel the resistance in him, the uncertainty, as well as the tamped need that made his limbs tremble.

She shouldn't tempt him. But her will was not quite as strong as his, and fierce need had sovereignty over sense.

She parted her lips.

He moaned softly when she touched her tongue to his.

And as they spiraled slowly, deeply, irrevocably, hungrily into the kiss, she hooked her hands in her bodice and dragged it down to her waist.

She gently reached for his hands and drew them up to her bare breasts.

He drew in a sharp breath.

"Ginny." His voice was shredded with yearning. "Are you sure?"

But he'd already filled his hands with the satin weight of her breasts.

"I'm sure." Her voice was still rough from tears. "But no bargains. I just want you. It's just me and you."

When he dragged his thumbs hard over the stiff peaks of her nipples, she gave a little wild cry of stunned plea-sure. He half groaned, half growled, like an animal at last unchained.

She got hold of his shirt and tugged. Together they freed him of it.

She threw it across the room as if it were her enemy.

The aggressively male beauty revealed scrambled her thoughts like a punch to the head. The gleaming slopes of his shoulders, the biceps nearly the width of her thighs, the curling hair over pectorals as hard as a table, cut in facets, like a jewel. Before she could reach for him, he slid his hands to her back, lowered her to the settee, and closed his mouth over her nipple, licked, then lightly nipped the pink tip.

She cried out as pleasure pierced her. Her body arced up against him. "*Gabriel.*"

He circled her nipple with his tongue, then sucked. The onslaught of glorious sensation made her breath come hot and ragged.

"Fucking hell, the beauty of you," he rasped.

And while his lips were busy teasing her nipple, his hands were sliding her dress down over her legs, down and down. The air of the room was on the entirety of her skin. She was nude. He was not.

"I want to feel your skin against mine," she whispered to him.

Her wish was his command. He crouched, slid his hands beneath her, scooped her up, and effortlessly ferried her over to the bed. He abandoned her there for two seconds while he got out of his trousers, and then she was in his arms once again. She felt the primal shock of his cock, swollen, hard, and shockingly large, pressed against her thigh.

She turned to him at once. He engulfed her in his arms; she looped hers around his neck, reveling in the meeting of skin, the chafe of her nipples against his chest, the roughness of the curly hair of his thighs against the smoothness of hers. Their lips met, melded in an inebriating kiss, a searching, carnal dance of tongues as he set his hands free over her body. His palms and fingers roamed over the slopes of her buttocks, skimming along the sharp blades of her shoulders, down the pearls of her spine, slipping between her thighs to find the satiny, vulnerable skin there, feathering across her breasts, tracing filigree shapes over her nipples, revealing pathways of exquisite pleasure to her. She rippled, sighing, in thrall to it, asking for more. She felt as though she were being both claimed and introduced to herself.

She watched his face, riveted by, reveling in, his obvious rapt pleasure in the feel of her. His gray eyes were all pupil. He was a beloved stranger in that moment. It seemed shocking to her that she would willingly lie naked with someone who could easily crush her. It was equally shocking how very badly she wanted to taste and touch every inch of him. She had every intention of doing it.

He kissed her throat, where her pulse thumped. He traced the whorls of her ear with his tongue and she sighed, turning to aid him.

His hand glided over the black curls between her legs, then his fingers slipped between, and she moaned and gave a jerk at this new startling bliss. Her legs slipped open wider.

She was slick and hot.

"Move with me, Ginny."

Her hips seemed to know what to do, just as his fingers seemed to know what to do. He circled and stroked, like a magician calling bliss from every corner of her being to gather where his fingers danced, more swiftly, then harder. Until her skin felt made of bright cinders. Until her breath came in hot gusts. Frightened and exulted, she was hurtling toward something extraordinary, something she needed more than life.

"Gabriel . . . *please* . . . what is *happening* . . . *help* me . . ."

And she was screaming his name as if she'd been thrown over a cliff.

She was smithereens of bliss.

He held her as her body shook in the throes of release and kissed her throat, her lips, her breasts, as she floated up among the stars.

He bridged her, balancing on one arm, his cock gripped in his hand. She arched up, eager to take him into her body.

With a thrust he was inside it. She gasped.

So strange and beautiful, how her tightness softened to receive him.

She saw herself reflected in his eyes, which were hot and hazed.

"Sweetheart. You feel . . . so good . . . dear God . . . I don't want to hurt you. Hold on to me, love."

She dragged her fingers over his chest and he softly hissed in his pleasure. His hips drew back and thrust again. She obeyed; she wrapped her arms around him, locked her legs around his back, as if he were a comet she would be riding through the universe. She arched up to take him more deeply. The chafe of his chest against her nipples and the friction of his cock inside her colluded to bank again that shocking bliss; she chased it, knowing now where it would take her, her hands sliding down to notch against his buttocks, holding him closer, urging him on. She knew the wild triumph of watching his control slip away as he lost himself in her body. How his eyes went remote and fierce as their bodies collided ever more swiftly, each racing toward bliss.

"Gabriel . . . I . . . *please* . . . I'm . . ."

Her head thrashed back as a silent scream tore from her and shook her like a rag again. She distantly heard her own name on a harsh cry.

He spilled hotly on her thigh. She wrapped him in her arms so she could feel him shudder in the throes of his release.

He found a handkerchief on the table near the bed and gently cleaned her thigh.

Then he gathered her up. She curled up in his arms, her buttocks pressed against his cock, her head resting on his huge biceps. She turned to kiss it. Then bite it a little, because it looked delicious. Then she kissed it again.

His breath was soft on the back of her neck.

"Guinevere," he whispered. "Guinevere. You are precious. And I love you."

He said this as though these were the last words he'd ever say to her. As though he'd thought about it the way he'd thought about "beloved." He wanted her to know.

She'd been the strong one; that was her assignment. Her mother, desperate and knowing she was dying, had anointed her. For so long Ginny had not been allowed to be fragile, to come apart, to surrender. In choosing this, she had reclaimed herself.

You can decide the point of you, he'd said.

She rolled out of his arms and propped herself up on her elbows to gaze down at him.

They regarded each other somberly, searching for traces of regret or wariness.

Finally, she drew a finger along the clean, hard line of his jaw. His eyes went soft. What a luxury it seemed to touch him anywhere she pleased. "I'm not sorry. Are you?"

The ramifications of this night hovered on the outskirts of their awareness like storm clouds. Therein lay the only source of regret. Now that they knew what it was like to make love to each other, everything and everyone after would feel counterfeit.

"How could I be sorry for the sweetest night of my life?" He turned his head to lay a kiss on her palm.

She lowered herself to his side again, and his arms went around her. She drifted drowsily, allowing herself to feel only the heat radiating from this beautiful naked man, the blessed peace of her well-loved, sated body, the rightness of having given herself to him. The magnitude of what it meant to love him.

Presently she realized he'd fallen into a doze. The rise and fall of his breath against her back lulled her as though she drifted on a gentle sea. She didn't stir. She scarcely even entertained a thought. It seemed enough to exist in this miraculous moment and to experience being loved.

Gabriel murmured something unintelligible. There was a sharp edge of fear to it.

Suddenly he shot bolt upright with a hoarse cry, panting as though he'd been running.

He turned to her, his eyes wild and dazed.

They went at once relieved and grateful when he realized she wasn't a dream.

"I'm sorry." He rasped. "I just . . . sometimes . . . when I dream . . ."

"I'm here." She laid a hand over his heart and felt it thundering. She left her hand against him until the franticness slowed. And then she kissed his chest, gently, while he drew his fingers in a caress along her spine.

I'm here. It was what he'd said to her that day on the bench in the park. As though there was no danger he wouldn't defeat for her.

She'd never felt so safe.

What a privilege it would be to be the person he turned to when old terrors jolted him from sleep.

A serrated grief slashed her heart. She could not ever be that person.

"Your arse"—his voice had gone low and rough and velvet— "is spectacular. Two pearls, side by side. I love it very much."

She laughed and blushed furiously at his coarse eloquence.

"You are, in fact, so beautiful I think my head might explode. I cannot adequately absorb it." He trailed his hands up over her rib cage and claimed her breasts again.

She knew what he meant. She wanted to wallow in him.

She leaned forward and gently kissed his nipple, then traced it with her tongue.

"I like that," he said, his voice lulled. "Well done."

His cock was stirring again, and the responding heat between her legs gave a pulse, wanting him again.

He reached for a cravat dangling across his bedpost. "We can do something fancy, if you like."

Her heart gave an anticipatory leap. "All right. Perhaps not spanking, though."

"Not tonight." He wrapped the silky length of his cravat around her eyes and tied it loosely. "All right?"

"Am I going to walk the plank?"

"Ride it, of a certainty."

She gave a nervous laugh.

Everything was completely dark.

She was utterly at his mercy.

Which was unutterably thrilling.

"Here," he whispered. "Lie back, sweetheart." He urged her backward in his arms until her head rested on the pillow.

"Tell me anytime if you're uncomfortable."

For long moments, nothing happened.

All was silence, apart from the crackle of the fire. Anticipation ramped, and she supposed that was the point. Deprived of her vision for the moment, her other senses greedily came alive to the feel of the sweat drying on her skin, and the sheets on her back, and the delicious musk of a nearby sweaty man.

Then his hand slid softly across her belly.

She gave a start and moaned low and long, the pleasure honed by anticipation and surprise. It surged swiftly out from where he touched her, the way a rock displaces water. She felt it everywhere in her body.

He dragged his hand over the mound of her belly to her hip and back again.

And then suddenly his touch vanished from her skin.

Her heart beat with spiky longing for the next sensation.

She gasped when his mouth closed around her nipple, and he traced and teased it with his tongue, then sucked.

"*Oh . . .*" She gasped and drew her knees up.

"Good?" he whispered. Seconds later his fingers began trailing down the seam between her ribs, and twining in the curls between her legs, and the feeling was odd and gorgeously illicit, as if another man had come to join them.

He trailed kisses now from her breasts to her navel. She was mesmerized by the magical collusion between her skin and his fingertips. How would she ever have known?

"You are all over satin." His voice sounded drugged. "Your skin is the most decadent thing I have ever in my life touched."

But then his hands vanished from her again.

In the silence she could hear her own quickened breathing.

A guttural animal sound of almost shocked, agonized bliss when his tongue stroked where she was wet and aching.

He didn't stop.

Just in case he had any plans to do that, she thought she'd better say, "Don't stop. Oh, please don't stop."

He didn't. With relentless, merciless skill he used his tongue, and lips, and fingers to drive her to the brink of madness with pleasure heretofore unimaginable. Her breath sobbed from her until she shattered again, white lights exploding behind her eyes.

"I want you again. Please, Ginny. I need you now," he begged.

She reached for him, and as she took him into her body in the dark and he moved in her swiftly, urgently, she felt as though she had become something elemental. She was pleasure, she was the night, she was free, she was love, she was his.

They clung to each other in silence for a long time after he came.

She held him until his breathing settled into slumber.

She kissed his face softly. When she slid from his arms, she understood how Lucifer must have felt when he was evicted from heaven.

He untied her cravat blindfold at last.

She slid from the bed. She gathered her dress and felt herself returning to her body. And now she was Ginny, with all that entailed, and that meant she needed to return to her room and face what tomorrow would bring.

Chapter Twenty

He awoke alone the following day, stark naked, sideways across his bed, and chilly. His pillow smelled like her, and so did his skin. His cravat was trailing from his open hand. The memories came in such a vivid rush that his breath went short.

He forced himself to move when what he wanted to do was savor, and remember. But if the maids came in and found him like this he'd likely be evicted like the rules threatened.

He had an important meeting today. So he washed and shaved and dressed in crisp clothing. In the little mirror in his room he looked like a man who had shagged all night. It was a good look for him, he decided.

At ten o'clock, Farnham, Sydenham's footman, brought Marchand up to a room lined with bookcases and furnished in mahogany and gilt.

Sydenham rose from behind a fine desk—not nearly as fine as the one Marchand had in his office, he ascertained—to greet him.

"Mr. Marchand. Always a pleasure to see you. Imagine my delight when you wrote to me to request a private conversation.

Have you a business proposition in mind? Something juicy, perhaps?"

He gestured to a chair and Gabriel sat down across from him.

He didn't reply.

He merely regarded Sydenham wordlessly, expressionlessly. Fixedly.

Long enough for the earl's smile to drift away from his face and for unease to settle into his expression.

"I know what you did," Marchand said finally.

And because he noticed everything, he saw the minute tensing of the Earl of Sydenham's jaw. The spasm of muscle at his cheekbone. The twitch of a brow.

It wasn't shock.

It was guilt.

For a moment, it didn't seem as though the earl would respond.

"I beg your pardon, Marchand?"

"I know that you drugged the young Earl of Highgrove's brandy that night at Lucifer's Fall."

The earl's mouth parted slightly.

No sound emerged. His eyes had flickered to blankness for an instant, in shock.

Marchand continued calmly. "I know you put a so-called headache powder known to cause hallucinations in the earl's brandy. And then you proceeded to take advantage of his resulting incapacitation to win fifteen thousand pounds." He shook his head. "Hardly sporting of you, Lord Sydenham. Very, very, *very* against the rules you agreed to when you became a member."

Marchand's heart was now, in fact, thudding like a war drum.

He'd been seething ever since he'd confirmed this.

"Come now, Marchand." The earl gave a little laugh. "I've never known you to be irrational."

"We have a witness to your deed."

He'd told Ginny that he never lied anymore. But this lie was strategic, and necessary. He had Hogarth's word. And he believed him.

He wanted to see what happened to the earl's expression when he said it.

The earl was a novice at this sort of thing, clearly. He'd gone absolutely motionless for a few seconds longer than mere surprise would dictate. And that, Marchand knew full well, was the telltale sign of someone internally scrambling to get their story together.

"I can't imagine why you believe you have a witness for something that never happened," Sydenham finally said, with a little laugh.

"I have eyes everywhere on the betting floor. It's my responsibility to keep every single man in my establishment safe, after all. My reputation and my livelihood are staked upon it, as are the lives of some of the finest men in London. And when I made a few subtle inquiries, it was just a matter of the right person coming forward. We know for a fact that the only person from whom the young Earl of Highgrove accepted a drink was you. He was sober when he arrived at Lucifer's Fall."

The earl's mouth worked, but no sound emerged. He was clearly unaccustomed to thinking quickly.

"Oh, and also?" Marchand reached into his coat and retrieved two folded documents. "This is a signed statement from the apothecary from whom you bought the headache powder stating that you did indeed buy it from him and were indeed aware of its properties. And this is the receipt with your signature on it. Dated a day before the event."

He unfolded both of them and held them up so the earl could read them. Sydenham leaned over his desk to peer at them.

Color fled his face, leaving it gray.

"These documents are not proof that I did anything."

Yet he couldn't seem to tear his eyes away from them.

Marchand ignored this.

"I take it very, very personally that a young man who paid for a pleasant experience, someone who not only trusted *me*, but trusted *everyone* there, was so grossly abused."

Sydenham finally risked looking up at Marchand then.

He recoiled from the look in his eyes.

"Come now, Marchand," he cajoled, sounding hoarse. "I only meant to have a bit of fun. A sprinkle of powder couldn't have killed the lad. Call it an initiation, of sorts, for a new member. I thought it would be amusing, and it was! I've never seen anyone dance on a billiards table before, have you?"

Marchand prayed for restraint. His hands twitched to close around the man's throat.

"Anything could kill anyone, given the right conditions, Lord Sydenham. Ask me how I know." He smiled almost tenderly.

The earl went still. For the first time, rank fear flared in his eyes.

"The main thing is that what you did wasn't sporting at all. In fact, I consider it cheating." Marchand said this silkily. "And I think you know how I feel about cheating. And what I do to cheaters."

Sydenham was dead quiet now. A neat row of sweat beads had appeared at the earl's hairline.

"But I'm giving you two choices. You can tell Miss Woodville that you've decided to tear up her brother's vowels out of the goodness of your heart in order to honor your *friendship* with her parents"—he gave that word the most ironic frisson imaginable—"and resign your membership from Lucifer's Fall. If you choose not to do that, I will ban you without comment from Lucifer's Fall and strike your wager from the books, as per our rules regarding cheating, and allow the ton at large to talk as they may. If questions are asked about the reasons for your absence, I will not hesitate to answer them truthfully. In both instances, you will forfeit your membership fees, which will become the property of Lucifer's Fall. Either way, you're never welcome on the premises again. And if I witness or hear about any comment, protest, or slander regarding me or the Woodvilles from you, concerted steps will be taken to stop it."

A long, long silence followed.

"I can ruin you, Marchand." The earl's belligerence was unconvincing. His voice shook.

"You're certainly welcome to try." Marchand smiled politely. "I do wonder, however, Sydenham, what you think I'm unwilling to do in order to exact retribution."

And with that, he saw the fight leave the earl. The man was sickly pale and resigned.

Had the ancient, festering wound of losing Ginny's mother to his rival driven the earl to this? Had he remained close to Ginny's father only for the opportunity to be near Ginny's mother? Was he witnessing how thwarted love could warp a man? A chill traced Marchand's spine. Such a long time to grieve a lost love.

"I'll just sit right here while you write the letter to Miss Woodville, shall I?"

Sydenham's hand trembled as he reached for his quill.

* * *

A few hours later, Marchand witnessed the crushing weight of the debt lift from Ginny when she read Sydenham's letter. The very shape of her face and the way she held her body transformed, softened.

He'd given it to her in the little park in front of the Grand Palace on the Thames, because that's where she was when he'd returned from the earl's house. And for a shining, futile instant, he imagined coming home to her every day, to a garden just like that one. Longing sliced right down through him.

Finally, she closed her eyes and exhaled at length.

She sat silently, clearly refamiliarizing herself with how the world felt now that a sword suspended by a single hair, à la Damocles, wasn't dangling over her.

They sat quietly together.

It made his throat tight with emotion. Gratitude, and guilt, and grief.

Did he deserve the guilt? Did he blame himself at all? Should he?

Should he extend to himself grace?

He didn't know the answers.

He had created the only kind of life he'd known how to create. Her brother had walked in and gambled their life away.

If that debt had never existed, he never would have met Guinevere Woodville. He'd known a weak moment or two when he'd wondered whether that would have been more merciful for both of them.

But at last he'd fixed it.

Now she was free to go home, negotiate marriage settlements for her sisters, and marry the third son of a duke, should Francis get around to proposing. If that's what she wanted to do. She would fulfill her mother's final wish for her. She would have the life she'd long anticipated, as secure a life as fate would allow anyone.

He'd done what he could to take care of her, and that was really all that mattered.

"I've had another surprise, too," he said. He produced Hogarth's letter, which had at last arrived.

"I agreed his plan to pay off his debt by teaching was a sound and fine plan, and I've written to tell him so. I will have contracts drawn up for him to sign soon."

He was hard-pressed to imagine a greater pleasure than the expression on Ginny's face in that moment. Amazement and pride and relief. "Do you see, Gabriel? He's a good person, isn't he? I'm so proud of him."

"He is," Marchand confirmed. "You did a good job raising him, Ginny."

"So . . . it's over? All of it? Just like that?"

"Just like that. I've stricken all of your brother's debts from the books at Lucifer's Fall. You are all free."

He lost himself in the luxury of her gaze for a moment.

"Gabriel . . ."

"Yes?"

"Did you have anything to do with . . . any of this? With Sydenham's decision or Hogarth's proposal to be a teacher?"

"Sydenham had a change of heart, Ginny." He said this gently but firmly. "And Hogarth is a fine young man who made a mistake, and I approve of the way he intends to see it right. And didn't you find *three* heart-shaped stones? Surely it was all bound to turn out fine in the end."

She didn't reply. But the slight, tender curve of her smile told him she didn't believe him.

God, she looked lovely today. Irresistibly pristine and proper, in a high-necked yellow walking dress and a straw bonnet tied with a matching ribbon. But anyone who had the wherewithal to look closely could see how thoroughly loved and ravished she'd been last night. The faint lavender shadows beneath her eyes. Her lips just a little pinker and fuller, swollen from endless kissing. The drowsy, sultry heat in her eyes when she looked at him.

He risked tracing her lips with a finger. She kissed the tip of it.

He could hear voices nearby—it sounded like Dot, and perhaps Helga—or he would have stolen a kiss.

When he heard the wheels of a hack approaching, he pulled in a resigned breath.

"I hate to leave you now," he said quietly. "But I've business that cannot wait. I'll see you tonight in the sitting room, Miss

Woodville. And you've a standing invitation for eleven o'clock in my room."

* * *

That night, Ginny and Marchand listened to Mrs. Pariseau read from *The Arabian Nights Entertainments* in the presence of all of her new friends from the Grand Palace on the Thames.

Then Ginny bid everyone a fond farewell. She would be leaving for Sussex the following morning on the mail coach, and that meant she needed to rise very early, even earlier than the maids. She needed to finish packing her trunks and valise this evening.

She was hugged and cheek-kissed and patted (Daniel did the patting), and she basked in the shower of genuine affection while Marchand looked on.

"You'll have to return to fetch your donkey. But I'm happy to look after her while you're away," Mr. Delacorte told her.

"Thank you, Mr. Delacorte. I know she's in good hands."

She turned to Marchand.

He bowed to her. "It's been a pleasure, albeit a brief one, Miss Woodville."

"Likewise, Mr. Marchand." She curtsied sedately.

* * *

At eleven o'clock that evening, Ginny appeared at his bedroom door in her night rail. She'd thrown a pelisse over it.

His door was already ajar. She pushed it open, closed it, and locked it.

She threw off the night rail and pelisse, kicked both aside, and went naked into his arms.

They made love wordlessly, with a desperate, thorough, tender savagery. Licking, kissing, clawing, sucking, colliding. Sighs, the slide of hands over skin, their names moaned in begging cadences, and the crackle of the fire were the only sounds.

Finally they lay, spent and sweaty, side by side, hands twined, in silence.

"I cannot bear the thought of never seeing you again," she whispered finally, anguished. "And I cannot imagine never seeing my family again. And that's what might very well happen if I stay with you."

His heart shot into his throat.

He'd asked nothing of her and demanded nothing of her. He had resigned himself to taking what he could, and to the pain of missing her when she was gone.

This was the first time she'd mentioned she'd even thought of staying with him.

He scarcely dared breathe, let alone speak.

He considered what to say.

"I meant everything I said to you in the hall the other day, Ginny," he said carefully. "About what I will give you. What I will do for you. There is nothing I wouldn't do for you." Too many endings were nigh; he could not bear the miracle of hope's resurrection only to watch that die again, too.

She was quiet. They both sensed the heaviness in the room.

He dragged his hand along the eloquent curve of her waist to the swell of her hip. "Sometimes, Ginny . . . I think you would feel better about this if I was just a little ashamed of being what I am."

"Never." She was indignant. "Do *not* put words in my mouth, just because you want to goad me into an argument so we feel less sorry about parting."

That made him smile. She was too bloody smart, and so effortlessly able to stand up to him. How he enjoyed it.

"Then perhaps you are a little ashamed of *yourself* for loving me."

It mordantly amused him that she actually paused to think this over. "I swear to you, that's not true. I'm not ashamed of you, and I'm not ashamed of myself. I think you are remarkable, and I love you."

"Tell me another word for it."

She considered this, too. "It's fear."

"Fear of shame," he countered relentlessly.

That was the crux of it, and it stopped her cold.

"You don't under—" She stopped herself.

His temper stirred. "You know very well I understand. You wish you didn't have to make a choice, and I wish you didn't have to make a choice, but you do. Because whether you want to view it that way, you do have a choice. I am who I am, and you are who you are. I will give you the whole goddamn world. But I can't change who I am."

She half laughed, half groaned. "You've *ruined* me, Gabriel. You've ruined *me*. Not just because of this . . ." She gestured at the bed. "But for anyone who is . . . bearable."

He laughed shortly. "Oh, have I now? Sorry to be the bearer of bad news, Miss Woodville, but you were ruined when I met you. That is, maybe your sisters *are* delicate and precious and your brother is sheltered, because you bravely bore the burdens that turned you into someone who could love only a man like me. Maybe you developed like whiskey in a barrel while your siblings remained chamomile tea. And maybe that isn't fair. But when I met you, you were already meant *only* for me."

The possessive, claiming words had the ring of prophesy. They thrilled her to her core and yet scared her, too.

If he was right, what did it mean for their futures, if they remained apart?

The silence was long and fraught.

"Stay with me," he whispered. His voice was frayed, aching.

She knew how much it cost him to risk saying that.

"I can't."

He squeezed his eyes closed as if a vise were clamping his heart.

"But I also can't imagine never seeing you again," she whispered.

He threw an arm over his eyes. "All right," he said evenly, tightly. "Picture, if you will, this version of the future. You'll marry the third son of a duke. I will secretly fuck you when you visit the ton because I am and always will be absolutely helpless to resist you until the end of my days, because I have *never* known this kind of pleasure with a woman, and you will naturally be helpless to resist me. Because I will take from you, Ginny, anything you're willing to give me. Whenever you want to give it. You will have his children. And you will think about me when he's on top of you."

She was appalled. "That's horrible! You're horrible!"

"*Yes*. And yet you love me, so what does that make you?"

She began to softly weep. Gabriel let her do it, even as every tear scored his heart like claws. Even as he half hated himself. Even though all of this pain had been expected. Neither one of them apparently knew how to suffer this in any noble and dignified sort of way.

"You're not horrible," she said finally, thickly, wearily. "I'm sorry. I just don't want to hurt you and I still don't know what to do. I just know that I must leave for now."

He stroked her damp hair away from her face. His throat was tight.

"No, I'm sorry, love. I fight dirty when I'm hurting or scared. But I don't want to hurt or scare you."

His voice was thick. He had never confessed such a thing to anyone else in his life, but that was because no one else had ever been able to strip away all of his defenses in such a way that he'd never felt safer.

"I know. I think you know that I can take it. At least we know how to apologize."

He gave a soft laugh.

"I do understand why you need to leave. Please know that all I truly want is for you to have what you want, whatever you decide that may be. I will abide by it. Come back to me if you can."

She kissed his forehead. She kissed his eyelids, one at a time. Then his temples. With each kiss she hoped to soothe a little more of his heartache.

When she finally laid her lips over his, he captured them with his own, greedily, latched his arm around her, and took the kiss deep, and searching, thoroughly claiming, until they were both restlessly aroused.

As he did, her hand wandered over his chest. Traced the gullies between the muscles, savored the powerful rise of them.

She took her lips away from him to drag her tongue down his throat, followed by her fingers. She traced her tongue around his nipple, then nipped. His legs shifted, stirred, at the sharp rush of pleasure. "Ginny," he whispered. Mesmerized.

Never, ever had anyone made love to him this way. With devastating tenderness and innocently carnal abandon.

The flat of her hand smoothed over his belly; as his cock stirred and swelled, she slipped her hand between his thighs and stroked. His legs dropped apart to abet her as she took the head of his cock into her mouth, traced it with her tongue, sucked.

He groaned raggedly. "Oh Christ. Please. Yes."

She licked and stroked and sucked until he was as hard as lumber.

"Inside you. Ginny, I want to be inside you."

She rose up over him, and he showed her how to guide his cock into her.

When he was seated her head went back on a gasp.

He groaned low in his throat.

"Move with me, sweetheart."

She did, but with evil languor, rising slowly, slowly up, sinking back down to take his whole length. Teasing herself, teasing him.

He gripped her hips and thrust up.

She refused to let him control the speed. She tortured him with leisurely skill, gazing down at him like a conqueror.

He was mesmerized by the sway of her breasts. By the sheen of sweat on her pearly skin. By the hazed, passion-drugged intensity of her beautiful eyes. By the surprisingly talented cruelty with which she was driving both of them mad.

Finally, she moved faster.

He thought his head might explode.

He tasted his own sweat as it poured down his face. He moaned like a man being killed as nearly unendurable waves of pleasure were banked and banked. "Love, I'm *begging* you."

He thrust up again, reaching to stroke where they were joined.

Her head fell back on a cry. She set both of them free.

In a frenzied collision of hips they drove each other to the brink and at last, at last, over it.

His bliss came at him like an andiron. He blacked out briefly, her name a harsh cry, an anguish of ecstasy. He nearly fucking wept.

He was undone.

She collapsed over him.

He slid his hands down the satiny skin of her back. Over the curve of her arse.

He slipped from her and gathered her in his arms.

Their rough breath mingled as dawn peeked through the gap of his curtains.

"Gabriel, you are precious, and I love you. Now and forever," she whispered.

She kissed his mouth softly one more time.

He watched her without a word as she quietly dressed.

She gently closed the door behind her when she left.

* * *

Mr. Pike brought her trunk and her valise out to the park in front of the Grand Palace on the Thames in the pink light of dawn. He offered to wait with her, but as luck would have it, Mr. Marchand was up early, too. He told Pike he would be happy to wait with Miss Woodville.

Mr. Pike, who was far from naive, left them to it.

Neither one of them could say a word.

Everything had been said.

And then a hack rolled into view, and Marchand hailed it.

He helped the driver load her trunk and valise, and then he turned to her.

"Ask your mother for a sign," he said shortly.

"I will," she promised.

"I love you. Godspeed, Guinevere."

He kissed her mouth, swiftly and hard. Heedless of who might see.

(Gordon the cat and the driver of the hack were the only ones who did.)

And for one final time, he closed the hack door.

It took Guinevere Woodville away from him.

* * *

Marchand sank down on the little bench in the park and closed his eyes. He tipped his head back and let the rising sun touch his lids, his throat. All of it felt gentle on his raw spirit: the little park, the breeze, the cat winding around his ankles. The birds starting up their songs.

He wanted a home like this.

All along he'd thought St. Giles had prepared him only for a life in hells. When really, viewed from another angle, with one twist of the kaleidoscope, it had prepared him for the heaven that was loving Guinevere Woodville.

He'd learned that he didn't need to keep climbing up those ladder rungs forever.

Loving and being loved was all the distance he needed from his past in St. Giles. It was everything he'd needed for so long.

His soul was downright bruised from the infinite stretching it had done lately. But he'd long ago learned that love and pain lived hand in hand, and the privilege of loving was worth any price. Michael had taught him that.

It wasn't that he had no fear of what might happen next.

But he was at peace.

Because he knew Ginny was a gambler at heart.

He'd already set their forever in motion. It would be ready when she came to claim it. To claim him.

What she didn't know was that he held one final card. He'd refused to play it, even though he was certain it was the winning one. Even though it might have kept her here.

Because that wasn't the way he wanted to win.

Chapter Twenty-One

Ginny made the final leg of her journey back to the Wood-ville house in a horse-drawn cart, courtesy of a neighbor who'd seen her disembark at the coaching inn. He left her and her trunks at the foot of her drive, by her request. She stood and stared at her home, a grand pile of pale gray stone, soft and worn and well-loved as the sitting room at the Grand Palace on the Thames.

But her heart, which had ached with a near unendurabil-ity the entirety of the trip home, at last lifted a little. Even though she could see William nibbling on the flowers around the fountain.

How would she feel if she was never welcome within its walls ever again?

It was her brother's home, in truth; it was her brother's pre-rogative to decide who would be welcome within its walls. She could not imagine him shunning her. After all, he'd offered to work for Marchand.

She walked up the drive, her valise bumping against her leg.

The door of the house burst open.

All of her siblings, who clearly had been watching from the

upstairs windows, tumbled out of the house and fell upon her with hugs and kisses.

"I fixed it" was the first thing she said to Hogarth. "I fixed all of it. Everything is fine now."

His expression went stunned, as though he'd taken a blow to the head.

The color drained from his face.

"Get him, girls! I think he's going down!" she said.

Felicity got one arm and Fiona got the other and Ginny got her arm around his back. They lowered him to a sitting position on the edge of the fountain.

William paused in his flower munching to sniff him.

"Ginny, what did you fix?" Felicity asked brightly.

Bless Hogarth for not saying a word. He must have been so worried, and it must have been a struggle not to confide in them.

"Oh, just some things to do with the estate."

She didn't want her sisters to know. They never, ever needed to know.

"He's been forgetting to eat," Fiona fussed over her brother. Who did indeed look thinner.

Ginny could imagine why. "Will you two run into the house and bring Hogarth and me something to drink and perhaps a little bite to eat? I just want to sit here for a minute. It's a beautiful day."

Felicity seized up Ginny's valise and both girls skipped off.

They really were sweet, lovely girls, who deserved every happiness, and bloody Marchand was right. She was whiskey, and they were chamomile tea.

Hogarth bent double and breathed. She patted his back.

"Oh, Ginny. Bloody hell. Thank you. Dear God. I'm luckier than I deserve to be," he said.

"Too right you are," she agreed.

"So what happened?"

"The Earl of Sydenham tore up your vowels." She decided that was as much information as she needed to share. "And Marchand shared with me your plan to teach the children from the workhouse. I think that's a very fine idea, Hogarth, and I'm so proud of you."

But Hogarth was frowning at her. He was unfortunately every bit as smart as she'd told Marchand he was. He was clearly puzzling over something.

"Did Marchand have anything to do with Sydenham's decision?" He was eyeing her with peculiar intensity.

She hesitated. "I think he had everything to do with it."

And just like that, her eyes filled with tears.

"Ginny!" he said. Alarmed.

She swiped at her eyes. "I'm just a bit tired from the journey."

He frowned at her so darkly and so skeptically that she nearly laughed.

"Are you unwell?" He was so worried, and it was so sweet.

"No. I'm . . . I'm a little sad, though."

He looked as though he intended to say something, then thought better of it. "Do you want to tell me about it?" he asked gently.

She shook her head. It was true: She didn't *want* to tell him. Perhaps she would, at some point. Perhaps she would need to.

He slung an arm about her instead, and they sat together.

William came over and shoved his big face into their shoulders, asking for pats. They obliged him.

"I'm looking forward to teaching boys and girls, actually. It was so very good of Marchand to arr—agree to it."

She stared at him. Her breath stopped.

She was fairly certain she knew what Garth had almost said: *arrange*.

And possibly he had said it on purpose.

"It *was* good of him," she said slowly.

A wave of the warmest, sweetest love for Gabriel swept through her and stole her breath so thoroughly she couldn't speak for a moment.

"Hogarth . . . " she said carefully. "I think Gabriel Marchand is a good man." Her heart beat with nervous speed.

He eyed her intently. He seemed to be considering this. "I think you may be right," he said gently. "Believe it or not."

That was all she was going to say about it for now.

"I think you should do all the talking during the marital settlement discussions, Garth. I'll make sure you're prepared. I'll go with you. But you're the earl, and the official head of the family now, and I think you should take on that role and everything that goes with it. I will help, if you need help. But I want you to do it."

"All right," he said. "I can do that. You've carried us for so long. I am so grateful. We all are."

"I haven't minded." Her voice was hoarse. "You all mean everything to me." How would Hogarth's expression change if she told him about Gabriel?

Would she lose them forever if she married a beautiful rogue?

She leaned her head on his shoulder.

Felicity and Fiona emerged from the house lugging a little

picnic hamper, and they all sat in front of the fountain and ate tea cakes and fruit and cheese, sharing bites with William.

* * *

Back in her own bedroom at last, she unpacked her valise and trunk, which Hogarth and their man of all work had fetched from the drive.

Like a madwoman she sniffed carefully every dress she'd worn when Gabriel held her or kissed her, hoping against hope to find some trace of his scent on them. She found nothing.

She put them away in her clothes press. Every single one of those dresses was a veritable museum of memories. All she needed to do was look at her goldenrod pelisse and she would see him gazing across at her, comparing the stars in the sky to her freckles, trying and failing not to fall in love with her.

Next, she opened up her valise to retrieve her hairbrush and stockings.

She went still.

Something was wedged into the bottom of it. A little box of some sort she didn't recognize. She wondered if one of the maids at the Grand Palace on the Thames had tucked it in there.

She reached in, pulled the string that held it closed, and lifted the lid.

Inside, tucked inside cotton wool, was the shepherdess she'd seen in Fleegle's Emporium of Wonders.

The one who had belonged to Henrietta Parker! The one whose friends had all been used for skeet. Gabriel must have gone back for it.

She gave a little happy cry when she realized it was wrapped in one of his handkerchiefs.

She gently unpacked the shepherdess and gave her a spot on her window ledge.

Then Ginny sat at her window, watching the lowering sun through the trees in the rambling park behind their house. She held the clean, soft, bright loveliness of his handkerchief to her face and breathed him in. She closed her eyes. Her heart felt a thousand times too big for her chest. Her head ached from fatigue and from weeping too much lately.

"I love you, Gabriel," she said aloud, fervently. Willing her words to sail through the ether and to reach him, sink right into his heart, wherever he was tonight, lonely and missing her. "I love you I love you I love you."

She retrieved from her reticule the heart-shaped stone she'd found outside the earl's house and transferred it into a wooden box on her writing desk that held the others.

She gently stirred and sifted them through her fingers.

She looked out at the view she'd known and loved her entire life.

"Mama," she said aloud. Her voice was graveled. "If you're listening . . . we did it, Mama. Felicity and Fiona are getting married to lovely men. I did what you asked me to do. So I wonder, would you mind terribly if I asked for something for myself?" She paused to pull in a few breaths. "Because I'm in love with a man. His name is Gabriel Marchand. Oh, but you would like him. He's the kind of handsome that stops your breath. He's brilliant and strong and caring and competent and passionate and very funny. He loves me, too, more than his own life. And I know he'll take care of me. Maybe you understand. Maybe you loved papa that way, too. But Gabriel doesn't have a title. He's not even a gentleman. He owns a gaming establishment. Are you gasping right now? Are you appalled? I hope not. That would break my heart." She cleared her throat. "But I may never be accepted into polite society ever again if I marry him. I should be very fair and tell you that Francis Balfort would like to marry me, too. And, as you know, he's the third son of a duke."

She paused.

"The thing is, Mama . . ." Her voice broke. "I do not think I can do without Gabriel. I do not think I could bear to go on. You know I'm not in the habit of saying such things. I go on, no matter what. It's what I do. And it makes my heart ache not to fulfill all of your wishes. I know you want what is best for me. But *he* is best for me. So if you could send me a sign to let me know that you approve, I should be so grateful."

Exhaustion overcame her.

She could barely keep her eyes open as she splashed water from the basin on her face, plaited her hair, and threw a clean night rail over her head.

She was asleep almost before her head hit the pillow, Marchand's handkerchief clutched in her hand, held against her cheek.

* * *

Ginny was very proud of how Hogarth acquitted himself during the marriage settlement negotiations for his sisters, which, over a span of days, were accomplished with surprising thoroughness and efficiency in a room filled with solicitors, the prospective grooms, and their fathers. It was a process that could take months, depending upon the estate, so the civility and speed with which it was all concluded delighted everyone.

She'd sat near Hogarth, mostly quietly—which was no mean feat, as she was very used to being in charge, and as she'd told Marchand, she quite liked it—while hard but cheerful bargains were driven about allowances and so forth for Felicity and Fiona.

Such an unsentimental yet ultimately loving thing to do, she supposed. It was meant to protect them, but it also enriched their husbands. There was no doubt about that.

A man who would pay any price for the privilege of being with her, Gabriel had said.

His voice was in her head throughout the entire process.

All parties parted happy and hopeful and excited about their futures.

A fortnight later, a radiant Felicity and Fiona were married in a joyful double ceremony in their parish church, which was packed with family and townspeople who had watched the Woodville siblings grow up and were pleased to see them at last successfully leaving the nest.

Francis had come for the wedding, too.

The sight of him amazed Ginny into breathlessness: How absurdly, dangerously gossamer their connection seemed to her now, and how flimsy the reasons to marry him. How on earth had she ever lightly contemplated committing the rest of her life to him?

The notion of lying sweaty and sated across his naked body seemed so inconceivable she could scarcely breathe for panic.

He was the same sweet, admiring young man he'd always been. If he noticed anything different about her, he didn't remark upon it. This struck her as shocking, since her spirit felt so utterly transformed—or rather, her spirit had at last fully bloomed. He could see her only through the lens of the life he'd lived, which meant he could not know her heart.

It wasn't his fault that her heart had chanced upon its own true mate.

And then the moment she'd dreaded occurred: He'd asked if he could call upon her and her brother in a week's time at the Woodville house.

Her gut went cold.

"Yes," she told him. Her voice shredded from nerves.

His eyes had gone meltingly soft. He'd been emboldened to take her hand. "Thank you, dear Ginny."

Yet again she confronted, with dread, the ticking of a clock toward a decision.

* * *

She had not found a single stone heart in the three weeks since she'd been home.

Her eyes had been so frequently on the ground that she had crashed into a pillar, a tree, a settee, Mrs. Haddock, accidentally stepped on a cat, and collided with William.

In her time away from Gabriel her feelings had not ebbed or faded even a little; longing had cut a deep channel through her, and like a river, it flowed endlessly. His presence was nearly as vivid to her as if he stood at her side.

The absolute certainty of his love, the absolute conviction

that he would come to her at once if she needed him, had changed the very way she moved in the world. Every breath seemed richer and deeper and freer, every moment safer and more peaceful, because she was surrounded at all times by the invisible eiderdown of his love.

And the thought of him yearning for her all this time was nearly unbearable.

A little flame of fury at last ignited in her heart every time she looked for a sign and didn't find one.

Each passing day without a sign fanned it higher.

She had not asked for a thing in her life for eight years. One little sign! One little sign that she should claim her own happiness, even if it looked different from everyone else's. Was it too much to ask?

Apparently, it was.

And perhaps it meant that she shouldn't.

Perhaps it was her mother's way of protecting her. Perhaps there was wisdom in it that she could not currently see.

Perhaps . . . perhaps it was a decision she would need to make all on her own.

You can decide the point of you, he'd said.

And when she bravely tormented herself by imagining life without Gabriel, a life married to some other man, her heart contracted into a tight, hard fist. Protecting itself from the very notion.

She had known the rambling park behind their house in every season, and the sky was blushing with the dawn when she sat at her writing desk and sifted through her stones one more time.

She could have sworn she heard her mother's voice.

What does your heart tell you, Ginny?

Goose bumps rained over her arms when she realized the truth:

Her *own* heart felt like a stone without him.

And she knew this was her sign.

Chapter Twenty-Two

"I didn't know when to tell you. Please forgive me if you feel as though I ought to have told you before the weddings. Because I *am* telling you. I'm not asking you."

She had hastily gathered her worried siblings for a family meeting in the Woodville drawing room, before her sisters could go off on wedding journeys to the Continent.

She told them about Gabriel Marchand.

She told them about St. Giles, and about his son, Michael, and about Lucifer's Fall. She told them how he had gone out of his way, even risking his life, to help her solve a very serious problem about the estate, and that he had at all times kept her safe. She told them he was funny, kind, wise, admirable, noble, and brave, and that he smelled wonderful.

She left out a good deal, and steadfastly refused to embellish with details, but Felicity and Fiona, eyes wide, mouths agape, hung on her every word as if it was the kind of vivid tale Mrs. Pariseau read aloud in the sitting room.

Instead of "happily ever after," she concluded by saying, "I love him very much, and I want to marry him."

"Oh, my good heavens. How romantic! He must be so in love with you," Fiona breathed.

"Sick with love over her, I should say," Hogarth confirmed.

Ginny looked at him sharply. But apparently, just like the secret of his disastrous wager, he was going to keep to himself why he believed this about Marchand.

"Ginny," Felicity said. "Of course you would fall in love with someone like that. Francis is far too ordinary for you. I've always thought so."

Fiona nodded vigorously.

Ginny was surprised to hear that they thought she shouldn't marry someone ordinary.

"And he's rich?" Fiona wanted to know.

"Very," she confirmed.

"Well, if anyone in my new family objects to him . . . that's simply too bad," Fiona said loftily, with a pretty shrug. "They cannot and will not stop me from seeing both of you."

"Likewise," Felicity confirmed.

They all suspected it wouldn't quite be that easy. But if there was anything the Woodville siblings understood, it was things that were not quite easy.

"Well, I'm the Earl of Highgrove," Hogarth said. "I'm the head of the family. You have my blessing. Marchand is a good man, Ginny. I like him, though I confess I'm also a little bit afraid of him. He'll take good care of you and your children. I suspect he would kill for you. You deserve someone who would do that, anyway."

Ginny closed her eyes and exhaled and they all gathered around to embrace her. And she held on to each of them tightly.

And that left Francis.

She decided it was kindest to tell him in a letter, rather than subject him to the humiliation of visiting with the happy expectation of an enthusiastic acceptance of his proposal.

Dear Francis,

I have cherished our friendship, and it has been an honor to be esteemed by a person as fine and kind as yourself. It therefore grieves me greatly to share news which I fear will hurt you, and perhaps forever cost me your regard.

I have fallen in love with another man, who loves me in return. While this recent development has taken me quite by surprise, our feelings for each other are genuine, profound, and permanent. I cannot now conceive of a future without him, or with any other man.

I felt it would be unconscionable to wait another day to tell you.

I greatly regret causing you any pain. I swear upon all I hold dear that it was never my intent to mislead you with regards to my nature of affection, if this is indeed how you feel.

I wish for you the joy of the true love that you deserve. May life shower you and your family with blessings.

I will always think of you warmly.

Yours sincerely,
Guinevere

Her palms went clammy as she read the letter. The moment she sent it, her destiny would be sealed.

Finally, she sprinkled it with sand, took a deep breath, and squeezed her eyes closed against the image of Francis's face when he read it.

How she loathed the very notion of hurting him. How unfair that claiming her happiness might cost someone else theirs.

But how did she know what lay in store for Francis? Like Marchand said, life was a tide that rolled in and out.

And it seemed to her that she was a little mad to send this letter before she'd even had a proposal. She supposed it was possible that Marchand had expired suddenly, or eloped with an actress. Where would that leave her?

Grateful for her time with him.

She would simply spend her life spoiling her nieces and nephews. There could never be anyone else for her.

I'll take whatever you're willing to give me, Gabriel had said to her.

Her trepidation dissolved into a peaceful certainty.

She gave one of the Woodville footmen two shillings to deliver the letter to Francis at his father's estate.

By the time he read it she would be on a mail coach to London.

* * *

"Are you sure this is where you'd like me to leave you, miss?"

The hack driver sounded dubious, and a little concerned.

"Of course," Ginny reassured him. "It's kind of you to ask, thank you. I'll be fine. I'm expected."

This last part wasn't entirely true. She was arriving unannounced. But she *was* reasonably confident of her reception.

And as the hack drove away, the handsome Grecian-style building that she'd only visited once before, the day her life had changed forever, was once again before her.

Her heart already galloping as if it couldn't get to him fast enough, she took a long, long breath and moved toward the entrance of Lucifer's Fall.

It was surprisingly very quiet, and some premonition made her halt.

And that's when she saw that the windows were boarded.

Her heart gave a lurch.

She stared. Confused.

And then icy unease crept over her skin like a frost.

She inched closer to the building, dread quickening her breathing now.

The elegant sign that said "Lucifer's Fall" was gone. She stared, her mind blanking, at the bare place it used to occupy next to the entrance.

No bulky, glowering guard stood at attention near the entrance.

Something was terribly wrong.

She could now hear the panicked rush of her breath in her ears.

She froze, flailing inwardly. Horribly disoriented.

She jumped and whirled at the sound of a cough.

She hadn't noticed the man standing to the far left of the entrance. His girth was nearly as imposing as Mr. Delacorte's and the excellent fit of his coat and the shine on his boots suggested he was prosperous, if not officially a gentleman. He was reviewing the time on a gold pocket watch and impatiently shifting from foot to foot.

"Sir . . ." she ventured.

He looked up, startled. And then he gawked at her, clearly utterly nonplussed to see a young woman alone in front of an obviously deserted, boarded-up gaming palace.

"Madam," he replied cautiously. He tipped his hat, revealing a balding pate.

She swallowed because her mouth was parched with fear.

"Sir, can you tell me . . . did . . . did . . . something happen to Lucifer's Fall?"

"Oh, it's closed, forever, madam. Lucifer's Fall is no more." His brow furrowed in a faintly disapproving, fatherly sort of way.

And just like that, the bottom dropped out of her world.

She needed something to lean on; her legs were threatening to give way.

"Why on earth are *you* looking for Lucifer's Fall, young lady?" he pressed.

That was really none of his business.

"But . . . I just . . . it *can't* be closed." She could scarcely hear her own voice over the ringing in her ears.

"Well, clearly it *can* be, because it is. Surely you can see for yourself." He gestured broadly at the building, seemingly affronted that she didn't believe him.

Surely this couldn't be happening?

Was this her punishment, then, for leaving?

Who did she think she was, to believe she could bargain with fate?

"But . . . when did that happen?"

"Oh, must be well-nigh a month ago."

A month ago! Right after she'd left Gabriel!

How surreal that this man before her could sound so *blithe* about what constituted the end of her world.

"But . . . but what about Mr. Marchand? Where did he go?" She was nauseous with terror now.

"Oh, God only knows where *Marchand* has got to," the man said, irritably.

He again consulted his watch.

She gave another start when she became aware of voices calling to each other very nearby. It sounded like two men engaged in a passionate debate.

"Steady! Back it up, back it up. What the *devil* are you doing, Jenkins? This thing don't bend, for God's sake!"

She stared, astounded, as a man dressed in workman's trousers, heavy boots, and a cap emerged from the alley between the former Lucifer's Fall's building and the building adjacent. He was walking backward in a crablike crouch, his hands behind his back. In them he balanced one end of what turned out to be a long, rectangular slab of wood, about three feet tall.

A few moments later, another man in workman's attire appeared—Jenkins, no doubt. He was supporting the weight of the back end of the slab. All in all, it was a good ten feet long, if she had to guess.

They didn't see her as they gracelessly swung their cargo about.

She staggered backward as she dodged out of their way.

They maneuvered the slab until it was horizontal with the front of the building. Then lowered it gently to rest against the wall and stood back, swiping their gloved hands in that universal gesture of satisfaction with a job well done.

On it, in tall, regal gold letters, the slab read:

The Marchand Academy

Her breath stopped. The words seemed to shimmer with portent.

It was a sign.

In more ways than one.

A blast of hope thawed the frozen knot of her heart. Goose bumps spangled her arms.

What was *happening*?

She whirled at the sound of yet another man's voice coming from somewhere in the alley. "We're going to need at least two ladders to hang that, lads."

And just like that, her heart soared like a flung discus.

"*Three* would actually be better, because that sign is so fine and heavy." The voice, closer now, sounded pleased about this. "I think we can borrow a ladder from—"

At last the man belonging to the voice came into view.

"Oh, *that's* where you've got to, Mr. Marchand," the supercilious fellow with the watch said, with great relief. "I've been waiting for you, sir. The carpet delivery will be here any minute and your signature will be needed."

The poor man might as well have been a ghost.

Marchand clearly couldn't see anything at all but Ginny.

They drank each other in with their eyes.

He looked precisely the same as he had in all the dreams she'd had about him while they were apart. In other words, overwhelmingly magnificent.

The men all around them had frozen, sensing something momentous was afoot.

"Gentlemen," Marchand said finally, without looking at any of them.

Understanding that to be a command, all of the men scattered at once, disappearing from view.

When they were at last alone, Gabriel slowly paced to her.

"Gabriel . . . what on . . ." Her voice was thready from the emotional whipsawing she'd just withstood.

"I confess this has been in the works since before you left." His voice was low and gruff. "I offered Lucifer's Fall members a choice: I would refund the balance of their memberships for the year or they could donate them to the Marchand Academy. More than half donated, if you can believe that. It seems I've a knack for persuasion." A ghost of a smile here. "Soon, at least forty, perhaps more, children from workhouses will be housed and educated here. I've interviewed teachers for all subjects and hired most of them. Your brother is one of them. The classrooms will be on the bottom floor and dormitory rooms in the upper floors. Lord Kirke is working on legislation that would partially fund this and other institutions like it in perpetuity. For now, I can easily afford it, in large part because the membership fees alone will fund tuition for children for at least fifteen years."

She covered her mouth with her hands. Speechless with pride and dumbstruck with happiness. She lowered her hands. "Gabriel. Oh, my God. This is extraordinary. I'm just . . . how . . . it's perfect. It's beautiful. It's *perfect* for you."

"I like the sound of chancellor for my new title. What do you think? I haven't yet officially decided."

She shook her head slowly in wonderment. "A splendid word."

"I didn't tell you before you left, Ginny, because I wanted you to be certain that you loved me as I am. And *I* needed to be certain that you loved me as I am. Was I wrong not to tell you?"

She left him in suspense for two seconds.

"Well. That was risky."

"Said one leaper to another. For here you are." He said this with a dazed wonder. "You came looking for the worst man in London. You clearly want a first-class rogue."

She smiled. "Fair," she conceded.

"Are you sorry not to find him?"

"Who says I didn't find him?"

He gave a short laugh. "What will you do with me now?"

Her slow smile was all randy promise.

She pulled in a deep breath. "For what it's worth . . . I love you precisely as you are, Gabriel, and I will love you in any incarnation. Now and forever."

He fell quiet. His throat moved in a swallow.

His eyes were shining suspiciously.

She knew he had a clean handkerchief on his person. She had a feeling the occasion was going to demand it.

Because her own eyes were burning.

"So why don't you tell me why you're here, Ginny," he asked quietly.

The wind lashed the spirals of hair at her temple against her eyes while she gathered sufficient courage to speak.

"You told me you would take from me anything I wanted to give you. Do you still mean it?" Her voice trembled.

He gently captured one of those spirals and drew it between his fingers. "I mean it," he said softly. "Anything."

She took a breath to steady her nerve. "I want to give you all my days. And all my nights. I want to give you children. I want to give you a home. I want to give you *all* of me. Forever."

What an extraordinary gift it seemed to be able to make Gabriel Marchand look as brilliantly happy as he did now.

"Do you by any chance also want to give me your hand in marriage?"

"If you'll have me."

"Oh, I'll have you, Guinevere Woodville."

He folded her into his arms, and she latched her hands around his neck, and they clung to each other like a pair of shipwreck survivors who had finally washed up on shore.

The way he kissed her, with a thoroughness that turned her knees to smoke and her blood to lava, made it clear he'd missed her every single moment of every day she'd been away.

"God, I love you," he whispered against her throat. "I've missed you so. And I've been carrying something about with me, in case you need an unmistakable, forever sort of sign."

He released her gently and reached into his coat pocket.

"Hold out your hand, Ginny."

She'd never yet regretted obeying when he asked her to do that. So she did.

His hand trembled as he slid onto her finger a delicate gold ring.

It was crowned with a little diamond, precisely in the shape of a heart.

Epilogue

I publish the banns of marriage between Mr. Gabriel Marchand of St. James's Parish, London, and the Honorable Miss Guinevere Woodville of Balcombe Parish, West Sussex. If any of you know cause or just impediment why these two persons should not be joined together in holy matrimony, ye are to declare it. This is the third and final time of asking."

A gasp soughed through the church at the first reading of the banns.

Gabriel had been cautious about the notion of being married in Ginny's parish church, simply because he had more than an inkling of how controversial their match might be viewed. But Ginny wanted to make a bold, unequivocal public declaration. She wanted the people she loved, most particularly Gabriel, and the people who had watched her grow to womanhood to know how proud, how happy, how grateful, how staggeringly lucky she felt to be marrying him. How blessed she felt to have found her heart's true mate. She wanted Gabriel Marchand to feel irrevocably *chosen*.

But unease and uncertainty had rustled through the church

after the first reading of the Banns. The haste of this astonishing engagement struck many as unseemly; most didn't know Marchand's name and the few who did were aghast. The Honorable Francis Balfort was known and well-liked and it had long been assumed that Ginny would marry him. It would have been the most appropriate match imaginable.

Ginny and Gabriel kept their heads high and their expressions peaceful.

After church on the first reading of the banns, Guinevere introduced him to the townspeople only as the chancellor of the Marchand Academy, but no one had ever heard of the institution (though it would only be a matter of time before all of England had heard of it). Marchand looked for the most part exactly like what he was, which was someone who had met untold difficult challenges head-on and had perhaps conquered a lot of them by fighting dirty. They found it impossible to fault his manners, however. And many of them found it impossible to look away from him once they'd gotten that first look.

And the man was clearly *besotted* with Ginny.

It was admittedly very difficult not to thaw in the presence of a besotted man.

So in the weeks between the three consecutive Sundays upon which the banns were read, Marchand did what he did best: He charmed and beguiled and impressed. He traveled between London and Sussex, but he spent most of his time in Sussex. He went to the village pub and bought rounds and played darts. He learned and remembered the names of local families and all their family members and servants and even their pets. He held babies and played with children. He asked for advice about raising sheep, which the Woodville family intended to do at the estate they had inherited, and about a horse he intended to buy. He laid the groundwork for being the perfect husband for Guinevere Woodville with the thoroughness he'd laid the groundwork for becoming a lord of the demimonde.

And then there was her brother, the Earl of Highgrove's steadfast, quiet, stubborn, unflagging support of their match. "I know of no better man," Hogarth told everyone at every opportunity.

Her sisters had postponed their own wedding trips to attend Ginny and Gabriel's ceremony. Their husbands were at first wary of and cold, even disdainful to Marchand, which Ginny found painful. They had grown up with Francis and were loyal to him (who had gone off on a long, soul-searching trip to the Continent). They were, in fact, quite stunned at this turn of events.

They soon found themselves slowly, reluctantly, drawn in by Marchand's charisma and his obvious good intentions, which had nothing of obsequiousness to them. "I understand how you feel and I don't expect you to love me," he told them frankly. "But I love Guinevere, and I would do anything for her family. And that includes you, from now on. I do hope we will one day become friends. And if the notion of that remains unpalatable, then I hope we will abide in mutual respect, as allies. For you can count on me in that regard, in all things." It was difficult to deny that he looked like the sort of man one wanted on one's side, rather than the opposite.

By the third and final time the banns were read, all the faces of the churchgoers were nearly as radiant as the bride-to-be's. Everyone was impressed (and, they told themselves, not surprised) with Miss Woodville's wherewithal in finding the perfect partner. She'd always had such a level head, that girl!

After all, everyone loved a good transformation story.

The following Sunday, Guinevere Woodville and Gabriel Marchand became husband and wife in the village church. They were surrounded by Ginny's family and all of their new friends, and it was as joyous an occasion as her town had ever seen.

Mr. and Mrs. Marchand were going to be *very* busy in London. So off they went.

The dormitories of the Marchand Academy would be decorated very like the rooms at the Grand Palace on the Thames, they decided together. A home should feel like a *home* for the children. The common areas, too. The days after their wedding were full of plans and preparations, exhilarating progress, laughter, and enjoyable clashes of will they always sorted with more laughter or passionate kisses.

Their nights were torrid.

Together they learned to play with the elasticity of desire. To master everything from a long, slow build to shattering crescendos to swift ferocious bonfires of lust. Every curve, angle, and slope of their bodies was explored, claimed, and savored with fingers and palms and tongues and lips. They reveled in the infinite ways in which sex was a language to express every gradation of their love for each other.

Ginny was quite surprised and delighted to learn that a variety of positions could be employed. This was very useful in the instances she wanted to be taken swiftly and immediately, skirts hiked, her bare arse pressed against a wall, her husband thrusting expertly as he murmured filthy endearments in her ear. And during occasions when they found themselves with a few minutes to spare, she would surprise him by dragging him into an empty room at the former Lucifer's Fall, lock the door, reach for the fall of his trousers to tug it open, and drop to her knees before him. With her mouth and hands she would make him moan. "God, Ginny, just like that, don't stop."

Sometimes they sprawled nude on Marchand's comfortable bed on a velvet counterpane like a pair of pashas and simply luxuriated.

He never did do anything with ropes. But now and again they liked to do fancy things with a cravat.

The lust, like the love, only seemed to replenish a thousand-fold.

Six months after they were married, she discovered she was pregnant.

They were ecstatic. But as the months went on and her belly swelled and the baby thumped about in there, Marchand grew quieter, beset with a sleepless, nervy tension and an almost overwhelming possessive protectiveness.

And she knew old fears had him in their grip.

"Listen to me," she whispered to him, stroking his forehead one night. "I am never, ever leaving you. Ever. And neither will the baby."

But they both knew love itself was no protection. Just look at Apollo and Eros and Daphne.

On the most harrowing and miraculous night of their lives, Gabriel St. James Michael Marchand arrived.

He was named for his father, for the place where Gabriel

had found a heart-shaped stone to give to Ginny, and for the brother he would never have a chance to meet. He was a staggeringly perfect baby, probably the best one ever born. And he proved to be a funny, enchanting, willful, mischievous child.

Marchand held his baby and his wife and wept at the miracle that allowed him to love and protect them for the rest of his days.

Gabriel soon had another brother. And then a sister, and then another sister.

And they eventually had lots of cousins, too.

Hogarth's sensitivity, intelligence, and kindness turned out to be precisely what a vivacious, beautiful, very confident, and very wealthy American heiress yearned for. He married her four years after Ginny married Marchand. Hogarth blossomed in his wife's company; the new Countess of Highgrove melted in his.

And after years of torturous uncertainty, the Woodville finances not only recovered, but became positively robust, and would remain that way for generations to come.

* * *

Politicians. Printers. Poets. Blacksmiths. Farmers. Silversmiths. Sailors. Teachers. Scientists. Doctors. Explorers. Shopkeepers. Husbands. Wives. Artists. Factory owners. Bankers.

Over the next several decades, many of them began storied careers and happy lives at the Marchand Academy. There was also one highwayman, but the people he robbed always remarked that he was very well spoken and possessed considerable dash.

Children at the Marchand Academy were taught to read and write English, French, and Latin. They were taught manners and deportment and etiquette, and to think critically and to debate effectively. Fed, clothed, housed, protected, and respected, they flourished. They were given opportunities to learn trades and to meet people who would help them prosper far, far away from places like St. Giles. Though many returned to extend a hand to others there, too.

Where Gabriel had once imagined a gaming hell on every corner, within a decade, there were three Marchand Academies in England rescuing children from workhouses and funneling dazzling little citizens into English society. Gabriel and Ginny presided over all of them. Mr. Ogden became a beloved headmaster of one of them. The Earl of Highgrove remained a fencing and mathematics tutor many years after his debt was paid, because he was good at it and the children loved him.

And courtesy of the Michael Marchand Memorial Scholarship, every year at least one student from the academy was sent to Oxford or Cambridge.

It was everything Ginny and Gabriel loved: a vast canvas upon which to fling passion, care, ingenuity, and bossiness. People struggled to say no to either of them, and they lost all reticence when it came to asking for things for the children in their charge. They worked in tandem with politicians like Lord Dominic Kirke and Mr. Jonathan Redmond to protect the rights of the most vulnerable. They entertained in their London home frequently, inviting their friends from the Grand Palace on the Thames, who were less surprised than either Ginny or Marchand expected at the news of their marriage. As Delacorte had mentioned, men often left there with a wife.

And when, after fifteen years of marriage, Gabriel was awarded a baronetcy for his exceptional public service, he finally joined White's, because it ironically amused him to do so. But he could scarcely have a drink there without critically assessing how much better he and Ogden could have run the place.

* * *

When Mr. Peck returned to collect his little family—Mrs. Peck, Daniel, and baby Roger—to bring them back to Northumberland, everyone actually watched them go with some degree of misty-eyed fondness. (Mr. Delacorte's degree was admittedly slightly less misty.)

The week prior, Captain Hardy, Lucien, and Delacorte had taken Daniel down to the docks. While the two ships in the Triton Group's fleet were still undergoing repairs at the shipyard in Dover, there were plenty of others just offshore to admire.

They found Daniel's unbridled, giddy delight in all of it— the sights and sounds, the seagulls, the ocean—exhilarating. *Everything* was new to him and it made all three of the men feel brand-new, too, as if the world was just beginning. As if it still contained wonders.

It also made them feel old and learned.

They were all a bit wistful and pensive when the Pecks departed.

"Well, I'm not sure I'd *mind* filling the ballroom with babies," Lucien allowed carefully that night in the smoking room.

Captain Hardy gave an almost pained laugh.

After a long silence, Mr. Delacorte said, "I've had a letter from the Earl of Highgrove offering to give his donkey to me."

"Congratulations, Delacorte," Bolt said warmly, as if he'd just announced he was going to be a father.

* * *

The morning after they said their goodbyes to the Pecks, Dot took the contents of the Epithet Jar—which had been nice and jingly thanks to her recent chess lessons with Mr. Delacorte!—to buy the morning papers and have a little wander around the market stalls that appeared twice a week before she was expected back at the Grand Palace on the Thames.

She'd reserved twenty pence of her own wages to buy something frivolous. Her last such purchase was the little journal that she'd christened "Dot's Thoughts."

Today she thought she might want a handkerchief or a ribbon. Something pretty and soft.

On a table scattered with what looked like ordinary detritus of daily life, things like clay pipes and plain hair combs and drinking mugs, her eye landed on a little vase. It was white, patterned with blue vines and flowers; a pair of lovebirds sat among them.

It seemed to snuggle right into her hand when she gently picked it up.

It was one of the loveliest things she'd ever seen.

"It's ten pence, miss," the merchant told her. "Pretty thing, ain't it? Felt I couldn't charge more fer it, as it's got funny dark lines on the bottom."

Dot peered; indeed, on the bottom were what looked like a set of six scribbled lines. It seemed like something that Daniel Peck might do to a vase if he got hold of ink and a quill.

It would look lovely on her writing desk next to her little wooden donkey named Fate, which she'd been mysteriously gifted, and her Dot's Thoughts journal. Last night she'd written in it, "Mr. Pike believes I can be a story writer." She'd stared at that sentence in wonder.

Ironically, she'd been unable to write another word after that.

Then again, that sentence seemed a story unto itself.

The vase perfectly matched the blue-and-white rag rug next to her bed. She wasn't entirely certain why, but she always noticed colors and she liked them to feel just right.

She took an expenditure of ten pence *very* seriously.

But lovebirds!

Surely it was a sign.

"I'll have this then," she'd told the merchant.

He wrapped it carefully up in newspaper, and she tucked it into her little net bag just as the sun was peeping out from behind a cloud.

She knew she'd best hurry. Captain Hardy and Lord Bolt especially liked to have the newspapers first thing—they shared them throughout the house and with all the guests, because they were expensive—and the maids expected her in the kitchen, because she read the gossip sheets aloud there every day.

Quite a few of the guests at the Grand Palace on the Thames had appeared both on the front page and in the gossip pages, which was always exciting. Not a day went by when she wasn't astonished and grateful for her life here.

She burst through the door in time to walk through rainbows.

But she was walking perilously too fast.

Her slightly damp soles slid over the slick marble floor.

To her horror, she stumbled.

And fell.

Time seemed to slow as her package shot up, up, toward the chandelier, spiraling right into the rainbows. The vase was destined to become smithereens.

But Mr. Pike was on the first-floor landing, lurking. Because even though Dot thought it was her secret, he knew that Dot liked to walk through the rainbows on clear days. And when he was able, he would watch her, his breath held, as she spun in that delicate shower of color.

She was a maddening, stubborn, enchanted being, impossible to fathom, and for some reason this both irritated him and made him want to fathom her. She had once accidentally nearly knocked him out cold with a wicked right hook, which embarrassed her to this day. She made him feel both ordinary and uncomfortably extraordinary.

So he saw her race back into the boardinghouse, and he was there when she slipped, and he saw her package go flying straight up in the air.

Her wild cry of grief pierced him.

Mr. Pike hurdled over the banister, landed hard on the marble floor, stumbled forward, caught the package in his hands as it was coming down, and pulled it into his chest as gently as if it were a baby.

Then he rolled over and lay flat.

Dot froze, dumbstruck by the miracle.

And absolutely horrified that she was once again the reason Mr. Pike had landed hard on a floor.

She clambered over to him and knelt. "Mr. Pike! Oh, my goodness! Thank you! Speak to me! Are you all right?"

"What did I save?" he asked.

He was still cradling the vase against his chest.

She took it from him gently and unwrapped the newspaper to show him.

The miracle of its rescue gave Dot courage. It was, of a certainty, kismet.

"I found it for ten pence at the market stall. It has lovebirds on it."

He gazed up at her.

"It's very pretty," he said. But he was looking at her when he said it. Not the vase.

And now her heart was thundering.

"You might want to have a look at the market stall, Mr. Pike, in case that's the sort of thing you'd like to buy for your sweetheart."

His eyebrows flicked in puzzlement, then his face cleared.

"I don't have a sweetheart," he told her carefully.

Dot smiled slowly down at him.

She'd always known something magical would come from standing in a rainbow shower.

Acknowledgments

My gratitude to my editor, Shannon Plackis, and the supportive, talented team at Avon/HarperCollins; to my agent, Steven Axelrod, and his wonderful staff, Lori Antonson and Elsie Turoci; to Helen Kunic Davis and Bobbie Jo Fersten, the wittiest, sweetest friends, cheerleaders, and support team an author could dream of—I appreciate you so much; to the incredibly kind authors who have said such beautiful things about my work, including Julia Quinn and Katherine Center; to all the delightful members of The Pig & Thistle After Dark for your warmth, wit, and enthusiasm—you're such a joy!— and to the many readers who have shared their love for my books on their socials in such creative, unique ways—it means more than I can say.

About the Author

USA Today bestselling author and RITA® Award winner **JULIE ANNE LONG**'s books have been translated into eighteen languages, have been nominated for numerous awards, and have appeared on dozens of "Best of" lists. NPR named her Pennyroyal Green series one of the Top 100 romance series of all time. She currently lives in Northern California.